Wyatt

A LUCKY RIVER RANCH NOVEL

JESSICA PETERSON

Also by Jessica Peterson

THE LUCKY RIVER RANCH SERIES

Texas cowboys do it best.

Cash (Lucky River Ranch #1)

Wyatt (Lucky River Ranch #2)

Sawyer (Lucky River Ranch #3)

Duke (Lucky River Ranch #4)

Ryder (Lucky River Ranch #5)

THE HARBOUR VILLAGE SERIES

Small town romance with a smoking hot southern twist.

I Wish I Knew Then (Harbour Village #1)

I Wish You Were Mine (Harbour Village #2)

I Wish We Had Forever (Harbour Village #3)

THE SEX & BONDS SERIES

An outrageously sexy series of romcoms set in the high stakes world of Wall Street.

The Dealmaker (Sex & Bonds #1)

The Troublemaker (Sex & Bonds #2)

THE NORTH CAROLINA HIGHLANDS SERIES

Beards. Bonfires. Boning.

Southern Seducer (NC Highlands #1)

Southern Hotshot (NC Highlands #2)

Southern Sinner (NC Highlands #3)

Southern Playboy (NC Highlands #4)

Southern Bombshell (NC Highlands #5)

THE CHARLESTON HEAT SERIES

The Weather's Not the Only Thing Steamy Down South.

Southern Charmer (Charleston Heat #1)

Southern Player (Charleston Heat #2)

Southern Gentleman (Charleston Heat #3)

Southern Heartbreaker (Charleston Heat #4)

THE THORNE MONARCHS SERIES

Royal. Ridiculously Hot. Totally Off Limits…

Royal Ruin (Thorne Monarchs #1)

Royal Rebel (Thorne Monarchs #2)

Royal Rogue (Thorne Monarchs #3)

THE STUDY ABROAD SERIES

Studying Abroad Just Got a Whole Lot Sexier.

A Series of Sexy Interconnected Standalone Romances

Lessons in Love (Study Abroad #1)

Lessons in Gravity (Study Abroad #2)

Lessons in Letting Go (Study Abroad #3)

Lessons in Losing It (Study Abroad #4)

Where to Find Jessica!

- **Follow my not-so-glamorous life as a romance author on Instagram @JessicaPAuthor**
- Follow me on TikTok!
- Check out Jessica Peterson's City Girls, my reader group on Facebook for giveaways, serious discussions of seriously hot guys, and more
- Check out my website, www.jessicapeterson.com, for a list of my books, my recommended reading order, plus lots of other goodies
- Follow me on Goodreads
- Follow me on Bookbub
- Like my Facebook Author Page
- Drop me a line at jessicapauthor@jessicapeterson.com

❀ Created with Vellum

For those of y'all with hearts like wild horses.
Don't let them rein you in.
(But if a cowboy wants to tie you up and have his way with you,
well…)

Cowboys Cry Too

TWELVE YEARS AGO

GROWING UP IN CATTLE COUNTRY, you learn early that gambling is a way of life.

You bet the rain will come and the rattlers won't bite.

You play the odds and hope you chose the right breed, the right time, the right pasture.

You go all in on the belief that there is honor and goodness in tending to the land and the animals that live off it. The knowledge that it's all a crapshoot, that the sky can fall at any minute, lives inside your blood. And yet you're still somehow unprepared for the moment tragedy strikes.

"This wasn't supposed to happen." The preacher's hand lands heavily on my shoulder. "I'm so sorry for your loss, son."

Looking up from my feet, I swallow the ache in my throat and paste on a smile. I might be eighteen, but I still need my parents. I have no idea what we're gonna do without them.

"Thank you, Reverend Ford. That means a lot to us."

How many hundreds of times have we parroted that line this week as friends and neighbors came to check on us here on our family's ranch?

How many hundreds more will we have to say it tomorrow, the day of our parents' funeral?

My older brother, Cash, catches my gaze from across the room. Sitting on the lopsided sofa alongside our three younger brothers, he looks as uncomfortable and lost as I feel. I keep waiting for Mom to use whatever sweet treat she just whipped up as bait to lure me to help her in the kitchen, where Shania Twain is playing on Mom's little portable speaker. But her call never comes.

"I've told the city council for years that we need better lighting downtown," Reverend Ford continues. "You boys need anything, you holler, all right?"

"Yes, sir. Thank you for stopping by."

"Least I can do." He glances at the sofa and shakes his head, letting out a heavy sigh. "Five of y'all. My goodness."

"We'll be all right."

Aunt Lollie, Mom's sister, emerges from the kitchen as Reverend Ford makes his way to the front door. She frowns when she sees me. "Wyatt, honey, you need to eat. A neighbor just brought over some fried chicken that looks good."

My stomach lurches. My mouth fills with a familiar, sour-tasting rush of saliva.

Mom and Dad died on impact after being hit by a car five days ago. They were crossing Main Street on foot when they were run over by an elderly man with an expired license who wasn't wearing his glasses. My parents were on a rare date night, the two of them able to get out of the house because Aunt Lollie was visiting from California and she'd offered to watch my brothers and me.

Ever since we got the news, just the thought of eating makes me want to puke. But I still manage to keep the smile on my face. My brothers are watching me, and I know if I fall apart, they will too.

My head throbs with the effort of keeping everything—the anger and agony—inside. I do my best to ignore the pain, hardly able to breathe around the lump in my throat.

"I'm okay. Thanks, Aunt Lollie."

"Honey, you need your strength. Tomorrow's going to be a long day."

"She's right," Cash adds. "Please eat, Wyatt."

"There's some of that sheet cake left that I made," Lollie says.

Cash nods. "And the enchiladas Mrs. Wallace brought over."

"Those are so good," Duke says, his voice cracking.

He and Ryder are twins. They're my youngest brothers— only fourteen years old.

Way too fucking young to lose their parents.

We're all too young.

My eyes burn, blurring with tears. I blink them away. "That your evil plan, to get me fatter than a pig on Sunday?"

That gets a chuckle from Ryder. The heaviness in my chest lifts before falling back onto my breastbone like a ton of bricks.

"I'm gonna go check on the front pasture. Irrigation was acting funny earlier." I hook my thumb over my shoulder. "I won't be gone for more than a few minutes."

Lollie looks at me for a long beat. "Don't go far."

"I won't."

"Don't get into trouble," Cash calls as I make a beeline for the front door.

"I will!"

Now Ryder and Duke are laughing. Sawyer, who's two and a half years younger than me, laughs too.

Good. They deserve a little happiness after all the terrible shit that's gone down this week.

Stepping outside into the warm October evening, I make sure the door is closed behind me before I collapse into a crouch and gasp at the air like a man dying of thirst. Tears leak out of my eyes.

I can't fucking breathe inside the house.

All week, I've been slowly suffocating as I politely greet neighbors bringing food and condolences.

All week, I've tried to lift my brothers' spirits by keeping them busy and making them laugh.

All week, I've pretended like Mom and Dad aren't really gone. I didn't lose my mentor, the man who'd taught me everything I know; Dad's just at the feed store in town, and he'll be back any minute. Mom's heart wasn't pushed out of her chest cavity when she was hit by a car going thirty-plus miles per hour; she's out watering her garden. The pumpkins are huge this year.

Reaching inside my shirt, I run my thumb along the delicate gold ring that hangs from a chain around my neck. It's Mom's wedding band, which I dug out of the ziplock bag filled with her things that we got from the hospital. I don't know why I took it. I think—maybe I like having a piece of her with me, however small.

Cash is the smart one, and he got into college, no problem, when he graduated high school two years ago. Me, on the other hand? I didn't even apply to college. I graduated last May, and I've been cowboying full time here on Rivers Ranch ever since. Really, I've been cowboying since before I could walk. Rivers Ranch has been in my family for over a hundred years, and I'm not sure I ever want to leave.

I just don't know what my role here should be. Cash is a natural-born leader, and he's getting his degree, so I never doubted he'd take over as foreman and owner when Dad was ready to hand over the reins. But where does that leave me? How do I put my stamp on my family's legacy?

What happens now that my parents are gone?

Mom and Dad were smart, hardworking people who grew into incredible mentors for me. They were my guiding lights my whole life, and now I miss Mom so much that I could scream. Everyone said I take after her in looks and in personality, both of us extroverts. We shared a love of food and books about the Wild West. When she brought home *Little House in the Big Woods* by Laura Ingalls Wilder from the library, I climbed in her lap, and together we read my first chapter book. We have so much in common.

Had so much in common.

I look up at the sound of an engine, my hand dropping from the ring. Glancing across the front pasture, I see a truck kicking up a cloud of dust on the dirt road that connects our house to Highway 21.

My heart skips a beat when I see that the truck is a tan Ford F-150. What would John B, our veterinarian, be doing here at this hour? Far as I know, the herd doesn't need medical attention. Was there some kind of emergency? He already came to offer his condolences earlier this week. Maybe he's checking in on us?

Rising, I lift my arm and wipe my eyes on my shirt. That's when I hear it—a vaguely familiar song playing on full blast. It's coming from the truck.

My heart skips another beat when I recognize the opening notes of "Yellow" by Coldplay.

I'm down the front steps and on the driveway before I know what's happening. Holding my hand against my forehead, I squint against the light of the fiery sunset and nearly choke on my heart when it leaps into my throat.

Sally. My Sally.

Holy shit, she came.

I watch, pulse drumming, as the truck rounds a curve and heads my way.

Oh, it's Sally all right. My best friend's got both hands on the wheel, her long, dark hair flying around her face.

I smile, my chest cracking open. I've never been so happy to see someone in my entire life.

She pulls to a stop in front of me, the heat of the engine hitting the front of my legs. She turns down the music and smiles, the dimple in her left cheek popping.

I'm momentarily struck speechless.

She's *here*.

When did she get so fucking pretty?

Sally was always a cute girl. But while she's been away at college, she's grown into a beautiful woman with big brown eyes and a full, soft-looking mouth. Her cheeks are pink, probably from the heat, and her hair's gotten longer since she left. Wavy tendrils frame her round face in a halo of brown that burns to gold in the sun.

Or maybe I just didn't appreciate how pretty she was until she left. I haven't seen her since mid-August, when her parents moved her into her freshman dorm in Waco.

"Hey." She holds up a six-pack of Coca-Cola. "I got the Coke. You got the Jack?"

The Cokes are the old-fashioned kind, the ones that come in glass bottles. I see a bottle opener tucked into the red-and-white cardboard holder. We agreed when we were eleven that glass-bottle Cokes tasted better than the ones that came in plastic or aluminum.

A sudden, searing pressure builds behind my eyes and inside my chest.

I clear my throat. "What are you doing here? Don't you have exams?"

Being the smarty-pants she is, Sally got a full ride to Baylor University, a prestigious college that's a long drive from Hartsville. She's got big dreams of becoming a veterinarian like her daddy, and getting good grades is really important to her.

When she called me after hearing the news about my parents, Sally said she was buried in preparing for some midterms she had coming up. It didn't sound like she'd be able to make it to the funeral.

She tilts her head. "I'm here to get you drunk. Obviously."

"Off my own liquor?" Now I'm grinning, too, despite the emotion clogging my windpipe.

Sally dropped everything to be here.

She dropped everything for me.

Her eyes dance as they search my face. "I know you have some hidden around here somewhere."

"I do." I reach for the handle and open the door. "Your exams—please don't tell me you—"

"Got them moved to next week on account of the major family emergency my best friend is having. Yup."

I climb into the truck and pull the door shut behind me. "You didn't have to do that."

"Nah." She playfully lifts a shoulder before pulling on the gearshift to put the truck in drive. "But I did, so now you have to tell me where your stash is."

"Usual spot." I point in the direction of the hay barn.

We're quiet as the truck bumps over the uneven road. The rifle John B keeps tucked underneath the front bench clanks against the heel of my boot. I reach down and carefully set it farther back so that it stays put.

For a minute, I feel normal again. I can pretend life is the same as it was a year ago. Sally's here. It's Friday night. We're gonna get buzzed and listen to music and talk shit about our high-school teachers. Life is simple. A little boring, sure, but good overall.

I can't stop looking at her. I've missed this girl like crazy. Just being with her, not even talking—neither of us feels the need to fill the silence—makes me feel safe. Like I can finally relax.

Finally let my guard down.

She drives to the back of the barn. I jump out of the truck and dig a half-empty bottle of Jack Daniel's and a pack of Marlboros out from underneath the seat of Dad's old tractor.

My chest twists. He was alive when I hid my stash here last weekend.

Now he's not, and I don't know how to process that. Accept it. Because I refuse to believe the strongest, biggest, most capable man I know could die in the snap of a finger, just like that.

Sniffling, I don't bother to hide my tears as I climb back into the truck, the cigarettes tucked inside my pocket, the whiskey held underneath my arm.

Placing the whiskey between my knees, I wait for Sally to put the truck in drive again.

Instead, she turns to me and wraps me in a tight, warm bear hug. It ain't the polite kind of hug I've shared this week with people like Lollie and Reverend Ford.

This hug is fierce—her face buried in my shoulder, her arms clasped around my neck. I can smell the flowery scent of her lotion, the same kind she's used for as long as I can remember.

Anyone else hugged me this way, it'd be awkward.

With Sally, it's just what I need.

I open the floodgates and let out the sob I've been holding for…Christ, feels like forever.

"I'm so sorry, Wyatt." Her raspy voice is muffled against my shirt. "So, so sorry. I haven't stopped thinking about you or your brothers. I love you, and I feel—my God, I'm hurting so much for y'all. I love you. I love you. I love you."

I cry harder. Part of me is embarrassed to lose it like this. Tears and snot are everywhere.

Sally, though, just tightens her grip on me. I cry, and she cries, and we hold each other for what feels like a small eternity in the front seat of her daddy's truck.

Outside the open windows, birds chirp, and a breeze rattles the yellowing leaves on the giant old oaks that border a nearby pasture. A cow lows in the distance. The earthy smell of hay fills the air.

I don't get how the world can be the same as it ever was, but life as I know it is over. Dad is gone. Mom is *gone*, and now I'm struggling to figure out what the hell I'll do without her.

When I'm finally able to breathe again, I pull back, sopping up tears with the pad of my thumb. "Sorry."

"Stop that shit." Sally wipes her eyes too. "Cry all you want with me. I promise I'm not going anywhere—mostly because you're the one with the liquor and I need a drink after my long-ass drive."

I let out a bark of laughter. "Using and abusing your best friend? Shameful."

"Told you college wouldn't change me."

I laugh again, my heart swelling to fill my chest. At home, I make everybody else laugh. Nice change of pace to be the one laughing.

Having a good time feels so effortless when I'm with her. I don't have to put on a show or pretend to be something I'm not.

I can be myself, be a mess, and she won't bat an eye.

Speaking of messes, my nose is running. I wipe it on my sleeve, but that doesn't help much.

"Should we go for a swim?" I ask without thinking. "Weather's kinda perfect, and I need to get all this snot off of me."

"You do." Sally scrunches up her nose. "It's bad."

I tug a hand through my hair. "Gee, thanks."

"What? I'm just being honest. I'd love to go for a swim, but I didn't bring my suit."

I shrug, ignoring the press of heat in my center at the idea of seeing Sally's bra and panties. I've seen her in a bikini plenty of times. This won't be any different, right?

"We'll just go in our underwear. I promise I won't look."

Her eyes catch on my mouth before she quickly looks away. "Now who's being shameful?"

"Please? C'mon, Sally. My parents just died."

"See?" She scoffs, even as she puts the truck in drive. "Shameful."

Smiling, I reach for one of the Cokes. "I'll take care of our drinks."

Sally turns up the music, and together we belt out off-pitch lyrics to Coldplay as we head across the ranch. She parks in our usual spot on a bluff overlooking the river and kills the engine. The clean, cool scent of the water fills my head as I hand Sally a bottle of Coke. I drank a few sips of it on the drive over to make room for the whiskey. I was careful not to pour too much into Sally's bottle; she likes to get her buzz on, but she hates feeling out of control.

I make a mental note to text Sawyer or, if he doesn't answer, Cash. One of them will give us a ride home so no one's drinking and driving.

Sally sips her drink and falls back into her seat with a sigh of contentment. "I've missed this."

The view through the windshield is spectacular, especially at this time of day. The Colorado River winds its way through the Hill Country landscape, a thick blue-green ribbon of quiet, slow-moving water. It reflects the light of the dying sun, which sets the sky on fire in shades of pink and orange, tinged with purple at the edges.

A hazy half-moon is just visible above our heads.

"Ain't been the same around here without you." The Jack Daniel's hits my bloodstream. Maybe that's why I'm suddenly aware of the throb in my lips.

Sally lifts her hips and tugs at her teeny-tiny denim shorts, adjusting the hem so it doesn't ride up. My eyes graze over her bare thighs. Her skin is milky white, a startling contrast to my own. Mom used to joke her sons were born tan. We have a lifetime spent outdoors in the South Texas sun to thank for that.

Sally, though, spent most of her time indoors, studying so she could make her plans for the future happen. Reason number five million why I can't be checking her out like this. My life is here in Hartsville. Hers is gonna be in some big, fancy place where all the big, fancy jobs are.

And, yeah, Sally is also my best friend. Has been since she punched Billy Hanover in the face for bullying me in second grade. I'm no genius like her, but even I know the friendship we have is special. As her friend, I'd never want to hold her back or keep her from chasing her dreams.

I need her now more than ever. Which means I absolutely, positively can't fuck this up by wanting her like *that*.

Like I very much want to down this Jack and Coke and get to swimming so I can pull her against me in the water. Wrap her legs around my waist—

Stop.

Reaching for the pack of Marlboros, I ask, "School still goin' okay?"

"School's going great. My classes are anyway. I love my professors."

"But?"

"But I still feel pretty homesick sometimes."

"You do have deep roots here. I get that." I put a cigarette in my mouth and dig a lighter out of my pocket.

She furrows her brow. "Since when do you smoke?"

"Since all the cool kids started doing it."

"Gross."

My thumb stills on the strike of the lighter. I meet her eyes. "This really gonna bother you?"

"Yes, you killing yourself one cancer stick at a time really does bother me."

There's a catch in my chest. Sally *cares*. Now that my

parents are gone, she might be the only person in the world who cares about me so deeply. So sincerely.

I pluck the cigarette out of my mouth and put it back in the pack. My hand shakes a little. *What the fuck?*

I'm gripped by the acute need for space. Air. Downing the rest of my drink, I put the empty glass in the cupholder and reach for the door. "I'm goin' in."

Her eyes follow me as I hop out of the truck and reach over my head for my shirt collar.

She sticks her head out the window. "You're not getting, like, totally naked, are you?"

"Nah." I yank off my shirt and smirk. "Just mostly."

Her eyes flick over my bare torso before locking on mine. She holds my gaze for a beat too long.

And I hold hers for another beat, and another, my skin suddenly feeling two sizes too tight.

Even from several feet away, I feel the heat passing between us.

I tell myself I'm imagining it. Sally doesn't want me that way. She's too smart. Too ambitious. Small-town cowboys don't turn her on.

I blame the grief and the alcohol for all the mixed-up shit happening inside me right now.

Her eyes finally flick to the gold chain on my chest. She frowns. "Is that—"

"Mom's ring. Yeah." I reach up and poke my pinkie through the circlet of gold. It's so small it doesn't even get past my first knuckle. "I liked—I needed—I had to keep her close. Sounds weird—"

"It's not weird. It's sweet." Sally's throat works on a swallow.

Of course she'd say that.

Of course she'd understand.

I'm more than a little self-conscious as I head for the rope swing dangling from a tree on the top of the bluff. I quickly toe off my shoes and lose my jeans so that I'm wearing only my boxers.

Then I grab the rope, step back, and take a running leap over the edge.

My heart thunders inside my chest as I swing out over the water. The familiar way my stomach dips has me laughing and hollering like an idiot. I hear Sally laugh, too, right before I let go of the rope and drop into the river.

The water hits me in a cold, bracing rush. I'm instantly alive, reveling in the pleasure of spreading my arms and legs and just *being*. I float in a starfish pose for several heartbeats and let myself sink, the chain around my neck catching on my lips.

Down here, it's just me and my heartbeat. No hollowed-out numbness. No pain. No thought other than, *this feels good*.

When my lungs start to burn, I kick up to the surface. I shake my hair out of my eyes. The sun has set, but the blue tinge in the air still glows with subtle light.

I immediately look for Sally up on the bluff, but she's nowhere to be found.

"You coming?" I shout. "Water is perfect."

"Close your eyes," she shouts back.

I notice the rope is pulled taut toward the bank. She must've grabbed it, and now she's waiting her turn to take the leap.

Did she strip too? Or did she do the smart thing—she always does the smart thing—and keep her clothes on?

"They're closed," I lie.

"You promise?"

"No."

"*Wyatt.*"

"All right, all right." I squeeze my eyes shut. "They're closed."

A moment of silence. Then a high, happy shout, a sound that hits me square in the chest.

Can't help it. I open my eyes and see Sally falling through the air, her face split into a smile.

My stomach seizes when I see she's only in panties and a bra.

They're white. Innocent-looking enough.

But then she turns a little, and I see the curve of her ass cheek.

A thong. I nearly bite off my tongue.

Sally is wearing a fucking thong. And while it might be white, it's edged in lace. Same as the bra.

My dick pulses.

Holy God, am I getting hard for Sally?

I absolutely cannot get hard for Sally. What is wrong with me today? Why can't I get a grip on, well, everything? My body, my feelings, my thoughts? This was a bad idea.

Our eyes meet just before she hits the water.

Or maybe this was the best idea ever.

"Wyatt, you liar—" she yells, the sound cutting off when she plunges beneath the surface.

My pulse drums an unsteady beat as I wait for her to reappear.

I wait.

And wait.

A flare of panic ignites in my center. Kicking my feet, I turn in the water, frantically looking for her. "Sally? This isn't funny. Sally! Where—*oompf!*"

Hands find my stomach and push hard, sending me skidding through the water. Sally's head breaks the surface a couple of feet away, her brown eyes on fire.

"What was that for?" I sputter.

"Being a shithead." She splashes me. "What happened to not looking?"

I splash back. "I…was just making sure you were okay."

"Shut up."

"You shut up." I splash her again.

She shakes her head, her body undulating in time to the strokes of her arms in the water. "Why are you like this?"

"Because."

Sally grins. "Because you miss me?"

More than you know. "Sometimes."

"Just sometimes?"

"You miss me?" I'm vaguely aware this conversation is starting to feel flirty. Which is confusing. And awesome. And confusing.

Have Sally and I always flirted and I didn't know it? Or is this new?

"Sometimes," she replies, lips twitching.

I'm gripped by the sudden, fierce urge to kiss her.

Before I can process that—before I can drown myself so I don't do something very, very stupid—Sally does it for me. Drowns me, that is. She puts her hands on my shoulders and pushes me down. She rises out of the water as I fight her, laughter bubbling up the sides of my rib cage.

The last thing I see before I let her push me under is her nipples poking through her bra.

Bless.

I hear her laughing, too, and despite the terror I feel over the possibility of falling for my best friend out of the blue, I'm filled with this blindingly warm sensation. Trying not to suck in lungfuls of water, I picture a literal sun bursting to life inside me.

That's how it feels, being touched by Sally. Laughing with her.

Being loved by her.

Without thinking, I wrap my hands around her waist and pull her down with me. Her body feels solid and soft.

So fucking soft.

I wait for her to push me away, to unhook my fingers from around her middle.

She doesn't.

In fact, she puts her hands on my waist, her pinkies curling around my hips. My body lights up at the contact, but we don't go any further.

Instead, we hold each other underneath the water for a beat. And another. I kick my feet to keep us from going too deep.

The quiet is soothing, even if the desire pounding through me is anything but.

Even if the creeping knowledge that something's changed between us, that some big shift just happened, won't quit looping through my head.

Just when I'm about to burst with the need for air, Sally uses her hands to gently push me up to the surface. I don't need the help, but I take it anyway, keeping my hands on her so I can take her with me.

We're both breathing hard when we emerge from the water. The light catches on Sally's eyelashes, the fullness of her lips.

There's a sudden, sharp drop in my chest. She's so damn beautiful.

"I do miss you," I blurt. "All the fucking time, Sally. I worry you'll forget about me. I'm happy you're living your dream—don't get me wrong. But life...it's suddenly all so different, you know? My parents died. And right now, with you, is the first time I feel like I might not die too."

She blinks, her eyes getting misty. Her hands move up, dropping from my torso so she can wrap her arms around my neck. We kick, our legs brushing underneath the water as she pulls me in for a hug.

My brain short-circuits at the feel of her tits pressed against my chest.

My heart stops beating at the feel of her warm tears leaking onto my shoulder.

"You're not gonna die," she says thickly. "I won't let you. I miss you too, Wyatt. Sometimes...God, at school, it gets lonely, and I find myself wanting to be back on the ranch with you so badly that I can't sleep."

My pulse is going apeshit at the idea that Sally has missed me as much as I've missed her. Guess part of me really did worry she'd forget about me. That she'd fall in love with some asshole frat guy and never come back.

"You need to sleep if you're gonna ace your classes, Sal." My voice is different. It's deeper. Rougher.

Sally pulls back, her bottom lip caught between her teeth as she searches my face. "I'm doing just fine in that department. Which is why my professors let me move my exams."

"You really didn't have to come."

"You really think I'd leave you alone to face this?"

Everything inside me melts. I squeeze her harder, resisting the urge to press my lips to her throat. "You're like sunshine, you know? Sounds cheesy, but it's true. I always feel so much better when you're around."

Her swallow is audible. "I'll be your sunshine anytime, Wyatt."

I should end this conversation right now. Thank her for her kindness and get dressed. Get her home safe. The cold water's burned off my buzz; I'm fine to drive.

But when I try to unwrap my arms from around her body, I can't.

When I try to tell her we need to go, I don't. The words refuse to come out of my mouth.

My entire being rebels at the thought of letting this girl go. Every single one of my cells screams at me to keep her here, to make her mine.

That's when I know I'm in love with her.

Could be the grief talking. Could be the feel of her body wrapped up in mine.

But in my heart of hearts, I know that somehow, over the course of an hour, maybe less, I've fallen in love with my best friend. Or maybe I've been in love with her all along, and the realization is only hitting me now.

And because I'm in love with her, I have to let her go.

So I don't lean in and kiss her.

I don't throw her over my shoulder and carry her out of the water and lay her down in the back seat of the truck.

I don't tell her how I feel.

I don't do any of that.

Instead, I paste on a smile and pry my hands off her waist.

"C'mon, Sunshine," I say. "It's getting dark. Let's get you home."

CHAPTER 1

Sally

KING OF HEARTS

PRESENT DAY - NOVEMBER

CHECKING out the cowboy across the bar, I have one thought and one thought only—*Damn, I've missed this.*

Thick, tan, tattooed forearms rippling with muscle and crisscrossed with large veins—check.

Stetson and a pair of broken-in Wranglers, which are topped off with a clean white tee that stretches across his broad chest and shows off his enormous biceps—check.

Scruffy, obscenely handsome smirk—*check.*

My heart flutters when he looks up from chatting with the gorgeous blonde at his elbow and turns that smirk on me. This cowboy is the complete opposite of the serious, seriously entitled guys I went to college and veterinary school with, and I am *here* for it.

Maybe that's why I'm in the middle of the longest sexual drought of my life. Up until this summer, I wasn't hanging out with any cowboys.

The cowboys I grew up with are generous and honest to a fault. They say what they mean, and they don't play games. They certainly don't make you feel self-conscious, like you're asking for too much or you're not cute or cool enough. Having lived in a handful of different places over the course of my studies, I've learned how rare that kind of man is.

The cowboy across the bar holds up his first two fingers in his approximation of a wave. "Hey, Sunshine."

I manage a smile, my face burning. "Hey, Wyatt."

You'd think I'd be immune to my best friend's extreme hotness by now, even though I've been away from Hartsville more often than not over the past decade. He and I have been friends for—goodness—over twenty years now. Wyatt Rivers *should* be like a brother to me.

Only the raging crush I've had on him since the second I hit puberty makes my feelings for him anything but fraternal.

The supermodel type beside him hanging on his every word is Exhibit A as to why I've never acted on those feelings. Wyatt is way, *way* out of my league. He was always Mr. Popularity, star of our high school baseball and football teams, while I was the nerd who played violin, had braces, and spent her free time assisting her dad, a veterinarian, with calls on ranches across the county.

Wyatt is also very much a free spirit. Or playboy, depending on who you ask.

He'd be the perfect hookup, if only he wasn't my best friend. I don't have time for a boyfriend; last week, I was offered my dream job in Ithaca, New York, so I'm not sticking around in Hartsville. But while I'm here, I'd like to be able to get out of my head and have some really great sex—work out some of the frustration I've felt lately about, well, everything.

My experience in that department has been lackluster at best.

I lost my virginity at twenty-one to my boyfriend at the time, and the sex was unexciting to say the least; I only orgasmed when I took care of it myself. He blamed me, saying he'd "be more into it" if I was adventurous and lost a few pounds.

The next guy I dated insisted I always went down on him, but he never returned the favor.

"I just don't love it," was his explanation, which made me feel like the grossest, unsexiest person alive.

Was my body *really* that much of a turn-off?

The last boyfriend I had—this was during my residency about a year ago—didn't seem interested in having sex with me at all. When we did hook up, it was always quick and to the point. I tried to be adventurous with him—tried to incorporate more playfulness, more foreplay—but he always said he was "too tired," thanks to the round-the-clock rigors of our program. Which I didn't entirely understand because I was in the same program and I was tired, too, but never too tired to have sex. His lukewarm reaction made me feel pretty shitty about myself.

Years of disappointing experiences have left me feeling anxious and excruciatingly self-conscious when I'm with men. I feel like I need to constantly watch what I say, what I wear, what I eat. If I could be a little less of *this*, a little of more *that*, maybe the magic will finally happen.

It hasn't, and now my confidence is hanging by a thread. It's gotten to the point that I'm so self-conscious around guys I end up overthinking myself out of a great time. I try so hard to be what I *think* a guy wants that I can barely talk to someone, much less hit on them. I don't enjoy sex because I'm always in my head about whether or not *he's* enjoying it. At some point, I just gave up trying to date.

But now it's been almost a full year since I've done anything with a member of the opposite sex, and I feel like I'm coming out of my skin. A vibrator can only get you so far. I'm legitimately worried I've forgotten how to kiss someone. I know I've forgotten how to pick someone up.

Most of all, I've forgotten how to have *fun*.

I put on a smile when Tallulah—The Rattler's owner and

bartender—hands me a spicy margarita on the rocks, the glass rimmed with just the right amount of Tajín.

"How'd you know I wanted—"

"The Tajín?" Tallulah glances over her shoulder at Wyatt. "Lover boy over there ordered it for you."

Rolling my eyes, I bite back a smile. "Of course he did. Here's my card. You can keep it open—"

"He took care of that too." She waves away my card. "C'mon, Sally. You've been back for months now. You oughta know that man isn't gonna let you pay for a damn thing while you're here."

And *this* is why I often wonder if my standards for men are just too high. Has Wyatt, with his forearms and his Stetsons and his generosity, ruined me for everyone else?

I've been living in New York for the past three years, where I did my residency in large animal surgery at Ithaca University. Before that, I'd attended veterinary school in Chicago, and before that, I'd completed my undergraduate degree in Waco. Guys bought me drinks in those places, but they did it with the implied expectation that we'd have sex, or I'd at least go down on them. But of course my orgasm was an afterthought, if they thought about it at all.

Cowboys are a different breed. Makes me wonder what the hell I'm gonna do when I move back to New York at the end of December. When I completed my residency at the Ithaca University Hospital for Animals back in May, I applied for my dream job to be a surgeon there. Dad and I always talked about how great it would be to work at a university, where I could practice *and* teach, maybe even do the kind of research that would lead to breakthroughs in the field. In the meantime, I returned to Hartsville without the job offer to figure out my next steps.

I'd missed Texas like crazy over the years, so I didn't mind moving home, even if it meant living with my parents. I love my hometown. I also love the veterinary work I've gotten to do alongside Dad in the area.

But when my adviser called me earlier this week and offered me the job at Ithaca University, I immediately accepted it, even though the conversation gave me a stomachache. The pay is great, the position is prestigious, and it will set me up as one of the top equine surgeons in the nation. The job security alone is worth it. Never mind the real impact I can make there—from performing life-saving surgeries to teaching others how to provide top-notch veterinary care. Dad said it was his dream to be that kind of groundbreaking surgeon, but his grades weren't good enough to make it happen. It's one of his biggest regrets.

I start January 1. Which means I only have so many ladies' nights at The Rattler left. Only so many days to get my cowboy fix so I can go back to Ithaca University sated and steady, ready to live out my dreams.

In other words, getting this job offer has kicked my search for no-strings-attached fun with cowboys into high gear.

It's also brought my anxiety to new heights, but I think once I get cute guys in Wranglers out of my system, I'll be ready to move back to New York.

I'll finally feel excited about the next chapter in my life. Love is something I'm definitely looking for in the long-term. When I think about my future, I always picture having a partner in life. Someone to help shoulder life's burdens and celebrate its joys. Someone to start a family with and grow old with.

In the meantime, though, I just need to blow off some steam.

"Thank you for the drink," I call over to Wyatt, even as I give him a pointed look.

He just shrugs, still smirking. "It's ladies' night. Cheers, Sally."

"Cheers."

It's a Tuesday night at The Rattler, Hartsville's one and only dive bar. It's our only bar, period, which is why there's already a crowd here at half past five.

The space, with its sticky floor and clapboard walls and ceiling, buzzes with conversation, country music pumping through the speakers. I know I'm biased, but the vibe in here is unlike anything I've experienced anywhere else. There's this energy in the air, this sense of anticipation, that makes you feel like you're about to have a damn good time.

Ladies' night has been a time-honored Tuesday night tradition at The Rattler for as long as I can remember. Tallulah marks the occasion with half-priced tequila drinks.

I don't always make it out. Our days begin early; Dad has coffee going by four, and we're usually out the door not long after that, on our way to the first of many appointments and calls he'll get.

By the time supper rolls around at five p.m., I'm beat. But tonight, my libido won out over my exhaustion. I'm not going to scratch my fun-with-a-cowboy itch if all I do is work and sleep. And being around Wyatt more often than not—he's a cowboy on Lucky River Ranch, where Dad cares for the herd and the horses—has taken my sexual frustration to new heights.

Sipping my margarita, I watch Wyatt make the pretty blonde laugh while simultaneously buying another girl—this one a redhead—a drink. He's smiling, a Shiner Bock in his hand, as a third girl approaches him. They clearly know each other. Wyatt smiles, says something that makes her giggle, and then wraps her in a tight, flirty hug, the kind that has her going up on her tiptoes to plaster her body against his.

To be fair, he is a tall guy—six-two—with long legs and the kind of pecs that would make a Hollywood casting director cry. At five-three, I basically have to leap into the air to give Wyatt a hug.

The woman holds him for a beat too long before stepping

back, her hand lingering on his chest, his arm lingering around her waist.

He talks. She keeps giggling. The other two women wait patiently for him to return his attention to them at the bar.

Really, Wyatt got this sunshine thing all wrong. He's the one who's the sun. The rest of us just float in his orbit, waiting our turn to bask in his warmth and attention.

I watch in wonder as he seamlessly brings the third girl into his conversation with the first two. Now Wyatt is telling a story, and *all* the girls are giggling. The blonde playfully slaps his shoulder, and he responds with a flirty nudge of his elbow.

The man is a master.

He's fun without being cheesy. Forward without being creepy. There's an ease to the way he casts his spell over these women, a confidence in his movements, that's epically, lethally sexy.

Wyatt is getting laid tonight, no question. Ignoring the twist of jealousy in my gut at the idea of him taking *any* of these women home, I force myself to look away.

Lucky for me, my friend Mollie—who also happens to be Mom and Dad's employer, as she's the owner of Lucky River Ranch—picks that moment to walk into The Rattler. Cash—her fiancée and Wyatt's older brother—is right behind her.

Like usual, Mollie is dressed to the nines in a miniskirt and metallic-purple cowboy boots.

And like usual, Cash drapes an arm over her shoulders, letting everyone in the bar know she's taken.

Smiling, I wave at them. You'd never know from the lovey-dovey way they act now that a few short months ago, they absolutely hated each other's guts. Amazing how quickly things can change.

"I'm sorry he's here." Mollie aims a smile at Cash. "I know it's supposed to be girls' night—"

"But somebody's gotta make sure no one bothers y'all."

Cash's voice is gruff, but his eyes are soft as he looks down at Mollie.

When I decided earlier this afternoon that I'd find a second wind and give ladies' night a try, I asked Mollie to be my wingwoman. She landed a hot cowboy, so I figure I have something to learn from her. She and I have gotten close since I've been home. Plus, she's always down to have a good time.

"Pretty sure that's why Sally's here, Cash." Mollie tilts her head. "To get bothered by hot guys."

"I'll make sure they're the right kind of hot guys then." Cash glances across the bar at Wyatt and shakes his head. "My brother sure as hell ain't one of 'em. Who's he talking to?"

Mollie squints. "Don't know. Flavors of the day, I guess."

"Of the hour, more like it," Cash murmurs.

I smile tightly at the oldest Rivers brother. "Please tell me you have some friends you can introduce me to."

Stepping away from Cash, Mollie loops her arm through mine as she surveys the crowd. "There're some *cute* ones here tonight."

"Hey," Cash says.

Mollie just waves him away. "Oh, please, you and I both know you're the cutest of them all. The grumpiest, too, but that's neither here nor there."

She's not wrong. I love Cash dearly, but he definitely growls a lot.

I will say, he's been almost pleasant—pleasant for Cash anyway—ever since he and Mollie got together.

See? That's the power of good sex. Love too, I guess, but let's not put the cart before the horse.

I need a fuck that's not fictional, as rude as that sounds. I need to take advantage of being in such close proximity to so many gorgeous guys with big hands and bigger…hearts. All of a sudden, I have an end date for my stay in Texas, so it's time to make shit happen.

A gust of cool air hits the back of my legs. I turn to see a broad-shouldered man in a cowboy hat and a striped button-up stride into the bar.

My stomach dips. It's Beck Wallace, a horse trainer who works on his family's ranch about twenty miles away.

He's really, really handsome. He's not as tall as the Rivers boys, but he's still tan, ripped, and wearing a Stetson. He's got a head full of dark, thick hair and a scruffy beard-mustache situation going on.

When he smiles at me, I feel sparks catch inside my skin.

I also feel myself already getting inside my head. *Do I play hard to get, or do I go right up and talk to him? Would he be into a girl with that kind of confidence? Or would he want a nice girl, one he got to chase?*

All these questions—along with my desire to put on the perfect performance—fill me with anxiety. Our interaction hasn't even happened yet, and I'm already dreading it.

I already feel…defeated, and kinda dead inside.

Mollie pulls me closer. "Ask and you shall receive. C'mon. Let's go say hello."

Before I can respond, she's pulling me toward Beck.

He and I grew up running in the same circles, but because his family's ranch is in a different town, we didn't go to the same school. We were only officially introduced a month or so ago, when Beck came to deliver a horse to Lucky River Ranch that Cash had purchased. I immediately developed a little crush on him.

Beck's a charming guy. He's also a rock star at his job. After I examined the horse Cash had bought, it was clear that Beck and his family bred some of the finest quarter horses this side of the Rockies.

I should not be this nervous to run into him. Then again, I'm nervous around all guys. Except Wyatt, of course. But he doesn't count. I think I've internalized the idea that because Wyatt is *so* much hotter than me, *so* much cooler, I don't have a shot in hell of ever catching his eye. Which means I can just be myself around him. I'm not at all self-conscious around him. I don't second-guess myself the way I am right now.

It helps that Wyatt and I grew up together. There's a level of comfort between us, of camaraderie, that I hope will never ever go away.

I manage a smile as Beck holds out an arm, clearly inviting me in for a hug.

"Hey, darlin'! How you been?"

A million thoughts whip through my head as I look up into his green eyes. *What did that blonde do again with Wyatt? Do I press my boobs against Beck's chest? What if the boobs are too much? I feel like he'd be into boobs. What guy isn't? I don't want to give him the wrong idea though. But, wait, I actually do want to give him that idea. Isn't that why I'm here? I can't always be the nice girl—nice girls don't get laid. But if I* don't *play the nice girl, will he want to see me again?*

Mollie is looking at me expectantly.

"Hey there." My scalp prickles with heat as I try my best to mimic the blonde's smooth, easy, flirty hug. I move forward, reaching up, and Beck immediately recoils.

"Ow."

I look down to see that I'm stepping on his foot. Both feet actually.

Great freaking start.

My face is on fire as I jump away. "Oh my God, I'm so sorry—"

"Don't sweat it. You're not doing The Rattler right if your boots don't get a little scuffed up from being knocked around."

"Amen." Mollie cuts me a look. "I hope that means we'll be seeing you on the dance floor, Beck? Sally gets a break tonight from being the star of the show." She nods to the empty stage on the other side of the bar.

My mom is the drummer for Frisky Whiskey, a local band that plays here every Friday night. When I'm in town, I moonlight as a backup singer and violinist.

"Hardly the star," I reply.

"I've seen you up there, doing your thing. You're great." Beck is still smiling at me—a good sign. "I don't have a musical bone in my body, so I'm always so impressed when people can sing or play an instrument."

I swallow, *thank you* on the tip of my tongue. But a bit of Tajín gets stuck in my throat. Suddenly, I'm choking, my eyes watering as I sip more tequila in an effort not to cough.

But, oh, do I cough. Loud enough that I catch Wyatt looking up from his threesome—or it's a foursome, I guess, if you include him—and scrunching his brow while mouthing, *You okay?*

I hold up my thumb. "All good. Just went down the wrong pipe."

"You really all right?" Beck's eyebrows are pulled together. "I can get you some water if you need it."

I shake my head. "Water's the last thing I need."

"You sure?"

"Well, yeah." I suck down the dregs of my margarita, all the while wondering at what point interacting with men had become the opposite of fun. "I'm clearly a mess, so I probably need something a little stronger. You know, to, um…"

"Loosen up a little?" Mollie looks at me.

The sympathy in her eyes makes me wish the ground would open up and swallow me whole.

"Yes, that. Exactly. It's been a long day. I mean, we've all had long days, am I right? Because days here are long. And hard. Not that there's anything wrong with long and hard things. I just—oh. Oh wow, that…came out wrong. I was just trying to say that, sometimes, I enjoy things *because* they're long and also hard—"

"How about we get you another margarita?" Mollie begins pulling me back toward the bar before offering Beck a smile. "We'll be right back."

CHAPTER 2

Wyatt

COWBOY KILLER

I'VE GOT two girls on my left and one on my right.

They're easy on the eyes. Fun to talk to.

But the only girl I'm interested in right now is the one across the bar, who looks like she's about to puke.

The Rattler's bar is U-shaped. When I'm in my usual spot by the back, I can see clear across the other side of the counter. That's where Sally is holding her head in her hand, her cheeks bright pink as she blinks and blinks again.

My stomach twists.

Shit, she upset? Why? What the fuck happened over there with Beck Wallace?

I'd seen Mollie drag Sally that way. Or maybe that's just me thinking—hoping—Sally was dragged. Beck's a good guy, but that don't mean he's good enough for my best friend.

"So, Wyatt," Brianna, the girl on my right, says, "you have a date yet for the potluck?"

Sipping my beer, I keep my eyes on Sally. She's saying something to Mollie, who has a hand on her shoulder. Sally looks up. I let out a sigh of relief when I don't see any tears. Still looks a little queasy though. I know she wouldn't want me meddling—she made it clear when we were texting earlier that she was having a girls' night with Mollie—but I'm having a hard time resisting the urge to march over there and fix whatever's the matter.

"Not yet, no. What about you ladies?"

Every year, Hartsville comes together to host a charity potluck. Everyone dresses up, brings a dish, and participates in a silent auction, bidding on various items donated by community members to raise money for our local animal shelter.

Caitlin's lips twitch. "Not yet."

"I'm single as hell." That's Lennon, a redhead who works at the pharmacy next door. "And I'm definitely ready to mingle. I'd love to go, but no one's asked me. Care to rectify that, Wy?"

I've never gone to the potluck, mostly because it's a little stiff for my taste. But I like Lennon. She's fun, and she's suffering from a bout of unrequited love for a bull rider who came through town a few months back.

In other words, she's perfect. Not interested in anything serious, but always game to party.

But Sally's clearly having a shitty night, and I can't concentrate on anything else. Maybe she'll hate me for getting involved, but whatever. I don't like not knowing what's going on with her.

I glance at the tattoo of a sunrise on my left forearm. Sally's remarked on it in passing, but she doesn't know I got it for her. She also doesn't know about the other tattoo I got for her, the one on my leg. That one, more than the sunrise, is a dead giveaway of how obsessed I am with my best friend.

"Excuse me, ladies." I put a hand on Caitlin's side at the same moment she puts one on my stomach. "I'll be right back."

"Promise?" Lennon grins.

I grin right back. "Promise. Y'all don't talk to strangers, you hear?"

"Wouldn't dare," Brianna says.

It takes me a minute to work my way through the crowd. Ladies' night is in full swing, and The Rattler is packed. No surprise there. The guy-to-girl ratio in Hartsville is about ten to one—those are the results of my very (un)scientific study of our male-dominated ranching town—so you bet your bottom dollar that every cowboy, ranch hand, and farrier is out tonight, looking to get laid.

I'm not one to judge. I'm not sure I've ever needed a mind-blowing hookup more than I do right fucking now. The girl I've been in love with for twelve years—the girl I can't touch—has been back in our hometown since the end of August, and being around her so much has made me more heartsick than I've been in a long-ass time.

Sally's returned to Hartsville plenty over the past decade. She came back during her fall and spring breaks, or for a week or two here and there in between internships over the summers. But this is the first time she's been back for an extended period since we were eighteen.

This could also very well be the last time she's in Hartsville for a while. Since Sally got her dream job, John B talks all the time about the impact she's going to make on the practice of veterinary surgery. I imagine that means she won't have much time to visit us little people.

The idea that Sally might not come back for *years*—

Yeah, I'm gripped by the selfish impulse to finally make her mine.

But that's not right, and it sure as hell ain't fair. Sally and I were never meant to be. I'm a simple man who loves his family and his hometown. The Rivers have deep roots in Hartsville; my great-great-grandfather bought the land that became our ranch over a hundred years ago, and it's been in the family ever since. My parents were incredibly proud of our legacy, and they were hell-bent on passing it on to my brothers and me.

I never want to leave. Even if I did, I'm not sure I could. I'd miss my brothers, even though they're a giant pain in my ass most of the time. And leaving Hartsville would mean leaving the memory of my parents behind. They live on through the people and places in this town that they loved, and that's something all the money in the world can't replace.

Our family's ranch fell into disrepair after they died. My brothers and I just couldn't afford the upkeep, which is how we ended up working on Lucky Ranch—it was a way to make some money so we could hang on to our property. Broke my heart to see our land go untended, and we dreamed of bringing it back to life one day.

Now my brothers and I are finally able to make those dreams come true. When Mollie and Cash mended fences and fell in love, they decided to combine her family's neighboring place, Lucky Ranch, with ours, Rivers Ranch, to form Lucky River Ranch. Mollie's dad, Garrett, had struck oil on their property back in the '90s, and he quickly became a rich man. Mollie and Cash are plowing some of that money into much-needed renovations on the Rivers' side of the ranch.

Needless to say, I was born in Hartsville, and I'm gonna die here too. Still, part of me wonders what I'd do if Sally asked me to move with her to New York. Not like she ever would. But I think about it sometimes.

I find myself wishing I had kissed her that day down by the river twelve years ago. Maybe she would've kissed me back. Maybe we would've figured out a way to be together.

Maybe we'd still be together. Married. Living with our babies and our dogs in the home we made on my family's ranch. But for that to happen, I'd have to get over this fear I have of letting people in. Of opening myself up to someone, even my best friend. The pain of losing somebody you love is fucking terrible. I was not okay after my parents died, falling into a deep depression that lasted for years. I got another taste of that darkness after losing Garrett earlier this year. Time seems to be the only cure.

But losing Sally? Yeah, I don't think I could survive that.

Living on the ranch is also *my* dream. Sally doesn't want to settle down, least of all in Hartsville. She's too intelligent, too gifted, to live a quiet life in a small town. She deserves the world.

She does important work that literally saves lives. I have no right to claim her.

And yet that's what I find myself doing in every fantasy, every daydream. I claim her like a caveman possessed by a horny demon. I'm not sure I've ever used my right hand more than I have in the past few months since Sally came back.

Still, I manage to play it cool when I find my way to Sally's side. I've had more than ten years of practice pretending to not want her.

I cross my arms and lean a hip against the bar. "Who is he, and where can I find him?"

"Not funny," she replies, even though her full mouth curves into a half grin.

"I promise I'll only beat him up a little."

"I'm going to beat *you* up a little if you don't go back to doing whatever it is you were doing over there." She gestures to the three women eyeing us.

My pulse skids. Sally was watching me? Did I detect a little jealousy in her tone?

But that's just crazy. Sally is practically family. Her parents, Patsy and John B Powell, took me under their wing after my parents passed, along with Garrett Luck, who was very much a father figure to my brothers and me.

Bet Sally considers me family too. Which is why she'd never be jealous of me talking to other girls. She doesn't want me the way I want her. Period, end of sentence.

And that's a good thing.

That's the *right* thing.

Only the idea that Sally thinks of me as a brother ties my stomach in a knot. Why do I feel like that means I've fucked up somehow when, really, it means I've done everything right?

Aw, Sunshine, I'd do you right. Every time.

Shoving that thought aside, I shift my weight. "I'm not going anywhere until you tell me what's wrong."

"I'm just an idiot." She presses her thumbs into her eye sockets. "I don't think you can fix that."

I give her a gentle nudge. "You couldn't be an idiot if you tried."

"That's the thing. I did try. And I totally fell on my face." Sucking in a breath, she straightens. "You make it look so easy."

"That's because I am easy." My lips twitch.

Sally rolls her eyes. "You know what I mean. Anyone you want, you get."

"Who do you want?"

"I don't know." Sally scoffs. "Anyone. I've been thinking about it, and I decided I need to"—she tilts her head one way, then the other—"blow off a little steam while I'm in town."

I stare at her. "Does that mean what I think it means?"

"Stop looking at me like that. I'm allowed to have needs."

"You're allowed to have anything you want. But last I checked, you were into the long-term thing. Boyfriends and shit."

I've never seen Sally troll The Rattler for a hookup before. Granted, she hasn't spent a ton of time in the dive bar over the past twelve years, but this is still out of character for her.

"I *was* into the long-term thing. I still am in, like, a big-picture kind of way. But now that I know I'm leaving Hartsville, I obviously can't start something serious. I figure I'll just have some meaningless fun while I'm here."

I feel the words she doesn't say like a punch to the gut. *I don't want anything serious because I'm leaving for good.*

She's leaving to go live in a cute college town, where she'll fall for some Yankee dickhead and never come back.

I run a hand over my scruff. Do I tuck tail and run? I don't want to talk to Sally about who she'd like to fuck.

But some sick, mean part of me is dying to know who—what—she wants.

Some mean part of me wants to be the one to give it to her. Who better to *blow off a little steam* with than the town heart-breaker?

I don't take pride in the title. Yes, I have fun. A lot of it. But I also feel like the butt of a joke at this point. I'm thirty years old, for Christ's sake. I'm also a little...lonely, if I'm being honest, now that I've moved out of the bunkhouse and into my own place on Lucky River Ranch.

When Mollie and Cash joined forces, they gifted me the 1920s Victorian farmhouse Mollie's great-grandfather had built. It's simple but beautiful, having been meticulously renovated and maintained by Garrett, who preferred the farmhouse to the giant but sterile New House, which he built as a gift for his then-wife Aubrey. It was their main residence on Lucky Ranch for a little while, a six-thousand-square-foot behemoth where they planned to raise their family. But not long after they moved in, their marriage crumbled, and Aubrey took Mollie and moved to Dallas. Garrett moved back to the farmhouse, where he lived until the day he died. Now the New House is a gathering place of sorts for the ranch's employees, Patsy turning out three meals a day in its massive kitchen.

I'd like to settle down. Find a real partner in life. Seeing Cash and Mollie pair off has only intensified my desire to find my person.

I've never seen my brother happier.

I've never been more jealous. I try to keep it to myself. Envying what my brother has makes me feel ashamed. Cash has had a hard road, and he deserves to be happy.

Jealousy ain't my style.

But I'm jealous of my brother. And whoever Sally's looking to take home tonight…and every night.

I absently tug Mom's ring across the chain hanging from my neck. "So you wanna hook up with one of these winners?" I eye a nearby ranch hand, who's already so drunk that he's pretending to reel a woman in with an invisible fishing pole.

Sally scoffs again. "You can't be serious. *You*, of all people, have no right to judge me."

"I'll be the first to admit, I'm no saint." I hold up my hands. "I'm just looking out for you. Don't want you getting burned."

"I'm a big girl. Beck Wallace isn't going to burn me."

My heart lurches. So she does want Beck. Why him?

Turning to lean my left hip into the counter, I paste on a smirk. "He ain't nearly smart enough to get under your skin."

Sally's shoulders rise on an inhale as she glances across the bar. I follow her gaze to see Brianna, Lennon, and Caitlin watching us intently.

"See?" Sally asks. "You get attention, even when you're talking to another girl."

"Well, yeah. That's how it works."

"How what works?"

"You gotta play the game. Jealousy is a powerful aphrodisiac."

Sally turns those big brown eyes on me. They shine with a funny little spark, igniting the flecks of gold in her irises. "Really?" Her flat delivery of the word drips with judgment and something else. Something that sounds suspiciously like…curiosity?

"Hey, I don't make the rules. I just play by them."

She grins. "Hate the game, not the player. That *would* be your MO."

"C'mon, Sunshine." I've missed how much this girl makes

me smile, despite the seriously *un*funny things happening inside my chest. "You could never hate me."

"Show me, Wy."

My heart does that lurching thing again. "Show you what?"

"How to play. It's been forever since I had fun like that."

Heat rips through my skin. Sweat prickles along my scalp and inside my collar.

God almighty.

This girl don't know what she's asking.

She doesn't know that asking me to *show her* has me thinking about showing her lots of things. Most of them involving nudity and my face between her legs.

Legs that are very much on display in tight jeans. She's wearing a pair of fire-engine-red Bellamy Brooks boots, which hug her calves like a second skin.

"I'm not helping you get laid, Sally," I manage, bringing my beer to my lips.

"I'm not asking, Wyatt." She's still grinning.

There ain't a thing on God's green earth I wouldn't give this girl.

And, yeah, maybe the thought of making Beck Wallace jealous appeals to me, even if Sally's endgame doesn't.

Tonight, Sally will be in my arms.

Tonight, she'll only have eyes for me. That's enough.

That has to be enough, because the whole point of me doing this—showing Sally how to play the game—is for her to ultimately end up in someone else's bed.

Who knows? Maybe seeing her with Beck will finally make it click that she and I aren't meant to be. It'll suck, but it'll be like ripping off a Band-Aid. Once it's done, it's done.

I'll be done with the world's most serious case of unrequited love.

"You wanna learn from the master"—draining my beer, I set it on the bar—"you gotta do as I say."

"Ooh." Sally wiggles her shoulders in an adorable fake shiver. "I like the bossiness, Wy."

I nod over her head to the dance floor. There's no live band, but the playlist tonight is a vibe, filled with the kind of country that makes you wanna move. It's a mix of new artists and '90s greats—from Shaboozey to old-school Alan Jackson. Couples flock to the floor, along with girls in groups of two or three.

"Let's go." I push off the bar and motion for her to walk in front of me.

Sally digs her teeth into her bottom lip. Her eyes are soft now. "Thank you."

"I ain't going willingly."

"Yes, you are. And I love you for it."

My heart lifts. *I love you too, Sal.*

But then I'm crushed by a familiar sense of disappointment when it hits me that her words don't mean what I want them to. Sally loves me as a friend. But I'm *in* love with her. Big fucking difference.

I watch her turn around and follow her onto the dance floor. Morgan Wallen is playing. Sally holds up an arm, swaying her hips to the beat, and I resist the urge to put my hand on the small of her back. On her hip.

She looks *good*. Mostly because she moves with confidence. Makes me puff out my chest a little, knowing she's comfortable enough with me to let loose.

But then she glances over her shoulder. I follow her gaze and see her glancing at Beck. He's looking at us—a good sign. Sally, though, goes stiff, her arm falling to her side—a bad sign.

"Hey."

Her eyes dart to mine.

"Stop looking to see if Beck is watching us. You look at me. Only me. Got it?"

Sally's long, dark lashes flutter as she turns around to face me. Even in her boots—they've got a good heel on 'em—she's so short I still have to bend my neck to make eye contact.

"I see how this works for you."

Is her reply a little breathless? Or am I just imagining it?

I step closer and smirk. "How so?"

"You're...good at making a girl feel like...like she's the only person in the room."

"Take notes."

She puts a hand on my chest and gives me a playful shove. "The cockiness doesn't help."

"Yeah, it does." I grab her wrist and put her hand back on my chest. "There. That's good. Let him see how much you like to touch me."

Uncertainty flashes across her expression. Her eyes flick over my shoulder.

"Nuh-uh. Eyes up here, Sunshine. And the other hand on my waist."

Sally hesitates, but then she does as I tell her. She's stiff again—clearly in unfamiliar territory—as she puts her hand on my side in an awkward position. Her palm is cupped near my rib cage so that only her fingertips touch me.

Hell no. This middle school dance shit ain't gonna do it.

So I grab her hand and move it to my belt, pressing it against my hip so that her palm flattens out. My body leaps when one of her fingers dips inside my waistband for half a heartbeat. This girl makes me weak in the fucking *knees*.

"Sorry!"

"Don't be." I clear my throat. "I like a good fondle."

She's smiling again, the discomfort melting from her face, and there's a catch in my chest. "You a master of that too?"

"I am indeed. Which is lucky for you because—and I say this with love—you've got some practicing to do."

Sally bites her lip. "Fondling is not my area of expertise, no."

"You just save the lives of animals and shit."

"Some shit like that, yeah."

I sway to the music a little. Just enough so that she doesn't realize when she starts swaying again too.

Dang, I *like* her hands on me this way.

I wanna put my hands on her. But that'd be crossing into dangerous territory. Beck'll be watching us whether or not I touch Sally, mostly because I'm about to show her a damn good time.

And a beautiful woman having a good time at a bar? No man in his right mind can resist that.

Sally's doing a good job of keeping her eyes locked on mine. The extended eye contact is unnerving, but I...kinda like it. Feels like I'm edging myself. How much can I take before I pop a woody and come in my pants like a teenager?

Sally and I have danced together before, but it doesn't happen often enough. She's usually either working or up on the stage, performing with her mom.

For a split second, I allow myself to fantasize that this is real. That Sally is looking at me like this because she wants me, and I'm gonna make her smile and laugh and sweat while we take turn after turn around the dance floor. Then I'm gonna take her home. Lay her down. Give her what Beck Wallace can't.

"You good if I give you a spin?" Because I'm a masochist, clearly.

Sally scrunches her brow. "Yes. You don't need to ask."

"A guy should always ask if it's okay to touch you."

"Okay, Dad."

I grab the wrist of the hand she's got on my chest. When I wrap my first finger and thumb around it, I'm struck by how delicate she is here. How small. The pads of my finger and thumb touch with room to spare.

I can feel the uneven beat of her pulse against the inside of my thumb knuckle.

"*Daddy* is fine. *Dad* is not."

Sally lets out a bark of laughter. "I'm scared to ask if you're serious."

"I'm dead serious when I tell you not to call me Dad again. C'mon, Cinderella. Time to dance at the ball."

Letting go of her wrist, I curl my hand around hers so that our tangled fingers are clasped against my chest. Her palm is warm. The kind of soft that makes my chest tight.

Her gaze wavers, falling to our hands before moving back up to my face.

"What?"

"Your calluses." She runs her thumb over the top part of my palm. "They're insane."

"Too rough?"

Her brown eyes glitter. "Yeah. But I think I like it."

"Do not elaborate." I bite the inside of my cheek. I pull our hands over her head, forming a bridge with our arms. "C'mon, Sunshine. Give me what I want."

"Yes, Daddy."

Dear God. "What did I tell you about—"

"I thought Daddy was okay?" Her eyes dance.

She's teasing me, and I fucking love it.

When am I gonna stop feeling like a lovesick asshole?

"Changed my mind. It's definitely not okay." I give her hand a tug, encouraging her to spin already. "God forbid my brothers overhear you calling me that."

Sally turns, a big old smile on her face as she mouths the words to a Post Malone country song. She glances around the bar as she moves, her gaze catching on something—someone—before returning to my face.

"He's watching," she says, definitely breathless this time. "Beck."

My gut clenches. Instinctively, I pull her close and wrap an arm around her waist, pulling her flush against me. "Good."

"Your girlfriends are watching too. I hope I'm not stepping on any toes?"

I look at our feet. "Not yet."

"Aren't you clever?" she deadpans.

I look back up to see her grinning at me. "Sure am."

"Cocky."

"It's working, isn't it?"

She lifts a shoulder. "It is actually." Her eyes go wide. "Oh. Oh, Wy, wait. I think it's working too well. He's coming over."

My head snaps around so fast that my neck cracks. Sure enough, Beck is heading our way, his eyes narrowed playfully as they devour my best friend from head to toe.

"Do you not want him to come over?" I bite out.

"No, I do. I definitely do. I'm just—now I'm nervous."

He makes *her* nervous? Man doesn't deserve to lick her boots.

I don't realize I'm squeezing Sally's hand until she lets out a little yelp.

"Sorry, Sal, I—"

"You're lookin' good out here, Sally." Beck glances at me. "Mind if I cut in?"

I do fucking mind.

I mind so much that I gotta resist the very strong urge to punch the guy in the mouth.

But that would upset Sally. It would also give me away. And, yeah, I was young when my dad died, but I'll never forget him telling me over and over again that Rivers never start fights.

We do, however, always finish them.

So I drop Sally's hand, and I step away. "Y'all have at it."

She's looking at me, a deep groove between her eyebrows. "You all right, Wy?"

"I'm great. Why wouldn't I be?" I clap my hands. Jesus, now I'm the one who's stiff and awkward, and just—I gotta get outta here. "You good, Sunshine?"

She nods, the movement a little too quick.

I meet her eyes. *Don't be nervous. You got this.*

Her lips curl into a smile. "All good."

Beck takes her hand. Sally turns that smile on him. A piercing ache slices through my center.

I can't watch. So I turn and stalk off the dance floor. From the corner of my eye, I catch Brianna waving at me. I don't wanna be rude, but I can't stay here.

I need to be alone.

I'm a few feet shy of the exit when I feel a hand on my arm. I glance over my shoulder to see Cash glowering at me.

It's all I can do not to roll my eyes. I get why he doesn't want me crossing any lines with Sally. The Powells are like family to him too—not to mention the fact that they're essential to the operation of Lucky River Ranch.

"What were you doing with Sally over there?" Cash asks.

I shrug, like the two of us don't know how down bad I am for her. "Before you get your panties in a wad, know that she's the one who asked me to dance."

Cash tilts his head, his eyes hard. "Y'all were awfully close."

"We're friends. We were talking. I'm allowed to talk to her, Cash."

"Way you looked at her wasn't exactly friendly."

I'm not gonna deny that. Doesn't mean I gotta confirm how I feel about her though.

"You know we're both adults, right?" I say. "What we do or don't do isn't anyone's business."

"And you know I'm only looking out for you." His expression softens. "I just don't want anyone gettin' hurt."

Too late for that.

"You don't have anything to worry about. She doesn't want me like that. Look, she's out there with Beck right now. We're safe, all right? Everything is fine."

I'm not fine though as I push out into the chilly November evening.

I don't feel fine as I climb into my truck and immediately lunge for the glove compartment, shoving aside several packs of gum to find what I'm looking for.

The first drag on my Marlboro has me feeling lightheaded. Smoking is a gross habit, and I hate it. Except when I don't. Rolling down my window, I fall back against the seat and close my eyes.

I don't want Sally to leave Hartsville. But she sure as hell can't stay. I might very well end up a dead man if she does. Wanting her this way—being around her—is killing me. It's torture.

The worst, best, sweetest kind of torture there is.

CHAPTER 3

Sally

BONES

LIVING with your parents at the ripe old age of thirty, albeit temporarily, is not ideal.

It's especially not ideal when your dad is a veterinarian who is basically on call twenty-four/seven, three sixty-five, and he knocks on your door in the dead of night.

"Hey, Sal? I'm sorry to wake you, honey, but we have an emergency. A foal was kicked by her mama, and sounds like her leg might be broken."

The sound of his voice yanks me out of my deliciously deep REM cycle. One of the many benefits of working on ranches: you sleep like the dead.

Prying open my eyes, I grab my phone off the bedside table. No wonder I feel like I was asleep for ten minutes—it's three thirty in the morning. I went to bed a little after eleven, after I got home from The Rattler. Late for me.

I am exhausted. But baby horses with broken bones can't wait.

"I'm awake, Dad." I reach up to turn on the lamp.

I blink as my childhood bedroom comes into view. My parents have preserved it as a kind of museum exhibit, an ode to my teenage obsession with Peeta from *The Hunger Games* and the color periwinkle.

It's sweet they haven't touched it. And a little weird, but I guess that comes with the territory of being an only child. There's comfort in knowing I'll always have a home base. A place to land when I'm feeling lost or sad or alone. I'm lucky.

And very, very tired.

Also, did I *really* ask Wyatt to show me how to pick someone up last night? My heart skips several beats at the memory of the way his fingers locked around my wrist, his eyes steady on mine.

The craziest part? It worked. Beck and I danced to not one, but two whole songs together before I finally lost my nerve and disappeared into the ladies' room with Mollie and her friend Wheeler. I would've danced with him more, but I felt so painfully self-conscious that it kind of ruined the whole thing for me. I wish I could be a little more carefree around him. A little bit more relaxed. Maybe then we'd *both* have a good time.

"I'm already dressed," Dad says. "Coffeepot is on. We'll take it to go, and I'll fill you in on the drive."

As much as my dad's been on my ass lately about, well, everything, I have to smile at his thoughtfulness. He means well. Loves well too.

Shivering, I throw on jeans, a T-shirt, a sweatshirt, and thick socks. I have no idea if we'll be working in a barn or outside this morning, and doing my veterinarian thing in the frigid temperatures of upstate New York has taught me to always dress in layers and prepare for the worst. It doesn't get nearly as cold here in South Texas, but it sure as hell isn't comfortable outside in the dead of night in November.

Popping out my retainers, I brush my teeth and try not to think about Wyatt. I could very well be performing surgery in the next half hour. I need to strategize. Go through my mental catalog of the things I gleaned from that pair of articles I read last week, the ones about tweaking the double-plating technique I've used to repair equine compound fractures.

Putting down a foal is not something I want to do this morning. Or ever. Which means I have to fix her leg.

But I'm tired, and my mind keeps wandering to the warm, firm slab of muscle I felt when I accidentally slipped a finger inside Wyatt's jeans. The man is jacked, no two ways about it.

I'm pretty sure he wears briefs; I felt their thick, silky elastic waistband. And the way he looped an arm around my waist—how confidently he moved, how smoothly—

"Sally, honey, coffee is ready! We best get a move on!"

I jump at the sound of Dad's voice from downstairs. Rinsing my toothbrush, I pull my hair back into a ponytail and turn off the light.

Time to get to work.

Mom is already on her way to the New House at Lucky River Ranch, where she's the chef and she feeds its dozens of employees breakfast, lunch, and dinner five days a week. So it's just me and Dad in the same F-150 he's driven for as long as I've been alive. I made sure all my surgical supplies and the portable X-ray machine were still in the back before we left.

I sip my coffee as we drive through the dark, heat blasting. "Where we headed?"

"The Wallace Ranch."

My stomach plummets. That ranch belongs to Beck and his family. They run an incredible horse breeding program there, and rumor has it they want to start training barrel racers there too. Dale Wallace, Beck's dad, is even building an arena on their property.

Because they're such a big operation, they have their own veterinarian on staff. Vance is a little younger than Dad—in his late forties—and he's a kind man and an excellent doctor. If he can't fix the problem, you know it's serious.

"The fracture is complex, then." I take a bigger sip of coffee, even though it scalds my tongue.

"Yep. She specifically asked for you."

"Who?"

"Ava Bartlett. She's a new trainer over there—just started this week. I think she was a barrel racer for a while. Anyway, she called me in a panic, saying Vance was stumped. He told her you were the person to call."

My chest lifts at the compliment. In many ways, I feel more confused about my future than I ever have. I just can't seem to get excited about the job I just accepted. But this—my reputation, my hard work—I'm damn proud of it. I love what I do.

Also nice to feel needed by the community I grew up in and love with all my heart.

"See how good that feels?" Dad asks, glancing at me. "What I'd give to be the go-to person for this kind of thing. You possess talent and brains that I never have. I'm glad you're not gonna waste it staying in Hartsville."

Now my chest is twisting. I reach over to pat Dad's arm. "Life is good here and you know it. Besides, you're the go-to guy for other things that are just as important."

He lifts a shoulder. "I suppose. But the thought that I coulda been better, coulda done more with my life…" He sighs. "Hard not to dwell on it sometimes."

When my adviser called last week to offer me the job, Dad was so proud, so excited, he literally had tears in his eyes. Beneath his excitement though, I also detected a hefty dose of regret. I know that was a call *he* had hoped to get but never did. I understand why he's so invested in my career—this job is an opportunity he missed out on—but at the same time, it puts a lot of pressure on me to take advantage of that opportunity.

I also wonder if Dad is a little jealous. He loves his work and appreciates the beautiful life he and Mom have built in our small town, but he never had the support, financial and otherwise, that he's always provided for me. I wonder if *he* wonders how far he could've gone in life if his parents had been a little more involved in his education. They were ranchers who, according to Dad, "didn't have two pennies to rub together." My grandfather never finished high school, so it was a big deal that Dad not only went to college, but to veterinary school too.

I know he's proud of that fact. I also know Dad is a smart, ambitious guy, and his regrets about his career haunt him in a way he doesn't want regret to haunt me. I have to remember that the pressure he puts on me comes from a good place.

I have to remember that once I get cowboys out of my system, I'll feel worlds better about moving back to New York.

Finishing my coffee, I grab Dad's phone and call Ava back on speaker. She fills me in on what happened—the foal, named Pepper, was accidentally kicked by her mama—and then she FaceTimes us from the foal's stall.

"Aw, poor baby," I say. "Looks gnarly."

"Do you think you can fix it?" Ava asks. "Vance didn't sound hopeful."

I bring the screen closer to my face, narrowing my eyes. I'll need X-rays to confirm, but it looks like Pepper fractured her metacarpal bones. I immediately start to visualize the fix —two steel plates to stabilize the bone, along with several screws. Luckily, I don't think we'll need to use cables.

"I don't want to make any promises, but I'm coming up with a plan. We'll be there in…" I look at Dad.

"Twenty minutes."

"Okay, great." The relief in Ava's voice is palpable. "See y'all soon."

The Wallace Ranch is second only to Lucky River Ranch in terms of facilities and beauty. Even in the dark, I'm able to see how organized and well-maintained Wallace Ranch is. Neat fences line the paved driveway that leads up to an enormous and beautiful white barn.

"Jesus." I duck my head to peer up at the barn through the windshield. "I feel like we just drove onto the set of *Yellowstone*."

Dad grins, his face creasing. "You know, I've been told I look like Kevin Costner."

"You're handsomer than he is." I lean across the center console to press a kiss to his stubbly cheek. "Let's go."

I'm relieved to see just Ava and Vance when we walk into the barn. As much as I want to flirt with Beck, I need to focus right now. Having a hot cowboy in the vicinity would definitely make that difficult.

"Y'all, thank you so much for coming out here so early." Ava's brow is furrowed, her full mouth turned down in a frown. "Poor thing was howling so loud that it woke up the bunkhouse."

I'm struck by how pretty Ava is, despite her oversized coat and the knot of messy blonde hair on the top of her head. Like many barrel racers, there's a pageant sort of beauty to her looks—perfect skin, dramatic brows, and large eyes framed by long, dark lashes.

"Pepper is in good hands." Dad nods at me. "Did I tell you Sally is going to be a surgeon at Ithaca University?"

Resisting the urge to roll my eyes—Dad can be a little obnoxious with the bragging—I look at Vance, who appears relieved.

"Impressive. We're so glad you're here, Sally," he says.

"Seriously." Ava uncrosses her arms. "Y'all can follow me."

I'm careful to keep my footfalls quiet as we approach the stall. Pepper is tucked into the far corner. I can immediately tell she's in distress by the rapid rise and fall of her sides. She's holding up one leg—the injured one—and as I peer into the stall, I can see she doesn't appear to have an open fracture; there's no blood or bone poking through her white-and-gray speckled coat.

Her huge, liquid eyes meet mine in the low light. The naked pain in them makes my chest cramp.

When I look over my shoulder, Dad is right behind me. He wordlessly holds out my headlamp and stethoscope.

"Thanks." I plug the stethoscope into my ears and put on the headlamp. Turning on the light, I head for Pepper, Dad beside me.

I do a quick exam, listening to her heart and stomach. She's skittish, but I press a hand to her side and murmur, "That's a good girl. There we go. We're gonna make you feel better, all right?"

She calms down enough for me to examine her foreleg, Dad and Vance gently holding Pepper in place while I do my thing.

"There's not a lot of swelling, which is a good sign," I say. "No ligament damage that I can tell. And the blood supply doesn't appear to be interrupted. Let's get some X-rays and go from there."

That doesn't take long. The pictures tell me what I already knew—this poor baby has multiple fractured bones. She'll definitely need the plates and screws.

I'm already visualizing how I'll stabilize the joint. Surgery on horses is extra complex because they're working animals. The fix has to enable Pepper to do what she was bred to do—work on a ranch—or else she'll be of no use to the Wallaces.

Which means I have to get this right.

Ava's face falls when I tell her the news. She swallows hard, eyes glazing over with tears. "Not good, huh?"

"I think I can fix it actually."

"Really? Because that's a bad break." Her unspoken words hang in the air between us—horses who have this kind of break are usually put down.

"I can't guarantee a full recovery." I loop my stethoscope

around my neck. "But I've repaired dozens of fractures like this one, and the prognosis is good. If you'll give me permission, we can operate right away."

Vance's eyes bulge. "But the vet office isn't open until—"

"We'll operate right here." I grin at him. "Have you ever done standing surgery before?"

He shakes his head.

I roll up my sleeves. "We'll sedate sweet Pepper so she's nice and calm, and then we'll use local anesthetic so we can operate. She'll be standing right here in the barn the whole time."

"And the recovery?" Ava asks. "What will that look like?"

Dad nods toward the exit, his way of telling me he's going to get the equipment I need. I tip my head, and when he disappears, I turn back to Ava.

"I think we'll need to use a full limb splint for her. Then it'll be box rest for a bit. Nothing too crazy."

Ava slowly shakes her head. "This is wild. In all my years on the circuit, I've never heard of anything like this."

"Ithaca University teaches all the cutting-edge techniques!" Dad shouts from somewhere.

This time, I do roll my eyes. "I'm sorry about him. He's—"

"Really damn proud of you, Sally." Vance smiles at me. "As he should be. Mind if I assist?" He motions to the foal.

"I'd love that. Here, let's go wash up."

CHAPTER 4

Sally

HOT TO GO

I'M SWEATING BULLETS. My legs and back ache from squatting, and my eyes are gritty.

But when I look up from the bandage I just wrapped around Pepper's foreleg, I'm surprised to see thin yellow light streaming through a nearby window.

Pepper's surgery was a challenge. I debated where to insert the screws, and getting the angle of the plates just right had me cursing like a sailor. My feet hurt so badly that I feel like I'm about to fall over.

At the same time, the procedure seemed to go by in the blink of an eye. My body is tired, but overall, I feel…peaceful. Proud.

Best of all, Pepper no longer has that pained, haunted look about her. She blinks lazily, still sedated, before she noses at the hay at her feet.

"I like your smile." Dad's eyes twinkle as he packs up the portable X-ray equipment. "You did good, Sally."

Vance just shakes his head, staring at Pepper. "That sure was something. I know I already asked you so many questions, but I'd love a debrief if you have time. These are techniques I'd really like to learn. You saved a life today, Sally."

My chest swells. "Couldn't have done it without an assist from you and Dad. I'd be happy to teach you."

"She's good at that, isn't she? Teaching?" Dad gives me a look. "Which is why she needs to be at a university, not in a barn in the middle of nowhere."

The joyful feeling in my chest dims. Truth is, I love working in the barn. I love teaching too. Most of all, I love being surrounded by our little makeshift team. Dad was handing me tools before I even told him I needed them. Vance kept me talking, asking about my residency, the goat cheese I've been making now that Lucky River Ranch had goats, how I liked playing in a band with my mom. And Ava was there to fill us in on Pepper's bloodline, making us all laugh when she shared Mrs. Wallace named the horse Pepper because she liked to read spicy books.

I feel like I had a real support system of people who genuinely cared about the horse and about me too. I feel appreciated.

I feel good.

Makes me realize how I feel like just another cog in the machine at Ithaca University. It's a super-professional environment, but it feels sterile in comparison to Hartsville. Then again, it probably feels that way because I haven't been there long enough. My residency lasted three years, but that's a drop in the bucket compared to the years I've spent in Hartsville. And I haven't found a "squad" in New York like I have here, people I know and work with easily. I'll eventually find those people in New York, though. I just need to give it time.

Still, I continue to force my smile. "Thanks, Dad."

"Well, I for one am glad you're here." Ava holds out a gallon-sized jug. "Some cider Mrs. Wallace made from the harvest. The orchard is apparently overflowing this year."

I'm smiling for real again as I tuck the jug into the crook of my arm. Say what you want about small towns, but never in my ten-plus years at school has someone given me a gift for my services. Much less a thoughtful one.

This is why I love Hartsville. And this is why it's always so hard to leave.

"This stuff is delicious," I say. "Please thank her for me. I think I'll use it to make some mulled cider."

"You put whiskey in that cider?"

"Of course I put whiskey in my cider. Key is to use a lot of it."

She grins. "I like you."

"You have to stay warm out here somehow."

"There are lots of ways to do that on a ranch. Especially if cowboys are around."

Vance chuckles. Dad turns red.

I blush a little, too, but I'm able to laugh, despite the image of Wyatt on horseback streaking through my mind, his hat on his head and a lasso in his hand. Man rides harder and faster than anyone I know.

I'd bet good money he does the same in bed.

I email Ava and Vance a detailed summary of Pepper's post-op care plan. Then Dad and I climb into his pickup and head home, the gallon of cider tucked carefully behind my seat.

On the drive, Dad gets a call from a nearby rancher about a horse that's not eating.

"Sounds like colic," Dad says when he hangs up. "I'll drop you back at the house, and then I'll head over to Jordan's to handle the horse."

"You sure?"

"Of course. You should get some sleep. You did awesome, Sally. Really, you have so much talent. I can't wait to watch you soar in New York."

My heart swells at his obvious pride. I'm proud of myself too. I love how happy my success makes my dad. But I'm starting to wonder if my definition of success is the same as his.

I flip down the visor against the strengthening sun. With the light no longer blinding me, I can see just how blue the sky is. My window is cracked open, letting in a crisp, clean breeze.

It's going to be a gorgeous fall day here in South Texas.

How many more days like this will I get? I'm supposed to start my job in Ithaca in a month and a half. It will be beautiful here when I leave. But Ithaca? It will be a gloomy, frozen tundra.

My chest hurts when I think about it, so I try not to. Only Dad seems intent on reminding me of my duty to honor the "talent" I have.

"I know you don't want to move into your apartment until after the holidays," he says, referring to the two-bedroom place I'm renting just off campus in Ithaca. "But since your lease starts December 1, Mom and I thought the three of us could fly up there early as a little Christmas present for us all. I'd love to get to visit Ithaca again, and we could start moving you in."

I turn my head to look out the window. The view of Hill Country is spectacular from this stretch of Highway 21—pale earth, green cacti, the orange and fiery-red leaves of the gnarled oaks dotting the undulating landscape.

Home.

"Y'all don't have to help me move in," I reply carefully. "I'm not in college anymore."

"We'd like to be there for you, Sally. This is an exciting time for you, and we're excited too."

Talk about twisting the knife.

"That's sweet of y'all. Thank you. Let me think about it, all right?"

He glances at me. "Don't sound so thrilled."

"I'm sorry. I really do appreciate the offer. Thank you. I'm just tired." It's a lie, but I yawn nonetheless.

Sighing, Dad turns his attention back to the road.

I'm going to be actually, legitimately tired once I start my job. It'll be balls to the wall from the get-go: twelve-hour shifts, tons of overtime, eighty-hour weeks. Lots of stress. Just thinking about it makes my stomach twist.

Needless to say, I'm not going to have a lot of free time. I have to have fun while I can. Only problem? I'm not great at fun.

However, I *do* know someone who, in his own words, is a master at it.

My stomach does a somersault when I remember the hot glimmer I saw in Wyatt's eyes last night when he called me Cinderella and spun me around the dance floor. Beck clearly couldn't stay away once I had Wyatt's attention. And I couldn't help but notice how comfortable I felt with Wyatt. When I was with Beck, I was a nervous wreck, overthinking every little thing. But with my best friend, I was able to have fun.

I was able to be carefree.

What if…

This is crazy and inappropriate and just plain weird, but what if I asked Wyatt for another lesson-slash-date? Just so he can teach me to let go and have a good time with a guy? A fake date would also have the added bonus of making other guys jealous.

My pulse skips a beat when I remember the potluck is coming up. Wyatt wouldn't be caught dead at such a wholesome event, but every other cowboy in Hart County will be there.

Bet Wyatt looks *really* good dressed up, but that's neither here nor there. Does he even own a suit jacket?

I glance at the jug of cider behind my seat. Glance at the clock. It's only nine, but that's practically the afternoon on a cattle ranch. Wyatt and the other cowboys have been up for hours at this point.

Dad drops me off at our house. "Try to get some rest, all right?"

"Love you." I grab my cider, open the door, and hop out of the truck.

"Sally," he warns, clearly suspicious of my sudden burst of energy.

I look up at Dad with a grin. The warm sunshine pours over my head and shoulders. "I'm getting a second wind."

"Rest, sweetheart."

"I'll see ya later, Dad." I close the door and scurry inside the house, wondering if my parents have an extra bottle of Jack Daniel's around.

I don't know if I'll actually have the courage to ask Wyatt to be my fake date to the potluck. Just like I don't know if going through with this dumbass plan will make me feel worse or better.

All I know is, I have to do *something*.

And I know if I ask Wyatt to get his mid-morning buzz on with me, the answer will be yes. The guy can never say no to a good time.

Come to think of it, he can never say no to me either.

CHAPTER 5

Wyatt

DIAL DRUNK

I'M ALREADY GRABBING my rope and urging my horse, Joker, into an all-out sprint when Sawyer shouts, "You got her, Wyatt?"

"Oh, I got her."

Joker and I make a beeline for the rogue calf who's apparently intent on driving me up the wall today. This is the second time since sunrise that she's tried to make a run for it.

Joker's hooves thunder on the hard-packed earth. My heart thunders in time to his stride. I didn't get near enough sleep last night, but you wouldn't know it from the rush of hot, urgent energy coursing through my body.

Squeezing Joker's sides with my legs, I drop the reins and use both hands to ready the lariat I'll use to lasso the calf. My shoulders and biceps sing as I take the looped rope in my right hand and whip it in a circle above my head. I hear its *whoop, whoop, whoop* every time it rotates just above my ears.

"Look at that smile!" Duke yells as I hurtle past him. "Boy, that ain't gonna last when you miss!"

"I ain't missing!"

I wish I could say I'm not one to brag, but there's no use lying. I'm the best damn cowboy this side of the Colorado

River. No one can outride or outlasso me. Not even my older brother, Cash, who was basically born with a Stetson on his head and a rope in his hand. Too bad he's not here to see this. He and Mollie went to Dallas this morning to lay the groundwork for the launch of her next boot collection.

A grin splits my face as Joker and I hit just the right distance from the calf. I release the lariat. My heart leaps into my throat as I wait the split second it takes for the circle of rope to land around the calf's neck. When it lands, the calf struggles, pulling the rope taut. Joker holds his ground while I leap off him with a happy yell.

The calf struggles. She's strong, but I'm stronger. Ryder hops off his horse, too, and together, we tie up the calf's legs with another rope we call the piggin' string. We give her a few minutes to calm down before we let her loose.

By the time we're done, I'm covered in sweat and out of breath. The cloud of dust we kicked up has yet to settle, making my eyes sting. But the calf has rejoined the herd and is now merrily munching on some grass.

I can't stop smiling. "Eat that, motherfucker," I say to Duke.

He rolls his eyes, the side of his mouth curling into a smirk as he trots closer. "You got lucky."

"He actually didn't." Sawyer puts his hands on his hips. "Wyatt came home alone last night. Saw it with my own eyes."

Ryder stares at me. "Are you sick?"

"Shut up." I yank off my hat and wipe my brow on my sleeve. "I was tired, is all. Been a long week."

"It's Wednesday." Ryder blinks.

"So?"

"This have anything to do with Sally?" Duke asks. "I saw y'all dancing last night. Looked…cozy."

Sawyer screws up one eye against the sun and the dust. "I thought I heard her call you Daddy."

Heat crawls up my neck. Sally did call me Daddy, and now I can't stop thinking about it. My dick throbs at the memory.

I bite back a wince. I've been on the verge of a half chub ever since it happened. Kept me up way past my bedtime, wondering if Sally had gone home with Beck after I left.

I wondered if the eager way she'd touched me—the heat in her eyes—was real, or if she really was just faking it to get that dickhead's attention.

No wonder I smoked like a chimney on the drive home. My chest is still heavy from all the cigarettes I long-darted out my truck's window. I only smoke when I'm stressed or drinking, but even the occasional cigarette is terrible for you. I need to quit. Go cold turkey.

I tell myself quitting will be easier after Sally leaves for New York. I won't be so stressed then. Or horny. Or angry with myself for being such a fucking coward and not telling my best friend how I feel. But being honest would mean opening up—risking decimation—and I don't do that. Avoiding my feelings might not be the smartest way of protecting myself, but it does mean I avoid more hurt.

"We got work to do." My voice sounds gruff, even to my own ears. I clear my throat. "And y'all remember what Mom said about gossip."

"*Gossip is the Devil's radio*," Sawyer replies.

Duke grins. "*But nature's telephone.*"

My chest twists. Mom had a big heart and was always telling us the importance of kindness, but she also had a wicked sense of humor. I'd like to think I inherited all of that.

God, I miss her.

Grabbing a piece of gum from my saddlebag, I pop it into my mouth and climb back into the saddle. "Don't make me pull rank, y'all. Let's get to it."

Garrett Luck made Cash foreman of Lucky Ranch when my brother was barely twenty years old. Cash was green as a blade of grass—we all were—but Garrett was patient with us, and taught us everything he knew about running a cattle ranch.

I miss him too. His death from a massive heart attack this spring shocked us all; he was only fifty-six and in great shape. Cash took it the hardest, but all of us Rivers boys felt the loss of our adopted father figure acutely.

Sometimes, I wonder if we're cursed, like every parental figure in our lives is going to be taken away.

Like everyone we love really is going to leave.

When Cash and Mollie became co-owners of the newly created Lucky River Ranch, they made me foreman. My older brother—bless his black heart—left big shoes to fill. He's a hard-ass, but he's always been fair, and he pushes us to do our best. He had no problem getting people to take him seriously.

Me, on the other hand? I couldn't get my brothers to take me seriously if I paid them. And I mean that literally because as their boss, I really do pay them now.

Case in point: Duke snickers at my threat. Ryder climbs back in the saddle, but pulls his phone out of his pocket. Sawyer is on *his* phone, thumbs flying over the screen. But that's allowed because he's got a three-year-old daughter, Ella, at home.

Still, if Cash told the guys to get a move on, they'd get a move on.

"Y'all."

No one so much as glances my way.

"*Y'all.*"

Only Sawyer looks up at my bark. "Sorry, Wy, just checking in with Ella's teacher. We're all good. Back to the barn?"

"Back to the barn. Sawyer, you and I are gonna meet with the farrier. Those clowns"—I motion to the twins—"can muck stalls."

Ryder finally looks up from his phone. "Aw, man—"

"Shoulda listened. I won't ask again."

Giving orders is weird. I still haven't decided if I like being in charge. Don't get me wrong, I'm grateful for the opportunity. And the pay raise. I don't mind the extra work. But things have changed so much so quickly around here. I wonder if I have what it takes to do Lucky River Ranch justice. I'm a good cowboy. Good brother. Decent poker player too.

But a leader? A boss? I don't know if I can take myself that seriously. No one else does.

We've brought in the herd now that winter's approaching, so we're able to ride back to the horse barn since we're close enough. I don't mind it one bit. I suck in lungfuls of crisp, cool air as the boys and I cover the distance in a trot. The breeze is refreshing in the best way, drying my sweat. The sun feels good on my shoulders, my back, my thighs.

The land around us is a kaleidoscope of colors. The changing leaves; the flawless, wide-open sky; the pale rise of canyons in the distance—it all makes my heart beat a little faster.

Glancing at Sawyer, I take in his narrowed eyes, the way he chews on his bottom lip. I know he's thinking about Ella. I also know he's tired as all get-out, but he'll never complain because he loves being her dad.

I look at Duke and Ryder, who finally fucking listened and are following us to the barn. Despite the chill in the air, their shirts are soaked with sweat. They mouth off a lot, but they do work hard.

We make a good team. And maybe that's enough.

It should be enough, being surrounded by people who know and love me. Working my dream job in a place this beautiful. Continuing to build my family's legacy.

But there's still this ache in me, this longing for more. I know that's ultimately because I'm too chickenshit to let people in—to let them truly know me. Being *the* Wyatt Rivers is a mask I wear. The guy who's the life of the party, the one who gambles and fucks and jokes—it's a caricature I created, a way to keep people at arm's length.

I've got too many responsibilities now to risk falling into the darkness—to risk falling down on my family when they need me most.

My brothers and I crest a hill, the horse barn and its corral coming into view in the little valley below. Everything about the Luck side of the ranch is beautiful, including the barn. It's enormous, a circular crow's nest dotted with windows rising from the center of its gabled roof. The barn is painted a rich chocolate brown, and Mollie had Lucky River Ranch's new horseshoe-shaped logo painted in yellow above the huge doors that mark the main entrance.

But it's not the barn that makes my heart beat faster.

Nah, that flutter's on account of the familiar figure I see hanging out by the corral, her chestnut hair gleaming in the sun.

I put my gum back in its wrapper. Then I'm urging Joker into a sprint again before I even know what I'm doing, the two of us thundering down the hill.

"I see you, *Daddy*," Ryder calls from behind me, his voice laced with laughter.

I raise my arm and flip him the bird.

I should probably play it cool. Try to at least make it *look* like I'm not nursing a raging case of unrequited love and/or blue balls. Sally is probably the most dangerous person of all to be around right now. If anyone can see behind my mask, it's her. I let her see me, the real me—the heartbroken, devastated boy who'd just lost his mother—that day we kinda, sorta skinny-dipped in the river, and look how that turned out. When she left the day after the funeral, I felt so destroyed that I was sure I'd die from it.

But then my best friend holds a hand up to her forehead and grins, her dimple so deep that I can see it from here.

Fuck being cool.

I don't miss the way her eyes flick over my body when I pull Joker to a stop beside her, just far enough so that the dust we kick up doesn't get on her clothes.

"Ma'am." I touch my fingers to the brim of my hat. "Wasn't expecting to see you out here today."

Sally is at Lucky River Ranch a lot. It's awesome. And awful. If she's out here at the barn, it's because she's tending to our animals. As foreman, I would know about that. If she's not with the animals, then she's in the kitchen at the New House, helping Patsy prepare a meal.

It's not totally out of character for Sally to visit us cowboys unannounced. But her just showing up like this has alarm bells going off inside my head.

Or maybe that's just last night's leftover vibes coming back to haunt me. Everything about my interaction with Sally felt undeniably real, and I'm still recovering from the emotional hangover that gave me.

Sally holds up a gigantic thermos. "I made mulled cider."

"You spike it?"

"Of course I spiked it. Thought y'all might want to warm up after working in the cold."

This girl. Her kindness. Her thoughtfulness. That pretty smile. And the whiskey I know she put in that cider. It'll be Jack Daniel's. My favorite. *Our* favorite.

Aw, Sunshine, how could I not fall head over boots for you?

I smile down at her. "Cold's not too bad now that the sun's up."

"You sayin' you're gonna make me drink alone?"

I love how her accent gets thicker the longer she's home.

"I got work to do. I'm the boss now."

Her dimple makes another appearance. "You are."

"My brothers would chew me out for playing hooky."

"I bet they would."

"It's not even noon."

"You do love a scandal."

I tilt my head, my heart squeezing at her good mood. "You got an answer for everything today, don't you?"

That mean she got laid last night? I absolutely don't need to know if Sally got laid last night.

Shit, I'm dying to know. The thought of another guy touching her, not taking his time with her—

I see *red.*

The sunlight catches on her eyelashes. "You gonna drink with me or not?"

"Are we invited?" Duke rides up beside me.

Sawyer tips his hat. "Hey, Sally. Everything okay?"

Sally strides forward and runs her hand over Joker's glossy brown neck. "Y'all tell me. Wyatt here is about to turn down my cider. Yes, it's spiked, and, yes, I used whiskey."

"You really must be sick," Ryder says to me.

Sally scrunches her brow. "Wait, Wyatt, are you not feeling—"

"No. Yes. I'm not—fuck, I'm fine." Only I'm not as I watch Joker nuzzle his nose into Sally's hand. Christ, even my horse is in love with this girl. She's relentless. "Sally, when have I ever told you no?"

"That mean we are invited?" Duke asks.

I slide off Joker. "No."

"Aw, man—"

"You got stalls to muck, don't you?" I give my brother a pointed look.

His shoulders slump. "Whatever. Nice to see you, Sally."

"I brought plenty, Wy." She pauses. "It's fine if he stays."

But the hesitant way Sally says that tickles my sixth sense. She need to talk to me alone?

Something is up. Fuck, fuck, *fuck*, she did sleep with Beck, didn't she? He hurt her?

"Nah, y'all really do need to go muck those stalls. And here, untack Joker while you're at it. I'm gonna check in with the farrier."

Sawyer nods at my horse, then turns to Sally. "Y'all enjoy the drink. Holler if you need anything, all right?"

"Sounds great. Thanks, Sawyer."

He meets my eyes before he takes Joker's reins and hands them to Ryder. Then the three of them disappear into the barn.

Go figure. Just when I'm ready to wring my brothers' necks, they do me a solid and read the room for once.

Don't know why Sally wants me alone. But I'm gonna find out—right now.

"Should we head down to the river?" I ask.

She runs her tongue along her bottom lip before taking it between her teeth. "Let's do it."

CHAPTER 6

Sally

LOVE ME LIKE A COWBOY

DESPITE THE COOL breeze blowing through the ATV's open windshield, I'm sweating bullets on the short drive.

I don't think I was this nervous when I took the boards to become a certified veterinarian. Then again, I wasn't sitting next to a broad-shouldered cowboy with thighs like tree trunks and eyes so blue that they seem to glow in the shade of the ATV's roof.

I was doing *so* well back there at the corral. I was fun, a little flirty. Totally confident. Wyatt looked so damn good on horseback that it was difficult for me to focus, and when he flirted back, my knees got wobbly. But I persevered. I convinced him to have a drink with me.

But now that we're alone and the time to ask him to be my kinda-sorta fake date is suddenly right in front of me, my heart is in my throat. I run my clammy palms over my jeans in a failed attempt to dry them.

How much spiked cider is too much spiked cider before lunch? Asking for a friend.

"You all right?" Wyatt glances at me, brows lifted. "You seem a little...keyed up." He says it so casually, like I'm not about to jeopardize our friendship and make a total fool of myself by asking for a wildly inappropriate favor.

Everything about Wyatt is casual. Cocky. He's got one wrist draped carelessly over the steering wheel. His knees are spread, and they almost touch the dash because he's that tall. That big.

He took off his hat—it's on the seat between us—and now his long, shaggy hair lifts in the breeze. I detect the faintest hint of wintergreen in the air; Wyatt is addicted to gum. Not like I mind because he always smells fresh and delicious, except when he smokes.

"I, um…had an early morning."

Wyatt changes hands on the wheel. He uses his left to drive while he pulls the right through his hair, making his bicep bulge against the sleeve of his denim shirt. "Were you playing doctor without me again, Sunshine?"

I involuntarily squeeze my thighs together, but I still manage to laugh. "We got a call a little after three. A mama accidentally kicked her foal and broke the poor baby's leg."

"Aw, man, that's rough." Wyatt cuts me a look. "But you fixed it, didn't you? The foal's leg?"

"I did, yeah. Two plates and six screws later, she should be right as rain."

"Just another day for you." Grinning, Wyatt offers me his fist. "Saving lives by screwing."

God, I love how this man makes me laugh. I give him the fist bump he's looking for. "Only doing my part."

"No wonder you brought that." He nods at the thermos cradled in the crook of my arm. "You deserve a drink. Hell, I do too. I *am* your biggest cheerleader."

"Thirsty work for sure."

"There's a lot about me that's thirsty, yeah."

I lift my elbow and nudge him in the ribs. "Gross."

"I am as God made me."

"And God will most certainly *not* bless the broken road that led us to your thirst traps."

"What thirst traps? You need to be on social media to post those."

"Not having an Instagram account doesn't make you any hotter, Wy."

Except it does. It most definitely, definitely does.

His face splits into a smile. "Then why you blushin', Sal?"

I decide to ignore that question. "I'm just talking about you. The way you walk into The Rattler like you own it. The way you talk to women. You're like a live-action thirst trap—"

"It's actually cute how red you get."

"It's the sun, okay? And being up at three."

Have we always been this flirty? I feel like we're usually playful, and yet—

I don't know, something feels different between us right now. I could be imagining it on account of my extreme, *extreme* nervousness. But I wonder if our little not-so-fake flirting routine on the dance floor last night amped up the, er, *energy* between us today.

Then again, I am in the midst of a very long, very serious sexual drought. Maybe I've just reached a critical level of dire need that makes me hyperaware of any male in the vicinity.

Wyatt turns his attention back to the windshield. "You said, *we* got a call. You're talking about you and your dad, right? Like y'all were, well, together? When the call came? Like in the same house?"

I furrow my brow, my stomach flipping.

Wait a second. *Wait.* Does Wyatt think I left The Rattler with Beck last night?

Why would Wyatt care? And why won't my stomach stop flipping at the idea of Wyatt being jealous? That's just ridiculous.

"Of course we were in the same house. Thanks for the

lovely reminder that I live with my parents and sleep in the same twin bed I've had since I was three."

"Welcome," Wyatt says, his expression relaxing.

If I didn't know any better, I'd say he almost looks relieved.

The scent of the air changes, a clean earthiness filling my head. We climb one last hill, and the Colorado River comes into view, a broad stretch of blue-green water that cuts a meandering path through the arid countryside. The strong afternoon light glints off its rippled surface, and I can just hear the quiet, gurgling rush of the water above the sound of the ATV's engine.

I inhale a lungful of the familiar smells. For a split second, my exhaustion and nervousness lift. I'm fifteen again, and my best friend, Wyatt Rivers, is beside me. There's no weird energy. No looming moves thousands of miles away. I don't have a care in the world other than filling the hours of a crisp November afternoon with more of this: fresh air, family. Familiar rituals that are simple but satisfying.

I really don't want to leave.

Being with Wyatt always feels like coming home.

Heat hits the back of my eyes, my chest squeezing. I look out the open window as Wyatt parks the ATV on the crest of the ridge overlooking the river.

He kills the engine. Without a word, he reaches for the thermos and unscrews the blue plastic cap. The scent of cinnamon, along with a hint of fiery whiskey, fills my head as he turns the cap upside down and fills it with cider.

He holds out the cap to me, steam rising off the cider's surface. His eyes flick over my face, and his smirk disappears, a pair of indents appearing between his brows.

"What's on your mind, Sal?"

I hate how easily this man reads me. *Knows* me.

I love it so much it hurts.

Wyatt's fingers brush against mine as I take the makeshift

cup from him. The heat between my legs blares to new life at the quick, casual, and yet somehow hot-as-hell contact. I remind myself that Wyatt's like this with everyone.

Still can't help but feel special. Singled out.

Wanted.

I gingerly hold the cup, heat stinging the pads of my fingers. "Nothing. Everything."

"Lucky for you, we got all day." He rests his bent elbow on the doorframe, his hand gripping the ATV's roof. "Talk to me."

"I had a really good morning." I blow on the cider. "And it's making me not want to go back to New York."

It's the first time I've said that out loud. Feels...nice, if I'm being honest.

Wyatt's chest rises on an inhale. "Well, yeah. It's heaven out here right now." He gestures out the windshield. "No one in their right mind would wanna leave. You'd feel different if it was the dead of July, a hundred ten degrees, and you were stuck doing preg checks all day. Much as you love sticking your arm up cow butts."

I laugh for what feels like the millionth time today. "I do know my way around cow butts."

"You're a goddamn expert. And because you're an expert, you'd get bored real quick."

Bringing the cider to my lips, I lift a shoulder. "Maybe. Or maybe I'd still love it, despite the heat and the excessive amount of ass jokes people make when I'm around to break the ice."

Tilting back the cup, I let the cider hit my lips. It's hot, fragrant. Equal parts strong and sweet.

"Good?" Wyatt's gaze flicks from my eyes to my mouth and back again.

I smack my lips. "Fall in a cup. Here."

I pass him the cup and he takes it, rotating it in his enormous mitt of a hand so that his lips hit the same spot mine did. He didn't do it on purpose. But a quiet yet potent rip of electricity courses through my skin nonetheless.

What I'd give to have his mouth on mine.

I am suddenly starving for this man's touch. Any man's touch really. Wyatt's touch is at the top of my list, but obviously that's not happening, so I'll take what I can get.

Who knows when I'll have the opportunity to satiate that hunger again? The second I'm back in Ithaca, I'll be hitting the ground running. There won't be time to go out or meet people. And I can't jeopardize my career by hooking up with a colleague. I've also been there, done that. Got the *This guy made me feel like shit* T-shirt.

I either speak my mind or forever hold my peace.

Wyatt makes a shockingly sexy, deeply satisfied rumble of pleasure as he swallows the cider. "Damn, Sunshine, that's delicious."

You're delicious, I think as I watch him take another long swallow before handing the cup back to me.

I tilt it back and swallow what's left in a single audible gulp. The cider singes my tongue, the whiskey setting fire to my blood.

"I have a favor to ask." I reach for the thermos and refill the cup, grateful for the excuse to not look at Wyatt.

"Answer's yes."

"Let me ask it first."

"Answer's still yes."

Goddamn it, leave it to Wyatt to make me smile, despite the tightly wound feeling in my chest.

"Last night, your little trick worked—you pretending to be into me to get Beck's attention."

"You go home with him?"

The sharpness of Wyatt's tone has my head snapping in his direction. His eyes are narrowed, mouth a tight line.

"No. But I—I think I could go home with someone like him if, you know…" Swallowing, I look away. Look down at the steaming cup of cider in my hand. "If I could just get out of my head a little and have fun with him. With guys in general, I mean. The way I have fun with you."

His expression smooths ever so slightly. "You sayin' I'm the best time you've ever had?"

Grinning, I lean over to gently elbow him. "I'm saying you have a way of making me feel comfortable in my own skin. I'm able to have a good time with you without overthinking things, which is what I do when I'm with other guys."

His forehead scrunches. "What do you overthink?"

"What *don't* I overthink?" I scoff. "I get so self-conscious when I'm trying to flirt. Like I can't get out of my own way. I worry that I talk too much or not enough. *Am I coming on too strong? Am I wearing the right thing?* Saying *the right thing?* I try so hard to be what I *think* guys want me to be that I can't just...be."

"Maybe you're hangin' with the wrong guys, then."

"I think I just need to take a page out of your book and learn how to let loose a little. If I could feel as comfortable around other guys as I am around you..."

"Right." He smiles tightly. "You'd be able to have fun with them too."

My heart dips at the emptiness of his smile. It doesn't touch his eyes. There's no way Wyatt is jealous because he thinks of me as a sister. Maybe it's annoyance I see in his expression? Which I get. With any other guy, I'd immediately back down. Dash home with my tail between my legs.

But I'm determined to get my confidence back. I have to learn to stop overthinking everything, or I'm never going to have a good time with a member of the opposite sex. I'm never going to have good sex, period.

Ultimately, I'm never going to get excited about leaving Texas for New York, which would be a big fucking problem.

It's now or never. And didn't Wyatt already say yes? I have nothing to lose.

That's not true, and you know it.

Shoving that thought aside, I take a deep breath. "I bet you've already had fifteen people ask you to go to the potluck, but of course you're not going because you're, well, you—"

"I wasn't planning on going, no."

I look up and my stomach swoops at the strange, almost-feral look in Wyatt's blue eyes.

"But you wanna ask me to be your date, then yeah. Answer's yes. How many times I gotta repeat myself?"

My heart flutters, and I feel a tickle in the back of my throat. "Don't change your plans for me. I have an ulterior motive." Oh God, best to just come out with it. "If you pretended to be my date—like, maybe if I have fun with you, it will give me the confidence boost I need to have fun with other guys…"

A muscle in his jaw tics. "Why're you doing this, Sally? You want to be with Beck, ask Beck to be your date. He'll say yes."

My face burns with embarrassment. "I can't. Not without getting all uptight about, well, everything. I feel like I need a lesson in how to just…let loose and have fun on a date. And, well, who better than you to teach me? You're always having fun. And it seems like you make girls feel really, really good about themselves—they can't get enough of you."

Silence.

Awful, painful silence that rings with my best friend's judgment.

The shame that fills me as Wyatt stares me down is unlike anything I've experienced, ever. I am hot and prickly all over. Sweat breaks out underneath my arms and along my scalp. He looks…not disappointed exactly. But certainly not pleased.

And do I detect a hint of that jealousy from before? That

can't be right though. Why would Wyatt ever be jealous of who I'm hooking up with?

I knock back the cider with a shaky hand. "You know what? Forget I asked. I'm sorry. I didn't mean to offend you or make you uncomfortable—"

"Sally—"

"Please forget I ever mentioned it, okay?" I somehow manage to refill the cup. "Friends don't ask you to fake date them. And I want to be a good friend to you, Wy."

From the corner of my eye, I catch his expression soften.

"You're the best friend. Literally."

"Ha."

"Why this sudden need for, well, *that*?"

The urge to be honest—truly bare it all—grips me. I blame the whiskey.

I already told Wyatt how I was feeling about going back to New York. If anyone found out I was having doubts, my parents especially, I'd be in hot water.

But no one is going to find out because Wyatt can keep a secret.

"It's been a while since I was able to have fun with a guy, whether it's at a bar or in bed." I swallow, hard. "My mind is just this jumble of panic when I'm around men. I end up chasing them away, which sucks but I figured whatever, I'll just focus on work for a while. But now…God, Wyatt, I feel like I haven't been touched in forever. Touched *well*, you know? And going without that for so long, it makes you…" I struggle to come up with the right word to describe how I've felt lately. "Sad. Anxious. I doubt myself constantly. I need to make a course correction, reverse the momentum, or I'm afraid…"

"Afraid of what?"

I swallow hard. "That I'll believe the worst about myself— the lies my doubt tells me when I hit a low, or I'm feeling especially lonely. That I *deserve* loneliness."

More silence.

I pass the cup to Wyatt, and he takes a long, thoughtful sip before running his tongue along his upper lip. The movement is slow, deliberate, and my body pulses when I imagine how that tongue would feel on my own lips.

How it would taste.

I blink, looking away. Honestly, *what* is *wrong* with me today? Maybe I really am fifteen again, awash in hormones and haunted by the desire for a deep, good kiss.

Speaking of goodness—I was a good student. I am a good veterinarian. I'll be a good employee. I've always been a good friend and a good daughter.

But what do I have to show for being so damn good for so damn long? A job I'm not sure I want and a raging case of whatever the female version of blue balls is.

I blink at the familiar press of heat in my eyes.

"You're spiraling, aren't you?" Wyatt's voice is different.

Deeper and yet somehow softer too.

My nipples pebble. "No. Just questioning all my life decisions and wondering if I should live off the grid and raise alpacas instead."

"Assuming makes an ass out of you and me, you know."

A bark of laughter escapes my lips. "An ass joke. I get it."

"I do have a nice ass."

Don't I know it.

"What am I assuming?" I ask.

"That raising alpacas would be fun."

"Ha."

"You don't deserve to be alone. No one does." Wyatt's eyes meet mine over the rim of the cup as he sips the cider. "You're too smart to let this shit knock you around. Trust yourself, Sal. Sounds to me like you know what you want. You know you deserve better. You just gotta have the balls to ask for better."

"As luck would have it," I say with a scoff, "I don't have any balls."

"You did just ask me out."

"And you turned me down!"

His eyes go wide as he swallows. "I said yes. Twice. Three times. More than that."

"But that was before you knew what I was asking for."

Wyatt lets out a breath through his nose, those blue eyes raking over my face. "Do I love the idea of fake dating you, or whatever you're calling it? No. But I get where you're coming from, and I want you to get what you need so you can feel better. And once you feel better, I know you'll absolutely crush it at your new job."

I blink, heart skipping a beat.

Could this actually happen?

What if it worked?

"You really don't have to."

"I know. But I will. For you."

The sincerity in his words—in his eyes—has me feeling short of breath.

Wyatt pretends to be happy-go-lucky all the time. And while I do think he genuinely likes to have fun and make people laugh, I know Wyatt swims in deeper waters than he lets on. He's been through some shit. I saw firsthand how losing his parents at eighteen affected him.

Deep down, he's still the hurt kid who sobbed in my arms not far from this very spot.

Deep down, he *cares*. A lot. But he rarely shows that side of himself.

He's showing it to me now, and it's all I can do not to reach across the ATV and kiss the shit out of him.

"So it's a fake date." I tuck my hair behind my ear.

Wyatt looks out the windshield. The breeze blows a stray lock of dark blond hair off his creased forehead. "It's a fake date."

"The potluck starts at seven, I think. I can pick you up at six—"

"Nah, Sunshine. That ain't how this is gonna work." The playful, cocky gleam in his eye is back. "You date me, you don't drive. You definitely don't make the plans. I'll buy some tickets. Then I'll come grab you, and we'll have some of that fun you been missin'. Sounds like we have a lot of lost time to make up for."

If only he meant that literally.

I'm just buzzed enough to smile and say, "I like the sound of that."

"I'mma show you how fun is done. How it should be done." He reaches over to put the cap back on the thermos and flashes me a handsome smile. "Hell, you'd better hope I don't ruin you for everybody else, Sal, because I'm real good at this shit."

That's exactly what I'm worried about.

CHAPTER 7

Wyatt

AIN'T NO HOLD'EM

GLANCING UP FROM MY CARDS, I peer through the haze of cigar smoke at Colt Wallace.

He's sitting across from me at the large, round table in The Rattler's basement. There's a Macanudo clamped between his teeth. A glass of Blanton's single-barrel bourbon, neat, sits at his elbow. His Texas Rangers cap is pulled so low that I have to strain to see his eyes.

He looks like any other cowboy at this table. Could be his brother Beck's twin for how alike their features are.

What is it about the Wallaces that caught Sally's eye? Cowboys have never been her type.

Then again, she hasn't been around Hartsville all that much. Maybe she's just never had the chance to throw down here in town.

I blink when Sawyer clears his throat beside me. His eyes flick to my cards, which I've let wilt in my grip to the point that I'm about to reveal my hand to all eight players in the weekly poker game I've hosted for—wow—five years now here in the basement.

That conversation I had with Sally earlier has totally

knocked me off my game. The ugly part of me is jealous she's set her sights on someone—anyone—else. I also feel a little angry. Hurt, too, that she wouldn't consider me for a real date. Her insinuation that I'm the king of casual, meaningless sex was more than a little insulting.

But the rational part of me knows I've never led anyone to believe any different. It's not Sally's fault that she doesn't know the one-night stands and dance-floor make-outs have left me feeling hollower and more alone than ever. Really, who the hell was I to tell her no one deserves to be alone? 'Cause I'm sure as hell lonely, but I ain't doing jack shit to fix that. Maybe deep down, I also believe I deserve the loneliness I feel.

Ultimately, it's not Sally's fault I'm hurt. That's on me, because I've been too chickenshit to tell her the truth.

Truth is, I'd let her use me until I got nothing left.

Also hurt, hearing how messed up she feels around men. Makes me wonder who the fuck made her second-guess herself that way. How could she not know how perfect she is? How witty and smart and sexy? She deserves to have a good time as much as anyone else.

If I gotta be the one to remind her how it's done…

Well, I'll do it.

I got no choice when it comes to Sally Powell. If she's unhappy, I'll move heaven and earth to make her feel better.

I'll do whatever it takes to make her see she's perfect just as she is. And then I'll let her go, just like I did twelve years ago.

I take a deep, unhurried inhale through my nose. Firm my hold on my cards, then lazily drop my elbows to the table, like I don't have a shit hand that jeopardizes the four hundred dollars' worth of chips I have in the pot.

I get dealt bad cards as much as anyone else. But I've learned to make my own luck.

"Fake it till you make it," Dad used to say.

He was the one who taught me how to play Texas Hold'Em. The game started out as a way for Dad to occupy my brothers and me when it was too wet or cold to be outside.

After he died, I insisted we continue playing it as a way to keep his memory alive. When my brothers and I lived in the bunkhouse on Lucky Ranch, John B and Garrett would join us after supper, and we'd play until we couldn't keep our eyes open.

I won. A lot. Not because I was a particularly skillful player, but because I was—am—an excellent bullshitter. My poker face is second to none.

Once we started playing for money—pennies at first, small bills—I slowly amassed a war chest of cash. I liked the money, so when my old friend Tallulah took over as owner of The Rattler a few years back, I approached her about hosting a not-exactly-legal poker game every Wednesday night in the basement.

The space ain't fancy. But the exposed brick walls and low lighting give it a speakeasy vibe, and the liquor is free—I cover the drinks—so we're all drinking top-shelf shit. Don't hurt that I usually walk away with a wad of hundreds in my pocket.

Needless to say, Wednesday night is the highlight of my week.

Was. It was the highlight of my week, until Sally finished her residency and came back into town. Now I look forward to seeing her more than anything.

A familiar ache grips my heart and squeezes as I watch the players around me fold, one by one. I guarantee they have better hands than me. But as long as I stay relaxed, crack jokes, I'll be the last man standing.

Finally, it's just me, Sawyer, and Colt left in the game. I feel Colt eyeing me from across the table.

"What're ya thinkin' over there, Wyatt?"

"I'm thinkin' I'd like to buy myself a nice steak dinner with your money."

He smirks. "Sounds tasty. Although I think you'll be the one treating this time, 'cause I got a good-lookin' hand here."

"Why haven't you gone all in yet then?" I nod at the chips sitting by his drink. "You know I'm tryin' to pay for Ella's college. Haven't put nearly as much as I'd like to in her 529."

"I think y'all are doing just fine in that department now," he replies.

He's not wrong.

When Mollie and Cash created Lucky River Ranch, they made my brothers and me stakeholders in the company that owns and operates the ranch. Revenues are split more or less evenly between Mollie and all five of us Rivers boys.

It's a wildly generous setup. Too generous, in my opinion. Cash agrees with me. We fought Mollie on it, mostly because the ranch she brought to the table was so much bigger and generated so much more revenue than our old Rivers Ranch did. Yes, in our family's heyday, our ranch had rivaled Lucky Ranch in scope and size. But that hadn't been the case for decades.

Still, Mollie insisted we all had an equal stake in the newly formed Lucky River Ranch. "No one works harder than y'all," she said when we recently sat down in our attorney Goody's office to sign the paperwork. "I've seen firsthand the love you have for this land. Each of you is an essential part of our legacy, and your ownership stake should reflect that."

Now, all of a sudden, I'm a wealthy man.

Wish I could say that having that money hit my account was as much of a thrill as I'd hoped. Don't get me wrong, I'm grateful. When my parents died, they left behind a mountain of debt they'd accumulated trying to keep Rivers Ranch afloat. My brothers and I had to bust our asses for a long, long time to claw our way out of that hole.

I never wanna be broke again. And I won't be, thanks to the enormous revenue that the ranch's multiple income streams—cattle, oil, development—spin off.

But now that I have the money, it's just thrown my loneliness into stark relief. What's the point of having that kind of cash if you don't have anyone to share it with?

"Wy?" Sawyer's looking at me. "Your turn."

I need to stop spacing, or I'm gonna lose for the first time in…well, for as long as I can remember.

Glancing at the table, I see that Sawyer's folded. No surprise there—he's a conservative player. Has been since Ella was born.

"Let's see just how good that hand of yours is, Colt." I shove my remaining chips into the center of the table, the stacks toppling into a pile with a series of quiet *clicks*. "I'm all in."

Colt grins, and unease slices through my center as I watch him push his chips into the pot. There's gotta be north of four grand on the table right now.

And somehow, before Colt even lays down his cards, it hits me that I really have lost. Not just the hand. But Sally too. Her asking me to be her fake date was the perfect opportunity for me to ask her if she'd be my real girlfriend.

Her telling me she hasn't been touched in a while—*has she ever been touched the way I'd touch her?*—was the perfect opportunity for me to show her how it was done.

She wants the shit that I'm good at giving, and yet I didn't say a fucking word. I just agreed to her plan and have been an angsty, distracted mess ever since.

But I can't be honest because I can't fuck with her head. Sally needs to go back to New York and become the world's best veterinary surgeon. I know she's capable of great things. She's second-guessing her decision to return to Ithaca University now, but I know she'll regret not taking a chance on herself.

Being honest with her about how I feel wouldn't do either of us any favors. Especially now that I know she's having doubts about the job she's worked toward for basically her entire life.

Fuck me for falling in love with a girl who was never, ever going to be mine.

Colt wears a shit-eating grin as he lays down a straight flush. The table erupts in hollers and whistles, and then I feel all eyes turn to me.

Usually, I'd relish the attention. I'd add to the drama by pausing or pretending to be taken off guard.

But tonight, I'm too tired to give a shit. I'm the opposite of relaxed and fun and easy, and I don't care who knows it.

My mask slips. I throw my cards across the table and shove up to my feet. Everyone stares at me in stunned silence.

"Wyatt?" Sawyer's brows are pulled together. "You okay?"

"I'm...not feeling great." I nod at Colt. "Enjoy the steak."

Then I turn and dart up the stairs.

The night is cold and clear, the sky lit up with so many stars that it makes me dizzy to look at them. My breath is visible in a small white cloud as I open the passenger door of my truck and rummage around inside the glove compartment.

I'm taking a long, deep inhale of my cigarette when Sawyer emerges from the bar, hands in his pockets.

I wait for him to rib me for smoking. Instead, he does what brothers do and goes right for the jugular.

"You're not sick. You're in love with Sally."

I take another pull on the cigarette, the nicotine making my chest tighten and my head buzz. I don't say a word.

"And y'all had fun today on your little ride down by the river, and you're realizing that the more you're around her, the more you want her, and that ain't ever gonna stop. But you think you can't have her because you'd be holding her back."

I drop the hand holding my cigarette against my leg and look up at the sky.

"For the record, I think you're wrong. You couldn't hold Sally back if you tried. No one can."

"What does that mean?"

He lifts a shoulder. "Sally's a grown woman. She's the one who gets to decide what's good for her and what's not."

I think about the joke I cracked with her earlier about assuming making you an ass. Am I being an ass, too, assuming I need to stay out of Sally's way?

Sally is a great fucking friend. I want to be great to her too. I don't know when doing that became so complicated.

"She's going to New York. And my life is here, Sawyer. It's where I belong. I'm gonna stay in Hartsville forever, if only so I can be a pain in your ass for the rest of our lives."

My brother cocks a brow. "We'll be just fine without you, thank you very much. Why're you so scared to leave?"

"I don't know." My turn to lift a shoulder as I hold my cigarette between my thumb and forefinger and take a drag. "I feel like Rivers stay put. Leaving…" I swallow the sudden tightness in my throat. "It feels like the coward's way out. And I love it here. I love what I do. I love y'all, even though I hate you sometimes."

Sawyer is quiet for a long beat. "You know, you're not gonna let Mom and Dad down by choosing a path that's different from theirs. You don't owe them anything, Wy."

My eyes burn. I've always felt like I have no choice in the matter—that I have to stay in Hartsville because I owe it to my family's legacy.

What if I did have a choice, though?

Why is Sawyer always fucking right? I've never hated him more than I do right now.

"Don't we though? They worked their fingers to the bone to make sure we had a place in this life. It was in their goddamn will—they passed the ranch to us. We have a responsibility—"

"To be happy." Sawyer's eyes gleam in the lights outside the bar. "That's it. That's all they wanted for us. As a parent, I can tell you that's all anyone wants for their children—for them to be happy. To be who they are and do what they want."

My fingers sting. I look down to see my cigarette is burned almost to the filter. I take one last drag before putting it out in the ashtray on top of the nearby garbage can. These ashtrays are everywhere in Hartsville, leftover relics from the era of the Marlboro Man. Back then, every cowboy in these parts smoked morning, noon, and night, and no one lived past sixty.

I gotta quit.

"I want to be a cowboy." I shove my hands into my pockets. "But I also want Sally."

"See how simple that is?"

"But it's not. Not by a long shot."

"It can be. Why not tell her how you feel?"

Looking down, I kick at the gravel. The chain around my neck jostles as I move. I'm gripped by the crazy idea that it's Mom's way of wringing my neck from the grave.

Your brother is right. Tell her. She might not stay, but that doesn't mean you can't leave with her.

"She asked me to help her pick up guys," I blurt. "Wants me to show her how to have fun by pretending to be her fake date. Says it'll give her some much-needed confidence."

Another pause.

"Surely, you asked her to date you for real instead because the thought of her being with anyone else kills you? Because you're not afraid of your feelings and you've learned from

Cash and Mollie that putting yourself out there is worth the risk? But really, because pretending to date someone is the dumbest shit ever?"

"Like I don't know that."

"I'm serious."

"I know how stupid that sounds, Sawyer, trust me. But I guess..." I squint up at the sky. *I'm scared that losing someone again will do me in.* "I was in such a dark place for so long after Mom and Dad died. I hid it well—"

"But I knew." Sawyer swallows. "We all did."

"So, yeah, needless to say, I lost my nerve today with Sally. I don't want to go back there. To the darkness. If things don't work out, or she leaves..."

Sawyer peers at me. "Isn't your nickname for her 'Sunshine'?"

I scoff. "Ha. Hadn't thought of that."

"Move toward the light, brother. That's all I'm sayin'."

I cut him a look.

"Oh, you got it bad, boy," he says with a smile. "Lord save us."

"I'm beyond saving at this point, I think."

"Stop that shit. You actually cornered yourself into a nice opportunity here, Wy. Obviously, you can't let Sally get it on with randos. But you can encourage her to get it on with you."

"Because that won't fuck up our friendship or anything."

"That ship sailed years ago. You don't wanna 'be friends'"—he uses air quotes—"with Sally. You're worried you'll lose her if you tell her how you feel, but what do you think is gonna happen anyway if you don't say anything and she goes back to New York? She's gonna meet someone. Y'all will still be friends, but you ain't gonna see her but once or twice a year when she comes back to visit her parents. And don't think that guy of hers will like you calling or texting her the way you do now. Either way, Wy, you risk losing your friendship, and that will definitely send you back into the darkness. But if you're honest with her, then you have the chance to be with her how you really wanna be with her."

"I fucking detest you, you know that?"

Sawyer just smiles. "It's annoying when someone's right all the time, isn't it? All I'm saying is, you wanna be a good friend to Sally? Give her what she's looking for. *You*. Not some drunk guy at a bar. Not some asshole from New York." He claps a hand on my shoulder. "I know you think you can't be good to her. But you can. You've got a big heart, brother. Share that motherfucker with someone already."

I wipe my eyes, wincing at the way the acrid smell of the cigarette lingers on my fingers. Sawyer has a point. I just wish I knew *how* to share my heart. How to open up, despite the very real possibility that I'll get destroyed in the process.

Really, how do people risk so much with so little certainty of success?

Baby steps. The voice in my head that says that isn't mine. Well, it is, but it rings with a certainty—a sense of wisdom—I don't possess.

What *if* I dip my toe in the water of vulnerability and see what happens? Maybe I don't tell Sally how I feel right off the bat. Maybe I never do.

I have to start somewhere though. Fill the hole inside me by spending time with the person I love most and opening up to her as best as I can.

If I ever want to be happy, I have to at least try to change. Because I think part of me is still stuck in the dark, and will be as long as I keep wearing this damn mask all the time.

I'm just buzzed enough from my cigarette and the cocktails I had to ask my brother, "You got a blazer I could borrow? A suit maybe? Something a little dressy?"

If you had asked me a month ago if I'd be excited to go to this fucking potluck thing, I would've laughed in your face.

But now I can't wait. Hell, I think I might even donate a poker lesson to be auctioned off, hosted by yours truly.

I also make a mental note to send a keg or two to the event's organizers. I'm no cook, but I'm happy to provide adult beverages.

Sawyer grins. "I got a suit. Just promise me you won't get any bodily fluids on it, all right?"

CHAPTER 8

Sally

MARLBORO MAN

"SO, JUST TO CONFIRM"—DAD eyes me across the tiny kitchen island—"you and Wyatt aren't actually dating. Y'all are just going to the potluck tonight as friends."

Poking a sparkly hoop earring through my earlobe, I nod. "Exactly."

"But he's coming to pick you up." Mom lifts her mug of tea to her lips as her eyes flick over my little black dress and heels. "And your outfit is *fancy*. You look gorgeous, honey."

I grin as I guide the little plastic back onto the hoop post. "Thank you. The dress code is semi-formal, so—"

"Those earrings are new," Dad says.

"Yep," I reply easily, like I didn't pay an extra forty bucks in shipping just to get them delivered in time for tonight. I was sweating bullets until they finally arrived at the post office in town this afternoon.

Mom's eyes are kind when she adds, "That's a lot of sparkle for you. I like it."

Dad, though, wears this funny expression as he eyes the earrings, then my face. Do I detect a hint of annoyance? Anger even? I feel like he's been acting weird ever since I accepted the job at Ithaca University. Well, not weird necessarily. Vigilant might be a better word. It's like he's watching my every move, making sure I stay in line or something.

"You're too old for a curfew, right?" he asks.

"Right." I go up on my tiptoes to peck his cheek. "I'll let y'all know if I'm going to be late."

Dad sighs. "I feel like I should bring Wyatt inside when he gets here. I'll make sure he sees the gun safe and put the fear of God in him." He nods at the tall rifle safe tucked behind the stairs.

Rolling my eyes, I elbow Dad. "Don't you dare."

Ordinarily, I'd promise to behave. But I'm sick of behaving. I don't want to do anything stupid or careless, but I also want to have fun. Cut loose a little—or a lot.

And no one is better at having fun than my date.

Speaking of, my heart nearly pops out of my chest when the doorbell rings. Glancing at the clock on the microwave, I see that Wyatt is right on time.

Mom and Dad exchange a look I can't decipher. They're not huge partiers, so they're not coming tonight; they donated money instead.

It takes every ounce of my self-control not to run to the door. Instead, I give my dress a discreet tug and walk as calmly and confidently as I can to the front of the house. I wobble a little on my heels, and the new thong I bought rides up where it shouldn't.

I'm not exactly comfortable. But I do feel sexy. Who knows if I'll actually go home with anyone tonight? But I want to be prepared if I do. I shaved everything in the hopes of manifesting *some* sort of naked-with-a-cowboy situation.

I live in my scrubs and sneakers, so getting dolled up like this is a treat. I feel like a different person, like I'm actually a grown-up, red-blooded woman and not a perennially sleep-deprived surgical resident who barely has time to brush her teeth, much less blow-dry and curl her hair.

I grab my coat from the sofa and put it on. Then I open the door and—

Holy God.

Holy God in heaven.

Wyatt's handsomeness hits me like a wallop to the chest. He smiles at me from underneath the brim of a pristine brown felt cowboy hat I've never seen on him before. His scruff is neatly trimmed. He's wearing a sharply cut navy-blue blazer that molds to his wide shoulders and thick arms. Underneath that is a crisp blue shirt that matches his eyes.

It's the tie, though, that really does something to me. It's brown, same shade as his hat, and I'm gripped by the alarmingly strong urge to grab it and yank him against me. My body pulses at the imaginary sound of his deep, rumbly laugh as he stumbles into me. It's a sound I'd capture in my mouth, a sound that would morph into a groan as I kissed him and he kissed me back.

The scent of sandalwood, mingled with a hint of wintergreen, rises off his skin.

He looks me over, head to toe, and my stomach flips when his Adam's apple bobs on a swallow. Blinking, he hesitates, his eyes raking over me again, and again, finally landing on my face.

Another beat of heated silence stretches between us as his gaze searches mine.

Whoa whoa *whoa.* Is Wyatt Rivers at a loss for words?

No way is this man—this gorgeous, professional flirt—speechless right now.

Only he *is* speechless. He's not speaking, but he's sure as hell looking, a pink flush creeping up his neck.

It's kind of adorable, actually. And hot. It's so hot to be looked at this way that heaviness gathers between my legs with an insistent throb.

His attention makes me feel sexy. Confident. *Bingo.*

At last, he blinks and clears his throat. "Hey. Hi. Hello, Sally."

"Hi, Wyatt."

He holds out a paper-wrapped bouquet of pink and orange zinnias, his eyes flicking appreciatively over my dress yet again. "For you. You look—wow." He chuckles, and I swear I hear a hint of nervousness in the sound. "Wow, Sally. Beautiful."

Have I died?

Am I in heaven?

Have I ever felt prettier or happier in my entire life?

Wyatt was speechless.

And he's put in effort. A lot of effort. There are the flowers. And the only other time I've ever seen Wyatt in a suit was at his parents' funeral.

Wyatt does not get dressed up. Ever.

Except he got dressed up for me.

I expected him to show up in jeans and a cowboy button-up. *Nice* jeans and a *nice* button-up, yes, but nothing that wasn't part of Wyatt's ordinary wardrobe.

"Where the fuck did you get a suit?" I blurt, taking the flowers and cradling them against my chest.

Even though I'm a step up from Wyatt and wearing four-inch heels, he still towers over me.

"That's some language," Dad pipes up from somewhere behind me.

Wyatt flashes me a wide, white smile, the kind that makes the tan skin at the edges of his eyes crinkle. "Borrowed it from Sawyer. The hat though"—he taps the brim with his fingers—"I drove out to Lubbock earlier today and bought it. Gotta look my best for Sally Powell."

My stomach dips again. Lubbock is an hour and a half drive from here. Fake boyfriends do not drive three hours round trip to buy a new cowboy hat so they look good for their fake girlfriends.

That's something real boyfriends do.

My pulse riots. Does Wyatt want to be my real boyfriend?

Absolutely not. And yet—

"You know what they say about a man and his cowboy hats," Mom says, appearing at my elbow.

"Yes, ma'am, I do," Wyatt replies easily. "He only needs two of them—one for *his* wedding day, and one for his son's wedding day."

Mom turns to Dad and wags her eyebrows. "Or his daughter's."

Wyatt's gaze meets mine, a knowing, slightly teasing glimmer in his eyes.

Yep, he gets that I'm trying very hard not to roll my eyes at my parents' general ridiculousness. He gets that I love them, just like he gets that they still embarrass the hell out of me.

Wyatt doesn't care though. It takes a lot to ruffle his feathers.

"Y'all sure you don't want to bring any food?" Mom asks. "I'm sure I could rummage up something—"

"Two kegs of Shiner were delivered to the barn this afternoon," Wyatt replies. "Mrs. Biddle said she'd give me an asskicking I'd never forget if we brought anything else."

Mom laughs. "How generous of you."

My heart hiccups. Since when is Wyatt Mr. Community Star?

I'm smiling when I say, "How like you to donate beer."

"And a poker game." He smiles back. "How much you think a lesson in Texas Hold'Em, taught by yours truly, is worth?"

"Hmm." I tap my finger on my chin. "Five bucks?"

His eyes dance. "Sold, if you're the one buying."

Dad leans forward, his shoulder brushing mine. "I know y'all are grown adults—"

"Please, don't," I say, blinking when Mom takes the flowers from me.

"I'll just go put these in water. Wyatt, they're gorgeous. Y'all don't hurry home!"

"But no drinking and driving, you hear?" Dad continues. "Gets so dark out here at night. Actually, the earlier you can have her home, the better."

Wyatt nods. "Yes, sir."

"Don't wait up." I peck Dad's cheek again. "Seriously though, I've been living on my own for a really long time. I'll be fine. Love y'all."

Stepping onto the front porch, I loop my arm through Wyatt's and yank him toward his truck. I can smell the hint of a wood fire in the air. Leaves crunch under our hurried footsteps, filling my head with their crisp, dry scent.

"We got all night, sugar," he drawls with a chuckle. He's his old bullshitting self again, and for some reason that gives me a vague feeling of disappointment. "Why the hurry?"

"Call me *sugar* again, and I'll be hurrying your ass right off a cliff."

"You been hangin' with Mollie, haven't you?"

It's a running joke that Mollie and Cash started out wanting to push each other off one of the many cliffs that dot Lucky River Ranch.

"Of course I've been hanging out with Mollie. She's my new favorite person."

"As long as I'm still your number one."

I grin. "Always."

Although I might or might not want to be Mollie when I grow up. If only I could fall in love like she did instead of falling on my face.

Wyatt might have just come into a boatload of cash, thanks to the newly formed ranch he and his brothers and Mollie own and operate. But he still drives the 1980 Dodge Ram pickup he bought for five hundred bucks when he was in his early twenties. He's restored it piece by piece over the years, and now its new tires, chrome finish, and Carolina-blue paint gleam in the deepening twilight.

I give him a look when he follows me to the passenger side.

"What?" He reaches for the door and opens it for me. "I'm your date. I open your door. You'd best get used to it."

And here is the vulnerable Wyatt again. The guy who doesn't hide his goodness, his concern, behind a joke or a crude line.

This is the guy who makes my heart do a hundred back-flips per minute.

"You'd best"—*stop being so damn good at this*—"not boss me around, cowboy."

He clasps the top of the doorframe in his hand and leans into me, his full mouth pulled into a grin. "Bet you'd like being bossed around."

I cross my arms, unable to keep myself from smiling. "How much are you willing to gamble?"

His eyes glimmer. But it's his mouth I can't stop looking at.

"How much you got?"

Giving him a shove, I laugh. He laughs, too, and it strikes me just how excited I am for tonight. Nervous? Yes. But if I'm already having this much fun with Wyatt, I think the potluck is going to be a really good time.

I always have a really good time with this man, and that's exactly what I need—a reminder that I'm capable of confidence, of wittiness. I *can* be myself around a guy. I just need to practice with Wyatt so I can eventually be comfortable around other men too. So I can just *be*, no fucks given.

"Everything I made being a resident. So, like, fifty bucks," I say.

"I ain't takin' your money, but I will take you out." He nods at the passenger seat. "Get in, or we'll be late."

My nerves take over the closer we get to the potluck, which is being hosted at a neighbor's barn fifteen or so minutes away.

What if there are no cute cowboys there? What if things get awkward between Wyatt and me? What if they're the opposite of awkward?

He looks *so* good in that suit.

So. Fucking. Good.

If he wasn't my best friend and totally, completely out of my league, I would one hundred percent jump his bones right now.

Using one hand to guide the truck into the gravel lot outside the barn, Wyatt cranks the gearshift into park and kills the engine.

The nighttime quiet fills the cab.

Is it just me, or is the silence between Wyatt and me suddenly thick, alive with anticipation?

"We should talk about what you're okay with." His eyes flick over my legs, lingering on the spot where my bare thigh peeks through the slit in my dress. "In terms of, you know, touching and…stuff. I don't know if it'll put you in your head or…"

I force out a laugh, cringing inwardly at the high, shaky sound of it. "I'm okay with touching and stuff. We did it at The Rattler the other night, and it actually helped me get out of my head."

His eyes meet mine. "Tonight, I need you to be more specific. Tell me what you want me to do so I can do it."

A rush of heat floods my face. I like this serious version of Wyatt too much.

I need a drink. Badly.

"To be honest, Wyatt, I'm not sure what to ask for."

"Jesus, Sal, have you *ever* been on a date before?"

"I mean, I have. It's just been a while. A long while since I had fun on a date. I forget how to do it."

He frowns. "You forget, or the guys you were with forgot how to treat you proper-like?"

"Proper-like?" I scrunch my nose. "All right, Pa from *Little House on the Prairie*."

He blinks, his eyes going soft. "Are you complimenting me with that reference?"

"Of course I am." I smile, even as my heart twists. "I remember very well how obsessed you and your mom were with Laura Ingalls Wilder."

"Yep." He reaches for his mom's ring, which he still wears on a gold chain around his neck. "It's how Mom taught us to read chapter books. She started reading *Little House in the Big Woods* out loud to me, then had me read it to her. You know, me trailing my finger underneath every line as I sounded out the words." He mimics the motion. "She was so patient."

"A true saint for putting up with you."

"No shit." He pauses, giving me the impression he has more to say. Then he sucks in a breath through his nose. "Anyway, back to you and the clueless douches you've dated who made you feel the opposite of relaxed."

I eye him for a long minute. "We can talk about your mom if you want. I'm in no rush to go inside."

"And here I thought you were in a rush to get laid."

Chuckling, I reply, "You're not wrong about that."

"Lemme help you figure out what you want then." He nods at my clasped hands, which are resting in my lap. "We'll start with holding hands. You still good with that? If memory serves, we did a lot of it at The Rattler."

"You're real smooth at changing the subject, but don't think I don't notice when you do it." I search his face. "You can fool a lot of people, but you can't fool me, Wyatt Rivers."

His eyes take on a liquid gleam. It reminds me of the look I saw in Pepper's eyes before I operated on her—the sheer terror, the pain.

My heart squeezes. Wyatt will talk about his parents in

passing, but the only time he's shared the full force of his grief with me was that day right before his parents' funeral. At first, I thought him avoiding the subject was a survival tactic, a way of pushing through those first few awful weeks. But then weeks turned to months, and months turned to years. The years turned into a decade, and Wyatt has never opened up again. Not once.

I know he's still hurting. He hides it so well, no one would ever guess he's in pain. I just wish I understood why exactly he's so scared to share that pain with me, his best friend.

Wyatt clears his throat. "I'm not trying to fool you, Sally. It's just—" His Adam's apple dips. "It's hard, you know? Talking about her without, yeah, totally falling apart. I don't wanna fall apart. Not tonight, when you got so dressed up and look so beautiful. You want me to remind you how to have fun, remember?"

My eyes fill with tears, but I manage to blink them back. "Fall apart with me another time then?"

He laughs. "Maybe. I don't—I won't make promises I can't keep, Sal. But maybe."

"I'll take maybe. Maybe is good."

"Maybe you wanna let me hold your hand again?"

"Yes." I nod. "I'm definitely still good with that."

Wyatt reaches across the cab, the sleeve of his jacket pulling back to reveal the silver cuff links he's wearing.

Jesus, he *really* went all out.

I literally start to sweat when Wyatt carefully but confidently slips his first two fingers into the crook between my thumb and forefinger. My blood jumps at the contact. He pulls my hands apart and clasps my left one in his right. He firms his grip so that our palms are flush. His skin is warm, and his calluses are so large that they scrape against my skin in a way that's foreign and thrillingly, shockingly *tender*.

Wyatt maintains eye contact the whole time. I know he's just making sure I'm okay, but—

He's making sure I'm okay.

More than that, he's making sure I actually like this.

It's been so, so long since someone cared about me this way.

It makes me feel like I'm alive again, like I'm a full human being. One who deserves touch and fun and good sex and freedom and connection. With Wyatt's hand on me, I'm not just a workhorse, a competent member of a team, a set of skills. I'm a soul. A body.

A being that exists only in the here and now.

My pulse beats a frantic, needy beat inside my skin. *More. More.* I could go for so much more of this.

"I see those wheels spinning," Wyatt says. "For this, you gotta let your body do the talking. It'll tell you what it wants."

"I feel weird that you and I are discussing my body like this."

"Sunshine, this whole fuckin' thing is weird. Might as well embrace it."

I furrow my brow, momentarily distracted from the pleasant, almost-silky feeling coursing through me. "Since when are you so on board with pretending to date me?"

He lifts a shoulder, the whisper of fabric just barely audible over the thump of my heartbeat. "You know I ain't the type to do anything halfway. You want a fake boyfriend? Well then, I'm gonna be the best damn fake boyfriend you ever had, sugar."

Without thinking, I twine our fingers. "You're not gonna quit with the *sugar*, are you?"

He laughs. "You gotta let me make fun of you a little bit."

"If you promise it's just a little, *little* bit." I pinch the fingers on my free hand together.

Wyatt smirks, his blue eyes going dark. "Ain't nothin' little about me, sugar. If the sound of that scares you, you'd better find yourself another fake date."

Aaaand now I'm picturing just how big Wyatt is. I've heard rumors. I mean, the guy is huge *everywhere*. Makes sense he'd be huge there too.

Need rips through me, sending a bolt of lightning straight to my clit.

"Are you doing this on purpose?" I manage.

"Doing what on purpose?" He's still smirking.

"Making me blush."

"You're pretty when you blush."

Fuck, now I'm blushing harder. God*damn* him.

"Stop it," I say in all seriousness.

But Wyatt is never one to be serious. "Stop what?"

"Being so good at this."

"Sugar, by the end of the night, you ain't gonna be asking me to stop."

I laugh. "Be honest. That line ever work?"

"Yep." His eyes dance. "It workin' on you?"

"Hell no."

His accent gets thicker when he's flirting. I realize mine does too.

Guess you can take the girl out of Texas, but you can't take the Texas out of the girl.

"How about this? You take my lead tonight. Anything makes you uncomfortable, you just tug on your ear. Like this." Wyatt plucks at his earlobe. "I like the earrings, by the way. The sparkle suits you."

"You don't have to compliment me." I put my free hand on my face. My skin is hot, almost feverish. "We're not inside yet."

I imagine his eyes are burning when he replies, "I know. But I want to compliment you. You really do look beautiful, Sal."

"Thanks. You really do look handsome, Wy."

The smirk is back. "I know. Ready?" His eyes flick to the barn.

I've been ready to get laid *proper-like* for what feels like a lifetime.

I'm also so, *so* not ready to be on this cocky, gorgeous, foul-mouthed man's arm all night. Seems too dangerous.

Too good to be true.

But that's the thing: none of this is true. It's all fake. I'm pretending to flirt with Wyatt in the hopes it reminds me how to have fun and not think so damn much.

If only the decades of friendship Wyatt and I share didn't make this kinda-sorta date feel so deliciously real. We're still holding hands, like it's the most normal thing in the world for us to be touching this way. It feels…right.

Good.

Really good.

"I'm ready," I say.

And he smiles. It's not a smirk. Not a silly expression. It's a real smile, the kind he lets touch his eyes, and my heart swells.

I love the real Wyatt. I need to bring him out more often.

CHAPTER 9

Wyatt

CALL MY BLUFF

I FEEL like I'm floating as I jog around the hood of my truck in an attempt to open Sally's door before she does it herself.

Not only does she look stupid gorgeous in her dress and heels, but she also gave me space to talk.

She allowed me to open up just the tiniest bit. Granted, it was only to basically say I didn't want to open up at all when she asked about Mom. But it still happened. And instead of filling me with terror or regret, sharing even that small piece of myself with Sally felt liberating. I feel physically lighter.

She didn't judge. She didn't run. In fact, she clearly wanted to know more. While I'm not prepared to give her more, there's comfort in knowing she'll stick around to hear it.

Maybe it really is about baby steps.

Also, Sally lit up like a goddamn firecracker when I held her hand.

That's all it took. A single touch, one gesture, and you'd think I had given her a fistful of diamonds for how happy she looked.

My palm still pulses with the memory of how warm and soft her hand felt in mine. I didn't miss the spark of heat that danced across her eyes as she twined our fingers. Even through the windshield, I can see how pink her cheeks still are.

If she looks like this, happy and bewildered and alive, after holding hands for all of five minutes, how fucking beautiful would she be after I laid her down? After I hooked her leg over my shoulder and spread her wide and made her shout my name?

My dick twitches. I silently curse. These trousers are a lot more tailored than I'm used to, which means sporting even a half chub runs the risk of public humiliation.

I pull open Sally's door at the same time she pushes.

"What'd I say about me taking the lead?"

Wrapping her coat around her, Sally shivers. That a good shiver or a bad one?

"I told you, it's been a while. Give me a second to remember how this date thing works, all right?"

I'm not all right.

It's not all right that she literally can't remember the last time she was taken on a proper date. Has anyone ever treated Sally Powell the way she deserves?

How do I not know the answer to that question?

It suddenly hits me—the enormity of all that I missed out on in her life while she was gone and I was wallowing in grief. Yet another example of how me pretending not to give a fuck about anyone or anything bit me in the ass. I never asked about her love or sex life. Frankly, I didn't want to know because I was so in love with her. Hearing about the guys she'd met, the parties she'd gone to, would kill me. I mentally filled in the blanks and tried not to think too hard about it.

Now I realize I should've asked, if only so I could look out for her. Remind her that she could—and should—ask for so much more than what some drunk-ass frat boy with a sense of entitlement as big as his trust fund gave her.

But it ain't my place to make that choice for her, is it?

Choose me. Goddamn, Sunshine, I'm dying for you to choose me.

Some sick, twisted part of me is a little relieved that no one's measured up yet. That I'm the only one who can make her feel at ease in her own skin.

I'm more pleased than I should be when I hold out my hand and she takes it, leaning into me as she climbs out of the truck, careful not to trip on her heels.

"You good?" I wrap my palm around hers, my blood stirring with familiar heat.

She gives me a tight smile. "I'm good."

"Remember, tug on your ear—"

"If it's too much." Her eyes glint in the darkness when they meet mine. "I don't think you have to worry. My current drought is so epic that I don't think *too much* exists for me right now."

I nearly bite off my tongue. "I feel like I should be worried if that's the case."

"You worried I'm gonna climb you like a tree?" She twines our fingers again and smirks. "Remember, Wy, just tug on your ear if it's too much."

What would she do if I bent down right now and threw her over my shoulder? Put her back in the truck, ripped off that dress, fucked her like the world was ending?

"You got some mouth on you, sugar."

"I'm not as sweet as I look, handsome."

"I kinda like *handsome*. Blond Bear Cowboy might be better—"

"Who's ever called you Blond Bear Cowboy?" Sally laughs, and my heart turns over.

"No one yet."

"I'll bet another fifty no one ever will."

"You callin' my bluff?"

She leans in, teasing. So close that I can smell the Crest

toothpaste on her breath. "Sure am, handsome. Hope you brought cash."

We've both used the same kind of toothpaste ever since I puked my guts out in ninth grade during fifth-period study hall—classic case of the Jack Daniel's flu—and Sally came to the rescue with a tube of Crest. I liked the way it tasted, so I asked Mom to buy me some. Been using it ever since.

Sally shivers again, and this time, I know it's because of the cold. How long have we been standing out here? A minute? An hour?

I give her hand a gentle tug. "Let's go. Feels better inside."

"That's a euphemism, isn't it?"

"Everything that comes outta my mouth is a euphemism. Best get used to it."

The annual Hartsville potluck and silent auction is already in full swing when we step through the barn doors. Sally gasps with delight as we take in the rustic barn of every wedding planner's dream. Fairy lights are strewn across the roof, and the wooden support beams are wrapped in brightly colored fall foliage. Candles glint from the dozens of round tables that fill the space, each one draped in a dark red tablecloth and set with china. The smells of mulled cider and smoked pork fill the air.

Waylon Jennings plays over the speakers, and Tallulah is behind the nearby bar. I overhear her agreeing to do body shots with some patrons if enough money is raised tonight.

Can't help but smile. This is Hartsville in a nutshell—a little bit classy, a lot country.

Guess you could describe Sally and me that way, too, if we were a real couple. Which we're not, obviously. But we're on theme without even trying.

Why do I get the feeling Mom is sending me another message? I'm not sure there is a heaven, but if there is, I hope she's too busy having a damn good time up there to keep up with me.

The idea that she's looking out for me from above makes me feel all warm and fuzzy, though.

There's a makeshift coat rack to our right. I drop Sally's hand and slip my fingers into the collar of her jacket, skimming her nape. "Let me take this."

"Oh. Yeah. Sure."

She unbuttons the front and rolls back her shoulders, allowing me to remove the jacket. It's heavier than it looks, some kind of thick black wool. Makes sense she'd have a serious jacket for those serious New York winters. Why anyone would want to live in that frozen wasteland, I don't know. I get why Sally doesn't want to go back there.

"So you *can* listen," I say, poking a plastic hanger into the sleeves of her jacket and hanging it on the rack.

She cuts me a withering look before turning her attention to her dress. She smooths it over her hips and thighs, giving it a gentle tug so that it puts her every curve on display.

My mouth goes dry. My best friend in a little black dress—

It literally knocked the wind out of me earlier when I picked her up from her parents' house. It's fucking *killer*.

The dress is tight, hugging her body. She's in incredible shape from her physically demanding job, and she's got a great ass, luscious hips, and these cute little tits that'd make the perfect handful.

I notice her nipples are peaked to hard, visible points, poking through the thin fabric of the dress. Almost like I'm actually touching her instead of thinking about it.

I should not be thinking about it. If I keep thinking about it, I'm going to think about sucking on those nipples, nicking them with my teeth through the fabric so it ruined her dress and no one would ever get to see her in it again—because to see her in it is to want her in an indecent way. I'm gonna think about the way her head would fall back, how she'd fist her hand in my hair and roll her hips—

Aw, shit, I'm gonna be hard in two seconds. I have to stop.

I wrap my real hand around her nape instead, giving it a squeeze. "A drink?"

"Fuck yes."

I smirk. "Such a lady."

"You were no gentleman until, well, tonight, I guess."

"Hey. *I contain multitudes.*"

She grins up at me, our mouths inches apart. "Another way of saying you're full of shit."

"You're too fuckin' smart for your own good, you know that?" I give her nape another squeeze. I could be imagining it, but I think I see that hot glimmer move across her eyes again. "Cider?"

"Sure, since you're driving."

"Yes, ma'am, I am. You have as much fun as you want tonight, sugar."

I look up just in time to see everyone within a twenty-foot radius suddenly avert their eyes from watching us. I see Duke and Wheeler together. She's in town a lot these days, working with Mollie on their cowboy boot company, Bellamy Brooks. Sawyer is chatting up a pretty girl I don't recognize. Goody is setting out dishes on the long food table.

Life in a small town: everyone is nosy as all get-out. Should piss me off. Embarrass me. Sally and I didn't talk about how we'd handle the gossip that's sure to circulate after tonight. Guess we could say we're having a fun little fling before Sally goes off to New York for good?

Instead, the attention makes me smile. A not-so-small part of me likes people thinking Sally and I are together. She's way outta my league, too smart and ambitious and successful for a ranch hand like me. She's the kind of good girl who knows better than to mess with Wyatt Rivers.

Only she is messing with me, and I fucking love it.

Fucking love the way Goody, who also happens to be Tallulah's wife, fights a grin as we pass her on our way to get drinks.

Fucking love the way Tallulah's eyes go wide and her face splits into a big old smile when we belly up to the bar.

But the thing I love the most? The disgruntled look on Beck Wallace's face when he spots us from across the room.

"Well, *hey*, y'all. This looks"—Tallulah's eyes flick to the hand I have on Sally's nape—"fun."

Without prompting, Sally slips a hand underneath my arm, bending her elbow so that she cups the ball of my shoulder. The motion has her curling her body into mine so we're hip to hip, her head tucked against my collarbone.

"The more fun we have, the more money we'll raise," Sally replies.

My skin ignites at the abundance of contact that is soft and yet somehow searing.

My heart though? That nearly explodes at Sally's sudden burst of confidence. The easy, casual way she touches me is sexy as hell, and it makes me think she knows what she's doing. She just needs to feel comfortable—desired—to do it.

That's my job then: make Sally feel so comfortable, so irresistibly sexy, that she does what she wants. She ain't clamming up or pulling back on my watch.

Not when I have so little time left to enjoy her company. Because even though this date is fake, the time I get to spend with Sally is real. And I love being around her more than I love pretty much anything else.

So I do what I do best. I pull her closer. Guide my thumb up the column of her neck, circling the spot underneath her ear. I hear her breath catch, feel her breasts press into my side.

Aw, yeah.

"I'll take a cider. Spiked, please," Sally breathes.

"And I'll have a Shiner Bock if you don't mind, Tallulah." Digging a fifty out of my pocket with my free hand, I drop it into the tip jar. "Silent auction going well so far?"

Tallulah nods as she grabs a glass and turns to fill it with cider from a fancy decanter. "So far, so good. I know your poker game is a hot item. Goody said there were ten bids last time she checked."

"Already?" I glance over my shoulder. "That's a surprise."

"Everyone wants to learn from the pro." Sally gives my shoulder a squeeze. "No one bluffs better than you."

"I don't know, Sal. You're giving me a run for my money."

Her eyes twinkle at the inside joke. "I am, aren't I?"

This is sick, right? Us joking about how great we are at pretending to be into each other?

Only I'm not pretending. Of course I'm good at this because I've been dreaming of touching Sally this way since I was eighteen.

What does it mean, then, that she's good at it too?

We take our drinks to our table. I lucked out; only Sawyer and Duke were able to make it tonight. Sawyer let our younger brother know that Sally and I might seem a little cozier than usual. In true Duke fashion, he ribbed me nonstop today about my fake date with my best friend, but tonight, he's too distracted by Wheeler to pay Sally and me much mind.

Dinner is over and the silent auction is just ending when there's a tap on my shoulder. My stomach dips when I turn and see Beck Wallace standing there, a sheet of paper in his hand.

"I bought your poker lesson." His eyes slip to Sally. "Any chance y'all want to play?"

"Tonight?" I drawl.

"Tonight, yeah. Figured why not since we're all here. We just need a deck of cards, but something tells me you got a few of those in your truck."

I watch Sally's expression flutter with hope. She smiles, shoulders rising on a quick, shallow inhale.

What the fuck am I doing, helping her get this guy's attention?

"I've actually never played poker." She glances at me. "I'd love to learn."

"He never taught you?" Beck asks, clearly surprised.

"Wasn't ever interested until now," she replies, still looking at me.

Why the fuck did I agree to this again?

I don't want Beck Wallace looking at Sally in her slinky dress and barely-there bra, much less touching her or taking her home.

At what point do I have to let her go?

At what point do I slip away and let them be alone?

Never.

At least, it ain't gonna happen tonight. Maybe that makes me a selfish bastard, but I don't care. I think seeing Sally leave with Beck might actually kill me.

I'll give myself one night—and one night only—to pretend that this date is real. To pretend that this girl is mine and that she's actually coming home with me. She's sleeping in my bed. Saying my name.

God, how good I'd be at pleasing her. If only she knew.

This is some kind of step. A big step, a baby one, a step back, a step in the right direction—I don't know.

All I know is, I want more Sally, and I ain't sharing.

"What do you say, boys?" I glance at my brothers. "Y'all up for a game of chance?"

Sawyer knocks back his whiskey. "I don't get out much, so, yeah, count me in."

"I'd love to give you all my money, sure," Duke deadpans.

Making sure Sally doesn't need another drink, I head for my truck.

CHAPTER 10

Wyatt

SHOULDA BEEN A COWBOY

SALLY IS TALKING to Beck when I walk back into the barn, deck of cards in hand. The cardboard edges of the box bite into my palm as I tighten my grip.

Yes, Sally connecting with other guys was part of the plan.

Yes, it was a plan I agreed to.

No, I was not prepared for the white-hot jealousy that streaks through me when I see her smile up at him like he hung the goddamn moon.

Enough of the pretending. Enough already of the hiding. Get her out of here and tell her how you feel.

"Y'all wanna play or what?" I toss the deck onto the table.

Duke pulls back, hooking a thumb in the direction of the parking lot. "What bit you in the ass out there?"

"The cold." And the fact that this stupid plan is actually working. "I'm about to turn into a pumpkin, so let's get the game moving."

"All right, Cinderella," Sawyer replies, mouth twitching.

Sally and I meet eyes. That's what I called her on our first kinda-sorta fake date the other night at The Rattler.

Determined not to read too much into that, I take my seat

and open the box. Out of the corner of my eye, I see Beck pulling out Sally's chair.

"Aw, thank you, Beck." She's still wearing that gorgeous, lit-up smile as she sits.

I can't help but notice how calm she seems around him now. Like the nervousness she had at The Rattler is melting away.

That's a good thing.

I tell myself that Sally feeling confident is a really good thing.

Why, then, does it feel so fucking awful to watch her right now?

Why do I reach for the leg of Sally's chair and yank her toward me like a possessive caveman, making her yelp? It's not like me to care. Scratch that—I do care. It's just not like me to *show* it. It's especially not like me to be so publicly possessive.

But as far as my brothers and Sally are concerned, this is all fake, so I'm safe.

Only I don't feel very safe at all when I pat my lap and say to Sally, "Your seat is here."

Duke lets out a bark of laughter that he tries to pass off as a cough. I cut him a warning glance before turning back to Sally.

Her long, dark eyelashes flutter. "Really?"

"You wanna learn how to play, don't you? You and I will play the first hand together. Cards'll be easier to see if you're on my lap. Plus, it'll be more fun this way."

Sally bites her lip. I'm gripped by the fierce, almost-frightening urge to grab her and put her on my lap myself. Let Beck know she's mine. For tonight at least.

He's gotta let me have a win. Just one. That's all I ask.

But then Sally shocks the shit out of me and does what I told her for once. She rises out of her chair, and her eyes glimmer as she saunters the two steps it takes to get to me.

Then she puts a hand on my shoulder and settles her weight on my lap before turning to the side and swinging her legs over my thighs, flashing a whole lot of smooth, soft skin in the process as the slit in her dress practically rides up to her belly button.

Fuck.

Me.

For life.

The scent of her flowery body lotion—I figured out it's jasmine—fills my head. My entire being leaps at her nearness. At the flirty, playful way she snakes her arm around my shoulders and shimmies her ass, giving me the friction I desperately want but absolutely don't need right now.

But her eyes, her smile, her general naughtiness, are the real turn-on.

She puts her other hand on my chest and asks breathlessly, "This better?"

"Much." The word comes out as a grunt.

Sally runs the tip of her tongue along her top teeth. "You gonna show me the ropes, cowboy?"

Can't. Stop. Staring.

At her mouth mostly.

Does she feel the buzzy, tight energy between us too? Or am I losing my mind?

The only thing keeping our faces more than an inch apart is the brim of my hat. I think about taking it off. I don't, thanks to the few remaining shreds of self-control and dignity I have left.

"What kinda ropes we talking about, Sunshine?"

"Toby Keith did say something about roping and riding going together." She's fighting laughter, and I fucking love it.

I wanna kiss you so bad it hurts.

"Interesting," I say.

"Y'all need a minute, or should I, uh, deal?" Sawyer asks.

The hand Sally's got on my chest moves to my nape. I bite

down on my cheek when she starts to toy with my hair. Goose bumps break out along my arms and legs at the tender, easy way she touches me, drawing her fingertips gently across my scalp.

"Yes." Apparently, I only speak in one-worded sentences now.

I opened the floodgates, didn't I, by holding Sally's hand back in the truck? I showed her how simple flirting could be, and she took that idea and ran with it.

Who knew she was a natural? She's clearly not over-thinking this. Instead, she's…present. Carefree even. The idea makes my chest soar.

I can feel Beck's eyes on Sally and me as my brother deals the cards.

Because I'm an asshole—why not stir the pot?—I curl my hand around her hip and use it to shift her a little bit more toward the table, her back to my front. Her hand falls from my nape, but this way, I'm able to rest my chin on her shoulder and murmur sweet nothings in hear ear about gambling like a degenerate.

"Okay, so those are the communal cards, and we can all use them." She motions to the five cards that Sawyer dealt face down on the table.

"Exactly."

"And these"—she takes the pair of cards out of my hand—"are just for us, and we use the communal cards to make the best combination."

"Right. We're looking for patterns—numbers, suits. Pairs of things, three of a kind. Flushes are what you really want because—"

"Flushes are five cards of the same suit, right?"

Sawyer's lips twitch. "Something tells me we're gonna have another card shark on our hands."

"We playin' with real money?" Beck asks. "Or is this just a practice round?"

Sally turns her head to look at me.

"Your call, Sally."

Her gaze flicks to my mouth. "I'm feeling lucky. Let's play for money."

"She's living dangerously tonight," Duke says with a smile.

Reaching down to give my thigh a squeeze, Sally replies to Duke, "Your brother is rubbing off on me."

I slip my hand inside my pocket. My fingertips meet with Sally's upper thigh through the fabric of my trousers, and without me having to say a word, she lifts her ass a little so I can dig out my money clip. I use my other hand—the one I still have on her hip—to guide her back onto my lap when I'm done. She leans forward, setting her elbows on the table as she considers our hand, pressing her ass into my lap, just how I like it.

I bite back a growl. I'm so turned on by this woman—so fucking attracted to her—that I literally have to count cards in an effort not to get a hard-on, even though you can only count cards when you're playing blackjack. Whatever. Focusing on the cards is the distraction I need right now.

I'm just stunned by the lack of awkwardness between us. This kind of silent communication—how our bodies automatically work in tandem, how *good* hers feels pressed against mine—is so hot that I must black out for a full beat. Next thing I know, the table is going through a round of raises and calls.

Sally leans back so I can see our cards after the flop, or the revealing of the first three communal cards. She turns her head, her nose nearly brushing mine as she holds her hand over her mouth and whispers conspiratorially, "So we have a two pair, right?"

"Right," I murmur, mentally begging my dick to behave as a wash of heat moves through me at the hint of cinnamon on her breath. I know—I *know*—her mouth would taste so, so sweet.

She'd taste sweet everywhere.

"What's our move? You think we play it safe or go for the glory and raise it big in case we get a queen of hearts?"

Of course she's a fast learner. And of course she ain't afraid to risk it all.

I dig my fingers into her hip. "You're good at this."

"I had a great teacher."

"That so?"

"Earth to Team PDA," Duke says. "Y'all gonna bet or what?"

Sally wags her brows. "I say we go for it."

"I say I like that plan."

"Sorry if I lose all your money." Sally sits up and pushes more chips into the pot.

I resist the urge to hold her down while I pump my hips upward. *I got some ideas on how you can work off that debt.*

We get a three of spades. Shit card. I can tell by the way Sally falls back against me that she's about to give us away. Nudging the brim of my hat back with my knuckle, I lean in. Stop just short of skimming my lips over the bare skin of Sally's neck, right where it slopes into her shoulder.

"You don't play the cards," I murmur. "You play the table."

I watch her roll her lips between her teeth before she runs her tongue along the fullness of her bottom lip. I realize it's her tell. She's thinking.

And then she twists her torso so that she's sitting up a little, our eyes meeting. She lazily reaches up and thumbs the side of my mouth, like she's wiping something away.

My blood surges.

She smiles. Turns her attention back to the table just long enough to throw another bill into the pot before turning back to me. "Raise."

Lord *above*, she's playing the fucking table, flirting with me to distract everyone from how terrible our hand is.

She's biting her lip, raking her eyes over my face. "I really do like the new hat, Wy."

From the corner of my eye, I see Beck throw his cards onto the table. "Fold."

"Thank you kindly, Sal," I say. "You know I bought it just for you."

"That so?" She bats her eyelashes. "You do know how to make a girl feel special."

Sawyer exchanges a glance with Duke. "This is a bluff, right? Surely, they're bluffing."

"I don't know what they're doing, but I don't got jack." Duke puts down his cards and runs a hand over his face.

"That's a shame," Sally says, her eyes still on my face. "We're gonna make out like bandits, aren't we, Wy?"

"Fifty whole dollars, Sal." At least, I think that is what's in the pot right now. I lost count somewhere around the time Sally sat in my lap.

She's relaxed. Playful. Like she ain't got a care in the world other than getting her money and getting home with her man.

What I'd give for that bluff to be real.

It could be.

While the flirting *isn't* real, my heart still swells at how well Sally and I play together. We make a damn fine team. Yeah, this is just a game. A stupid, meaningless game that I know I'm reading way too much into. But I can only imagine the things Sally and I could do if we banded together like this all the time.

Mom would have loved to see that.

The thought hits me out of nowhere. I know with bone-deep certainty that it'd have thrilled Mom to no end to see Sally and me do everything together. I'd be so good to Sally. She'd be good to me.

Only we're not good for each other. And that math, it don't compute. The kind of life I'm dreaming of isn't the life Sally wants.

Then again, I haven't asked her point-blank what exactly she *does* want. I've just assumed, like everyone else, that she wants to be a world-class veterinary surgeon.

But I'm starting to wonder, is that Sally's dream or her daddy's? Because she's expressed some angst about going back to New York. Is it my place though to dig into that angst? Would it be a selfish move on my part to explore it with her?

I'm not gonna be the one who holds her back. Keeps her from doing great things.

With a grunt, Beck pushes back from the table. "That's all I got in me, I think."

I watch him meet eyes with Sally. The certainty that he wants her to follow him sits like a two-ton weight in my gut.

The possibility that she'll actually do it makes me feel ill. I have to let Sally go with him—I know I do. I just—

I can't let her go.

I literally can't take my hands off of her.

This sudden burst of possessiveness is a *big* fucking step. Hell, it's a leap. The only reason I'm with Sally right now is because I promised to help her get into Beck's bed. I know that. All the flirting, the touching, the dressing up—we did it in the hopes of getting to this exact moment.

The moment he shows his hand. It's just a look. But it's a look I know well. He wants the same thing she does, and now the ball is in her court.

Sally starts to rise. "Hey, Beck, I'll—"

"Where do you think you're going, Sunshine?" I clamp my hands around her hips and yank her back into my lap. "You've just started a winning streak. Bad idea to walk away from the table now."

Her face flushing, Sally pulls her brows together, confusion written all over her expression as she turns to me. *What are you doing?*

She doesn't say the words out loud. She doesn't need to.

And for a million different reasons, I don't need to voice my reply. *I'm being a jealous asshole. I'm sorry. I can't help it.*

Am I actually sorry, though, when Beck walks away?

Sally stays put in my lap, and my hands dig into the delicious curve of her hips.

The image slams into me like a freight train—Sally's on my lap, facing away from me, like she is now. We're still sitting. Only she's naked, and she's playing with her tits as I guide her body up and down, up and down, her pussy's grip on me unbearably hot and tight as she rides my dick in a reverse cowgirl position.

The image is so vivid that I can see the way the muscles in her back bunch and release with every curl of her hips. Her hair is long and loose over her shoulders. Her tits bounce in her hands as she moves. I reach around and stroke her clit with my thumb, a slow, steady rhythm that has her gasping for air, her pussy tightening around me to an almost-painful degree.

"I should probably follow him though, don't you think? I feel like I'm missing an opportunity—"

"No." I say the word with so much force that it surprises us both. My mask has slipped yet again without me even knowing it. Good thing the barn is emptying out.

The confusion on Sally's face deepens. "Wyatt, he's about to leave."

I'm hit by an acute need for nicotine. Or sex with Sally.

Christ, I don't know what I need. All I know is, this girl ain't going anywhere with another man right now.

"Wyatt," she says, "are you okay?"

My thoughts whirl—*tell her he'll come back, say she's just upping the stakes, ask her to marry you*—but I can't make myself say the words.

Thank God my brothers are busy wondering what crawled up Beck's ass and died, so they don't witness my silent meltdown.

See? This is what happens when I let my guard down.

"Are you okay?" Sally's face is close to mine. Too close.

Not nearly close enough. I swear this girl is gonna kill me.

Pretending to not want her for another minute is gonna fucking *kill* me.

"Fine." Firming my grip on her hips, I slide her onto the seat of Beck's empty chair. "Go."

"Wyatt—"

"I'm sorry." I'm shaking as I shove up to standing and hook a finger into the knot of my tie, giving it a vicious tug. I can't breathe. "I'm—I know I'm being weird. I just—I can't. I can't, Sal. I'm sorry."

Then I turn and stalk out of the barn like it's on fire.

I'm on fire, and I'm so damn tempted to let the flames take over.

To let them take me out.

CHAPTER 11

Sally

CHANGE MY MIND

I STARE at the broad expanse of Wyatt's retreating back, my chest twisting.

What the fuck just happened?

I think—I mean, I have to be imagining it, but I think I saw hurt in his eyes. Hurt and something that looked shockingly like longing.

My stomach takes a violent nosedive. None of this makes sense. We were having so much fun playing poker. Too much fun maybe? Is that why Wyatt refused to let me go with Beck?

Or did Wyatt feel it too—the very real pull between our bodies as he and I flirted, touched, teased? The insistent throb between my legs is evidence of just how turned on I am—was—from the way Wyatt did that thing he does so damn well: making me feel like I'm the only woman in the room.

Tonight, he made me feel like the only woman he wanted.

Playing along was so, so easy. I wasn't worried about turning him off. I didn't overthink every word that came out of my mouth. He just taught me how to play, literally and figuratively, and so I played, egged on by the easy, confident way he handled me.

With his hands on my body, his words in my ear, I felt like I could do no wrong. He made me feel *that* desired. That safe.

And because I felt safe and desired, I was free to just *be*. It was fun as hell.

An ache takes root in the pit of my stomach.

I've wanted Wyatt for as long as I can remember. That's nothing new.

But the sharp-edged need I suddenly feel—coupled with the memory of his hands on my neck, my hips, the small of my back—that *is* new, and it makes me feel like I'm going to combust.

When I glance left, where Beck went, part of me thinks I should follow him. Wyatt is a grown man. He can handle himself. If he has something to say to me, he could've say it.

But the thought of leaving him alone right now—leaving whatever just happened unfinished, unexplained—gnaws at me.

I hang a right instead, stopping to grab my coat by the door. But stepping out into the chilly night air, I don't put it on. The cold feels good on my overheated skin.

The parking lot is mostly empty. It's later than I thought. Guess time flies when you're pretending to date your best friend.

Wyatt's truck gleams in the barn's floodlights. The passenger door is flung open. A movement inside the cab catches my eye.

A beat later, Wyatt emerges from the truck. He's still wearing his hat, and he has an unlit cigarette dangling from his lips.

That's a red flag. I've smelled tobacco on him before—Wyatt's the kind of guy who'll never turn down a party cigarette—but he's never smoked in front of me.

Anger, sudden and pressing, rises through my center. Ignoring the way the need inside me rises along with it, I make a beeline for him.

"Wyatt Benjamin Rivers, what the hell do you think you're doing?"

He looks up, the floodlights catching on his eyes. In the darkness, they look liquid. Stepping closer—too close, but whatever—I see that his pupils are blown out.

His cigarette bobs when he replies, "Aren't you supposed to be chasing Beck?"

"Shut up and tell me what's wrong."

"It's been a nice night, Sal. I showed you how to let loose, right?" Tilting his head, he brings his hand to his mouth. His thumb is poised on the strike of a red Bic lighter. "Let's not ruin it."

"You're ruining it by not talking to me." I duck my head so our eyes meet again. "I'm worried about my friend, and I'm not leaving until I know what's going on."

"Friend." He scoffs.

The lighter clicks, its flame throwing Wyatt's handsome face into planes of shadow and light. I'm captivated by his strong, straight nose. The fullness of his lips and the coppery tint of his beard.

He's beautiful.

But then he leans in to light his cigarette, and before I know what I'm doing I'm ripping it out of his mouth.

My fingers accidentally brush his lips, and a shock wave of heat bolts through me as I wobble on my knees. "What does that mean?"

His eyes search mine for a long beat. My pulse is frantic. At last his shoulders rise on a deep, resigned inhale, his hand falling away from his face.

"Means I don't love pretending to date you."

My heart falls. To my very great embarrassment, tears prick my eyes. "Oh. Okay. I, um, understand. Asking you to do that was"—I force out a threadbare laugh—"not okay. I'm sorry. But I thought—I mean, we were doing great in there. It really was fun—"

"That's just it." His eyes are pleading as they move between mine. "We crushed it. Beck definitely wants to take you home. How could he not? You were confident as all get out back there. You played poker like you had nothing to lose. Not to mention you're a total knockout in that dress." His gaze flicks down my body, a quick, hot perusal that draws my nipples to painfully sensitive points. "But I—Sally, if I'm being honest—"

"Please. Please be honest."

Because I love honest Wyatt. I love his playful side too. But the guy who isn't afraid to be vulnerable? He's the one who really captivates me.

He sighs again. Looks away, turning his head so I'm able to ogle the square, masculine line of his jaw. "I hate the idea of it—you going home with him. I got no right to say it, but it's been eating at me all night, and I—trust me, I know what I agreed to. I want you to get what you need, Sally. But the thought of you goin' to someone else to get it…" He keeps his head turned, but his eyes move to meet mine. "That don't sit right with me."

Everything inside me heaves. It's like a bomb detonated inside my circulatory system, sending shock waves of debris through every inch of my body.

Silence, electric and alive, blooms between us. Did Wyatt just say what I think he did?

Is he actually opening up to me?

Because that's one hell of a confession. And the raw, vulnerable look in his eyes—how he's clearly terrified, but looking me in the eye anyway—it's everything.

The fact that he's letting his mask slip—that he's not filling the silence with a joke or a line—is *everything*. Not to mention what he's confessing.

Does he really want me the way I want him?

"Wy," I say softly.

"Yeah." His reply is equally soft. Equally scared. "I know

you and me can't happen, but that doesn't mean I haven't been thinking about it all night. Longer'n that, if I'm being honest."

I have to be one hundred percent sure we're talking about the same thing here. "Thinking about…"

"Don't make me say it. You know, Sunshine. You know I wanna be your guy."

My heart flies right out of my chest. Just sprouts wings and takes off, leaving me unable to breathe, to think, to process.

Is Wyatt as turned on by me as I am by him?

Is he asking me to hook up with him instead of Beck? Surely, that's what Wyatt means when he says he wants to *be my guy.* He wants to be the person I go to whenever I have—ahem —needs.

I want to laugh at the absurdity of it. But there is nothing absurd about the frank lust in his eyes as he gives me a once-over.

Those eyes linger on my chest before moving to my face. "You're cold. Put on your jacket." He nods at my coat, which I have folded over my arm.

But I don't want to put on my jacket.

As a matter of fact, I would very much like to take some clothes *off.* Not put more on.

This is stupid. You're playing with fire. Be careful. Be careful. Be smart.

Hooking up with your best friend of twenty years is definitely not a smart move. There's a voice inside my head that says I'm conflating lust with love, which is exactly why I set my sights on a random cowboy in the first place. There's no risk of getting hurt. Of having my heart broken because I don't have enough time left in Hartsville to fall for anyone new.

But Wyatt? He's a heartbreaker. And he's not new. I've known him forever, and he is my favorite person on the planet. Which means crossing this line with him—becoming friends with benefits—has the potential to get messy.

It also has the potential to be exceptionally delicious. And if I've learned anything tonight, it's that taking risks is worth it.

Let's be real, I couldn't keep my hands off *this* Wyatt—the honest one—if I tried.

Time for me to be honest. Guess Wyatt's bravery is contagious.

"Put the jacket on, Sally," Wyatt warns.

I blurt the words before I lose my nerve. "I forget how to kiss. Wait, scratch that. I know how to kiss, but I don't know how to quiet my mind and just...get lost in the moment. Get lost in the kiss. I could use some practice."

He goes still. "Are you serious?"

"I mean, I feel like I can get by." A nervous chuckle. "But I wouldn't say I enjoy it—"

"Just *getting by* is depressing." Wyatt's jaw tics.

"Exactly." I step forward on unsteady legs. Hold up the cigarette. "You can have this back. But I'm not gonna stick around to watch you smoke it."

His nostrils flare as he looks from me to the cigarette and back again. I need to make sure he wants to cross this particular Rubicon too. Actions speak louder than words. And so far, all he's given me are, well, admittedly very sweet, alarmingly sexy words. But still, they're just words. He also hasn't made a move.

"Take it." I press it into his chest. "I'm sorry I said that about kissing. I've already asked you for too much."

He grabs my wrist, my blood rioting at the firm, confident way his fingers grip me. "Don't do that."

"Don't do what?"

"Assume that the answer's no before you even ask the question. Ask the damn question, Sally."

My lips twitch, even as I wonder vaguely if I'm going to faint. "Assuming does make an ass out of you and me."

"Ask."

Now it's my voice that shakes when I say, "Kiss me?"

"How do you like it?"

"I don't know. How everyone likes it?"

He sucks in a sharp, short breath through his nose. "I ain't asking you again, Sal. You gotta be specific, or you ain't gonna get what you're lookin' for."

I think for one panicked heartbeat, then another. *Stay out of your head. Go all in.* "I...want to feel something. I want to feel like time has stopped and I'm exactly where I'm supposed to be. Like I don't want to be anywhere else, with anyone else, because the experience of the kiss is so freaking delicious. I want to fall into it. I just...yeah, I want to *feel*."

"Ah. So you just want transcendence, then." He uses the knuckle of his first finger to tip back the brim of his hat, the way he did inside.

The teasing gleam in his eye makes me feel slightly less shaky.

"Something like that, yeah."

Since when did leaning into this man feel so natural? We don't normally stand this close.

Then again, we don't normally talk about kissing each other after a very flirty, touchy-feely game of Texas Hold'Em either.

Tonight is a night of firsts, that's for damn sure. Which is kinda cool. I feel like I'm getting a shot at my firsts all over again in a way. First date. First time meeting the parents.

And now, first kiss.

"Lucky for you"—*oh God, oh God,* Wyatt is slipping a hand onto my face, using his palm to angle my mouth up toward his—"I'm tight with God, and I'll have you saying his name often. Eventually though, I'd like you to say mine instead."

I love how this man seems to know when to make me laugh just when I need it.

My blood is rushing, and my head is spinning, and I'm so nervous that I feel like I'm literally going to burst. But there's something about this touch—the gentle, easy caress of his palm against my skin—that is both calming and wildly, indecently arousing.

I laugh, and then he's leaning in. The gorgeous, masculine slant of his neck is the last thing I see before he presses his lips to mine, his bottom lip positioned expertly between my own.

CHAPTER 12

Sally

COWBOYS MAKE BETTER LOVERS

WYATT CAPTURES my laugh in his kiss.

His slow, soft, deliciously warm kiss that's already so exquisite two seconds in that I have to close my eyes, overwhelmed by the sensation of *being kissed by Wyatt fucking Rivers.*

Holding me in place, he licks into my mouth. It's a deep, indulgent, almost lazy sweep of tongue. A bolt of lust cracks me in half, the heaviness between my legs almost unbearable in its intensity.

He sucks my top lip into his mouth at the same time, urging me to open up to him.

For a second, I hesitate. I wasn't lying when I said I forgot how to do this.

What if I'm slobbery? What if I'm too eager or not eager enough?

What if I just suck at kissing, plain and simple?

Wyatt, though, doesn't seem to have any qualms about his ability. Or mine. He continues to kiss me deeply, patiently, like we have all the time in the world. Like he's not afraid of spit, or slobber, or someone seeing us.

What *if* someone saw us? What excuse would we have

then? Beck is long gone by now. Clearly, this kiss has nothing to do with him and everything—*everything*—to do with us. Me and Wyatt.

His beard scrapes against my chin and cheek. I love the feel of it, how intimately rough the contact is. Without thinking, I reach up and press my fingertips into the thick, wiry hair.

A low, dark rumble rolls through Wyatt's chest. He likes that.

I do it again, running my fingertips over the hard ridge of his jawline, stopping to feather my pinkie along the top of his neck.

Another rumble. He's good at telling me what he likes.

Wait, does Wyatt actually like kissing me?

Yes. The answer comes in a hard, decisive heartbeat. This kind of passion, of hunger, can't be faked.

I'm determined not to fake anything either. I wait for my thoughts to rustle in that annoyingly familiar way of theirs— the second-guesses, the equivocations. The doubts.

Instead, my thoughts are shockingly…clear. Concise.

Confident.

Don't get me wrong, I'm scared as hell I'm going to fuck up my friendship with Wyatt. But I'm not scared to kiss him. Not when he's touching me like this, encouraging me to rise into his caress with *his* confidence. His silent assurance that everything is going to be just fine.

I stroke my tongue into his mouth. It's a baby lick, just deep enough that I can taste a hint of the clean, earthy malt from his beer on his tongue.

Yet another rumble, this one accompanied by him stepping into me so that our bodies are flush. My coat is in the way though, so I let it fall to the ground and put my hand on his face, arching my back so that our hips melt together.

I am throbbing everywhere as Wyatt spreads his legs and captures mine between them. His kiss becomes hungrier, his teeth sinking into my bottom lip before he gives it a tug. Fireworks erupt across the back of my closed eyelids.

Suddenly, I'm the one making a noise, a high, embarrassingly breathy moan that I try to mute but can't.

Wyatt chuckles, his hand finding my hip as he breaks the kiss to murmur into my neck, "Look at you, telling me what you like. Good job, Sunshine. Let your body keep talkin' to me, yeah?"

If only my heart were as brave. There's some irony here—the fact that I'm okay communicating what my body wants, but not what my heart, my soul, longs for.

I tell myself that's okay. At this point, I'll take what I can get. And I have to remember that I'm leaving. Even if Wyatt were open to falling in love—which he definitely isn't—it'd be a dumb move on both our parts.

It is pretty sweet, though, to think Wyatt likes it when I make weird noises. Judging by the way he presses a scruffy kiss to my jaw, he likes it very much.

More. That's all my body is saying right now as sparks erupt from the place where his nose nudges against the hollow beneath my ear. He inhales deeply, like he digs the way I smell.

Holy shit, am I actually getting this right? Does Wyatt actually think I'm sexy?

I grab his tie and yank his mouth back up to mine. He deepens the kiss right away, his tongue in my mouth, the fingers of the hand he has on my hip moving ever so slightly toward my ass.

I am a hot, hollowed-out mess, and I fucking *love* it.

Speaking of heat, it radiates off him in waves that smell like wintergreen and sandalwood. The contrast between the warmth at my front and the cold at my back makes me shiver.

"Aw, Sunshine, you are cold."

"I'm not—"

But Wyatt is already grabbing my hand. He's lifting me up

and tossing me on my back onto the front bench of his truck —the passenger door is still open—like I only weigh as much as the hay bales he throws around all day long. The seat is deep, and the windows are high up, meaning people won't be able to see us unless they're right beside the truck.

I yelp with delight. This time, I don't try to keep in the sound as he climbs into the truck—climbs on top of me—and closes the door behind him. Instead, I put my hands on his hips and watch, tilting my head back, as he straddles my torso with his knees and straightens to shove the key into the ignition.

The truck comes to life with a throaty growl that makes the bench vibrate pleasantly against my back. Wyatt cranks a dial, and heat blasts through the vents. He even goes so far as to aim the pair of vents nearby at me.

"That better?"

"Yeah. Yes. Thank you." My heart skips several beats as a wash of warmth moves over me.

Wyatt's body and his kiss are hot as hell. But I think his concern for me—for others in general—might be the sexiest thing about him. He's not afraid to show he cares tonight, and that display of vulnerability is the biggest turn on ever.

I watch Wyatt toss his hat aside. Then he shoulders out of his blazer, folding it neatly over the back of the seat.

He looks enormous in the moonlight, his shoulders and biceps straining against the crisp fabric of his blue button-up. Then he pushes a cassette tape into the tape deck—cassettes must be a Rivers thing, because every single one of the boys refuses to put even a CD player in their trucks—and I let out a bark of laughter when Sam Hunt comes on.

"Where the hell did you find *Montevallo* on cassette tape?" I reach for his tie again.

He falls over me, catching himself on the hands he plants on either side of my head. His hair falls into his face, and my stomach clenches at how it suddenly makes him look like an actual cowboy. One who's been out working cattle all day, unkempt and scruffy and *hungry*.

"I got my sources." His lips twitch as he leans in to kiss my neck.

A tingly rush spreads through my skin, the insistent beat between my legs spiking faster, hotter. I want him there.

It's forward of me to go from kissing this man to inviting him to lie between my legs. Ordinarily, with any other guy, I'd stop him.

This is, after all, only our first date. And good girls don't put out on the first date.

But being a good girl kind of sucks. And Wyatt said to let my body do the talking. I'm determined to listen.

It's liberating, not having to worry about what he'll think of me, whether or not he'll ask me on a second date.

There are no rules with Wyatt, and it's kind of the best thing ever. I'm able to be myself because he's unabashedly *himself* right now. He's not hiding how he feels or what he wants. And that makes me feel connected to him—safe with him—in a way I never do with other guys.

I let my leg fall through the slit in my dress. Wyatt, being the expert he is, reads me like a book. He lifts his knee, allowing my leg to fall outside of his. We do the same dance with my other leg, Wyatt kissing my neck all the while.

I am obsessed with neck kisses. Especially when he nicks me with his teeth. Scrapes me with his beard.

Then I'm spread-eagled, and Wyatt settles himself between my legs. Right where I want him.

He's heavy, broad, and my hip flexors sing to accommodate him, making my dress ride up my thighs. Wyatt reaches down to clamp a hand around my bare leg, pushing my dress up even further.

I roll my hips in a mindless search for friction, letting out a moan of frustration. Notching my knee at his hip, Wyatt spreads me even wider while his mouth works its way up to mine.

All that separates us now are his jeans and my thong. I wonder if he can feel how wet I am. Would my eagerness turn him off? Or would it drive him wild?

He presses his lips to mine. Opens me up with a luxuriously unhurried stroke of his tongue. My toes curl into the soles of my hideously uncomfortable sandals, and I rise on a wave of lust that feels like liquid sunshine in my veins.

This.

This.

This is what I want—to be with a man who knows how to kiss. To be with Wyatt Rivers, his hands all over me.

I cannot believe I am making out with my best friend.

I must be dreaming. This is too good to be true. At any moment, I'll wake up alone in my stiff twin bed, the alarm I set for five a.m. blaring.

But I don't wake up. Wyatt doesn't stop kissing me. So I decide to take advantage of the time I have with him and move my hands over his chest, his shoulders. I reach up and run my fingers through his hair, making him nip at my chin as he pins me to the seat with his hips, rocking against me in a slow, steady rhythm.

My clit pulses. Dear God, am I going to come from dry-humping alone? Even when guys have gone down on me in the past, I'm usually too anxious, too wrapped up in my thoughts, to orgasm. But here I am with Wyatt, ready to combust despite us both still having all our clothes on.

I think the danger of what we're doing is only throwing fuel onto my fire. We could be caught. We could take it too far and regret everything tomorrow. I could show up to work in the morning with a hickey. Or at the very least, some epic beard burn. Wyatt *has* been paying a lot of attention to my neck.

This is all so wrong, and yet I want more.

We make out for one song. Another. Another and another, and soon, I have no idea how much time has passed. All I know is that my lips are throbbing, and so is my clit.

I need more. Now.

To my very great surprise, Wyatt is an absolute gentleman. His fingers work lazy circles over my bare leg, but his hand doesn't move an inch further north. I'm constantly arching my back, rolling my hips, but he stays relatively still, slowly drinking me in with his mouth on mine.

I'm *aching* for sex. To be filled. Satisfied. Touched everywhere.

That transcendence Wyatt talked about? I'm not going to find it by playing it safe.

So I take a chance. I slip a hand around his torso and gather his shirt in my hand at the small of his back. I give the shirt a tug, pulling it out of his slacks. Flattening my palm on his bare skin, I press down, pushing him harder against my center.

At the same time, I grab his other hand in mine and guide it to my breast.

Wyatt growls—literally *growls*—biting down on my bottom lip before he sucks it into his mouth.

Then he rears back, lifting his body off mine, and for a second I panic.

Shit, I took it too far.

But suddenly his hips punch forward, and I gasp when he hits me *right* in my center with a protrusion that wasn't there a second ago.

My heart stumbles to a stop. He's huge. Hard.

Wyatt Rivers is hard for me.

"Sunshine, I got three legs right now." His breath his warm on my ear. "You keep this up, I ain't gonna be able to stop."

"What if I don't want you to stop?" I'm panting, dizzy with desire.

He already feels *so good*. How amazing will it feel when he's actually inside me?

"I'm not fucking you for the first time in the front seat of my truck." But he still swipes his thumb over my nipple. "That shit's for teenagers who can't control themselves."

Does that mean he actually wants to fuck me, just not right now?

Does that mean we'll get to do this again?

Because I think I'm already addicted to fooling around with this man.

"What about thirty-year-olds who can't control themselves?"

He laughs, pushing up onto his hands. I open my eyes to see him hovering over me, gaze glued to my face. "One of us has to be the adult in the room. Otherwise, it's not gonna be any good."

"What? The sex?"

"Well, yeah. Listen, no one wants to give you what you're asking for more'n me." His eyes stray to my body. "But I don't think either of us planned on this happening tonight. Let's take a beat, all right? I don't want you havin' any regrets in the morning."

Biting my lip, I hook my first finger into the knot of his tie. *I can touch him like this now.*

Wyatt and I just became more than friends.

The realization doesn't hit as hard as it should. I think I'm too keyed up. Too distracted by the beautiful man with the *very* large bulge who's still on top of me.

"I don't think anyone could ever regret kissing you."

"I'm good"—his mouth quirks up on one side—"but I'm not that good."

I touch my fingertip to his lips. "I call your bluff."

"You are the expert now." He nips at my finger. "You still wanna do this when you wake up tomorrow, then we'll do it.

But right now, I'm takin' you back to your mama and daddy's house."

"I'm gonna want to do it, Wy."

"Everybody wants to do it." He straightens, sitting up on his knees. He holds out his hand. "But it's not always the right thing. You said you wanted me to teach you. Consider this part of the lesson."

I take his hand and he twines our fingers. He helps me sit up, and then he pulls down my dress, smoothing it over my legs. The tenderness of the gesture makes my chest hurt.

"Wy?"

He grunts when he falls onto the bench on the driver's side. "Yeah?"

"Thank you."

"For what?"

"For the raging case of blue balls."

He lets out a big, booming laugh as he puts a hand on the gearshift. "Sugar, you got no idea the kinda hurt you're puttin' on me right now. I could chop wood with this thing." He gestures to his lap.

I lick my lips. "You could always teach me how to take care of it."

"Don't."

"Don't what?"

"Joke around like that." His eyes are dark when they meet mine. "It's like you want me to come in my pants."

I bite my lip. "Whatever you say, Daddy."

I expect him to laugh. Call me out on being a shameless dork. Instead, he blinks, nostrils flaring, and then his entire body jerks.

"Fuck," he bites out, covering his crotch with his hand.

I stare at him. "Wait. Did you actually—"

"Just come in my pants?" He grimaces. "Yes."

My turn to blink. I'm not sure what to make of this. Is it a compliment that I made him lose it like that? Or did I just embarrass him?

I don't know what to say. "I'm...sorry?"

"Ain't nothin' to be sorry for. Not your fault I was so turned on." He lets out a breath, and my heart takes a tumble when I see the corner of his mouth twitch. "Actually, it's totally your fault. I wanna hate you for it—"

"But you don't." I smile.

He grins. "Nah, Sunshine, I don't."

"Are you really not okay?"

"That's just...never happened before." He reaches for the gearshift. "I'll be fine. But use nicknames with caution, would you?"

I scoff. "Rich, coming from you."

"You sayin' my nicknames turn you on?"

"Maybe," I tease.

His eyes glimmer. "Good to know."

I'm smiling so hard, my face hurts. "I really do want to thank you for being the best date I've had in...jeez"—I blow out a breath—"feels like forever."

"You need to get out more, Dr. Powell."

"Good thing you're available, Mr. Rivers."

"For you?" Changing hands on the wheel so that he's holding it in his left, he puts his right hand on my thigh. "Always."

CHAPTER 13

Wyatt

YOU SHOULD PROBABLY LEAVE

BEST FRIENDS and blow jobs do not go together.

But you wouldn't know it from the very graphic, very vivid dreams I have of Sally on her knees, on all fours, or draped over my lap in the front seat of my truck, my dick in her mouth and my hand on the back of her head.

Just like in real life, in my dreams Sally is eager to please. She's passionate. Vocal. Vulnerable. No wonder I came in my pants like an amateur last night. The girl is on *fire.*

In my dreams, she becomes more confident the longer we touch, just like she did when we actually kissed in my truck. By the time I dragged myself off of her, she was all in, kissing me back like the world was ending.

More than that, she clearly cared about what I liked and how I was feeling, and that's what has me coming in my hand at six thirty in the morning on a Saturday as I relive a particularly explicit dream—the one where she comes from making *me* come.

The one where she shows up again and again, proving me wrong. People don't always leave. They won't always hurt you if you let them get close.

In fact, sometimes, they take real good care of you.

Did Sally take care of herself after I dropped her off at home last night? For some reason, I picture her using a vibrator. Something small and discreet, but also powerful.

She think of me while she used it?

Shoving the thought aside, I climb out of bed and turn on the shower. The house's old pipes creak. It'll be a couple minutes before the water warms up, but maybe that's a good thing. I need to cool my jets, literally, or I'm gonna end up doing something stupid. Like have sex with my best friend under the guise of "teaching" her how to have a good time on a date.

She's seemed to enjoy everything I've taught her so far. Still can't help but cringe at how much of myself I bared to her last night. Not with my words necessarily, but with my body. I couldn't hide my hunger.

Then again, I don't think she wanted me to because she didn't hide hers either.

And yet I still feel a sense of guilt that I didn't bare even more. I kept telling her to be honest with me, all while I was holding back an atomic bomb of a confession.

If we take things any further, she's gonna see the tattoo on my thigh—the one I got for her. And then what? I won't have any choice but to tell her I lied by omission.

I step into the ice-cold stream of water. It hits my skin like a hundred tiny knives, but I force myself to stand there and hurt. Only what I deserve for not being totally honest with Sally.

I need to grow a pair and tell her how I feel.

I need to tell her last night was a mistake. I'm desperate not to lose her.

But, God, it was good. So good that I can't stop thinking about it. Just like I can't stop thinking about how she encouraged me to talk about Mom. No one's really done that before. I think people are scared to bring up my parents, like they don't want to make things awkward or whatever. It's easier to just pretend like their passing didn't happen.

Sally, though, is never one to take the easy route. And I appreciate that about her more than she'll ever know.

Palming the tile wall, I lean into it and hang my head, letting the water course over my head and shoulders. It's getting a little warmer. Still not comfortable.

I loved how soft and warm Sally felt in my arms. Her mouth was hot and tasted sweet. Makes me think of how hot and sweet she'd taste between her legs. Even through our clothes, I could feel the pulsing heat of her center. She wanted to have sex as much as I did.

Is telling her I want more than a hookup the right thing? Or would that just be messing with her head? I'd never forgive myself if I was the reason she didn't go off and chase her dreams.

That's assuming an awful lot though, isn't it? That my confession might throw off someone as focused and ambitious and smart as Sally Powell?

Yeah, I'm gonna be a fucking mess when she leaves. But our separation might not affect her like that. It didn't in the past. Can sex really change that much, that quickly?

I don't know.

I do know I'm glad we didn't go any further last night. Of course I wanted to fuck Sally. I wanted it so badly that my body *still* aches with the desire however many hours later. But it all happened so fast.

One minute, I was Sally's fake date. I was asking her if she was okay with us holding hands.

The next, I was on top of her, capturing her moans in my mouth as I tried not to tear that fucking dress off of her.

My balls contract. I'm getting hard again. The water's finally warm, but I turn the tap all the way to cold. The skin on my neck and shoulders goes numb.

Cash would kill me if Sally did something stupid on my

account. John B would hate me forever. Patsy would never forgive me. By hooking up with Sally, I could very well tear our family apart.

It could also tear *me* apart. Bad things happen when I let people get close. Believing otherwise was just a dream—literally in my case. I have to protect myself.

Which means Sally and I have to stop. I have to tell her the sex we talked about last night absolutely cannot happen.

Sally wants to get laid, she's gotta do it with someone else.

I'm fine with her being with someone else.

I am fucking *fine with it*.

I get out of the shower and throw on a pair of jeans, a shirt, and my work boots. Then I tie a blue bandana around my neck. As foreman, I technically have weekends off. But there's always work to be done on a ranch, and I gotta do something to get my mind off Sally and the memory of those fucking thighs wrapped around my waist.

So soft. Soft and strong. Woman can ride a horse like nobody's business. She's at ease in the saddle, her body loose, her back straight.

Bet she'd ride me just as good.

Pushing my arms into my denim jacket, I pluck a hat off the stand by the door and shove it onto my head. It's too early for a beer, right? It *is* cold outside. Nobody would judge me if I put whiskey in my coffee.

I open the door—no one locks up around here—and nearly have a heart attack when I see Sally standing on my front porch. She's got two cardboard cups from the coffee shop downtown in her hands, and a big old smile on her face.

My stomach drops. But my heart, it swells, slowly unfurling like morning glory does when its flowers are touched by the sun.

"Hey." My voice sounds like gravel.

Sally, though, just keeps smiling, unafraid of my growling. "Hey. I brought you some coffee because, well, that's apparently my thing now, driving over to Lucky River Ranch at random times to bring you delicious, hot beverages. I promise I won't ask for anything this time."

She's got purple thumbprints underneath her eyes, like she didn't sleep much either. Her hair is pulled into a glossy knot on the top of her head. The strengthening sun catches on the stray strands framing her face and trailing down her neck, literally lighting her up.

Her lips still look a little swollen. My body leaps when I see a pink patch of skin on her throat. I did that. I marked her. She's so damn pretty like this, disheveled and tired, no makeup, illuminated like an actual angel. I can't find air to fill my lungs.

I am so fucking obsessed with you it's not even funny.

"I'm real happy to see you, Sally." I reach for the coffees. "Thank you kindly for bringing these."

There's a shyness to the way she looks at me from underneath her long lashes. "Do you hate me? For just showing up like this after…"

"Dumb question. I could never hate you. Especially not when you show up with caffeine." Our fingers brush when I take the coffees. My pulse jumps. "You wanna come in?"

Sally eyes the pair of nearby rocking chairs. "It's a beautiful morning."

So she's worried about what will happen if we go inside together too. That a good sign? Or a bad one?

That don't matter though, does it? We're not hooking up. I'm never putting my hands on her again.

Never ever, ever. Even if she is showing her hand by turning up like this, doing the difficult thing of facing the consequences of our actions rather than sweeping them under the rug. Takes guts to do that.

I love her for it.

"Not gonna be too chilly for you?" I ask.

"I'm good if you are."

Why am I thinking about Johnny Cash and how he said heaven was having coffee in the morning with June, his wife?

Might be just as dangerous staying outside with Sally as it would be going inside with her. 'Cause all of a sudden, I'm thinking about marriage and shit.

I'm not *good*. I really am in heaven. Which is a big fucking problem. Wasn't I just swearing up and down that I was gonna keep my distance? Tell Sally we can't do this thing, whatever it is?

"I'm great."

"Okay." Sally sits, and I hand her a cup of coffee.

"What'd ya get us?" I land in the chair beside her.

The sun slants onto the porch, and I stretch out my legs to feel its warmth. Birds flit through the trees nearby, filling the air with their chatter. The smell of freshly fallen leaves and woodsmoke is everywhere.

"Lattes. Two pumps of hazelnut, extra hot."

"A shameless appeal to my sweet tooth then."

She grins at me as she folds over the little drinking tab on her cup, securing it so that steam escapes from the tiny opening. "Yes."

I sip, and she sips. The latte is hot and sweet with just the right amount of hazelnut flavor.

It tastes like Sally.

Our eyes meet.

She thinking about the kiss too? What is she thinking in general?

She doesn't look teary or angry, like she regrets what we did. Neither of us drank much. And it was just a little making out. If I did that with anyone else, I wouldn't think twice about it. We're not in eighth grade anymore.

With Sally though, making out feels monumental. Probably because it is. We crossed a line I'd thought we'd never cross, and I admitted things to her I'd never thought I'd have the courage to say. Granted, I said them with my lips, my body, my hands. But Sally's a smart girl. She has to know I was very much into what we did in the front seat of my old Dodge.

An awkward beat of silence stretches between us, and I scramble to think of something to say.

Do I play it safe, make small talk? Pretend like it never happened?

Or do I jump in with both feet and tell my best friend I've been in love with her for over a decade? Ask her to stay at my place tonight and every night after that, please and thank you?

"So…about last night." Sally looks at me as she runs her free hand up and down her thigh.

I chuckle. "I'm glad you wanna talk about it because I do too."

"I loved it," she blurts. "Every minute, Wy. I loved every damn minute of it. You—everything—you are so, *so* good at it. That's what I came here to tell you. I was able to just be in the moment—I wasn't in my head at all—and that felt liberating in a way I can't quite describe."

Welp, there goes my plan to keep it in my pants. I let out a giant sigh of relief as my heart floats around my chest like a big, dumb, happy balloon.

Sally didn't like making out with me.

She fucking *loved it*.

Not only that, she ain't afraid to tell me she loved it. Makes me wanna be brave too.

Fuck not going for round two. If she's gonna give me the opportunity, I'll take it. I'll deal with the fallout later. This is a chance I have to take.

"You're one hell of a kisser," Sally continues. "I don't know if it was as good for you—I feel like I might have unfairly put you on the spot or pushed you—"

"Did you not feel just how much I loved kissin' you?" I slowly sip my coffee, like I'm not talking about my best friend turning me on so bad that I came in my pants. "Trust me, I wasn't pushed. You were better'n good, Sal. You were great."

Sally's cheeks flush pink as she smiles again. "Really?"

"Really. And I'd like to do it again. Whatever you want."

Her eyes go wide. "Are you serious?"

"Long as that's what you want too."

"It is, yeah."

"I have one condition."

"Name it."

"No more Beck Wallace. You want me to teach you how to stay out of your head, that's fine. But you ain't practicing it with anyone else."

Once she goes back to New York, she can do what she wants. Out of sight, out of mind. While she's in Hartsville, however, she's gonna do me and me only.

Sally looks away, her eyelashes fluttering. "I'm fine with that. That's…fine."

"You sure? I don't want to make you do something you're not comfortable with—"

"I'm sure, Wyatt." She looks me in the eye. "I definitely want to do this."

"Good. One more condition then." My heart hammers. "You gotta promise me we'll still be friends when this is over."

Because it will end. It has to.

But I won't think about that right now. Right now, I'm gonna pretend like January doesn't exist. Like November and December are gonna last forever, so I don't need to be scared of going all in. Sally's here to stay.

"Aw, Wy, that goes without saying." Sally reaches over and grabs my hand, her palm warm from being wrapped around her coffee cup. "You're my best friend in the world. When I got home last night, I literally couldn't sleep. I was so…excited. And happy. And I kept wondering if it was all so good because we're already friends, you know? There's a level of comfort there that I've never had with anyone else."

I lift a shoulder, my heart doing that hammering thing again. "Whatever the case, I'd like to think we're both adults. That we're going in with eyes wide open. Keep talkin' to me, yeah?" *And maybe—just maybe—I'll finally be able to really talk to you.*

"Like I could ever stop." Sally squeezes my hand. "Thank you, Wy. You really don't have to help me practice being confident—"

"But I want to." The breeze blows her hair into her face. Letting go of her hand, I reach up to tuck the strands behind her ear. I hope she doesn't notice that my hand's a little shaky. *I can't believe this is happening.* "Let me."

Her gaze goes hazy, eyes unfocused. A flicker of heat ignites low in my belly.

"Okay," she says softly.

I ain't about to waste time. I got a little more than a month to show Sally how a real man treats her. Five weeks—but who's counting?—to get my fill of her before I have to give her up.

Speaking of that, I gotta make sure we're on the same page here. Sally's just looking for a good time. A way to let loose. We cross any other lines, someone's gonna get hurt.

That someone is me, and I'm going to end up hurt no matter what happens.

I still force out the words. "Just sex, right?"

Sally blinks. My pulse thumps.

Ask me for more. Please, God, ask me for the world so I can give it to you.

Instead, she nods. "Just sex. Yeah."

"Okay then." I slap my leg in an effort to distract myself from the sudden pain inside my chest. "You got a lot going on today?"

"I do. There's a new journal I should read, and a surgeon I

really admire just released a podcast episode. I haven't done laundry in—sheesh—way too long. And Dad's always on call, so I like to be around to help out if he needs me." She bites her lip. "But if you gave me an excuse to bail, I totally would."

"How about…" I pretend to think it over as I grab her hand again. "You need to come check out the herd with me. Weather's good, and I saw a couple of heifers lingering at the back of the pens yesterday. I need you to triple-check that they're not sick."

"Sounds serious."

"It's not. But it'll give us an excuse to go for a ride."

Her lips twitch. "What kind of ride?"

"Whatever kind you want, sugar."

She rolls her eyes. "Jesus, you are a living, breathing one-liner."

"It ain't a line if it's true."

Those eyes flash. "Okay, I can't tell if you're actually joking or not."

"Finish your coffee"—I nod at the cup in her hand—"then find out."

CHAPTER 14

Sally

FRIENDS MAKE EVERYTHING BETTER

"SINCE YOU'RE A GAMBLIN' woman now," Wyatt says, threading his horse's reins through his gloved hands, "how about we race for some money?"

I'm on Penny, the appropriately named copper-colored mare I usually ride when I visit Lucky River Ranch. Wyatt and I tacked up at the horse barn, and now we're headed out into the glorious fall morning.

"We forgot to collect our winnings last night, didn't we?" I say with a smile.

Screwing an eye shut against the sun, Wyatt lifts his hips so he can dig into his front pocket. The motion draws my gaze to his thighs, which strain against the broken-in, faded denim of his Wranglers.

An image flashes across my thoughts—the muscles in those thighs tensing as Wyatt pumps into me, his breath warm on my ear as he murmurs, *Only you, Sunshine. You're the only one I want.*

Then again, he made it perfectly clear he just wanted sex. As much as that hurt—as much as I wish he'd asked for more —more is not in the cards. I have to get over that. I will get over that, if only so I can enjoy what Wyatt *is* willing to give me.

He holds up a wad of cash. "Sawyer grabbed it for us and dropped it in my mailbox late last night. Winner gets double?"

Wyatt is six-two, so he's got long legs. But they're thick, too, and so well-muscled that I can see the bulbous outline of his quadriceps through his jeans. The man is shredded, and—

Oh my God, I really do get to see him naked, don't I?

When? How? And what kind of delicious damage can be wrought by those quads?

Ever since he told me in no uncertain terms that he wanted to continue what we'd started last night, I've been wondering how it's going to go down. Part of me hoped he'd throw me over his shoulder and take me right to bed after we finished our coffee.

Another part likes the sense of anticipation that comes with not knowing what will happen next. It's edging at its finest.

By the time we get down to business, I'm going to be a hot, bothered mess.

I rock my hips in the saddle, my center aching for friction. "That'll just about empty out my bank account. But since I'm gonna win, I guess I don't need to worry about that, do I?"

Wyatt settles his ass back in the saddle and smirks. "You talk a strong game, Sunshine. First one to the fence in the south pasture?"

I look at him. He looks back. His blue eyes are piercing this morning, bright with laughter.

Laughter and lust. Because I know what lust looks like on him now. The tic of his jaw. The hard, fiery gleam in his eyes and the way they flick to my mouth.

"I'll take that fifty, cowboy."

Without waiting for a reply, I dig my heels into Penny's sides. She takes off at a sprint, my body rolling in time to her strong, even strides. The pounding of her hooves reverberates up my sides, a tickle that has me smiling like a lunatic as we rip past the corral and head out to the open pasture.

"You no-good cheater!" Wyatt calls behind me.

The breeze howls in my ears, the air cool and fresh. My hair flies everywhere, but I don't care. Heart thundering inside my chest, I feel the warmth of the sun seep through my clothes and into my skin. The familiar smells of sunbaked earth and leather fill my head.

For a second, I close my eyes and revel in the awesomeness of it all. There's nothing like it in the world. Upstate New York is beautiful in its own way, but there aren't wide-open spaces like this that invite you to ride like the devil just because you can. The sun also doesn't shine nearly as bright up there, especially this late in the year.

I also have virtually no free time at Ithaca University because I'm always, always working. When was the last time I rode for pleasure like this? Nowhere to be, nothing to do. Just me and my horse.

And my very, *very* sexy best friend. I glance over my shoulder at the thunder of more hooves, and I let out a yell when I see Wyatt quickly gaining ground.

I don't ride as often now as I did when we were younger, but I can still give Wyatt a run for his money. Literally, in this case.

Firming my grip on the reins, I guide Penny faster, faster still. She moves smoothly, her glossy mane glinting in the sun, and I can tell by the way she keeps her head held high that she's enjoying this even more than I am.

Isn't this the whole point of what I do? I perform surgery so animals like Penny can run wild and free, just like she is now. It's what she was born to do.

Maybe I was born to be wild and free too. Maybe we all are, every living thing.

That's paradoxically easy to forget when all you do is try

to fix the world and the living things in it, but you never get to enjoy any of it.

"That's it, Penny. Let's kick some cowboy ass."

But Wyatt catches up to us. "Cheaters never win!"

"Call my bluff then!"

"That makes no sense!"

"I know!"

"You were supposed to be my best student!"

"Maybe you're not such a good teacher!"

"Don't make me get out the ruler!"

"I wish you would!"

I'm laughing. We both are. I'm gripped by the crazy idea that I've never been this happy. Wyatt brings out the kid in me, and I guess I forgot what that feels like.

It feels like freedom and joy and possibility.

Wyatt takes the lead, his horse kicking up dust as they take off. I'm able to see just how good my friend looks in the saddle. He rides with a confidence that makes my blood rush hot. One hand on the reins, the other held out to the side, he's all cowboy cockiness in his hat and his jean jacket and the blue bandana he wears to keep the dust out of his mouth.

He turns his head and shoots me a devil-may-care grin. The handsome way his face creases, how blue his eyes are, how happy he looks too—it's like a kick to the chest.

What if I can't leave him?

What if we have sex and it's so good that I let down my defenses and actually admit to myself just how hard I've fallen for him, and then I'm too heartbroken to go back to New York?

Am I secretly dying for that to happen?

But that's assuming Wyatt would want me to stay. And it's pretty obvious that the only semi-romantic interest he has in me is purely physical. It's all he feels for any girl he's with. That's just him. As much as I'd like to think I'm different—

that he'd feel differently about me because we have so much history—I just don't think that's the case.

It hurts a little, if I'm being honest. But beggars can't be choosers. And aren't I getting what I asked for? I told myself I didn't want love. I want kissing and touching and really great sex, and Wyatt is offering me all that on a silver platter. I have no right to complain.

But I do have a right to feel my feelings. I just wish they didn't make this all so complicated.

I urge Penny into an all-out sprint, and we catch up to Wyatt in no time. His eyes flash with something like appreciation as we go nose-to-nose.

The fence comes into view, along with an enormous tree with bare branches that's fifty or so yards ahead.

"The oak," Wyatt shouts. "First one to the oak!"

Several heartbeats later, I reach up to slap a low-hanging branch at exactly the same time Wyatt does.

I still yell, "I win!"

"No, ma'am, you did not. I did."

Wyatt is breathing hard as he circles around the oak's wide trunk to face me. I can see the sweat glistening on his forehead and a slice of thick, well-muscled neck that peeks through his bandana.

I guide Penny forward, holding out my hand as I rub my thumb against the tips of my fingers. "I'll take my money now."

"You ain't gettin' jack because you didn't win."

"Don't think I won't reach inside that pocket myself." I nod at his jeans.

He lifts his eyebrows. "I'd like to see you try."

With a speed that startles both of us, I reach over and shove my fingers inside his pocket. The denim is soft, warm from the sun. He grabs my wrist and pulls out my hand, but when I try to pull back my arm, he refuses to let me go.

"Stop," I wheeze, my sides seizing with laughter.

"I know what you're really after."

"What's that?"

"A li'l bit of this"—he guides my hand to his chest, then moves it lower over his belly, *lower*, as he fights a fit of giggles —"and this."

I feel his abdominal muscles bunching as he laughs. He's so solid here, so broad and hard.

Somebody pinch me. I still can't get over the fact that I'm able to touch him like this.

I lift my hand a little and curl my fingers, tickling him, and he immediately twists in the saddle as he gasps for air. Seeing him laugh this hard makes *me* laugh hard. So hard that I can't breathe.

"You knew," I manage, "I'd do this. How did you"—I gasp—"forget how ticklish you are?"

"Because—" A beat passes. Another. "Bein' around you— makes it hard to think—sometimes."

My fingers go still. So does everything inside me as Wyatt's eyes lock on mine.

A breeze ruffles the long, shaggy hair at his neck. He's close enough that I can see the copper threads in his beard.

I don't realize I'm staring at his mouth until that mouth gets closer.

Much, much closer.

Wyatt's about to kiss me, isn't he? My pulse riots, and my lips tingle, and then—

"Hello, friends."

Wyatt and I immediately fall back at the sound of Sawyer's voice. I have no idea how we didn't hear him before, seeing as he's on horseback trotting toward us. Ella, his three-year-old daughter, sits in front of him in the saddle. She's wearing a pink riding helmet that matches her pink boots.

"Morning, Sawyer." I smile at his daughter. "And good morning, Ella. We were just…coming to find y'all."

Sawyer's lips twitch. "That so?"

"Ella ride with Uncle Wy?" The little girl reaches out for Wyatt. "Ella loves him."

"Uncle Wy looks like he's busy trying to get someone else to ride him." Sawyer clears his throat. "I mean, ride *with* him."

"Can you not?" A flush works its way up Wyatt's neck.

Sawyer looks at me. "Only because I like Sally so much. Sorry if we interrupted y'all."

"You didn't interrupt anything," I reply far too brightly. "Wyatt owes me money, so—"

"She tried to steal it by digging in my pocket."

Sawyer grins. "There's a joke in there about pockets and rockets, but I won't make it since there are children present."

"I hate you," Wyatt says wearily.

Ella kicks her feet, still holding out her hands. "Ella loves you!"

"Right! How could I forget?" Wyatt guides his horse toward Sawyer. With a small grunt, he lifts Ella out of Sawyer's saddle, pressing a noisy kiss to her cheek before settling her on his own saddle. "I love you too, Ellie Belly Boo."

My pulse hiccups. Because Wyatt isn't hot enough as it is. Now he's got to go and be adorable with his niece. I swear to God, I'm going to burst into flames before Wyatt and I so much as undo a single button on each other's clothes.

"Sally and I were going to check out the herd," Wyatt says. "Y'all want to join?"

"That's where we were headed too. That little sleepyhead" —Sawyer nods at Ella—"didn't wake up until after seven."

Wyatt curls his arms around her. "You needed your beauty rest, didn't you?"

"Go, go." Ella kicks her feet.

Wyatt laughs. "All right, all right, we'll go. You good, Sunshine?" He looks at me.

My mouth has gone dry. I swallow. I wish he'd stop being so relentless today. First the honesty over coffee, then the race and the laughter. The almost kiss and the sweetness with Ella. And now this, him checking in on me, making sure I'm okay after his brother *almost* caught us during that *almost* kiss.

Wyatt Rivers would make a really fucking great boyfriend.

Which doesn't compute because I don't think the man has ever had a monogamous relationship in his life. Only he asked me not to hook up with anyone else, didn't he? Which means we are, indeed, monogamous.

My heart swells at the idea, even as I silently chastise myself for reading too much into it. Yeah, we're monogamous in that we're not sleeping with other people. But are we in a relationship?

"I'm good."

We ride for another twenty minutes or so. I smell and hear the herd before we see it. That's what fifteen thousand head of cattle will do—the ground trembles, the air ripe with lowing and the scent of manure.

We crest a hill, and the breath leaves my lungs when I take in the view. Texas Hill Country stretches out before us in all its autumn glory. The pale earth is set alight by the colorful remaining foliage that clings to the trees. The Colorado River is just visible in the distance, a thick braid of deep blue water that reflects the more ardent blue of a clear, wide-open sky.

And then there's the herd, cattle as far as the eye can see. Brown cows, black cows, spotted cows. Longhorns and Angus. Some are huge; others are still young, less than a year old. I can pick out the pregnant heifers by their full udders and the way their bellies bow out, making them look like walking barrels on legs.

"The moo-moos!" Ella shrieks, pointing.

Wyatt tilts his head, shielding Ella's face from the sun with his hat. "Should we go see them?"

"Go, go," she replies.

He taps his cheek. "Only if you give Uncle Wy a kiss."

Grinning, Ella kisses his chin, then scrunches her nose. "You scratchy, like Daddy."

Don't I know it.

My face felt a little raw this morning. Mom even commented on how red my throat was when I came downstairs. I had to scramble to make up some excuse about an allergic reaction to my new face wash.

I am so, *so* ready to have my own place again. I just wish my next apartment weren't in Ithaca, New York.

Really, I wish my next apartment were here instead, and that I was renting it with a certain cowboy.

Wyatt takes the lead down the hill while Sawyer and I follow several paces behind.

"Looked like you and Wyatt had a good time last night." Sawyer keeps his voice low. "You know he told me—"

"I know." I'm blushing again. "I get it, Sawyer. It's really weird that we're pretending to date. But Wyatt's doing me a solid, which I appreciate."

"Y'all are awful good at pretending."

I shrug. "We know each other well, which helps."

"Right. And you wouldn't consider actually dating my brother because…"

My face is *burning*. "Because Wyatt is Wyatt. He's not interested in dating anyone. Least of all me."

Sawyer turns to look at his brother. "I wouldn't be so sure about that. I think Wyatt does want to be with someone. He wants to settle down. He's just afraid to put his heart out there after what happened with our parents."

My own heart twists. "That makes sense. No one wants to experience that kind of pain—the loss—again."

"You bring the best out in him, you know. He's always happiest after hanging out with Sally Powell. That's how it was with him and Mom. They were tight, two peas in a pod with their books and their sweet teeth. Sweet tooths? What's the plural there?"

I laugh. "No clue."

"I need to ask Cash. Point being, I don't think he's ever let anyone get close since she died. Anyone except you."

I glance at the cowboy in question. Wyatt's holding the reins in one hand, like he always does, his other arm wrapped around Ella. He's leaning down, saying something in her ear, and I can just hear her giggle over the sounds of the herd.

My eyes sting. Blinking, I wipe my nose.

"You all right?" Sawyer asks. "I didn't mean—"

"Please don't apologize. Thank you for saying that. I just —sometimes I forget how well y'all love each other. How well y'all know each other."

Sawyer smiles. "We know you too, Sally. We love you too."

Shit, now I'm really going to cry. One of the million reasons why I will always love Hartsville—being *known* the way Sawyer describes.

Outside of this small town—at least in the places I've lived —so few people care to even say hello, much less get to know you as a person. There's a sense of community here I haven't found anywhere else.

I'm sure it exists in other places. But I'll never have the same roots—the same relationships that span decades—that I do here. Maybe that's why I'm having such a hard time getting excited about being in New York long-term.

"I love y'all too, Sawyer." *And I'm in love with your brother, but I'm still not sure he wants what I want.*

I'm still not sure there's a way for us to be together, even if Wyatt feels the way Sawyer says he does.

"Just don't automatically take Wyatt out of the running, is all I'm asking," Sawyer says.

I furrow my brow. "Out of the running?"

But then we're at the bottom of the hill, and the shouts of

the cowboys who are already out here drown out any other sound. I'm grateful for the distraction, even though I'm dying to continue this conversation with Sawyer.

It's easy to fall into cowgirl mode once we're riding among the herd. I love using my body this way; I'm going to sleep like a baby tonight. Muscle memory comes back full force, and I'm able to help Wyatt cut a few lagging heifers from the herd. Penny has great cow sense—meaning she can recognize the cows' movements and respond accordingly—which makes my job much easier.

I hop off my horse to examine the heifers while Wyatt and Ella stay on horseback and keep the heifers separated from the herd.

"These mamas are just carrying around a lot of baby," I say, getting back on the saddle. "Y'all got some healthy calves coming."

Wyatt grins at me before turning to his niece. "You ready for some baby cows, Ella?"

Ella doesn't respond. Instead, she glances between Wyatt and me, her big blue eyes wide with curiosity. Almost like she's picking up on the tight but happy energy between us.

An image flashes across my thoughts—another blue-eyed baby, this one with a shock of dark hair, like mine.

What the actual fuck?

I urge Penny into motion, willing myself to forget whatever the hell that was.

Wyatt and Ella stay beside me as the sun climbs in the sky. Wyatt points out several cows my dad and I recently treated. Each one appears to be thriving. We talk about the brush and the grasses growing in the pasture, and Wyatt asks which plants he should add or subtract to make the pasture more nutritious for the herd.

"You ain't even been in Texas for the past twelve years, but of course you know the answer to that question," Wyatt says after I gave him a list of plant species native to the area that the cows might like.

I shrug. "I told you I miss it here. Sometimes, when I'm really homesick, I research this stuff for fun."

"Christ, you really have missed it then."

"I do. A lot."

"But less than you used to, right?"

"No." I shake my head. "More."

Wyatt narrows his eyes. He's quiet for a beat, careful to keep Ella upright while she munches on a granola bar Sawyer gave her for snack time on the go.

"Well," Wyatt says, "it'll get better."

That's just it—I don't think it will get better. I'll always miss days like this, time spent with my favorite people in the world, in my favorite place in the world.

I'll always miss Wyatt. And after what Sawyer said...

I wonder if Wyatt will miss me too.

CHAPTER 15

Wyatt

FUN WITH LASSOS

WE HEAD BACK to the New House, where we reheat the lunch Patsy left in the fridge. She doesn't work on the weekends, but on Fridays, she'll stock our fridge and pantry with enough food to tide us over until Monday.

Sally, Sawyer, Ella, Duke, and Ryder and I descend on the smoked brisket, slaw, and homemade mac 'n' cheese like a pack of starving hyenas.

When I'm done, I sit back and watch Sally chat with my brothers about everything and nothing—her epic bluff during last night's poker game, preparations for the upcoming calving season in January, that episode of *Parks and Recreation* that had us howling.

I love that she's here.

I love what a great team we make, working cattle.

I love how sweet she is with my niece, giving Ella her piece of Patsy's famous Texas sheet cake after Ella polished off her own in three huge bites. Then Sally helps Sawyer wipe Ella down; we laugh when it takes almost half a pack of Huggies wipes to get her clean.

I love how Sally's ass looks in those fucking jeans.

The ride calm her nerves? She seems relaxed enough.

She did say she wanted more practice quieting her mind. Surefire way to do that is to get her body talking, right? Watching her in the saddle—the athletic roll of her hips while we were cutting cattle, the way the wind tugged at her hair—was the world's biggest cocktease.

I'm done waiting.

I still can't believe this is happening. My fantasies—the ones I've relived over and over again for almost twenty years now—are finally about to come true.

I'm fucking *shaking*.

We clean up lunch. Then Sawyer heads back to his place to put Ella down for her afternoon nap while Duke and Ryder head to the feed store in town.

Then it's just me and Sally in the silent, soaring expanse of the New House's kitchen.

Closing the dishwasher, I straighten. Wipe my hands on a towel while I watch Sally push the chairs in at the big farm table where we ate.

I drape the towel over the lip of the sink. "So…"

"So…" Sally tucks a lock of hair behind her ear. She looks windblown, her nose a little red from the sun. "I should probably get going."

"There's a horse I'd like you to check out first. Think she might be showing signs of colic."

"Oh. Okay. Yeah, when it gets cold like this, sometimes the horses don't drink enough water. I'll grab my stethoscope. Meet you at the barn?"

"Yeah."

Walking across the yard, I wonder if I should hop in an ATV and grab some condoms from my house. I wanna fuck Sally so bad my teeth ache.

I also wanna take my time with her. Edge her a little bit so when we do have sex, she'll be wild with anticipation. If I got condoms in my pocket, that ain't gonna happen. Not having them will force me to pump the brakes.

That's a good thing—I think.

I hope.

I just wanna please this girl, plain and simple. She ain't even been kissed properly. Not until last night anyway. Wonder what kinda nightmare she endured the last time someone put their fingers or tongue between her legs.

Yeah, we aren't gonna need condoms today. But some rope? That could be fun. Don't you need to have fun to experience the transcendence we talked about?

I hurry to the barn. Thankfully it's deserted, and it should stay that way. Saturday afternoons are typically quiet on this part of the ranch.

It's also warm inside.

My body feels wound tight, pulse drumming and skin hot as I grab a coil of rope from the tack room. I hesitate. Will this turn her off? Scare her?

Nah. If her enthusiasm last night was any indication, Sally's gonna like her orgasm with a side of play. She's braver than anyone gives her credit for.

I'm taking notes.

I position myself behind the open door so Sally won't see me when she walks in. Leaning my back against the wall, I get my lariat ready. I run my fingertip over the smooth, almost-whip-like texture of the circle of rope. Its familiarity makes me feel slightly less shaky.

She enters a minute later, passing me without even knowing it. For a second I allow myself to just look at her. The wisps of hair that feather the pale skin of her neck, her stethoscope looped around her nape. The way her body narrows at her waist but swells at her hips and ass.

Sally turns her head, looking for me, and the breath leaves my lungs when I take in the fullness of her lips, how her intelligent eyes are framed by the longest, darkest lashes I've ever seen.

God-fucking-*damn* it, she's beautiful.

As quietly as I can, I push off the wall and throw the lasso in the air. Raising my arm, I guide the rope in a slow, lazy circle. I wanna catch Sally, but I sure as hell don't wanna hurt her. Not unless she asks me to.

When she's ten or so feet away, I release the lariat. She hears it, but before she can register what's happening, the looped rope drops over her head and shoulders. I give it a quick, hard tug, tightening the lasso across her tits.

Damn, I'm good.

"Wyatt!" she yelps, eyes going wide as she glances at me over her shoulder.

I close the barn door with a definitive *thwack*. Gathering the rope in my hands, I slowly make my way toward her. "You ain't goin' nowhere, Sunshine."

A small smile works its way across her lips, her dimple popping. "What about the horse?"

"Horses are fine. I just needed to get you out here."

"Ah. So what lesson is this?"

"The Toby Keith one."

She smiles, the kind that touches her eyes. "So I'm gonna know how to rope and ride by the end of it, huh?"

I sidle up behind her. Keeping the rope taut, I lean in and kiss her neck. "If it's too much—"

"Not too much." Her voice is breathy. "But what if— someone might—"

"Catch us?" I nip at her skin, and she tilts her head, giving me better access. "I know. Better make this count then if we're risking it, yeah?"

She arches her back, burying her ass in the cradle of my hips. "Yeah. So what am I gonna be riding?"

Of course she's into this.

Of course she's being playful.

I am a dead man.

"My hand." Using said hand, I thumb her chin. "My mouth." Turn her head and guide her mouth up to mine. "Anything you need to get you where you wanna go."

I kiss her. My top lip is caught between hers, and her tongue glides through the seam of my open lips.

This woman.

This fucking *woman*.

She's learning to not only ask for what she wants, but to take it too.

Those are lessons she learned from me. *Me.* The guy no one takes seriously. The guy who'd never be good enough for Sally Powell.

But apparently, Sally seems to think I'm pretty damn good at this.

Just like that, I'm hard.

This time, I don't try to hide it from her. I press my erection into her back. My head is so sensitive that even through our clothes, I can feel how soft she is in the spot where her lower back curves into her ass.

Sally manages to reach behind us. Reach between us to fondle my dick.

"What can I do, Wy?" she pants. "Show me how to make you feel good. I wanna make you feel good."

She gasps when I give the rope a tug.

"How 'bout I show you how I'm gonna make *you* feel good? I'm doin' it already, ain't I? The rope on your tits?"

"Jesus, your mouth is filthy."

"Yes ma'am, it is." Placing a hand on her chest, I slip it inside the V of her denim button-up shirt. "Tell me you're gonna keep it busy."

Because she's smart as a fucking whip, Sally picks up what I'm laying down. "I'll—yes, I...have some ideas."

"So do I. Turns me on"—I thrust my hips—"to know you

want me as bad as I want you. And I want you bad, Sunshine."

She squeezes my bulge. "I want you, Wy. I can't—I haven't stopped thinking about last night—"

I growl and bite down on her neck, vampire-style. At the same time, I cup her breast, using my fingers to push down the rope so I can pinch her nipple through her bra. She yelps again, louder.

"You yell and get us caught—"

"What are you gonna do?" She's working her hand up and down my dick over my jeans now. "Maybe you need to keep *my* mouth busy, then."

A shock wave of need rips through me as the fantasy takes shape. Me pushing Sally to her knees. Binding her hands behind her back. Grabbing her head and shoving my dick inside her mouth, pounding into her until I finish. She swallows my cum, all of it, and when I lean down to kiss her mouth she murmurs, *I love the way you taste.*

Would she really like me being so rough with her? Would I scare her?

Would I turn her on even more? And what would she say if she saw the tattoo on my thigh?

"Oh, sugar, I plan on it." I thumb her nipple. It pebbles against the lace, tiny and perfect and achingly soft, and Sally's breath catches. "Lemme show you how it's done."

Giving her nipple a pinch, I kiss her neck as I unbutton her shirt. I trail my fingertips over the bare skin of her belly, her stomach caving as she lets out a little moan.

"That's it. Keep tellin' me what you like." I push my dick against her. "Feel how much that turns me on? Don't stop."

She moans again when I unbutton her jeans and pull down the fly. She's panting now, hips rolling against my hard-on, and I have to bite the inside of my cheek to keep the friction from making me lose my goddamn mind. 'Cause losing my mind would look an awful lot like me bending Sally over a nearby blanket bar and fucking her bare.

It'd look an awful lot like me telling her I want so much more than just sex.

I'm an animal. She's an angel. I gotta stay in control.

She don't make it easy. I slide my hand inside her jeans and find cotton panties, edged with lace. My heart skips a beat. These are similar to the ones she was wearing when we went skinny-dipping that day twelve years ago.

I wanted to get inside 'em then.

I can't fucking believe I finally get to do it now. My fingers tremble as I press them against her pussy through the cotton. She's hot. The fabric gets damp as I keep pressing, gently guiding her lips apart with my finger.

"Wyatt, oh my God," she breathes, her shoulders falling back against my chest.

I scrape my fingertip against her clit through the fabric of her panties. "Your body don't lie, huh? I turn you on."

"Of course you—*oh*. Yes. More. Please."

I slip a finger inside her panties, gritting my teeth when I feel nothing but smooth skin as I loop the fabric around my knuckle.

"What's this?" I grunt. "You shave?"

"I did. I don't usually, but I…thought it could be fun. I don't know—"

"Oh, Sunshine, you know." I work my finger up and down, pulling the fabric taut so that it's caught between her lips. My knuckle trails over her skin. My dick is in agony. "You fuckin' know more than you let on."

"You like it shaved?"

"I like it how you like it. And I think you bein' this way turns *you* on."

She nods. "Feels more—wow—sensitive this way."

Good God. This girl.

I imagine her exploring what feels best in her shower.

Shaving her pussy, then grabbing the showerhead to see what happens.

The idea just about sends me into a death spiral.

I give her panties a quick, hard pull, and her hips punch forward. Aw, yeah, she really is sensitive.

Then I pull the panties aside and dig my first two fingers into her swollen slickness.

"Jesus *fuck*," I bite out. "Soaked. What the fuck—why the fuck—how the fuck—Sally, fuck you for not tellin' me. I gotta take care this for you, Sunshine."

"Fuck you right back." She laughs, a breathless sound, as she goes up on her tiptoes while my fingers glide through her slit, front to back, front to back again. "When was I supposed to tell you? Over lunch with your brothers?"

Fair point. Still enrages me that she's been walking around like this.

"Never again," I manage.

Turning her head, she looks up and bites my chin. "Take care of it now."

In reply, I jerk my hips. At the same time, I push a finger inside her. She is so tight and wet I can't see straight.

I wanna fuck her here so bad I can't *see straight*.

Gently thrusting my finger, I flatten my palm so I hit her clit too. Her knee wobbles, and her pussy flutters around my finger.

"Close?" I murmur.

She nods her head, apparently beyond words.

I thrust my finger one last time before I pull it out to circle her clit. Sally shudders, then cries out when I pull my hand away altogether.

I bring my finger to her lips. "Taste yourself."

"Wyatt—"

"I ain't asking. Open your fucking mouth and tell me how you taste so I know what I have to look forward to."

Glancing up at me, Sally parts her lips. I insert my finger

into the hot heaven of her mouth. Looping the rope through my hand several times so it stays put, I use that hand to cup her breast, squeezing so that her nipple meets with my thumb.

"Yeah, I'm gonna fuck you here too," I nearly yell when she strokes my finger with her tongue, then sucks on it. "You'd like that, wouldn't you, Sunshine? You'd suck my dick just like this, and you'd love it. I'd make you love it."

She nods. My cock pulses. I stroke her nipple, and she nips at my finger with her teeth.

"Tell me what you taste."

"Me," she says, pulling back so my finger falls away. "You."

Her eyes are hazy. The pink in her cheeks is bright.

Something in me snaps.

I loosen the rope just enough so I can pull off her shirt. I unclasp her bra and toss everything to the side.

Stepping around her so we're facing each other, I can only stare. My lungs burn with the need for oxygen and my mouth goes dry, but I don't breathe. Don't move. I just look in wonder at the most beautiful woman on the fucking planet.

Her skin is soft, creamy-looking, dotted here and there with dark brown freckles. The way her tits are fuller on the bottom, her nipples pointing high, has me biting back a string of cuss words that'd make Lucifer himself blush. I love the way her torso curves into her hips. And those legs, the silkiness of her thighs—my God, how perfect.

Everything about this woman is *perfect*. Especially the way she looks me in the eye, her gaze somehow fiery and sweet all at once. She sure as hell ain't overthinking anything right now.

She's comfortable. With me. *Only* with me.

Breathe in. Breathe out. Breathe in…

Only I can't make my chest work. I'm on the verge of passing out, but I just—

I can't take it. Sally is *naked*. She's looking at me with desire in her eyes. My finger is still wet with her saliva. Her arousal.

This is actually happening, and it's so much better than I fantasized it would be.

"You all right?" Her voice is husky.

The sound wakes me from my trance. I suck in a lungful of air. "You're beautiful, Sal. So fucking beautiful."

Her cheeks flush pink. "I thought you were going to pass out there for a second."

"I was."

"You need a minute?"

I shake my head. "I need you." I give the rope a tug, tightening it over her tits. "Trust me?"

"Wyatt," she pleads, "I'm so close. Please."

I lean in. Press a gentle kiss to her mouth. "Tell me you trust me."

I don't know why I crave the words. Maybe I just crave Sally's assurance. Her approval. I don't ask anyone for anything, but this—

This, I need.

Her eyes meet mine. "Of course I trust you. I always have."

Now is not the time to take a deep dive into what it means that someone as smart and accomplished and honest as Sally Powell trusts me. What it means that she's putting herself in my hands because she believes I'm capable of taking care of her.

Maybe that means I am capable of taking care of her.

Maybe I need to trust myself as much as Sally trusts me. Maybe I can trust *her* not to hurt me.

I tie the other end of the rope to the beam that forms the corner of a nearby stall. Now Sally is literally tied up, her arms bound to her sides, the rope drawn taut over the swell of her breasts.

I'm a fool for you, I think as I drink in the sight of her panting, ready, waiting. Not for Beck Wallace. Not for some Yankee douchebag.

For me.

I love the slopes of her belly and the strong yet feminine lines of her back.

Walking around to face her, I adjust the rope so that it's tight over her nipples.

"Lean forward," I say. "Just a little one."

She does, and it pulls the rope tighter against her nipples. She whimpers. The rope slips a little—it's not very wide—but I move it back in place, brushing my knuckle against her nipple before settling it underneath the rope.

"Oh, Wy, I like that."

Tucking her hair behind her ear, I take her face in my hand. "Thought you might."

Then I lean in and kiss her mouth. She rises into the kiss, a little moan erupting in her throat.

I move my mouth down her neck, over her collarbone. I nip at the fullness of her tits, moving my tongue over the rope that has her nipples caught. She fights against it, drawing the rope more taut, and she lets out a hiss.

"That hurt?"

"In the best way, Wyatt."

The need between my legs twists tighter. I fucking love it when she says my name.

I'm gonna make her do it again, and again, and again.

I fall onto my knees, one leg at a time. I dig my hands into her jeans and panties and pull them down, revealing her sweet little cunt.

The scent of her arousal blooms between us. Holding on to her hips, I lean in and press a kiss to her belly. The wood floor bites into my knees as my mouth works its way south, until I finally place my lips on hers.

"Wyatt."

I glide my hands down and use my thumbs to open her. I lick inside her slit, my tongue catching on her clit.

"*Wyatt.*"

"You feel like velvet here." I deepen my kiss, gathering her clit between my lips. I taste salt and Sally, some kind of sweetness that makes my head spin. "You taste like heaven."

"You feel like—oh, Wyatt, this feels so good."

I guide one of my thumbs back and sink it inside her. At the same time, I flatten my tongue and roll it over her clit. Her hips rock in time to my strokes, her legs beginning to tremble.

Looking up, I see her back is arched, her tits straining against the rope. It digs into the soft flesh of her breasts, leaving indents that break my heart and make my dick scream.

Can't help but smile. She's a bowstring, literally pulled taut.

I duck my head and eat her pussy with an open mouth and eager tongue. I dip my thumb in, out. I suck on her clit. I nick it with my teeth and soothe it by blowing on it, making Sally yell.

"My *God.*"

"My name." I move my hand to her ass. Squeeze it hard. "I like it better when you say my name."

"Wy, please. Let me—*oh God.*"

I'm feathering my fingers down the length of the crease between her cheeks. "My fuckin' name, Sally. Only my name. Say it—now."

She meets my eyes. She's breathing hard. "Wyatt. Please, Wyatt."

Grinning, I flick my tongue over her clit and press my thumb inside her. Eyes locked on hers the whole time.

I know the moment she detonates. Her pussy clamps down on my thumb, and her eyes roll to the back of her head. This time, she shouts my name.

"*Wyatt!*"

I hold her body in my hands as she comes on my mouth. I watch in awe as she rides out the orgasm, a beautiful, shuddering mess who whimpers my name over and over as her pussy squeezes my thumb.

I'm not gonna last but five seconds when I put myself inside her.

At last, her eyes flutter. My chest cracks open when a smile breaks out across her face.

"You get an A, Wyatt."

"Damn straight I do." Pressing one last kiss to her pussy, I climb to my feet. I carefully untie the lasso, frowning when I see the marks it left on her nipples and breasts. I run my thumb over the red lines. "Aw, Sunshine, this don't look good."

"It's fine. It felt—Wyatt, it felt amazing. The friction of the rope, the little hit of pain…it was a lot, but it was also really, really good."

I lean down and kiss her breasts, paying extra attention to her nipples. She moans when I take one, then the other, between my lips, stroking them with my tongue.

"Better?" I murmur against her skin.

She nods. "Yes. Much. Thank you."

Straightening, I take her face in my hands and kiss her. It's a soft kiss, a deep kiss, the kind she couldn't seem to get enough of last night.

Was that really only yesterday?

How did so much happen in such a short amount of time?

How does it feel like we've been at this forever?

Because this kiss—it's already comfortable, broken in. I tilt my head right and she tilts left, our lips moving effortlessly in an unhurried game of tug and release.

No awkwardness. No rush.

Just a really fucking great kiss.

The heavy feeling in my balls becomes unbearable. If I don't make a move soon, I really am gonna come in my pants.

I'd much rather come in her mouth. Yeah, she'll see the tattoo. But I can always play it off as an ode to our friendship.

Or you could tell her the truth.

Breaking our kiss, I reach for my zipper. "Ready for your next lesson?"

Her eyes flash. "Yes."

"Good. On your knees, Sunshine."

CHAPTER 16

Wyatt

TANGLED UP

BUT SALLY, being Sally, decides to do her own thing.

Digging her teeth into her bottom lip, Sally reaches between us. I've already got my fly unzipped, so she slips a finger into the waistband of my briefs and slides that finger back and forth. Back and forth.

My dick leaps. I feel myself leaking everywhere.

"I knew you wore briefs," she says. "Could've sworn I felt them when I accidentally touched you there on ladies' night."

"Wanna fondle me now?"

She grins. "I do."

My heart lurches when she tugs my briefs and jeans down to my knees. My cock bobs heavily between us, but the silence that suddenly permeates the room is even heavier.

Sally is looking down. For a second, I wonder if she's too busy ogling my dick to see my tattoo. But then she's falling to her knees, falling back on her haunches so she can get a better look at my left thigh. Specifically the place where it meets with my groin.

Reaching up, she runs her thumb over the tattoo there, high enough up that it can only be seen when I'm naked.

Smaller than my other tattoos, it's a simple black outline of a vintage Coca-Cola bottle with the words *No. 7* written underneath it in old-timey Western font. It's a reference to the Jack Daniel's Old No. 7 whiskey we'd put in our Coke bottles as teenagers.

I hold my breath. Sally knits her brows.

"Jack and Coke." She glances up at me, her eyes lit up with something that looks a hell of a lot like joy. "Wyatt, did you get a slutty little thigh tattoo to commemorate—"

"The day you showed up for me when I needed you most?" I swallow, my throat thick. "Yeah, Sally, I did get a slutty little thigh tattoo to commemorate that."

She laughs, but her eyes are wet. "I wasn't expecting you to admit it so easily."

"I wasn't either. But…yeah. There it is. It's stupid, I know—"

"It's perfect." She leans in and presses her lips to the tattoo. My dick pulses when she tongues the sensitive skin. "When did you get it?"

Oh Lord. She's pushing me to confess even more.

No one ever pushes me. They know better. I don't budge. I don't open up.

I open up for her though. How could I not?

"I got it when you were away in veterinary school. Think I hit an all-time high of missin' you. Or would it be low? Either way, you'd been gone for so long…" I take her face in my hand, my heart thundering. "I had to keep you with me, I guess. In my own way."

She blinks. Then she turns her head and presses a kiss into the center of my palm, eyes locked on mine.

The gesture is tender, and suddenly so is the stuff inside my chest. Feels like she's touched on a bruise—an injury old enough to be familiar, but severe enough for the pain it causes to feel fresh.

Only I'm not sure it's pain. Or maybe it is pain, but Sally's tenderness slices right through it. Underneath, I feel...*relief*. Not the endless pit of agony I thought I'd find, but a calm so steady and so potent that it's like my body's been filled with pure oxygen.

Go there. Follow that feeling.

"You saved my life, you know," I huff out.

Her teeth find my palm. Her eyes flash with something I don't recognize. "Maybe you're saving mine too."

Before I can ask what she means by that, she wraps her fingers around my swollen length. I see stars as she firms her grip and gives me a tug.

"Talk to me. Tell me what you like."

I close my eyes. Silently count backward from ten while I try to breathe through my nose. "Think about the things I did to you. Think about what you liked."

That gives her pause.

"Trust me?" she asks at last.

My chest twists. I open my eyes. "Of course I trust you. I always have."

She smiles at her line, her eyes taking on a mischievous gleam. "Good."

Then she rises to her feet. She takes off my jacket and unbuttons my shirt. She drops them to the floor, and she guides my undershirt over my head.

My body *pounds* when she puts my hat back on my head before reaching for the rope. "Hands behind your back, cowboy."

Holy fuck.

Sally is gonna tie me up. The girl who told me she forgot how to kiss is *binding my hands behind my back*.

Other guys made her lose her confidence. I'm helping her get it back.

She also called me *cowboy*.

My heart swoops.

She wraps the rope around my wrists and ties it in a tight

knot. "I wanted to control the pace so badly, Wy. Like, I wanted to take a break when I needed it. But I couldn't because I was tied up, and that made it...just...so hot, Wyatt. So, *so* hot. Not as hot as your thigh tattoo—"

"Few things are," I say with a chuckle.

"But almost."

My shoulders burn from being pulled back like this. The rope chafes against my wrists.

I like it.

I like it even more when Sally gets back on her knees. She looks at my dick, then up at me. "Last time I did this, it didn't go well. I'm gonna need a lot of guidance. I promise you won't offend me."

Her willingness to learn—the way her hips flare out when she's seated like this—I can't take it. "I promise I'mma like what you do. Put your hand on me like you just did. That's it. Hold me tight."

She circles me with her fingers and squeezes, a pearlescent drop of pre-cum appearing on my head.

"Start by licking that up. I hope you like the taste of my cum, Sunshine."

"Oh?" She's teasing me as she sits up on her knees and leans in. "Why is that?"

I wanna howl when she presses her tongue to the slit on the underside of my head. Heat rockets through me, my hips jerking. "I want you to swallow me. All of me. You want me to pull out, I will. But I want to come in your mouth, same as you came in mine."

"Okay."

Okay. This woman is killing me.

"Keep licking. Lick it all up."

Not only does she lick up every last drop. She also licks her lips, like she's savoring me.

Meeting my eyes, she says, "More."

I pull at the rope binding my wrists. It bites into my skin, but I don't care. What I would give to grab her head right now. Hold it steady while I pump into her mouth.

But I can't. As frustrating as it might be, Sally's in charge.

"What next?" she asks, giving my dick a slow, hard tug.

I bite down on my cheek. "Spit on it."

Her eyes go wide.

"Yes, Sunshine, I really want you to spit on my dick. The more lube we got, the better."

"You really—"

"I ain't askin' you again. Spit on my dick, Sally. Then I want you to spread it around with your tongue before you take me inside your mouth."

She blinks. "Okay."

I growl at the sound she makes when she does as I told her. Her spit feels warm on my skin, made warmer when she licks ribbons of fire down my cock and back up again. Tip to root. Root to tip.

"That's—good, Sunshine. Really fucking good."

Her eyes flick to meet mine. "Ready?"

I've been ready my whole life to be loved by you this way.

"I am if you are."

In reply, she tucks her hair behind her ears and presses her lips to my tip.

Sensation bolts through me. My balls contract. At this rate I really won't last more than five seconds.

Maybe that's a good thing. I don't want this to be the first and only time Sally sucks my dick. The faster I come, the less she'll have to endure.

Only the enthusiastic way she opens her mouth, bobs her head, and takes half of me in on a single swallow makes me think, *Hell, she's actually enjoying this, isn't she?*

"So. Good," I sputter as she bobs up. Bobs down.

She scrapes me with her teeth and immediately pulls back, but I just laugh.

"It's all right. Try rollin' your lips a little so your teeth are covered. Perfect. You're fuckin' perfect, Sal."

She covers her teeth with her lips and goes in for another try. My heart keeps swelling the more she tries. If she's trying, she's comfortable. She's invested.

She's swirling her tongue around my head. She's sucking on it. Kissing it. She's putting her hands on my hips, and she's guiding me deeper. Then she's reaching between her legs to touch *herself*.

Lord have mercy.

The need for release coils low in my center. I thrust forward at the same time she bobs, and I go deep. Too deep, my head hitting the soft tissue at the back of her throat.

She gags. Her eyes water. My pulse skips.

"Aw, shit, Sal, I'm—"

But she just shakes her head. She swallows. Swallows again, taking me deeper, centimeter by centimeter.

She pushes her limits. For me. *With* me.

"Remember," I grunt, "you swallow."

In reply, she gently arcs her thumb over my Jack and Coke tattoo.

My entire body jerks. I'm overtaken by blinding, searing sensation that cuts through my core and has me coming in hot, hard spurts inside Sally's mouth.

There's a lot of it. I feel it. I worry Sally's going to choke, so I pull out a little bit, allowing her to swallow.

I watch the lines of her throat work as she does exactly that, my tip still in her mouth. Cum gathers at the corner of her lips.

"Look at you, doing so good. You look beautiful like this. So fucking beautiful, Sunshine, with me all over you."

Now I wanna come on her tits. On her stomach. On her back and between her legs.

No way five weeks is gonna be long enough to do everything I wanna do with Sally.

I'm gripped by the fierce urge to ask her to stay. Spend the night. Hell, spend the whole weekend. I can already picture it. First, I'll take her home. I'll clean her up in the shower, and this time the water will be piping hot. I'll have her put on one of my shirts—no pants or panties—and I'll light a fire in the bedroom. We'll fuck in my bed. I'll make her dinner. Make cocktails. I'll fuck her again. Then we can watch a show, maybe a movie.

We'll sleep naked. Wake up and fuck before coffee. After, too, because why the hell not? We'll have breakfast, and then I'll go down on her on the couch in my living room. We'll watch another show. We'll fuck again.

And then what?

We ain't riding off into the sunset, that's for damn sure.

Everyone would know. They'd find out about it somehow. Sally not going home to her parents' house is about as big of a red flag as you can get. John B and Patsy sure as hell wouldn't approve of their darling princess messing around with the likes of me. Cash would resort to murder, no question.

Would it be worth it though?

Clearly, something is wrong with me. Nice, normal, sane people don't consider lighting their life on fire just to *temporarily* keep a girl in their bed.

And that's what Sally deserves—a nice, normal, sane guy who wants the same things she does. She deserves the world. But I'm just a small-town boy whose hands are literally tied.

Sally can't stay. I'd be an asshole to ask her to.

Then again, she did agree not to be with anyone else—

Nope. Not gonna read into that. I can't.

I'm still vibrating with the aftershocks of my orgasm, but I'm able to bite out, "Untie me."

Nodding, Sally gets to her feet. I don't miss the way she winces, putting a hand on the small of her back.

"You okay?"

"Who knew blow jobs were such a workout?" She smirks,

and that's when I see the goose bumps that cover her skin. Her nipples are tight pink points.

She's cold.

Or, like me, she's completely, utterly overwhelmed by what just happened, and her body is going haywire.

She presses her tits against my arm as she unties my hands. My wrists smart, and when I look down, I see they're red.

"The rope got you too," Sally says with a frown, gently tracing her fingertips over the marks. She looks up. "We make a mess of each other, don't we?"

You got me feeling a whole mess of things I shouldn't.

I can't ask her to stay.

I can't tell her I love her.

But I can warm her up. Make her *feel* loved. Wanted. Needed.

Because that's what this fierceness feels like when I look at Sally and she looks back—need.

I need to keep this girl in my life. Once again, that means letting her go.

Or does it mean I screw my courage to the sticking place and tell her how I feel? 'Cause I'm already sick of all this pretending.

Does it mean I never let her go again?

The blood rushes back into my biceps and shoulders as I reach up to take Sally's face in my hands. She likes it when I do that.

"You okay?" she asks softly. "You're quiet."

Glancing over her shoulder, I see her stethoscope on the ground by her feet. I bend down to grab it and, straightening, I hold open the ear tubes before gently placing the silicon tips into Sally's ears.

I settle the metal bell on the center of my chest.

"Not quiet at all, actually," I say, grabbing her hand and placing it over the bell.

Sally's eyes go wide as she listens to the way she's made my heart pound.

"This is what you do to me," I whisper. "If you ask me, we make a mighty fine mess, Sunshine."

Then I press my lips to hers, and she smiles when my heart beats even faster.

CHAPTER 17

Sally

LIES, LIES, LIES

HIS KISS TASTES LIKE US.

I'm on his mouth and he's on mine, and the taste is lewd and earthy and incredibly intimate. Coupled with the sound of his heartbeat racing in my ears, it's overwhelming.

I start to shake.

Really, I've been shaking since Wyatt told me about his tattoo—the one I've never seen before.

"I had to keep you with me, I guess. In my own way."

The Jack and Coke is more than a tattoo. It's a confession. One that's so sweet, that's such a big deal for someone as locked up as Wyatt, that I can't help but feel like he really does want me in a way I never thought he would.

He's opening up bit by bit, and I never want him to stop.

I imagine that's why I surrendered to the wildness in me just now, to the burning curiosity that I'd never dare show anyone else. His bravery made me want to be brave. And instead of being grossed out or turned off, Wyatt came in my mouth.

He was so into it—so into *me*—that he couldn't control himself.

He was also really into the fact that *I* wanted to tie *him* up. I enjoyed it so much, so I figured he might too.

And now he's kissing me deeply, gently, smoothing the callous pad of his thumb over the corner of my lips to clean me up.

He's kissing me like we didn't just engage in various levels of obscenity.

He's kissing me like he *cares*.

This kiss—it tastes like love.

My pulse seizes, my knees going weak as the longing in my center takes on a sharp edge. *Could this be love?*

Could the tattoo, the honesty, the possessiveness, and the really great oral sex add up to Wyatt being in love with me the way I'm in love with him?

My heart turns over. Separately, those facts don't mean a lot. Well, the tattoo kinda does, but Wyatt has a lot of tattoos. Those facts taken together, though—I mean, is Sawyer right? Wyatt does have that sunrise tattoo on his forearm. Could that also be a nod to the nickname he has for me?

It has to be. In my gut, I know he got that ink for me.

Holy shit, does Wyatt want more too? But he said this was just sex. Could he have been lying through his teeth the way I was in that moment?

I don't know, but I kiss him back anyway. What else can I do? I could kiss this man for hours, for days, and still not get my fill.

I already know it's going to make leaving Texas suck that much more. Today has been perfect. The kind of day I'd dream about while I was stuck inside studying, or doing rounds at the animal hospital at Ithaca University. All day, I've had this gut-deep feeling that I'm exactly where I should be.

I loved having coffee with Wyatt. I loved riding with him. I loved working cattle together and being with his brothers.

Wyatt nips at the corner of my mouth, arcing his thumb

across my cheek. I'm learning kissing chemistry is real, it's rare, and Wyatt and I have it in spades. It's the best stress relief. Best way to spend a Saturday afternoon. And a Friday night. And hopefully some part of Sunday too.

Jesus, I already want to see him again, and I haven't even left yet.

I want to stay. Spend the rest of the afternoon and evening with him. If we were still just friends—only friends—I *would* stay.

Then again, if we were just friends, I probably wouldn't have come over to Lucky River Ranch today in the first place. My never-ending to-do list would've definitely won out over having coffee with Wyatt on his front porch.

The fact that we became *more* than friends is why I'm here at all. It's terrifying to think about what we're risking. But also a thrill to ponder what I'm gaining by putting myself out there like this. I feel like I'm actually *living* instead of working, or preparing, or organizing, or answering emails, or doing any of the one million tedious tasks that typically fill my days.

I don't know what Wyatt and I would do for the rest of the afternoon and evening. Hang at his place maybe? Shower together, watch TV, have lots of mind-blowing sex?

All I know is I want to be with him.

Wyatt breaks the kiss to wrap his arms around me. "Aw, Sunshine, you're still shakin'."

Are you in love with me, Wyatt Rivers?

But then what? If his answer to that question was yes, where would that leave us? I'm not sure I'm ready to face the obstacles that'd lie ahead.

Let's be real, I'm not even ready to face his answer. He said this was *just sex*. Leave it to me to make a mountain out of a molehill.

So I paste on a smile and say, "I'm a little cold, yeah."

His brow creases as he runs his big hands up my arms. "Let's get you dressed then. Here, take my jacket."

"I'm okay."

"You're not okay. You're freezing. Take the damn jacket, Sally."

He pulls up his pants, then helps me tug my shirt over my head and guides my arms into my jacket. Then he wraps me in *his* jacket, the nubby sherpa lining cozy and warm.

It smells like him. Like sandalwood and bonfires and dryer sheets. The yearning in my center takes on a sharp edge.

What kind of detergent does he use? And why does it bother me that I don't know that about him? I thought I knew everything about Wyatt.

Then again, I'm not his girlfriend. I've been to his place, but I've never had an excuse to be in his laundry room.

I'm down bad if I'm interested in knowing what Wyatt's laundry room looks like. He moved into the old farmhouse on Lucky River Ranch, the one that was built over a hundred years ago by Mollie's great-grandfather. It's been renovated, but if I had to guess, it probably doesn't even have a laundry room; the machines are likely tucked into a closet or kept in the basement.

I need to get a life.

I need to ask Wyatt if he wants to get naked at his place, now. But I don't. Today really has been perfect. I don't want to ruin it by asking for more.

I'm still shaking when we finish getting dressed.

Wyatt frowns. "Talk to me. What's goin' on?"

Pressure builds inside my chest and behind my eyes. Now would be a perfect time to ask my best friend to take me home with him. But I can't.

We can't.

"That was great, Wy."

"Of course it was great. Tell me why you're still shaking."

"I'll be fine. Really. That was just…the orgasm, Wyatt. Wow."

He smiles. "No shit. I can't feel my fuckin' legs right now."

"Want me to feel them for you?"

He bursts out laughing. "Anytime."

I meet his eyes. They bounce between mine as a beat of heated silence blooms between us.

Ask me to stay.

For a split second, I actually think he's going to do it. His expression softens, and I swear I can see the same longing that I feel written all over his face.

But then he clears his throat, shoving his hands in his pockets. "I'm not lettin' you leave until you promise me you're all right."

I'm so crushed, I can't breathe. Still, I manage to keep my smile from wavering. "Seriously, Wyatt, I'm great. Thank you."

"Stop thankin' me. You give as good as you get, Sunshine." He flashes me a wide white smile. "I mean that in the perverted sense."

"Everything you say *is* a euphemism."

His smile broadens. I smile back, and this time, it's a real smile because I love the fact that he and I share so many inside jokes.

We smile at each other like that for one beat. Two.

"Let me walk you to your car." Wyatt's voice sounds different. It's deeper. Coarser.

I shake my head. "I should run. Lots to catch up on."

Wyatt nods. "Yeah. Me too."

Another beat of silence.

My chest burns from where the rope bit into my skin. It'll probably leave a mark.

Wyatt keeps marking me. Is that another sign that his feelings for me run deep?

"See ya." I turn and bolt for the door. "Please tell Ella I had the best time hanging out with her today."

"Okay."

Reaching for the latch, I glance over my shoulder. Wyatt is looking at me, his eyes narrowed. His smile is gone. A pair of indents has appeared between his eyes, like he's confused. Or hurt.

I'm doing the right thing. This is what he wants. This is what I said I wanted.

Only I want more, and I don't know what to do about that.

I burst into tears the moment I'm in my truck. Starting the ignition, I turn on the heat and lean my head against the steering wheel.

I drive back home in a daze. Luckily, I manage to get ahold of myself as I get closer to the house; I don't want to tip Mom and Dad off that something happened. Mostly because I don't feel like talking about it. And Dad is so laser-focused on *me* being laser-focused on my job. He gives me my freedom, but I doubt he'd approve of me being tied up by Wyatt instead of listening to that podcast or reading those journals.

The smell of Mom's white chicken chili hits me the minute I step through the door. No doubt she has a pot of it bubbling away on the stove.

My heart clenches. One good thing about coming home tonight: I won't miss dinner. I know Mom made the chili especially for me. Topped with sour cream, cubed avocado, tortilla strips, and some shredded cheese, her white chicken chili might be my favorite meal of all time.

"Hey, honey." Mom looks up from the book she's reading on the living room sofa. "How was your day?"

I'm getting scary good at pasting on these smiles. "It was great." Looking down, I toe out of my boots. "Smells delicious, Mom."

"I was hoping you'd be home in time for dinner. How's Wyatt?"

Did I tell Mom I was hanging out with Wyatt today? Pretty sure all I said this morning was that I had some errands to run.

"I was with Wyatt last night."

"I know. And you were with him again today."

My stomach dips. I glance into the house. Dad is nowhere in sight. I didn't see his truck out front, but there's a good chance that just means he put it in the garage.

I pull my brows together. Keep my voice low when I ask, "How'd you know?"

"I just do." She nods at me. "And you're wearing his jacket."

"Oh. Yeah." I look down at it. "I was...chilly. He let me borrow it."

"Awfully kind of him."

I swallow. "Yeah."

Her smile fades a little. "You okay, honey?"

Grabbing the nearby banister, I nod. "Just tired. Holler when dinner's ready?"

"Of course." A pause. "You know I'm always here if you need to talk, right?"

My eyes film over. Part of me wants to confide in Mom. Another part is afraid she'll think the same thing Dad would. That a fling with a guy from Hartsville is fine, but anything more than that is a bad idea. I've spent my whole life in pursuit of the job I now have in hand. Mom and Dad sacrificed so much to help me make that particular dream come true, and I can't let them down now that we're so close to the finish line.

Mom loves Wyatt like a son. So does Dad. But even if they do love him like family, would they love him for me?

I can't stop thinking about that fucking tattoo.

"I appreciate that, Mom. Thank you."

Then I bolt upstairs, my legs feeling like lead weights as I move.

CHAPTER 18

Sally

ALL IN

CLOSING my bedroom door behind me, I crawl into my bed. There's a new soreness between my legs.

Wyatt and his magic fingers. He knew just where to touch me. Just the right amount of pressure to apply. The way he teased me, dipping the blunt tip of his finger inside me before using the moisture he gathered to play with my clit—

Even now, wrung out, an emotional wreck, I'm still hot all over at the memory of how it felt when that man had his hands on me.

I wish I could be cooler about this. I hate dwelling on one afternoon, one orgasm, one guy, like a lovesick teenager. It's embarrassing.

But so much happened in that one afternoon. Wyatt keeps giving me glimpses of the man behind the mask he wears, and now I want more. I want to see all of him. Know all of him.

"Of course I trust you. I always have."

"You saved my life."

"You're fuckin' perfect, Sal."

I can't stop thinking about the things he said. The things

he did. I'm brimming with feeling, and there's nothing I can do to keep it from spilling over.

Burying my head in the pillow, I let the tears flow. It just...hurts.

I'm being greedy, wanting *more*. Wyatt's already given me so much—all the attention and the patience I asked for. I need to be content with that.

I should be content with that, but I'm not, and the frustration it makes me feel—coupled with the confusion I feel about my future—only makes me cry harder.

Tap.

At first, I think I imagined the sound. Speaking of lovesick teenagers, for half a heartbeat I time-travel back to high school, when Wyatt would climb onto the roof of the front porch and rap his knuckle on my window. Together, we'd sneak out and hop in his truck, which he'd hidden a couple of hundred yards from the house behind a stand of gnarled oaks. Sometimes, we'd escape to the river, where we'd drink our Jack and Cokes and go swimming. Other times, we'd just drive, the music turned up loud as we crisscrossed Hart County, singing along to Mumford & Sons, Alan Jackson, Bon Iver.

God, how badly I wanted Wyatt to pull over and make a move on those drives. I was nursing a serious, unrequited crush on him back then—same as I am now—and as we drove, I'd fantasize about him reaching across the center console and putting a hand on my thigh. Just like he did the night he drove me home from the potluck.

Tap, tap.

I go still, holding my breath. Maybe I'm not imagining the sound.

Lifting my head off the pillow, I turn and see a dark silhouette in the window outlined against the fiery sunset that fills the sky.

Tap, tap, tap.

My stomach swoops. I'm pushing off the bed and quietly scurrying across my room before I know what I'm doing, careful to avoid the floorboard by my desk that squeaks when I step on it.

Wiping my eyes, I blink, still not sure what I'm seeing. At first, I think it's just a shadow, a series of shapes put off by the dying light. But then suddenly—thrillingly—the shapes come together to form a whole.

Oh my God, it's a cowboy.

It's *my* cowboy, and I'm so fucking happy he's here that I want to yell.

He's crouching on the roof, knees bent, heels up. He's wearing his cowboy hat, because Wyatt is always wearing his cowboy hat. His hand is raised, first finger bent against the glass.

Even his *outline* is handsome. Because that's all I can see with the sun behind him like this—the broad expanse of his shoulders, the slant of his wide neck, the thick curve of a bent knee.

He gives me a little wave when he sees me approach. I can't breathe.

My pulse is wild as I unlatch the window and pull it open, a gust of cold air greeting me. Without the glare of the glass between us, I can finally see his eyes.

They're bright. Full.

The concern in them is crystal clear as they rake over my face. "I knew you were upset. Why didn't you tell me?"

He keeps his voice low.

So do I when I say, "Why are you here?"

"Can I come in?"

"I'm okay."

"Quit lyin'."

I wrap my hand around his forearm. "Of course you can come in. Think you can fit through the window?"

"I'm not *that* much bigger than I was in high school," he says as I help him through the window.

He is though. His shoulders barely clear the window frame, and when he straightens to his full height, he looks like a giant in my low-ceilinged bedroom.

When was the last time he was in here? Ten years ago? More than that?

More cold air rushes in behind him. He smells minty, like the wintergreen gum he definitely chewed on the way over here. He closes the window, then turns back to me. I watch through a film of tears as he takes my face in his hands and thumbs them away.

"I came because I had a feeling something was up with you," he whispers. "I came because I shouldn't have let you go in the first place. I ain't gonna be the reason you're cryin' alone in your room. That stops tonight—you hear me? I wanna take care of you, Sal, but I can't do that if you don't talk to me. Did I hurt you? Are you sore, or…"

I can't find words. Or air. My blood thrums inside my skin, my pulse marking a frantic, uneven beat.

Now. Now. Now.

Wyatt is showing his hand. Offering another glimpse behind the mask.

It's time to show my cards. To admit that I lied when I told him I only wanted sex. I'm too in love with him not to be totally, completely honest.

"I'm not hurt, no."

"Okay…"

"I know I asked you for transcendence," I begin, and Wyatt laughs quietly. "Like, transcendence in the sexual sense. Sex—that's all I asked for. And I genuinely thought I'd be okay with just that. But today—tonight—don't get me wrong, Wy, it was great. Best I've ever had. Somehow though"—I shake my head—"it didn't feel like enough. And I should've said something, but I was terrified of making a fool of myself or, you know, scaring you off by being *that* girl. The one who wants to date after hooking up once."

"Twice." A muscle in his jaw tics. "We been together twice now. And you ever scare me off before?"

"Well, no, but—"

"This isn't any different." His gaze searches mine. His thumb finds my lips. "What're we doing here, Sally?"

My heart somersaults at the pleading edge in his tone.

"I don't know." I'm so nervous I feel like I'm about to pass out. But I press on, because I'm sick of feeling so mixed up. Sick of feeling like I've lied by not telling the whole truth. *My* whole truth. "All I do know is that I'm so happy you're here. I want you to stay. I want to be around you all the time. I want you to be my guy. Not just the guy I have a good time with. But the guy I call, and confide in, and come home to. You're my favorite human, Wy." I sniffle. "No one else even comes clo—"

He cuts me off with a hot, hard, searing kiss, tossing his hat aside as his mouth moves over mine.

I close my eyes, tears leaking out of them left and right. I let him open my mouth with his tongue, his lips. His heat.

This means yes, right? This means that Wyatt wants *more* too?

Holy shit, I can't believe Wyatt wants what I want.

I can't believe he's not running.

Actually, I do believe it. After everything he's said to me, the things he's confided, the things we've done, I do believe Wyatt is the kind of man who stays.

This is what a healthy relationship feels like. I'm allowed to be myself, and I'm getting what I want *because* I'm free to just…be.

I'm free, and I'm wild.

I fall into him, fisting my hands in the denim shirt that peeks through his vest. Relief pours through me, a steady, potent warmth that is such a shock to my system after the nerves and the confusion I've felt since leaving the ranch that I get dizzy.

I hold on to Wyatt for dear life until we're both gasping for air, my lips throbbing, my body tight.

"I'll be your guy." He nudges my nose with his. "If you'll be my girl. I want so much more than just sex, Sally. I was full of shit when I said that, and I'm sorry."

An effervescent rush fills my rib cage, like champagne is being poured into my veins. In reply, I yank him toward my bed, and together we tumble awkwardly onto the mattress. Biting back a laugh, I freeze when the bed frame groans beneath our combined weight.

"Sally?" Dad's voice sounds from downstairs. "That you? Everything all right?"

"I'm fine!" I shout back. "Sorry, just got in bed to read!"

"Okay. Dinner'll be ready soon."

"Okay!"

Wyatt rolls onto his side and bends his elbow, leaning his head against his hand. "We do this, we're gonna do it right. No more sneaking around. I wanna tell your parents."

I'm on my side now, facing him. My bed is so tiny that we barely fit. "Tell them we're dating?"

"Yes." His gaze is piercing in its clarity. "I respect the hell out of your mom and dad, and telling them we're together is the right thing to do."

"Okay. Yeah." I finger the top button of his shirt. "I think that's a good idea."

I press the button through its hole, but Wyatt catches my wrist. His grip is like iron.

"Nuh-uh. You want me to fuck you in this cute little bed?" He pins my wrist to the mattress and rolls on top of me, running his nose up my throat. "Then I'll fuck you in this cute little bed. But first, we come clean to your mama and daddy. Last thing I need is John B catching us and putting a rifle in my face 'cause he thinks I'm just messin' around with you."

I scoff. "Dad wouldn't put a rifle in your face."

"Let's play it safe, yeah?"

"Fine."

"I also wanna take you on a proper date before we…"

I grin. "Go all the way?"

His eyes dance. "You make it sound like I'm taking your virginity."

"If only you had."

"I wasn't ready for you then. I woulda fucked it up."

"Really? I don't know if I agree with that."

His Adam's apple bobs. "It's what I gotta tell myself, Sal."

My pulse skips. There's a confession in there—something he's trying to say—and while I'm ravenously curious to know what it is, I also feel the need to be gentle. Patient. There's so much happening right now as it is.

So I make a mental note to circle back to his thought and run my finger along his jaw, determined to stick to what's necessary in this conversation.

What's necessary is a discussion about the future.

"And we're not fucking it up now? I mean, do we talk about the fact that I'm leaving or…"

His jaw tics again against my fingertip. "I don't know what the right call is, Sunshine. I think we just gotta be brave and keep talkin' to each other. I think we live in the moment. Enjoy the time we got. And then we see what happens. Obviously, timin' is not ideal, but is it ever? All I can promise is that I'll do my best to make the most of every second I get with you, whether that's a month, a year, whatever."

A year.

Wyatt is talking about being together for a *year*.

I dig my teeth into my bottom lip, just to make sure I'm actually here and this is actually happening.

Of course my mind leaps twenty steps ahead. Would Wyatt come to New York with me? Is it right to even ask him to? His entire family is in Hartsville. He has deep roots here. And he absolutely loves what he does.

As far as I know, there are no cattle ranches in upstate New York. Even if there were, no cowboys could ever match the Rivers boys for skill, dedication, and heart.

What about little Ella? Wyatt and his brothers are extremely close with her. And they're just beginning to revamp the Rivers' side of Lucky River Ranch. I know Cash and Wyatt have had those plans in the works for years, and now they can finally afford to make their dreams come true for their family's property.

Is there any way I could stay in Texas then?

Just the thought makes my heart dip, but not in an alto-gether-unpleasant way. I could be happy here. I *am* happy here.

Would I be wasting my potential, though, giving up a position at one of the world's top veterinary hospitals to stay in a small town? There's plenty of work for me here in Hartsville. But could I do what Dad does for the rest of my life and be satisfied? What if I got bored?

Worse, what if I got resentful?

"Hey." Wyatt leans his forehead against mine. "Where you at?"

Closing my eyes, I swallow. "I'm really happy, Wy. Truly. I'm thrilled you and I want the same thing. Only I'm not very good at trusting that shit will just…work out."

"Trust is all we got now, Sunshine."

"I know. I'll try, Wyatt."

He presses his lips to mine, a soft, quick kiss. "Let's try together."

CHAPTER 19

Wyatt

MAN-TO-MAN

I DON'T SLEEP a fucking wink that night—or the next.

I'm the first in the kitchen at the New House at half past three on Monday morning. I blearily scoop coffee into the coffee maker and fill it with water, yawning nonstop while I wait for the pot to brew.

I'm dragging ass. But I also feel wired, gripped by this insane, nervous energy I've never experienced before rattling through my body like a dog that won't stop barking.

It's the worst combination ever. My knees ache, and my eyes feel like sandpaper.

Also, my dick won't stay down. That's been fun.

It's been less than thirty-six hours since I last saw Sally. But you'd think I'd been in the desert for forty fucking days and forty fucking nights for how deprived I feel.

For how nervous I am about the nice, normal conversation I'm about to have with nice, normal people.

Hello, parents. I adore your daughter, and I would very much like to date her. I promise I'll treat her the way she deserves. The end.

That's it. That's all I have to say to John B and Patsy.

They know me. They love me. Hopefully, that means they'll recognize that while I might have had my fun in the past, I'm serious when it comes to their daughter. They have to know I'd never intentionally mess with Sally or break her heart.

They have to know my intentions—my heart—are good. I'm opening up in a way I never have before, and that's all because of Sally. Surely, they'll see that.

Why then am I so fucking nervous?

Why can't I stop smiling like an idiot, despite those nerves?

"I want you to be my guy. Not just the guy I have a good time with. But the guy I call, and confide in, and come home to."

"I want you to stay."

Only been waiting twelve years to hear those words.

I meant what I said when I told Sally I hadn't been ready for her when we were younger. Not because I was stupid, necessarily—I did some really stupid shit, don't get me wrong—but because I wasn't ready to let someone in. I didn't know how to be vulnerable. I hadn't understood yet that trust was a two-sided coin. Yeah, you risk a lot when you trust someone not to break your heart, but you also have a lot to gain.

The poker player in me should've recognized that reward only comes with risk. Guess I needed Sally to teach me that lesson for it to really stick.

The coffeepot gurgles, letting me know it's ready. I pour myself a giant cup and load it with cream and sugar. The mug stings my fingers as I bring it to my lips, my eyes rolling to the back of my head at the first sip.

Ain't as good as Patsy's coffee, but it's still pretty damn delicious.

Sally and I agreed we'd chat with her parents first thing this morning. I wanted to see her yesterday. I wanted it so bad that I sent her a text before the sun was up, asking if I could take her out for another ride on the horses. She'd seemed to really enjoy that the day before.

Almost as much as she liked riding my mouth.

Goddamn, how much is this girl gonna like riding me? I'm fucking dying just thinking about it. I just don't want to be doing that shit behind anyone's backs.

I don't want to be anyone's dirty little secret. Not that Sally ever made me feel that way. But it'll be nice to date her out in the open.

To love her the way I've always wanted to love her.

I almost think she might love me too. She didn't just like my tattoo; she was *obsessed* with it. She appreciated the thought that had gone into it, the sentiment behind it.

She understood and definitely didn't seem turned off by it.

In fact, it seemed to turn her on in a big way.

I was all set yesterday to meet Sally at our horse barn, but then she got a call about an injured filly at a nearby ranch. She ended up spending the morning performing emergency surgery, and by the time she was done, I was tied up with a tractor that wouldn't start and then a busted irrigation pipe that had flooded a good bit of the southwest pasture.

Sally texted me *good night* at seven thirty, which I missed because I was helping Sawyer put Ella to bed. She doesn't want to stay in her room these days, so bedtime has been a struggle. When I offered to help, I swear Sawyer teared up for a second he was so grateful. And so exhausted, but I guess that's parenthood for you.

By the time I was able to respond to Sally a little after eight, she already had her notifications silenced.

I miss her.

I already have so many ideas for our first date. This Friday. My place because I want her all to myself. I also like that the commute between the dinner table and the bedroom is thirty seconds. Less if I throw Sally over my shoulder and take her there myself.

I don't cook, and I don't know wine, but luckily, I have friends who do. I've already drafted the texts I'll send Mollie and Patsy.

Speaking of Mollie, I'm gonna need to talk to Cash after my chat with the Powells this morning. Hopefully, he'll also see that I'm doing everything above board. I just need to convince him to trust me.

Sally does. And she's the smartest out of all of us.

Surely, my brother will come around. If he doesn't...well, he'll just have to get over it because I'm done wasting my time by not spending it with Sally.

I look up at the sound of the back door opening. My heart thunders when I see John B step into the kitchen.

He is alone, and he has a grave look on his face.

Shit.

"Mornin'." It takes effort to sound normal. "Coffee's ready. Can I pour you a cup?"

John B takes off his Stetson and hangs it on the rack by the door. He runs a hand through his thick gray hair. "Already had some, thanks."

"Patsy not with you?"

"She and Sally were a little ways behind me in Patsy's truck. I got an early start."

My heart is in my throat now. I take a long, slow sip of coffee and pray like hell John B isn't about to punch me in the nose. Does he already know? How did he find out? Sally tell him? Or someone else run their fucking mouth?

He puts his hands on the edge of the nearby countertop. "Sally said y'all wanted to talk to Patsy and me. Wouldn't say what it was about."

So that's why he's early. He has his suspicions about what Sally and I are going to say, and he wants to talk about it, man-to-man, before the girls get here.

Don't know if that's a good sign or a bad one.

"Sir, I want to date your daughter."

Just coming out with it is a gamble. But John B is a man of few words. He never beats around the bush. I'm hoping he'll appreciate me getting right to the heart of what I'm here to say.

There's an unpleasant tug in my chest when John B lets out a long, aggravated sigh.

"Look, Wyatt. I love you like a son. You've always been good to Sally and to Patsy and me. I know you mean well."

I bring my mug to my lips, hoping the coffee will wash away the taste of bile in my mouth. "But?"

He meets my eyes. "Every father believes his daughter is special. But Sally—she's got enormous talent and even more potential. I've been a veterinarian for over thirty years, and I've never seen someone even come close to what Sally can do. She's smart. She's intuitive. She has excellent bedside manner."

Do not think about how hot Sally is when she forgets her manners.

Do. Not—

Fuck, I'm already thinking about the way she spit on my dick and then licked it up like I was a lollipop.

"She's the best in the business," I manage, clearing my throat. "But we always knew she would be."

John B eyes me. "Exactly my point. Sally is meant for greater things than Hartsville could ever give her. I have a lot of regrets about not being able to achieve more in my career, and I'll be damned if Sally has those regrets too."

The dagger plunges deep. John B would never intentionally hurt or offend me—I know he has an appreciation for how good I am at my job, for how hard I work—but his words are like a knife nonetheless.

He said that Hartsville's not good enough for his daughter. But what I hear is that *I'm* not good enough for her. I'll only be another choice she'll regret.

Anger flares inside my gut. Doing my best to keep it in check, I sip my coffee. "I hope you know I would never limit Sally or try to tie her down. I respect the hell out of her talent. I also respect her opinion. She knows what she wants, John. We have to trust her to make the right choices for herself. You and I, we don't have any business meddling."

He stares me down. "Sally is going to New York, and she's going to take the job there. That's where her focus needs to be. You understand what I'm saying, don't you? Of course you do. You just said we can't meddle." He tilts his head. "Y'all are adults. I can't stop you from doing what y'all want to while Sally is here. But you have to promise me, Wyatt, that come the end of December, she's not going to be second-guessing our plan. She's moving to Ithaca."

And you're not going with her.

He doesn't say that last part, but he doesn't need to. I'm picking up what he's laying down. He's fine with Sally having her fun with me. But we can't get serious because apparently, he thinks Sally falling in love with me would mess with her head.

He thinks I'd hold her back.

"I'm not gonna lie to you, John." Looking down at the dregs of my coffee, I rotate my mug in my hands. "I'm offended by your insinuation that I'm somehow bad for Sally. No one wants to see that woman soar more than I do." I look him in the eye. "You have my word on that."

He looks at me for a long beat before he swipes his palm over the countertop. "I'm sorry. Wasn't my intention to offend you. But we all know you can be…a bit of a wild card."

I inwardly wince. He's not wrong.

Neither am I when I reply, "Not when it comes to Sally."

"I just need you to understand what a big deal this job is, Wyatt. I know Sally has her doubts about it. I'm not blind. Is being a surgeon at one of the world's top hospitals going to be easy? Hell no. But the sacrifices will be worth it. Getting the job, succeeding at it—that's the ultimate goal. Do. Not. Stand in her way." His face is red.

Wow, he's *pissed*.

"Have I ever stood in her way before?" I stare at him, pulse thumping in my temples. "Not once. Not a single time over the past twenty years have I *ever* prevented her from reaching her potential. I've never messed with her head before, and I'm not gonna do it now. Even if I tried, Sally wouldn't have patience for it. You and I both know she'd tell me to go to hell."

"Maybe." John B's jaw twitches. "Maybe not. But I have your word that you'll let her go when the time comes?"

Emotion clogs my windpipe, making it difficult to breathe. To think. I can't tell if I'm mostly angry or sad or what. I just know this conversation has left me ripped up and hollow inside, like a hurricane just tore through me.

I'm damn proud of myself for being honest—*mostly* honest anyway—with Sally after more than a decade of bottling up my feelings.

I'm stupid happy I get to date her and touch her and teach her. I'm beyond excited about the time we're going to spend together.

But John B's disapproval dims all that.

I didn't expect him to be thrilled about me dating Sally.

I also didn't expect him to basically tell me to lay off because, *clearly*, I'm not good enough for his daughter.

Clearly, I'm going to lead her down a path that will break her heart and wreck her spirit and spell out death for her very bright future.

Prove him wrong.

That voice inside me is a familiar one. It's the voice that's been pushing me to try new things lately. To *believe* new things about myself, the past, the world.

I could let John B's words crush me. Or I could let them motivate me to show him I'm not the wild card who will keep Sally from achieving her potential.

I'm the man who's gonna help her make her dreams come true. Every last one of them.

Setting my mug on the counter, I wipe my hands. "If that's what's right, then yes. Yes, I'll absolutely let Sally go."

John B opens his mouth, but thankfully, Patsy and Sally arrive, their cheeks flushed from the cold as they step into the warmth of the kitchen. Patsy sets down a bag of groceries at her feet.

Sally's eyes immediately find mine. There's a sharp, sudden drop in my chest when she smiles, her expression bright. "Morning, y'all."

Yep, fuck John B and his bullshit insinuations. I can be good to this girl.

I am good for this girl.

Crossing the kitchen, I nod at Sally's jacket. "Lemme get that?"

"Sure." Sally turns around and unzips it.

I smile when I see that it's a Carhartt. Sally can be fancy, but she's country too.

I fucking love it.

I feel Patsy's eyes on us as I help Sally take off the jacket. There's no awkwardness now, no hesitation. My fingers brush Sally's neck, and I see her bite her lip as she rolls back her shoulders. I pull off the Carhartt and hang it on a nearby hook.

"Such a gentleman," Patsy says.

Sally looks up at me, her eyes dancing. "When he wants to be."

"Here, Patsy, let me get yours too."

"I can do that," John B grunts.

"I know." Patsy grins. "But cowboys do it—"

"Please don't finish that thought," Sally says.

"Please do," I say with a snicker.

I hang up Patsy's jacket and pick up the groceries.

That's when she claps her hands, turns to Sally and me, and says, "So how long have y'all been more than friends?"

Sally's eyes go wide. I nearly drop the groceries.

"Seriously, Mom, you can't—God, you can't just blurt things like that." Sally cuts me a glance. "We're, um... we've—"

"Been official for all of three minutes now." I drape my free arm across Sally's shoulders and step forward, pressing my body against hers. "John B and I were just talkin' about it. Sally and I wanted to make sure we were all on the same page before we shared the news with anybody else."

"I knew it!" Patsy throws her arms in the air. "I knew it, I knew it, I *knew* it! Y'all have been acting mighty strange lately. And I coulda sworn I saw a hickey on Sally's neck the other—"

"It wasn't a hickey," Sally replies.

John B sighs. "I beg you, don't elaborate."

"Beard burn?" Patsy asks.

Sally's face is red as a beet, but she's smiling. "Yes."

"Oh, y'all, I'm so happy for you!" Patsy goes up on her toes and pulls us in for an awkward group hug. "I've only been waiting for this to happen for twenty years."

Sally scrunches her brow. "Twenty years?"

"Your second-grade teacher couldn't get over how insepa-rable the two of you were." Patsy falls back on her heels. "Apparently, Wyatt was always talking about you bein' his girlfriend back then."

"You didn't!" Sally gasps.

I chuckle. "I did. I hoped the rumor would get back around to you and you'd say yes, but I guess that never happened."

"Timing is everything," Patsy singsongs. "The universe

wanted you to get together now, and here we are! So when can we go on a double date?"

"Never," Sally teases.

I gently elbow her. "Aw, c'mon, Sunshine. That would be fun."

I glance at John B, who's watching us with a strange look on his face. He's glowering, but there's also this softness in his eyes when he looks at Sally.

Maybe because she's *glowing*. Eyes bright. Cheeks pink. Shiny, clear skin.

She's a bundle of happy, smiling energy, despite the fact that it's four fucking a.m.

She looks *good* in a pair of broken-in Levi's and one of the Lucky River Ranch sweatshirts Mollie and Wheeler designed.

"Ranches need swag," Mollie had explained.

Wheeler had nodded. "Cute swag. The best swag." Then she'd asked Duke to be the model for the men's stuff they designed.

They should've asked Sally to model for them, too, because she fucking rocks this shit. Paired with a ponytail and a pair of Ariats, the shirt and the jeans scream cowgirl.

Because Sally *is* a cowgirl. It's less an occupation and more of a state of mind.

"You all right over there, Dad?" Sally asks, curling an arm around my waist before she rests her head on my chest.

My pulse skips several beats.

"I'm all right," he says. "Y'all be smart, okay?"

Patsy cuts him a look before turning back to us. "Y'all be whatever you want. Obviously, safe sex is good sex—"

"I think it's time to make breakfast." Sally glances up at me. "Don't you, Wyatt?"

"I do, Sally. I could eat a horse."

Sally's eyes ignite. Her mouth curls into a secret smile. I know the reply is on the tip of her tongue—*Eat me instead.*

I know that because I know her.

I know she's quick and witty and she has a salty sense of humor.

Now I also know that she really likes it when I eat her pussy.

Yep. Next time she's thinking about that, we're gonna be in my kitchen, at my house. Instead of unpacking the groceries and helping her mama make bowls of cheesy grits, topped with fried eggs and brisket, I'm gonna sit Sally on the counter, I'm gonna get on my knees, and I'm gonna give her what she's asking for.

I'm gonna make her come, my name on her lips.

CHAPTER 20

Sally

A CROWDED TABLE

"AW, hell yeah. My brother finally grew a pair and asked you out." Sawyer holds out his arms, a gigantic smile on his face as he walks into the kitchen for lunch later that day. "Welcome to the family, Sal."

Wyatt finishes the last bite of his collards and shakes his head. "One, only I call her that. And two, she's always been part of our family."

"You can call me whatever you want, Sawyer." I rise from my spot at the table beside Wyatt and wrap his brother in a hug. "And thank you. We're thrilled. How'd you find out—"

"Oh, your mama's just a wee bit excited." Sawyer nods at Mom. "She might have shared the news earlier without necessarily meaning to."

She just shrugs from her perch by the stove. "How could I *not* be excited? Two of my favorite people are finding happiness together. It's a dream, isn't it?"

"Mom—"

"It is a dream, yeah." Wyatt looks at me and smiles.

I can't believe he's not more freaked out by Mom's big mouth and Sawyer's insinuation that I'd actually, legally become part of the Rivers family. That's a big step. A huge one.

But I really can believe it. I keep coming back to the idea that, yes, Wyatt really isn't scared of commitment. He wants to fall in love.

He wants what his parents had. The loving relationship. The trust. The respect.

And, yeah, one day, the ranch and the house and the kids. He's never said it out loud. But I know he'd thrive in that kind of life if he ever let himself have it.

As an only child, I loved going over to the Rivers' house. Sure, it was often chaotic and always loud. But it was always fun too. They all seemed so connected to each other. All seven of them sat down for dinner every night and for breakfast every morning, and they had all these cool traditions they shared. Mrs. Rivers would let the boys help her make home-made cinnamon rolls every Saturday. Mr. Rivers would take us on "adventures" in his ATV in the afternoons when it was too hot to be on horseback.

They'd have huge Christmas dinners and epic Easter brunches. Pumpkin-carving parties, cookie-decorating parties. Dance parties in their living room when it rained.

I loved being a part of it. It made my home life seem quiet and tame in comparison. I also think it made me want a bunch of kids of my own.

But then I grew up, and I became aware of the reality of raising a large family. It would be expensive. And stressful. I'd have to sacrifice my freedom. Forget travel. And I don't know how I'd manage a family like that while working the super-intense jobs I've always been after.

Even so, when I'm sitting down to a meal surrounded by the Rivers family, like I am now, I feel a tug. A longing for a table like this, filled with family like this. Only it's my *own* family I'm eating with. I'm in my own house, where my husband and I enjoy our own traditions.

Glancing at Wyatt, I can't help but think of all the fun traditions we already have. Our rides. Our drives. Our Jack Daniel's by the river. And the coffee we had on Wyatt's front porch—that could become a tradition too.

I've never wanted to get a tattoo before, but now I'm thinking about it.

I've been thinking about it a lot.

I'm filled with this bright, joyful sense of gratitude when I think about all the things we could add to our list of traditions. The wholesome things, and the not-so-wholesome things too.

So much ground to cover.

"My only question is, what took y'all so long?" Ryder is returning to the table after grabbing a second pulled pork sandwich from the platter on the island.

Wyatt reaches for my thigh underneath the table. My heart skips a beat when he squeezes, a flare of heat igniting between my legs. "Good question."

I wonder when my face is going to stop hurting from all this damn smiling.

"So? Tell us." Duke takes a huge bite of his sandwich.

Wyatt and I were at breakfast so early that we left the house before anyone else was up. He and I got some steers caught up on their vaccinations, and then we tacked up our horses to go check out a pasture that had flooded yesterday.

It was just him and me all morning, and it was heaven.

By the time Mom radioed in that lunch was ready, we'd been out riding for hours and not seen a soul.

But word travels fast in a small town. I want to be annoyed that Mom told everyone about Wyatt and me. Honestly, though, I'm kinda glad she did. It's nice knowing at least one of my parents is excited for us.

Dad disappeared after breakfast, and I haven't seen him since. I understand why he's not crazy about Wyatt and me dating, but really, he doesn't have to be such a curmudgeon about it. I know he's worried Wyatt's going to keep me in Hartsville. But that's not Dad's choice to make.

This is my life. And I'm learning that the more I take the wheel—the more I block out the noise of everyone else's opinions and do what feels right for me—the more I feel at peace.

Does Dad's disapproval rattle me? Of course it does. Do I still have conflicting feelings about my future? Yes. But behind all that—or maybe beneath it—is this warm, solid sense of *oh, thank God.*

Thank God I took a chance and let Wyatt in.

Thank God I did that, despite what everyone else thinks.

Thank God I chose myself—and keep choosing myself.

"Most of the story"—Wyatt looks at me, his hand still on my leg—"ain't appropriate for polite company."

Sawyer grins. "Good thing we're not polite."

"I think we just realized we were done wasting time." I can't look away from Wyatt. "We're not getting any younger. And, yeah, I decided I need to have more fun, and I never have more fun than I do with your brother."

Duke raises his eyebrows. "So that's what y'all call it. Fun."

"Say another word, and I'll pop you in the mouth," Wyatt replies, his eyes still glued to mine. "Sorry they're heathens."

"I'm not sorry," Ryder replies.

"Uncle Wy! Hello! Look, look, Ella made bunny ears!"

We all look up at the happy little shout that sounds by the door. Ella bursts into the kitchen. She's wearing a paper circlet on her head that's topped with tall pink-and-white bunny ears.

Wyatt immediately lifts her onto his lap, laughing. "Aren't we closer to Christmas than Easter?"

"Her class is reading a book about a bunny that likes to listen and follow directions," Sawyer explains. "Because we like to listen and follow directions, too, right, Ella?"

She just smiles, curling up in Wyatt's lap. He plucks the ears off her head and puts them on his own head.

"How do I look?" he asks her.

"Cute," I say, suddenly short of breath.

"A cute doggone idiot," a voice says.

Glancing over my shoulder, I see Cash step into the kitchen behind Mollie. I've been around the ranch long enough to know that they must've just come from picking up Ella from school. It's their way of giving Sawyer a little break during the week. Mollie fell head over heels in love with Ella, so she asked Sawyer if she could get more involved by doing school pickup once or twice a week.

My stomach dips. On our ride this morning, Wyatt told me about Cash confronting him many times about the way Wyatt looked at me in the past. I guess Cash is worried that if things end badly between Wyatt and me, my parents will want nothing to do with Lucky River Ranch.

Again, I understand why Cash is concerned. But I wish people would trust us. Our decision to be together might seem impulsive, but in many ways, this relationship has been years in the making. We waited until the timing was right to make our move. We're not stupid kids anymore; I'd like to think we know what we're doing.

Then again, is the timing right, or is it worse than ever? We each have so much at stake now. My career. Wyatt's family and his plans for the ranch.

Cash's gaze immediately darts to Wyatt and me. He frowns when he looks down and sees our legs touching on the picnic bench beneath the table.

We don't need to sit this close. We never have before.

It's a subtle clue, but it's a clue nonetheless.

"What's goin' on here?" Cash's voice is little more than a growl.

Wyatt cuts me a glance before handing Ella to Sawyer. "You got a second, Cash?"

I meet eyes with Mollie. I feel a rush of relief when she offers me a small, knowing smile. I haven't told her yet about the recent developments between Wyatt and me, but I was planning to after we chatted with my parents.

Maybe things will actually work out. Of course this news is going to rock the ranch's boat. We're our own little close-knit community here, and change is always difficult, even when it's *good* change.

"Outside." Cash tilts his head back toward the door. "Y'all finish your lunch."

"I don't need to get out my spoon, do I?" Mom warns. "Y'all are gonna behave. You know my rule about fights."

"They'll behave," Mollie says easily, patting Cash's chest. "I have a feeling it's happy news."

Wyatt rises, his brow furrowing when I rise too.

"It's our news," I say. "We share it together."

Cash groans. "I love you, Sally, but—"

"Whatever you say to him, you can say to me too."

Wyatt's expression softens with gratitude. He grabs my hand. *Thank you.*

I smile. *You're welcome.*

Wyatt helps me into my jacket. I wait for him to take off the bunny ears and put on his hat, but he doesn't.

"Even Cash can't be mean to a bunny," he explains with a smile.

We follow Cash out into the autumn sunshine. It's a bright, beautiful day, the air crisp, not a cloud in the sky.

It's a startling contrast to Cash's stormy expression.

"How long?" he asks.

Wyatt grabs my hand. "How long have we been dating or—"

"How long have y'all been sneaking around behind our backs?"

I give him a look. "That's unfair, Cash. We only started

telling people today. And we're telling y'all *because* we don't want to go behind anyone's back."

"If you say so." Glaring at me, Cash runs his tongue along the inside of his cheek before he turns to his brother. "And this is different from all your other flings because..."

Talk about awkward. Cash is putting Wyatt on the spot by making him confess his feelings for me all over again.

"Sally is my best friend. I know my history is working against me here, but people can change. Just look at you and Mollie. Y'all were hell-bent on hating each other in the beginning, but then you talked about your misunderstandings and realized y'all were more alike than different. Isn't that how it went?"

I nod. "Y'all are so cute together."

"Thanks," Cash replies gruffly.

"If you can change, then I can too," Wyatt continues. "I know you think I'm full of shit, but you have to give me a chance to prove you wrong."

Cash takes a deep, aggravated inhale. "It's my job to look after the ranch and everyone who works here. Y'all screw this up, y'all could screw us too."

"You don't know that." My chest tightens. "You said you loved us. Show it. Give us the benefit of the doubt."

A pained expression crosses Cash's face. "I want to, Sally. But I also don't want anybody gettin' hurt. You understand how this puts me in a bind, don't you?"

"It only puts you in a bind if you're assuming the worst will happen," I counter.

"Again, that's kind of my job, Sally. Hope for the best, anticipate the worst. And the worst that could happen is pretty damn bad. Y'all break up, Wyatt's devastated, you're heartbroken, and your parents decide it's time to retire because they fuckin' hate our guts for destroyin' their daughter. Aren't you supposed to be moving to New York in, like, a week or something?"

"End of December," I say.

"What's the plan then?"

Wyatt clears his throat. "We're getting there."

"And your daddy?" Cash says to me. "What does he think about all this?"

It's all I can do not to roll my eyes. "He'll come around."

Cash gives us a pointed look, as if to say, *See? Y'all haven't grown up.*

Wyatt is silent. Cash puts his hands on his hips and looks out across the yard.

Time to bring out the big guns.

"You and Mollie happened fast," I begin.

Cash kicks at the dirt. "Well, yeah. We had to work together a lot—"

"And y'all are total opposites."

"Where are you going with this, Sally?"

"You two fooling around could've definitely ended in catastrophe. What if things had ended badly and she fired you as foreman? What if she'd fired all of us because we were friends with you?"

A muscle in Cash's sharply cut jaw tics. He looks so much like Wyatt in that moment that it makes my heart hiccup. The genes these cowboys share are insane. Will their sons inherit that handsomeness too?

"Admit it, Cash. You risked more than just your heart when you hooked up with Mollie. But it paid off, didn't it? No one would've believed you if you'd said the two of you were going to work out, but y'all did. You knew she was different, and you knew you could be different too. You guys coming together ended up being even better for the ranch and for us than anyone could've ever imagined. Extend us the same grace. Please, Cash."

Cash's shoulders rise and fall as he heaves out a breath. He looks at Wyatt. Looks at me.

"You and Mollie," he says to me at last, shaking his head, "are so fuckin' smart, it's annoying sometimes."

Glancing at Wyatt, I can't help but smile when I take in the bunny ears on his head. He smiles back, and I feel a heady dose of that relief again.

Wyatt squeezes my hand. "You don't need to give us your blessing. But you do need to give us a chance."

More silence. A hawk glides low over the house, its shadow cutting across the yard. The warmth of the sun seeps through my jacket. My heart flutters inside my chest, light as air. I'm so happy, I could burst. This is happening. Wyatt and I are *dating*. Which I guess means he's my boyfriend now, doesn't it?

Not only is Wyatt my boyfriend. Everyone *knows* he's my boyfriend. And so far, no one's threatened to murder us yet.

So far, it looks like Cash is actually going to give us a shot to prove him wrong.

I get this floaty feeling inside my chest, like the hawk is soaring through my torso instead of the November sky. I get Wyatt, and I get to enjoy him out in the open.

I feel like I'm getting away with something. This is too easy. Too much of a delight. Didn't Shakespeare have a lot to say about delights having violent ends?

There is still so much we need to figure out. But it can't be figured out today, or tomorrow, or even the next day. We have to just...be, I guess, and see what happens.

It's like jumping off a cliff without a safety net. Totally terrifying.

It's also the biggest thrill I think I've had outside an operating room.

Cash shoves his hands inside his pockets. "Please don't make me regret trusting y'all."

————

Later that afternoon, I help Mom do prep work for tomorrow's breakfast. We decide to make Mrs. Rivers's cinnamon rolls—Cash kept the recipe and gave it to Mom—so we throw together some dough that will sit overnight, and chop the peppers and onions that will go in the frittatas that will accompany the rolls.

Mom stretches a sheet of plastic wrap over the dough bowl. "I'm proud of you, you know, for being honest with Wyatt about your feelings. I imagine it wasn't easy telling your best friend you had the hots for him."

Grinning, I scoop the peppers into a Pyrex container. "Thanks. I'm proud of me too."

"You know your father and I are always proud of you. We're proud of your accomplishments, obviously. But more than that, I'm proud of who you've become. You're a woman with backbone and character and courage. I think it's spectacular you're taking risks."

I blame the onions I just chopped for the sudden burn in my eyes. "I appreciate you saying that. I know Dad isn't thrilled about this whole thing."

"But it's not about Dad, is it? This is about you and what you want to do with your life. It's okay to disappoint him so long as you're not letting yourself down."

Swallowing, I nod. "Easier said than done."

"Of course. I remember being terrified to tell my daddy I was dating John. Those two did *not* get along at first."

I blink. "Really? How did I not know that?"

Mom grins as she opens the fridge and puts the bowl inside. "Because that's not part of the story your dad likes to tell. Eventually, your grandfather came around to the idea of us being together. But my daddy, he was hell-bent on me getting my education, moving to the big, fancy city. Which, to him, was Amarillo, but that's neither here nor there. Point being, he didn't want me throwing away my dreams to become some small-town boy's wife."

"Sounds familiar."

"Thing is, marrying your dad was one of my dreams. That's what your grandfather didn't understand—that being with John didn't mean giving up on my degree or my dreams for my career."

I press the plastic cover onto the Pyrex container. "How did you get him to understand that?"

"I showed him. I started my catering business right out of college. I was taking freelance recipe development gigs left and right. I built a great little portfolio for myself. And I did it all while married to your dad. Yeah, it was a far cry from Amarillo. But I was happy. I loved my life—still do—and I think that's because I let go of my dad's expectations for me and did what I wanted to do."

Crossing the kitchen, I wrap Mom in a hug. "I love you."

"I love you too."

"You say I have courage, but I'm not gonna lie to you, Mom. I'm terrified of what Dad would say…" I shake my head. "Never mind."

"Tell me."

I glance over my shoulder, making sure the kitchen is still empty. "I'm not feeling great about going back to New York, which I don't entirely understand. That job represents everything I've worked toward. It's everything I ever wanted. But now…I don't know. I'm starting to wonder if it's everything *Dad* wanted, and I just kind of adopted that dream as my own. I know how much he regrets not going further in his career, but…I just love it so much here, Mom. I can't imagine leaving Hartsville, and I'm not just saying that because I'm dating Wyatt. Even if he weren't in the picture, I'm pretty sure I'd feel the same way."

Mom holds me tighter. "I knew something was up. You haven't talked about the job much."

"That's because talking about it makes my chest hurt."

"Oh, honey. I'm sorry. Your dad means well, but I understand what you're saying. Maybe your dreams are different from Dad's, and maybe they're coming true a little closer to home than you thought. That's okay."

"But turning down the job at Ithaca University makes no sense."

"It only has to make sense to you."

Sniffling, I close my eyes. "Thank you for saying that."

"Be patient." Mom rubs my shoulder. "And get creative. Hartsville might be a small town, but there's a lot of knowledge here. A lot of cool things happening. You never know when you might come across an opportunity."

I nod. "I'll keep my eyes peeled."

"Good. I'm gonna hit the bathroom. Then you want to head home? Or are you and Wyatt—"

"Mom."

She holds up her hands. "Okay, okay. I won't ask. One final piece of wisdom: people will make you happier than a job ever will."

Mom heads down the hallway. I head for the sink. I'm turning on the faucet and opening the dishwasher when I hear the door open.

Wyatt steps inside the kitchen.

Stomach dropping, I take in the way his hair curls out from underneath his hat. The sleeves of his jacket and shirt are pushed up, revealing his thick, tattooed forearms. They're bronze from the sun and covered in a furry sheen of hair.

I drop the plate I'm rinsing. It lands with a clatter in the sink.

Wyatt looks up with a smirk. "Just who I was hoping to see. Sawyer said you were up here, helpin' your mama." He glances across the kitchen.

"She's in the bathroom."

"Good." He strides over to the sink and melts his front to my back, placing his hands on either side of mine on the lip of the sink. "You know I wanna take you home tonight, right?" he murmurs against my neck.

A wave of longing crashes through me at the feel of his body surrounding mine. Thick veins crisscross the back of his hands. His chest feels impossibly huge, impossibly solid as he breathes into me.

"You know I wanna come home with you, right?" I turn off the water, mentally cataloguing everything I'm going to throw in my overnight bag. Toothbrush, deodorant, the least ratty pajamas I own. I'm definitely leaving my retainers at home. Should I bring a razor in the off chance I stay more than one night?

Wyatt gives my neck a quick, tiny bite. "I need you to know it's killin' me not to invite you over. But you come with me, I'm not gonna be able to keep my hands off you. And I want to be intentional. Dinner first. Then—"

"Fucking." I get what he's saying, but my heart still falls a little.

"You got a mouth on you, Sunshine."

"You got some nerve, handsome, making me wait. When do you propose we go on this date?"

"Friday. I know Frisky Whiskey is taking a break on account of your drummer having pneumonia. My place. I'll make dinner."

Laughing, I turn around in the circle of his arms and put my hands on his chest. "But you don't cook."

"Lotsa firsts happening these days." Wyatt doesn't budge, keeping me trapped against the sink so that our faces are inches apart.

Less when he leans his weight into his hands, flattening his hips against mine.

"What can I bring?"

The need between my legs coils tighter as he hovers over me, a massive, smirking slab of cowboy. "Just the shit you'll need for a sleepover. Forget the jammies though. We don't wear those at my house."

"Okay."

"Okay?" His eyes get this hazy look in them before he leans in and kisses me. "Aw, Sunshine, you got me feelin' a whole lot better than okay."

"And you have me feeling like I have the world's worst case of sexual frustration. You keep doing this to me."

His turn to laugh. "Patience pays off."

"You'd better put your money where your mouth is, cowboy."

"Lucky for you, I'm real good with my money and my mouth." He kisses me again. "Friday. Five o'clock. I'll come pick you up."

CHAPTER 21

Wyatt

ALWAYS BE MY FIRST

I WONDER what Mom would think if she could see me now.

I'm wearing bright yellow rubber gloves. I'm on my hands and knees, a toothbrush in one hand and a spray bottle of Clorox in the other as I go to town, scrubbing the grout on the bathroom's tile floor.

I know she'd smile. She'd definitely approve of all the effort I've put in this week, preparing for my date with Sally.

Mama, you raised me right. Mostly, anyway.

Go figure, a toothbrush really does the job. It's a trick Mom taught us when we were doing our chores. Cash and I always got assigned bathroom duty, so I have plenty of practice.

Falling back on my haunches, I survey my work. I'm sweating and I smell like bleach, but dang if the bathroom don't sparkle and shine. The vanity is spotless, and so is the old claw-foot bathtub that does double duty as a shower. I even cleaned the windows and the walls and organized the vanity drawers to boot.

My heart twists. I really wish Mom were here so I could run my plans by her for the date. She'd have so many ideas.

Mom would love the fact that Sally and I are dating. She always adored Sally. But what would Mom have to say about my fears of letting my guard down?

Take your head out of your ass and realize not every relationship ends in tragedy.

I want to believe that. I'm trying to believe it.

"Ho-ly *shit.*"

I nearly jump at the sound of the voice by the door. Yanking my earbud out of my ear, I look up and see Mollie standing in the doorway. She's staring at the shiny tile floor, her mouth a perfect O.

"Ever heard of knocking?" I ask.

"I knocked for ten minutes, Wyatt. But obviously you were too engrossed in scrubbing the *floor* with a freaking *toothbrush* to hear me." She blinks. "Have the bleach fumes gotten to you? Do you have a fever? I fear you are unwell."

"You're funny."

"I know." She grins. "House looks great. I can tell you've been working hard. That's super cute, you wanting the place to be perfect for sweet Sally."

I swipe the back of my wrist across my forehead. Any spare moment I've had this week, I've been prepping for Friday's date night. Now that it's Thursday evening, I'm in total panic mode. "You think it's all right? I feel like I might buy one of those hand-held steamer things for the couch. Just in case—"

"You want to bone Sally there? So you need it to be fresh and clean so y'all can get it dirty again, only in a different way?"

I let out a bark of laughter. "Well, yeah."

She leans a shoulder against the doorframe. "I can't tell you how thrilled I am that the two of you are finally together."

"I appreciate that." I push up to my feet and bend backward, stretching my back. "Could you rub off a little on my brother? He still isn't acting right."

Mollie rolls her eyes. "I think Cash is being really annoying about this whole thing. I'm sorry. Trust me, I've talked to him a lot about it. He's coming around. I think he's being an overprotective monster because all these things he's dreamed about for years are finally happening and he's scared to lose it all again."

Swallowing, I nod. "I get that. Just wish he weren't such a dick about it."

"Being a dick is kind of his style," she replies with a smile.

I smile too. "And you like that because you're always up for a challenge."

"Well, yeah."

"Can I ask you a weird question?"

"I love weird questions."

"What made you decide to be with Cash? Like, what made you want to stick around? Not stick around Hartsville necessarily. But stay with Cash and figure out how to make it work even though y'all have wildly different lives."

"Well, for starters, he's great in bed."

I laugh, the heavy feeling in my chest lifting. "The bleach already has me woozy. Don't make me barf all over you."

Her smile softens. "Honestly? I fell in love with Cash because I could be myself around him in a way I couldn't with anyone else. He was patient with me, believe it or not, and he made me feel safe enough to explore parts of myself and my past I'd kept locked up. And because I opened up, he did too. The rest is…yeah, history."

"How did you do it? Open up?"

Mollie swallows. "I guess being around Cash—he brought everything to the surface. I couldn't keep it in anymore. I knew if I wanted to be with him that I had to show him my hand. I think he liked that about me, how I went all in."

Makes sense. "Appreciate the poker references."

"Thought you might."

I ponder her words for a long beat, circling my fear that I'm ultimately not good enough for Sally. Not smart enough or courageous enough. "What do you think Sally likes about me?"

Mollie's smile softens. She straightens, crossing her arms. "I think she adores everything about you, Wyatt. But most of all? I think Sally is a lot like me—we put so much pressure on ourselves to achieve, achieve, achieve. To get things done and get them done right, you know? But you're like a release valve for her. You care about how she feels and pay attention to what she needs." Mollie sighs. "My goodness, no wonder she's obsessed with you."

"She's not obsessed."

"Oh, Wyatt, but she is. I knew it the first time I met y'all that you were destined to be more than friends. The way you looked at her—the way she looks at you…" Mollie shakes her head. "It's really romantic when you think about it, the two of you being friends forever before you finally took the leap. Most guys wouldn't be nearly as careful."

I have a lump in my throat and I don't know why.

"Thanks," I grunt.

"Do you know what y'all are thinking?" Mollie asks. "About what you'll do after the holidays?"

I shake my head. "We don't. Probably stupid of us to start dating now, but better late than never, right?"

"Not stupid at all. I think there's a reason you guys didn't get horizontal until now."

We've actually only done things vertically, but God willing and the creek don't rise, that's about to change.

I've been on the verge of sexual insanity all week. Used my right hand plenty, but that's only intensified my hunger for Sally. I wanna go slow tomorrow, but I'm not sure how much I'll be able to hold back.

"And that reason is?" I ask Mollie.

"It's gonna force each of you to make a decision about your priorities. And maybe that's a choice you need to make before you can live the life you want. The universe is telling you something here, Wyatt. Listen."

Shit, am I really gonna cry?

"That's…a nice thought. Thanks, Mollie."

Mollie tilts her head toward the kitchen. "C'mon. I brought over a bunch of really expensive wine and my mother's china. You break it, I kill you. Or, really, she will. Got it?"

We both look up at the sound of the front door opening.

"Helloooo!" Patsy calls. "Mollie, I saw your ATV out front. I've got our supplies!"

Mollie squeals. "Wyatt, I freaking love that you enlisted Patsy to help. It's seriously so sweet of you."

I'm blushing. "Thanks."

"I can't wait for Sally to, like, burst into tears when she sees everything you put together for her. She's gonna die!"

"I hope she doesn't die."

"You know the French call orgasms *little deaths*, right?" Mollie loops her arm through mine.

I laugh. "I love you."

"I love you more. Now let's get you your girl."

———

The next evening, I hold the wheel in a death grip all the way to Sally's house.

I'm nervous. But it's more about me not reaching for the Marlboros I have in my glove compartment than anything else.

I've never needed stress relief more than I do now, though. I would kill for a cigarette. I haven't lit up since before I kissed Sally the night of the potluck, but if Sally hates smoking, then I'm done doing it.

Checking my reflection in the rearview mirror one last time, I head to the door even though it's only four fifty. I delegated most of my tasks at the ranch this afternoon to my brothers so I'd have plenty of time to shower and get ready. Guess I took a little *too* much time off.

I'm not sorry. Yeah, Duke bothered me a couple of times with phone calls about our pain-in-the-ass farrier. But other than that, things seemed to go just fine.

John B answers the door, because of course he does.

"Evenin', John." I hold out my hand. "How's it going?"

He warily takes my hand and shakes it. I wonder if there's anything more awkward than shaking hands with the man whose daughter is coming to your house for a sleepover.

He knows what Sally and I are about to do. I know. And, Lord, if it don't make me feel hot under the collar.

"It's going all right. Sally's just getting ready." He steps aside. "Come in."

The house is warm. Cozy. Smells good—there's something in the oven.

"Patsy told me you're gonna cook," John says after an awkward stretch of silence.

I dip my head. "Yes, sir, I'm going to attempt it. Not much in the way of restaurants around here, but I still wanted the meal to feel special. Pray for me, would you, that I don't screw it up too badly or burn down my house?"

That gets a chuckle from him. "I think you'll do just fine."

We both look up at the creak of floorboards by the top of the stairs. The breath leaves my lungs when I see Sally standing there. She looks fucking *gorgeous* in jeans and those red cowboy boots she wore that night at The Rattler.

Her lips are pink and full. They glisten. Some kind of lipstick or gloss?

Her dark hair is loose around her shoulders, and her eyes have this subtle sparkle around them that makes me think she's wearing eyeshadow.

I don't ever notice the makeup girls are wearing. But I notice everything about Sally. The flush in her cheeks and the self-conscious way she tucks her hair behind her ear, revealing the multiple piercings that dot her lobe.

Placing her hand on the banister, she smiles, her dimple popping. "Hey, Wyatt."

"He—hey, Sally." Didn't realize my mouth was dry. I try clearing my throat. "You look beautiful."

"I showered for you." She makes her way down the stairs. "You're welcome."

I manage to smile. "How lucky am I?"

I get an intense, not-altogether-unpleasant sense of whiplash. This almost feels like prom night—the pretty girl coming down her parents' stairs to join her nervous wreck of a date. All I'm missing is a flask of liquor pilfered from my parents' cabinet, and a corsage for her that color-coordinates with my boutonniere.

Sally and I didn't go to prom together. I went with random people, girls who had asked me and whose names I can't remember for the life of me. Sally ended up going stag with her girlfriends.

At the time, I didn't think much of it. But now I'm glad I didn't know I was in love with Sally back in high school. Being fully grown adults who appreciate how special our connection is—how rare—is better. Mostly because we don't have to lie to our parents about where we're sleeping tonight and who we're sleeping with.

Also, I know what I'm doing now. I was having sex back then, but I can't imagine I was very good at it.

Now though? I'm real good at it, and I get to be good to Sally.

"Pretty damn lucky," John B says.

Sally bites her lip when she descends the last step and looks up at me. "You're early."

"Course I'm early." I slide a look at John. "I couldn't wait to see you."

I haven't seen Sally since Wednesday, when she stopped by the ranch with John B to examine an injured longhorn. Our conversation was brief, but I did get to give her a quick kiss before she left.

We've talked on the phone. Texted some too. But nothing compares to being in the same room with her.

The smell of jasmine fills my head as Sally goes up on her toes and wraps me in a hug. "Hi," she murmurs.

Careful not to pull her too close, I circle her with my arms. "Hi."

She falls back, hands resting on my biceps. She's still smiling. "My bag's right there. Dad, I'll…see you later?"

I grope blindly for air. Has Sally ever been this lit up? This *happy?*

John B must notice it, too, because he looks at her for a long beat before he takes a sharp inhale. "Sounds good. Y'all have fun."

He cuts me one last look, as if to say, *Remember your promise.*

Then he disappears into the house, and Sally is reaching for the little black bag by the door.

"I got it," I say, leaning down to grab it before she does.

Sally is still fucking smiling when we're in my truck and on the way back to my place. "That wasn't awkward at all." Her voice drips with sarcasm.

"Not one bit. I don't know what the rules are for picking up your date when she lives with her parents," I tease.

She carefully pulls her hair out of the collar of her coat. "I think the only rule is, you get her the hell out of there as fast as you can."

"Mission accomplished?"

She's biting her lip again. "Mission accomplished."

"So…I did a thing." I switch hands on the wheel so I can put my right one on Sally's thigh. "Many things, in fact."

"Can I be that thing?"

"Of course you're going to be that thing. But I did other things for us to enjoy before that."

"Like?"

I smirk. "You'll see."

CHAPTER 22

Sally

WILD CARD

WYATT OPENS the front door of his house and holds out his arm. "After you."

I step inside and am immediately inundated by a magazine-worthy spread of cozy deliciousness. Or would it be delicious coziness?

Either way, I never, ever want to leave.

The house is small but beautifully proportioned—think thirteen-foot ceilings, hand-carved millwork, and big windows that let in tons of light.

But it's the tiny, beautifully decorated table in the kitchen to my right that has my heart doing a hundred backflips. The table is covered in a checkered tablecloth, and it's set with real china and a pair of candles. There's a charcuterie board on the countertop, alongside a big salad bowl that's filled with crisp-looking greens topped with what appear to be chunks of roasted butternut squash.

The oven hums. The savory smell of roasting meat fills the air. There's something oddly familiar about it.

Coldplay is on. A bottle of wine and two fancy-looking wineglasses are set out beside the sink.

Despite the massive amount of preparation that obviously

happened in the kitchen, the space is spotless. So is the living room that the kitchen opens up to. It's dominated by a huge fireplace, which is filled with wood.

I cover my mouth with my hand. I literally don't know what to say. What to do.

This is all so perfect, so romantic, I want to cry. I've been here a handful of times since Wyatt moved in, but he's never had it set up like *this*.

"Wy," I say weakly.

Setting my bag on a nearby console table, Wyatt slips his fingers inside my coat. "You like it?"

"How did you—where did you—the time—and the salad —the wine—do you even like wine—"

"I do actually." He presses a scruffy kiss to my nape as he pulls off my coat. "I've been thinkin' about this night all week. And thinkin' about this night had me thinkin' of you, which of course got me all hard and shit. My dick literally wouldn't let me sleep. So figured I'd make good use of the time."

I get this feeling in my chest. I can only describe it as a best-day-of-your-life feeling—so full of joy, of tenderness, that I'm about to burst.

Have I ever felt more special in my life?

Have I ever felt more seen?

This isn't some half-assed date, thrown together at the last minute. This took thought. Planning. A serious amount of effort.

The kind of effort you make for the people you love. Not *like*. Not people you have casual, kinda-sorta dig-you feelings for.

I feel weak in my knees.

How is this happening so fast? But really, it's not happening fast at all because it's taken us twenty-plus years to get to this point.

Maybe that's why I also don't feel nervous. I'm thrumming with anticipation, sure. But I don't feel the least bit self-conscious.

I feel pretty damn comfortable, like I always do when I'm with my best friend.

"Lemme pour you some wine," Wyatt says as he hangs my coat in a narrow closet beside the door. "Then I'll light a fire. Dinner should be ready in an hour or so."

I head for the kitchen, my legs feeling like rubber. "I can open the wine."

"You can, but you won't. Not when I'm around."

I still reach for the corkscrew, but Wyatt grabs it out of my hand. The muscles in his forearm flex as he pulls the cork out of the bottle in a smooth, well-practiced movement.

"Mollie came over yesterday," Wyatt explains as he fills the glasses with a good pour of wine the color of black cherries. "She showed me how to properly open a bottle, and then we drank it while she helped me set the table."

Just keep breathing. "You had Mollie over?"

"I did. Had to call in the experts."

"She's the fucking best."

"Cash lucked out." Wyatt holds out a glass and meets my gaze. "So did I. Cheers, Sunshine."

I take the glass, our fingers brushing. "Cheers, handsome."

His eyes stay locked on mine as I sip and he sips. I don't know wine super well, but my roommates and I drank our fair share of it back in veterinary school. The stuff we bought from Trader Joe's wasn't awful, but it wasn't great either.

This wine though? This is *excellent*. Bright, vibrant flavor explodes on my tongue. I can only describe it as fruity yumminess, the kind that makes you want to lick your glass.

"Damn."

Wyatt smirks. "Am I off to a good start?"

"You already know you're getting laid, right? You didn't need to pull out *all* the stops."

"But I wanted to."

The gray-blue light from the window catches on his irises, making them appear translucent, the color of the Texas sky at dawn.

Sliding a hand onto his neck, I lean in and close my eyes and kiss my man.

Wyatt Rivers is my man. For now.

I lick into his mouth and taste the wine. His tongue dances with mine, and we fall into a slow, easy, deep kiss that has my pulse thundering and my heart twisting.

Now was never going to be long enough with Wyatt, was it?

I want him forever.

I want to be kissed like this *forever*.

Wyatt growls, shifting so that his hips are angled toward me, pressing his body against mine. He cups my cheek in his hand and drinks me in. Awareness blooms between my legs, need gathering in my thighs, my abdomen, the back of my knees.

"You're"—Wyatt feathers his lips over mine before breaking the kiss—"making it awful hard to do things in the proper order, Dr. Powell."

I nudge his nose with mine because I do that now. I do what I feel like doing without worrying if it's too much or not enough.

"Ever had sex before dinner on a first date, Mr. Rivers?"

"I'm not starting tonight. On the sofa, Sunshine. Now."

But his fingers still linger on my face as I grin and step back, sipping my wine.

I fall onto the sofa cushions while Wyatt squats in front of the fireplace. His checkered button-up stretches across his shoulder blades as he moves, tossing more wood onto the pile, striking a match, waiting for it to catch.

Being a true cowboy, Wyatt is an expert at starting—and putting out—fires. This one flares to immediate life, the flames licking high up into the chimney. The homey smell of burning wood fills the room. Wyatt turns off the overhead lights, and suddenly I'm enveloped in this delightful little cocoon of flickering light and dancing shadows.

"You really know how to set the mood," I say, marveling at the room.

Wyatt smirks. "I have an ulterior motive."

I laugh at my line—the one I gave him when I asked him to be my fake date to the potluck. "I was hoping you might."

Wyatt crosses to the kitchen and grabs the charcuterie board, setting it on the coffee table in front of me. "Hungry?"

"Yes." I sit up on the couch. "This looks amazing."

"You eat. I'm gonna check on the pot roast real quick."

I blink. "You're making pot roast?"

"Your mom's pot roast, to be specific. I told her that I remembered it being one of your favorites, and she showed me how to make it. I figured it'd be a good thing for date night because all the prep work would be done by the time you got here."

I blink again. Shit, am I really going to cry right now? "You are relentless."

"You say that like it's a bad thing."

"It's the best thing." I gulp my wine and set the glass on the table, rising. "What can I help you with?"

Wyatt just shakes his head. "I got it. Sit your ass down and eat."

"You sure?"

Wyatt grabs an oven mitt off the counter. "I know what I'm doing—I think."

"I'm going to have sex with you even if you don't."

"I know." He smirks again as he bends down and opens the oven, all cowboy cockiness in his jeans and belt buckle and button-up.

He's a cowboy who *cooks*.

I drink my wine, and I eat delicious cheese, and I watch

Wyatt do his thing. He cracks a dirty joke as he tosses the salad. Gives the pot of mashed potatoes on the stove a stir. He places silverware on the table, and when he comes over to nibble on the charcuterie, I've already got a cracker ready for him. It's loaded with mortadella, a smear of creamy blue cheese, and a drizzle of local honey.

"Open," I say.

The smirk is back. "Yes ma'am."

I pop the cracker into his mouth, and he falls onto the couch beside me with an exaggerated moan.

"Okay, Mollie really knew what she was talking about when it came to this charcuterie business."

"Of course she did. Crazy how much she's shaken up things around here. Don't get me wrong, I've always loved hanging with y'all on the ranch. But now that Mollie's in the picture, there's so many exciting things happening."

"Lots of great progress for sure," Wyatt says.

"You have to be so, so proud of the work y'all are doing."

Wyatt nods, sipping his wine. "I am. I'm proud of a lot of things happening right now."

He meets my eyes, and my pulse thunders.

We sit and nibble and chat about everything and nothing. I get a yummy little buzz from the wine and an even bigger buzz from the playful, easy way Wyatt touches me. He puts a hand on my thigh. Wipes a crumb from the corner of my mouth with his thumb. Kneads my calf when I complain about a muscle I pulled there.

An hour goes by in the blink of an eye, and suddenly, the timer on Wyatt's phone is going off.

"That'll be dinner." He gives my calf one last firm squeeze, making my blood jump. "Let me just get the pot roast out of the oven—"

"How about I help make up our plates? And I'll refill the wine."

"I want you to relax, Sal."

"I want to help. Let me. It'll be fun being in the kitchen together, mostly because it'll give me a chance to grope you."

He wags his brows. "I like it when you grope me."

"Aw, handsome, I like it when you grope me too."

The kitchen is small, and we keep bumping into each other as we open drawers and reach for cabinets.

"Sorry," Wyatt says when his hand grazes my breasts as he grabs a wooden spoon. "Wait. No, I'm not."

My hand finds his ass as I'm reaching for the box of matches by the sink. "How inappropriate of me."

His hand slips between my legs as I'm lighting the candles, his middle finger trailing over the center seam of my jeans. My breath catches.

Wyatt grins. "Very inappropriate."

"The most inappropriate."

"I should probably stop now."

"You probably should."

He presses his finger against me, right where my clit is, and I see stars.

"Remind me why we're doing dinner first?"

"Because you said we were?" I'm panting.

A muscle in his jaw tics. "Gonna be a long night. You need your strength, Sunshine. Let's eat."

He pulls out my chair, and I stare at him for a full beat.

"What?" His voice is gruff. "Mollie trained me well. I asked her to show me how to be a good boyfriend, and, well, now I'm a fucking great boyfriend, aren't I?"

He's so cocky I can't stand it.

So *cute* that I cannot freaking stand it.

He called himself my boyfriend.

My heart skips several beats as that sinks in. I love, *love* the idea of being his girlfriend.

I swipe my index finger over his mouth. "You've been taking lessons too, huh?"

"I got a lot to learn," he says, eyes flickering.

I sit, and he pushes my chair in.

I look down at the plate of beautiful food in front of me. Look up at the beautiful man across from me.

Best night of my life? Possibly.

Best date I've been on? Absolutely.

"You know who you remind me of tonight?" I place the cloth napkin—*a cloth napkin!*—on my lap. "Your mom."

I didn't intend to bring up Betsy Rivers. It's clearly a touchy subject for Wyatt. But I feel like he'll appreciate the compliment.

Maybe—just maybe—he'll open up a little more.

Wyatt glances at me as he picks up his fork. "Oh, yeah?"

"Yeah. She was always in the kitchen making something for y'all. I remember her putting on her apron and turning on that little speaker she had—"

"The pink one, shaped like a gigantic pill." Wyatt laughs and shovels a forkful of pot roast into his mouth. "Good memory."

"Betsy loved her some Shania." I try my pot roast too. "Wow, Wyatt, that's delicious."

"You think so?"

"Hell yes. Thank you."

Wyatt grins. "But yeah, how many dance parties did we have listening to that album? The one with 'Man, I Feel Like a Woman!' on it?"

My heart swells. *He's doing it.* Wyatt really is opening up.

That's a big, *big* deal.

"Too many to count," I say with a smile.

He blinks, looking away as he eats his salad. "Mom was the best."

"You take after her. Cash is one hundred percent your dad—"

"Kinda scary when you think about how alike they are."

"No kidding. But you're Betsy through and through." I scoop up some mashed potatoes on my fork and hold it up.

"Case in point: these are her mashed potatoes, aren't they? Made with parsnips?"

He's blinking again, not meeting my eyes. "Only way to make 'em."

I slide the fork into my mouth. The potatoes are *delicious*, just the slightest bit sweet from the parsnips. "You're so right. That is so damn right, Wyatt, it's not even funny."

"They're good?"

"Best I've ever had. Just as good as your mom's." I smile. "She'd be so proud of you, Wy."

I watch his Adam's apple bob on a swallow. My eyes fill when I see his expression flicker. Shit, I took it too far, didn't I?

He clears his throat. "Thank you for saying that."

A beat of silence. I don't rush to fill it. The moment suddenly feels tender in every sense of the word. It's tender, as in it's sweet, but it also feels like I'm pressing on a sore spot.

Part of me wants to backtrack, to say, *Hey, it's all right if you don't want to talk about this.* But he already knows that. Wyatt can change the subject at any time.

I wait for him to do exactly that. Instead, he takes the stem of his wineglass in his hand and rolls it between his fingers.

He sniffles. "I miss her, you know?"

I dab at my eyes with my napkin. "I know."

"Sometimes—" He lets out a breath. "Sometimes, it hurts too bad just to *think* about how much I miss her. How much I've missed out on, losing her when I did. I can't—it's like I can't breathe when I think about all the years that have passed that she hasn't been around for. The things she wasn't able to witness, you know?"

This is an important moment. There's a breakthrough happening, and my heart is hammering, and I'm overwhelmed by the love and the *respect* I have for Wyatt.

I don't think.

I just get up, set my napkin on the table, and walk around to him. I loop my arms around his neck and settle myself in his lap. Just like I did the night we played poker together.

Seems like forever ago.

Seems like yesterday.

Wyatt immediately pulls me against him, holding me close, and I rest my forehead against his so that our noses touch too. I take a deep inhale, then slowly let it out.

"Let me remind you how breathing is done then," I whisper. "Hear the air go in and out? Now you do the same."

I put my hand on his chest. Feel it barrel out on his inhale. Feel it fall on his shaky exhale that courses over my face in a warm rush.

We sit like that for one breath, then another, and another.

"This is not how I wanted dinner to go," Wyatt says with a half-hearted scoff. "I'm sorry."

"For what?" I lift my head and look him in the eye. "I'm not going anywhere, Wy."

His eyes are a little frantic as they search mine. "You're not leaving right now." The words come out as a statement, but I know they're a question.

"I'm not leaving."

He swallows. "Why not?"

"Because you still owe me mind-blowing sex."

Wyatt laughs, the sound real and loud and relieved, and something breaks loose in my chest.

I love how I can make this man laugh.

I love you, Wy, and I'm gonna stay.

"That, I can do." He presses a kiss to my forehead.

"Your feelings don't scare me. You know what does? You keeping everything bottled up in here." I tap my finger on his breastbone. "So talk to me. I'm listening."

CHAPTER 23

Wyatt

BIG FEELINGS

I TALK.

It comes pouring out of me in a steady stream—the stories, the memories, the regrets. The things I wish Mom could've seen—Duke and Ryder graduating high school, Ella being born, Cash falling in love with Mollie—and the things I'm glad she didn't, like our ranch falling into disrepair.

Sally listens, her body tucked against mine. Every so often, she'll reach for her wine and we'll each take a sip. But otherwise, she's quiet. Not in an absent or bored way—there's warmth in her silence, a sense of understanding. I can't really describe it. All I know is, I feel heard. Seen.

Safe.

There's still part of me that expects her to bolt at any minute. Because that's immediately where my brain goes—whenever you get close to someone, you end up hurt.

Of course Mom didn't hurt or leave me on purpose. Rationally, I know this. But her death rewired a part of my monkey brain, and somehow, I've ended up with the misbelief that love inevitably equals pain. It equals losing years to the darkness of grief.

Love and darkness—they've been a package deal for as long as I can remember.

But Sally? She's not leaving.

She stays in my lap, and she listens. By the time I'm finished talking, she's running her fingers through my hair, and then she's drawing soft circles with her fingertip on my chest.

Little reminders that she's *still here*.

"You should run," I murmur into her hair. "That was...a lot."

"I'd rather stay."

"If you insist."

She laughs, a pretty, feminine sound I feel inside my rib cage. Then she sits up and does that thing where she looks me in the eye, her expression soft, gaze softer. "I admire the hell out of you, you know that?"

My heart dips. "Say more."

Another laugh. "How do you feel? After getting all that out?"

I suck in a lungful of air, tinged with the smell of the dying fire. "Lighter? Empty, but in a good way?"

"And how did you feel before?"

Swallowing, I think on that for a minute. "Too...full."

"You were scared to let it out. You've been scared for a while, yeah?"

"Yeah."

"But tonight, you decided you were going to let it out anyway. I think that's one hell of an accomplishment."

"Me crying is an accomplishment?" I smile though as I say the words.

"Totally. Cowboys cry, too, especially when they talk about their feelings."

I scoff. "I feel like we're always talking to Ella about how it's okay to have big feelings. Sometimes, I think adults aren't much better at handling that shit than kids are."

A flicker moves across Sally's eyes. The energy between us shifts. Takes on an edge of heat.

"What?" I run my hand up the side of her thigh.

"Self-awareness. It just might be the sexiest thing about you, Wy."

I glance at the table. "Are we done with dinner?"

Sally digs her teeth into her bottom lip. "We're done with dinner."

"C'mon then." Slipping an arm underneath her knees, I slide my other arm down her back and cradle her against me. "How you're still attracted to me after I babbled on like that, I don't know, but—"

"Are you kidding?" Sally's turn to scoff. "Take off my pants and see just how attractive I find your courage. Your honesty. Your way with mashed potatoes."

I'm always laughing with this woman. "Oh, yeah?"

"Yeah."

"Arms around my neck. I'm taking you to bed, Sunshine."

Because she's trying to kill me, Sally nuzzles her face against my throat and kisses me there as I carry her to my room. Electricity bolts through my skin, blood rushing to my dick, and I'm already hard by the time I set Sally down just inside the door.

I turn on the bedside lamp. Turn down the covers. I make quick work of lighting a fire in the fireplace. One of the benefits of having a house as old as this one is the multiple chimneys that kept the rooms warm before central heating was a thing.

Once the flames get high, I turn off the lamp. The fire fills the room with low, soft light and the sound of crackling wood.

Sally waits by the door. Her eyes have this funny look in them as she watches me approach.

"You okay?" I ask.

The fire snaps.

She swallows. "This is so perfect. Everything about this night has been perfect, Wyatt, and it's...overwhelming. In the best, most beautiful way."

I slip my hands inside her shirt, her belly caving at my touch. Her skin is impossibly soft. I lean in and kiss her mouth.

You're the one overwhelming me.

Sally rises onto her tiptoes to kiss me back. Her hands find the hair at the nape of my neck as my tongue finds the seam of her lips. I open her, my heart thundering at the needy little moan that sounds in the back of her throat.

My dick feels heavy. My skin is tight. I slide my hands up, my thumbs finding the swell of her breasts. She moans again when I feather my thumbs over her nipples, drawing them to sweet little peaks against the lace of her bra, which I unhook with one hand.

"Arms up, Sunshine. That's a good girl. Look how well you listen."

I guide her shirt over her head and slip the straps of her bra off her shoulders. Looking down, I take her tits in my hands and marvel at her naked beauty. The fire paints her skin in shades of red, auburn, gold. I gently press a finger to the dark freckle just above her left nipple.

When I meet her eyes, I see that they're heavy-lidded. Alive with desire.

"Beautiful." It's all I can manage. A single word.

Her lips curl into a hazy smile. "That's how you make me feel, Wyatt." She cups my cheek in her hand. "Beautiful."

My briefs dampen. I'm leaking.

I'm in love.

Then I'm kissing her, and she's unbuttoning my shirt while I unbutton her jeans. I use the bulk of my body to start backing her toward the bed, my thoughts ringing with disbelief that this is actually happening.

Sally is about to be in my bed.

I get to have her all night. All morning.

I get to love her the way I've always wanted to love her.

I'm rock hard between my legs, but there's this achy tenderness in my chest as I help Sally out of her jeans and panties. The contrast is a mindfuck.

It makes me feel wild, a little shaky even.

Ordinarily, I'd shut this shit down. Bury these feelings and fuck this girl like the mindless animal I am.

Only with Sally, I'm able to be a whole human being. I can be the flirt, the good friend, and an even better boyfriend, but I can also be the man who's grieving. Who's hurt. The man who wants to do the right thing, but doesn't know how.

It's liberating. I don't have to hold back or hide because I know Sally isn't going anywhere.

She's staying. For tonight at least.

In the light of the fire she looks like a goddess, all curves and flawless skin.

I curse when I see that she's shaved her pussy again. She looks so small there, so vulnerable.

I can already taste her on my lips.

Shouldering out of my shirt, I nod at the bed. "Lie down."

Sally does as I told her. I catch a tantalizing glimpse of her slit as she climbs into bed, settling herself against the pillows.

"This is really comfortable, Wyatt. Wow."

"I'm glad you like it."

I don't tell her I paid a fortune to have a new mattress, bed frame, and bedding rush-delivered this week. She'll find out eventually.

She'll know I'm crazy in love with her and I would do anything to keep her safe and happy and comfortable eventually. Only the best for my girl.

I shuck off my jeans and briefs, and Sally's eyes dart to my cock.

"You're huge." Her voice is hoarse. "I mean, I thought you were huge before, but now that I'm picturing it inside me…"

"You worried? I have lube if you think we need it."

Her eyes move up to meet mine. Then she slowly—*slowly*—lets her legs fall apart on the mattress, rumpling the covers underneath her thighs. "You tell me."

Fu-*uck*.

This confidence. This *dare*. It has me taking my dick in my hand and giving myself a hard, almost angry pull as I devour her pussy with my gaze.

She's spread wide, allowing me to devour every inch of her from her swollen clit to the dark pucker of her ass. My blood jumps when I see how she fucking *glistens* with arousal.

"Show me," I grunt, giving myself another tug. "I want you to touch yourself and show me how wet you are for me."

Her eyes flicker. I watch, pulse going haywire, as she reaches between her legs. She hisses when she runs her first two fingers over her clit, her tits pushing out on a sharp inhale as she circles her fingers.

"Jesus, I can hear how wet you are."

Sally's mouth falls open. "I am. For you. I want you here, Wyatt."

I'm three seconds from coming in my hand. Takes every ounce of self-control not to pump myself again. "Move your fingers lower. Show me exactly where you want me."

Oh Christ, she's doing it. Those fingers head lower. One dips inside her, and she rolls her hips, hungry for more.

"Here." Her teeth come down on her bottom lip.

She thrusts her finger easily in and out. She's slippery, so wet and hot and soft I really can hear it.

My God, I did turn her on.

Who knew the truth was such an aphrodisiac?

I have to grit my teeth as I watch Sally fuck herself with her finger. One of her hands finds her breast, and she plays with her nipple and rides her hand. In my bed. Eyes on my cock.

Eyes on my eyes.

I step forward so my thighs meet with the mattress. "Anything I gotta know?"

She pulls her brows together. "About—"

"I want you to take that"—I nod at her arousal before squeezing my leaking tip—"and put it here. Unless you think that's a bad idea."

"Oh." She blinks as she realizes what I'm asking, a small smile breaking out on her face. "Oh, wow, okay. I had my annual appointment recently. I'm good."

"I'm good too. As luck would have it, I got tested two weeks back." My balls are screaming. "You on birth control?"

"I have an IUD, yes."

"You gonna let me do what I want, then?"

A softness comes over her expression. "What do you want?"

"Everything."

She runs her tongue along the inside of her top lip. "I want that too."

"I got condoms. You wanna use 'em—"

"I trust you."

Bless.

I somehow manage to bite out the words, "Get your fingers wet. Really wet, Sunshine. Yes, just like that." I hold out my dick. "Now get me wet too."

I have to close my eyes when Sally lifts her fingers and leans in, all eagerness and excitement. My hips punch forward when she touches me, gently spreading her slickness over my head with her fingertips, mingling it with my pre-cum.

My eyes fly open when she licks me, her tongue lingering in the sensitive furrow on the underside of my head.

Her eyes lock on mine, and she slowly toys with me, swirling her tongue along my shaft before sucking my crown into her mouth.

My heart ricochets inside my chest, its rhythm uneven, the breaths I take unsteady.

Sally is *savoring* me.

She likes tasting me. Pleasing me. Having fun with me.

I bared everything to her today, and she still fucking wants me this way.

I lean down, my cock falling out of her mouth, and I take her face in hands that shake. I kiss her, taste the salt on her lips, and she whimpers, her hands finding my hips and pulling me to her.

My body throbs with the need to be inside her.

"On your back, Sunshine," I whisper.

CHAPTER 24

Wyatt

HEAVY

SALLY NODS, scooting down on the mattress. I climb up on the bed and settle myself on my haunches between her legs. Hooking my hands behind the back of her knees, I fold her legs against her chest and hold them up and open, spreading her wide.

"So soft and sweet here." Opening my mouth, I lean in and kiss her clit. I run my tongue down the length of her. Run it back up. "I love lookin' at you. Tastin' you."

She arches her back, digging her fingers into my hair. One of her legs starts to shake, and she closes her eyes. "Wyatt, I'm close. So close."

"You already came on my mouth. Now you're gonna do it on my dick. You're soaked, and so am I, so I don't think we'll need lube." I climb over her, catching one of her knees in the crook of my elbow. "But if it hurts or you want some, just tell me, okay?"

"I'll be okay." Her hands are on my waist now, her fingers trailing ribbons of fire along the length of my rib cage.

The way this girl touches me—the patience, the reverence—

Her breath catches, and her eyes flutter shut when I settle

some of my weight on her. I still hold myself up on my elbows, my abdominal muscles tensed so that my cock hangs between us, the tip pressing insistently into her belly.

Bare.

I'm about to make love to Sally bare. Nothing between us.

I'm in heaven. I can't—I just can't fucking believe this is happening. That I get to have her like this. Makes me feel like my chest is going to burst open at any minute.

Ducking my head, I capture her mouth in a kiss. I nip at her chin, kiss her neck.

She writhes beneath me, her hands curling into my ass and pressing me down so she can grind her pussy against my shaft.

I slip a hand between us. Slip a finger inside her pussy, thrusting it to try to stretch her a little.

She's ready.

She's still tiny here though. Extremely tight. Sally isn't a virgin, but it's been a while. I need to go slow.

She breathes my name as I finger her, pressing her tits against my chest. If only I didn't want to impale her on a vicious thrust and come all over her.

I'll do that next time. Right now, I *take it slow.*

I lift my hips so I can take myself in my hand. Thumbing my head downward, I press it to her clit.

"Wyatt."

I slide my head lower, notching myself at her entrance. "You'd best wait until I'm inside you to come."

"I don't—I can't—*please*, for the love of God—" She gasps when I look her in the eye and push inside her an inch, maybe less.

She's swollen, silky with arousal, but the pressure is already enormous. I search her face, heart thumping in my throat as I try to read her reaction. Her lips are parted, and her brows are curved upward, almost like she's in pain.

"You're—wow. Wait. I wanna do this, Wy, but…are you gonna fit?" she pants, looking down. "You're so big—"

"Does it hurt?"

She shakes her head, her hair swirling around her head like a dark halo on the white sheets. "Just feels tight."

"You need me to stop?"

"Don't you dare."

I reach up and take her hand, lacing our fingers. "It'll fit, Sunshine. You just gotta relax." I push a little deeper so that my broad head is all the way inside her. "Give it a minute. I promise it will feel good. You're such a good girl, being patient. Taking me like this."

Her other hand is on my arm now. She holds onto me, her grip fierce as she nods her head. *I trust you.*

Her eyes are on mine again.

Biting down on the inside of my lip, I sink a little further inside her. It's all I can do not to howl at how fucking perfect she feels. The bareness of it drives me crazy. The hot, slick grip of her pussy is unlike anything I've ever experienced.

I never fuck without condoms. Ever.

Had no clue the heaven I was missing out on.

Part of me feels like we're being reckless. I'm being reckless, making love to a girl who's taking off. She's gonna take my heart with her when she leaves.

Another part—a deeper part of me—feels like I'm doing the right thing for the first time…ever.

I'm baring *myself* in a way I always believed would decimate me. Destroy me.

But I don't feel destroyed. I feel put back together. And that's making me question everything else I've always assumed was true.

I feel Sally stretching around me, her tightness easing ever so slightly. The indents between her brows smooth over. I sink deeper inside her, and she whimpers.

"Want me to stop?"

"Absolutely"—she shakes her head for the second time, breathless—"not."

"That's my girl. You're doing so good, Sunshine."

I kiss her forehead and press further. She relaxes, bit by bit. I'm close to being sunk to the hilt. It's agony, holding back, but I do it until I'm literally shaking.

"I'm gonna go all the way in. Can you take a deep breath, just like you showed me?"

She sucks in air through her nose. At the same moment I rear back, then thrust forward so I slide into her on a slow, steady stroke that has me buried balls deep. Sally's eyes go wide, and then they water. I do what I can to soothe the sting: I kiss her mouth, her neck. I arc my thumb over the back of her hand, and I stay very still, waiting for her to adjust to the feel of me.

Our fit is tight. Sweat breaks out along my scalp and on my chest as I hold for one beat, another. She feels so damn good, it makes my blood riot. My body aches with the need to rut, to move.

But Sally is the one to move first. Closing her eyes, she nudges her hips forward. The movement is small but significant, and I smile.

"Feel better?" I ask, untangling my fingers from hers so I can reach between us.

"Yeah. Wy, you feel so—" She rocks against me and sighs. "Oh, so, *so* good. It feels full, but—yeah, *good*."

I roll my thumb over her clit. "Aw, Sunshine, that's what I like to hear. You're doing so good. I'm gonna make you feel so good when you come around my dick."

Her pussy flutters around me and I chuckle, even as my body seizes.

"Told you I was close," she pants.

"No shit." I continue to roll my thumb as I try a baby thrust. "Open your eyes, Sally. Look at me."

She does. I pull back, push forward, and this time, her

hips rise to meet my thrust.

"Wyatt," she pleads.

Her eyes are full of sharp-edged lust. There's something softer there too. Something that makes my heart turn over.

"You promise you meant what you said?" I ghost my lips over hers. "That you were gonna let me do what I wanted?"

She whimpers, "What do you want?"

"I wanna come inside you."

Her mouth curves into a small smile. "You don't wanna pull out."

"Good memory."

"That's a hard line to forget." Her fingertips glide up my arm to caress my neck. "Go. Don't stop. Please, I want—" Her breath catches when her pussy squeezes me. "I want all of you, Wy."

I circle her clit with my thumb. At the same time, I duck my head and take her nipple in my mouth. Biting down, I give her my first deep, hard thrust, the bed frame groaning in protest.

She closes her eyes and *comes*. Her pussy clamps down on my dick and her back convulses, body rising off the bed on a tidal wave of sensation.

She's breathing my name when I capture her mouth in a kiss. I close my eyes, and despite the frenzy of need inside my skin I try to memorize everything about this moment. The way she tastes like me. How her hips continue to roll as she rides out her orgasm, the rhythm uneven but insistent.

She bites down on my bottom lip before sucking on it. The caress is lingering, lazy.

Loving.

Electricity shoots up my spine. I thrust again and again, my hips jerking as I blindly seek release. Sally takes control of the kiss, her hands on my face, her knees drawing up around my hips, like she knows I want—need—to be held.

Goddamn, the way this woman cares. She sure as hell ain't afraid of letting someone close. Letting me in.

She's the one who's got faith.

She has it in spades. Despite my reputation. Despite the fact that our lives are heading in opposite directions.

Despite all that, she's baring her heart to me tonight.

A feeling of sweetness fills me. My kiss becomes messy. I'm losing control, my balls contracting. My strokes become uneven. They're shallow, then deep. Slow, then fast.

I bury my face in her neck. *You wreck me.*

She digs a hand into my hair in reply, her touch soothing as her fingers work slow circles across my nape. *You're okay.*

I curse.

I moan.

The release slams into me with the ferocity of a hurricane. I'm vaguely aware of the sounds I make through gritted teeth as pulse after pulse of vicious sensation grips me. I feel myself filling her, feel the hot drip of my cum.

I'm helpless. Boneless. Instead of fighting that, instead of trying to find my way back to a sense of control, I surrender.

All the while, Sally encourages that surrender, kissing me. Her hands are achingly gentle on my face. Her thumbs skate over my cheekbones, her pinkies tucked in the underside of my jaw in a show of steadiness I didn't know I was desperate for.

When I'm finally able to breathe again, I lift my head. That's when I realize I've settled most, if not all, of my weight on Sally.

"Shit, Sunshine. I'm sorry."

I try to lift myself up, but she immediately grabs my sides and pulls me back onto her.

"You're so warm," she replies, kissing my collarbone.

"And heavy."

She smiles, her big, beautiful, sated eyes flicking to meet

mine. "I'm still breathing, aren't I? Your heavy doesn't hurt me."

I scoff, shifting a little as an excuse to look away. I'm worried I'll tell her I love her if she keeps looking at me like that. I'm not scared to say the words. Wait, that's a lie. I'm scared shitless to draw that line in the sand. But I gotta come clean anyway.

I'm gonna come clean. I just don't wanna do it while I'm still inside her. Seems like a cop-out to admit such a monumental thing when we're both still mindless with lust.

So I kiss her neck and ask, "How do you feel?"

She presses her lips to my forehead. "I feel like I wanna do that again, Blond Bear Cowboy. And again."

I laugh, light flooding my chest. "How many more times exactly?"

"At least fifty…five thousand."

"You owe me fifty bucks, by the way." I look up at her. I have to.

She's smiling at me, lips swollen, cheeks bright pink.

"Remember our bet?"

She chuckles. "Holy shit, I forgot about that."

"I did just fuck your brains out."

"*Terrible* line." She gives me a shove, but she's still chuckling. "Do it again?"

She's so pretty I can't breathe.

"Lemme grab the Advil first." I kiss the corner of her mouth.

"The Advil?"

"Bet you're sore already, aren't you?" I pull out of her the tiniest bit, and her breath catches. "Yep. Advil. Take two. Better yet, three."

She blinks, her smile softening. "You're sweet."

"You're staying." I kiss her one last time. "C'mon. Let's go clean you up."

CHAPTER 25

Sally

MIDNIGHTS

I'M HOT.

I'm not in my bed.

I'm naked.

My body lurches into sudden consciousness. I open my eyes and am greeted by total darkness. The air is cold, tinged with the scent of a fire.

There was a fire because I'm at Wyatt's house.

I'm in his bed.

His deliciously comfortable, insanely enormous king-size bed, which smells like sex.

Turning my head, I am just able to see the outline of the nearby fireplace. The fire in it has long since died. Did Wyatt put it out? What time did that happen? Last thing I remember is Wyatt using a washcloth to wipe his cum off my belly and breasts—*oh my God*—after we had sex for a second time. I think—hope—I went to the bathroom too?

Yes, I remember I did, and then we climbed into bed and he pulled me against him, the big spoon to my little spoon. I must've drifted off to sleep.

As if on cue, an arm tightens around my middle. Is Wyatt dreaming?

My stomach dips, a quiet but insistent throb blooming to life between my legs as my senses blink awake. I wince. Despite that Advil I took, I'm definitely sore.

I'm definitely still wrapped up in Wyatt.

My throat tightens. I try to stay very still so I don't wake him. Judging by the darkness outside the windows, it's very late—or very early. Too early to be up, even on a ranch. Wyatt needs his sleep.

The sex. My God. It was so good that I'm struggling not to cry just thinking about it. How patient Wyatt was, how thorough and intense and *tender*.

It wasn't fucking. It wasn't even sex.

To me, it felt like making love. Which is a beautiful idea. Then again, I could be making things up. I don't have tons of experience. But the way he insisted I take that Advil, the way he looked me in the eye as he patiently pushed inside me that first time—

You're not making anything up.

His skin is warm. I can feel the press of his wiry chest hair against my back as he breathes deeply, evenly, his breath rustling the hair at the nape of my neck.

I can also feel something wet on my lower back.

The throb between my legs blares when I realize that Wyatt is leaking.

Not only that. He's hard.

This man is an *animal*. The only animal I've ever encountered that I can't wrangle. Wrong that I love that about him?

He's awake.

He presses a quiet, hot kiss to my shoulder. A full-body shock wave of need moves through me, my breath catching as his mouth works its way up the column of my neck.

How did I get so turned on while I was sleeping? Because I am ready *to go* after a single kiss.

Reaching behind me, I find him and wrap my fingers around his length. He's definitely hard, hot to the touch, and I slick my thumb over his head before giving him a slow, easy pull.

In reply, Wyatt cups my breast in one hand and glides the other underneath my rib cage and then between my legs. I see stars when he plucks my nipple at the same time he parts me with his fingers.

The caress is gentle, a little sleepy even, but my body still comes to life at his touch. He lets out a quiet groan when his fingers find my slickness. He circles my clit once, twice, and it feels so good that I roll over to face him and lift my leg, draping it over his hip. I take his dick in my hand and guide it to my center.

He hesitates. *You sure?*

I press my hips down so that he slips inside me. *I'm sure.*

Then he's rolling his big body on top of mine. I'm on my back, spread-eagled, when he impales me on a deep, unhurried thrust, sinking to the root.

I close my eyes against a blinding flash of pain.

Reading me like a book, Wyatt goes still. He leans his forehead against mine and waits one heartbeat, then another, before he thrusts again, gentler this time.

The pain dissipates. Pleasure rises in its wake.

I'm close, and I want to come with him inside me, so I snake a hand between us and play with myself.

Wyatt blows out a breath. I circle my hips, meeting him at the apex of his strokes. He still goes slow, just deeper now. He's steady. Controlled. I run my free hand over his chest, his stomach, his side, marveling at the way the huge muscles there bunch and release as he moves.

He is so fucking sexy.

I don't chase my orgasm for long. I find it when Wyatt casually throws my leg over his shoulder, deepening the angle of his thrusts. It hurts.

It's the best thing I've felt in my entire life.

My fingers make shallow, rapid circles over my clit as the

release washes over me. My heartbeat dissolves into my skin, racing, throbbing.

Wyatt grunts, and then I feel the now-familiar sensation of being filled with warmth.

When he pulls out of me, a rush of cum seeps from the place where our bodies were joined.

He doesn't say a word when he kisses my mouth.

Not a word when he helps me out of bed and cleans me up with a towel after I use the bathroom.

Really, is there anything left for us to say that our bodies haven't?

———

It's still dark when a sound wakes me.

I hear a soft rustling, and when my eyes adjust to the darkness, I see Wyatt's hand working underneath the covers.

I can't help but smile, even as my heart twists. He doesn't want to wake me. And I know he's worried that I'll be too sore to go for another round.

Grinning, I gently toss aside the covers and swat his hand away. Then I lean in and take him into my mouth. He growls, dropping an arm over his face as he lets out a series of discombobulated sounds.

When his hips start to jerk, I sit up and straddle his pelvis. I hold his hand, using it for support as I sink slowly onto his cock.

He twines our fingers when I take him to the hilt with a small cry. He gives my hand a gentle squeeze.

You're okay. We're okay.

He puts his other hand on my hip and guides my body up and down, up and down, a slow rhythm that gradually gets faster and faster until I'm riding him hard.

I'm not sure I can take more.

But I know I'll always, always want more with Wyatt.

———

The backs of my eyelids burn red.

Sunlight. A lot of it.

Oh my God, how late did I sleep?

Opening my eyes, I sit up with a start. The shutters are closed, but ardent sunshine pours through the slats anyway, coating Wyatt's bedroom in a golden glow I can only describe as autumn coziness at its best.

Glancing at his side of the bed, I see that he's gone. The door is closed. Was he called into work?

Shit, what if I got a call for work? I didn't think to set an alarm since it's the weekend, but I don't need to when I'm staying at my parents' house because Dad is around. He'll wake me up if someone needs me.

I grab my phone from the nightstand and flip it over. My stomach somersaults when I see that it's *ten o'clock.*

When was the last time I slept this late?

When was the last time I was up so late? Yes, I got sleep, but it was broken sleep. I had no idea you could be so turned on that it wakes you up in the dead of night. That's never happened to me before.

Then again, I've never slept with Wyatt Rivers before.

I sit up and the sheets fall, catching on my breasts. I feel a slight burning sensation there. Looking down, I see red marks on my chest, my boobs, even my stomach.

Beard burn.

Wyatt kissed me literally everywhere last night, and Lord, does it show. Between him coming all over me and now the beard burn, there's not an inch of my body Wyatt hasn't left his mark on.

The thought makes me weirdly emotional. It also turns me on in a big, big way.

Glancing at my screen, I'm relieved to see I haven't missed any calls or important texts. I did get an email from my

adviser at Ithaca University, however, which I should probably read—

"Mornin'."

I look up, and my heart falls a hundred stories when I see
Wyatt standing in the doorway. He's wearing a pair of
broken-in Wranglers, and...that's it.

Not a shirt. No hat. Not even a sock.

His bare torso is a sight to behold. Whorls of dark blond
hair cover his barrel of a chest, narrowing to a happy trail
that disappears into his jeans. His thick abdominal muscles
slope into sculpted hips that form a very distracting V
shape.

And his arms. My God, this man's *arms*. His biceps bulge,
putting his tattoos on prominent display. Thick veins run
down the inside of his elbows and spread out along forearms
the size of Wiffle bats.

He's also got a raging case of bedhead. His thick hair is
rumpled, sticking up every which way in a kind of ragged
golden halo that's somehow both adorable *and* sexy.

But it's the mugs of steaming coffee he holds in his hands
that really make my pulse skip a beat. The velvety smell fills
the room, and for several seconds I can only stare, phone
falling from my hand onto the bed with a soft *thunk*.

One side of his mouth kicks up in a smirk as he strides
into the room.

"Lose your voice from yellin' my name so much last
night?"

Laughter bubbles up inside me, and I resist the urge to
grab him by the throat and have my way with him right here,
right now.

"If memory serves, you were the one yelling mine."

"You surprised by that, Mustang Sally?" He holds out one
of the mugs. "All you wanna do is ride."

I'm so in love with you I can't breathe, I think, even as I keep
laughing.

All this smiling, this laughing, this longing—it fucking hurts, it's so good.

I take the mug from him. "Please don't start calling me that."

"Nah. I like Sunshine better."

His eyes meet mine. A beat of heated silence passes between us as those eyes flick to *my* bare torso. My nipples pebble beneath his attention—a fact he seems to notice because his nostrils flare.

"I like you in my bed."

I bring the coffee to my lips. "I like being in your bed."

"Stay."

"You see me going anywhere?"

He sips his coffee before setting the mug on the bedside table. My body leaps when he sits on the mattress beside me. He frowns when he sees the red marks on my chest. "You hurtin'?"

"No." I shake my head. "I liked it, Wyatt."

He gently takes my breast in his hand. His eyes darken, taking on a feral glint. "And between your legs?"

"A little sore. Nothing"—my breath catches when he thumbs my nipple—"too bad."

His jaw tics. "What would I find right now if I touched you there? Same as last time? The time before that?"

I nod, momentarily losing the ability to form words as he continues to stroke my nipple. Heat bolts through me, gathering in my clit.

"Can I—will you—"

His smirk is back. "You want me to touch you there?"

I nod. Wyatt takes the coffee from my hands. I reach for his jeans, but he pushes away my hand.

"You said you're sore. Let's give your body a little break, yeah?"

I keep nodding. He adjusts the front of his jeans.

"But you're—"

"Don't worry, I got plans for that. But first, you." He grins.

At what point do I tell Wyatt how I feel?

When can I ask him to marry me? Does he want to get married? Sawyer says he might.

Is it weird I'm thinking about that? Or am I crazy to believe the sex we're having—the date we enjoyed, the connection between us—is special? The kind of once-in-a-life-time opportunity to build a life with someone who *gets it*? Gets you?

Also, *how* does he look so *hot* when he lifts the covers and climbs onto the bed, settling himself comfortably on his belly with his head between my legs?

Putting his hands on the back of my thighs just under-neath my ass, he spreads me wide. Then he looks me in the eye and says, "I'm gonna make you come. Then I'll feed you. Then I'm gonna take you home."

My heart falls. Scrunching my brow, I dig my fingers into his wild hair. I'm feeling just brave enough to say, "What if I don't want to go home?"

"You have to go home if you're gonna get what you need for the week." Then he bends his neck and kisses my clit.

I yelp, my heart flitting around my chest like a humming-bird. "What do you—I don't understand. Stay for the week? Like, stay here?"

He lifts his head, eyebrows snapping together. "You think I'm lettin' you outta my bed after how good last night was? Sunshine, I'm still weak in the knees."

I'm smiling, and Wyatt is dipping his tongue inside me, and there's a soaring feeling inside my chest. Like I'm the hummingbird now, suspended in the air.

"So you're asking me to stay over all week."

"Telling you, more like it." But his eyes meet mine, and I see the question in them.

I giggle.

I giggle like a fucking teenager because what else can I do but give in to the silliness, the joy, that I feel right now?

"I'll stay."

"You'd better. But I got one condition. A request actually."

"Anything."

"Much as I hate to say it, I do have to let you out of my bed so you can sleep in yours. Just for tonight."

I scrunch my brow. "So you—"

"Want you to sleep at your parents' tonight. Yeah. Trust me, I ain't crazy about the idea either. But it's important to me that your parents see I'm doing right by you. Feels a little disrespectful to kidnap you right off the bat. They'll think we're having a nonstop fuck fest."

"But we are having a nonstop fuck fest."

He smirks. "Just one night. That's all I'm asking. This way, you'll have more time to pack. And you bet I'll be on your doorstep first thing tomorrow to bring you back here."

I don't want to leave. But I love that Wyatt is trying to do the right thing here. If we are going to be together for the long haul, we'll have plenty of time for more sex.

I nod. "Okay. Just one night."

"Just one night. Then you're all mine."

He flashes me a handsome smile of white teeth and full lips, and it's in that moment when I know—I *know*—I'm not gonna be able to leave this man at the end of December.

Maybe—

Hell, maybe I won't.

CHAPTER 26

Sally

COME TO JESUS

MOLLIE PICKS up my call on the first ring. "So…how was it?"

Closing the bathroom door behind me, I drop the lid onto the toilet and sit. "The date was in*sane*—"

"Of course the date was insane. I helped Wyatt set it up. I'm talking about the sex."

I laugh, my heart skipping several beats. "That was insane too."

"Bet he did you *so* right, didn't he?" Mollie sighs. "I'm telling you, Sally, these cowboys are in a league of their own. I've never experienced anything like it."

I'm downright giddy when I reply, "Neither have I. I'm not sure I'll ever recover."

"Oh, you will. And then you'll want more."

"I already do."

"The addiction is real. Can I design the boots you'll wear for your wedding? Oh my God, I can already see them. White —no, pale blue because they'll be your something blue, with a cute little rising sun on them because Wyatt calls you Sunshine—"

"I think you're getting a little ahead of yourself." I'm laughing, but my pulse still skips several beats.

"I don't. I think part of the reason Cash has been so pissy about y'all hooking up is that he knows how obsessed his brother is with you, and he's worried Wyatt is going to royally fuck everything up because you make him that stupid."

"Ha. I wish I had that power."

"You do though. Aw, Sally, I can hear in your voice how happy you are. I'm thrilled for you, truly. Thrilled for me too. One of my best friends is also going to be my sister-in-law."

"You're ridiculous."

"I know. But that doesn't mean I'm not right."

Am I ever going to stop smiling? I feel like my smile hasn't quit since Wyatt handed me a cup of coffee this morning and then made me come on his mouth. It's almost dark now, so that was hours ago.

My face hurts. I'm exhausted.

And yet I wonder how the hell I'm going to sleep because I really am so happy. So excited, too, and *so* horny.

"I love what an optimist you are," I say. "Thank you, sincerely, for helping set everything up. It really was perfection. The wine, the food, the china—I felt so special."

"Mission accomplished then. I wish you could've seen how adorable Wyatt was when he asked your mom and me to help. He was so nervous. You could tell how much he wanted to get it right. Between you and me, Cash said he doesn't remember Wyatt going on a date with a serious girlfriend before. Like, ever."

My stomach dips. I put a hand there in the futile hope I can catch it. "Wow. I...don't know what to say to that. I know he's never really had a serious girlfriend, but I had no idea he hasn't *dated*."

"Not until you. He wants to be with you, Sally. For the long haul. I know it. You know it. We all know it."

I want to tell her she's being ridiculous again. Want to protest, say I don't believe my relationship with Wyatt could become so shockingly, suddenly serious.

But it has. And I do believe Wyatt is in it for the long haul.

As if I need further evidence, my phone chimes. Pulling it away from my ear, I see that it's a text from Wyatt, asking if I remembered to take another dose of Advil to help with my soreness.

Now the question isn't *does he want me*, but *how do we make this work?*

"I want that too." I keep my voice low. Mom and Dad have the TV on downstairs, but I can't risk them hearing me. I want to figure this out on my own without their meddling. Dropping my head into my hand, I whisper, "What do I do, Mollie?"

Mollie thinks on this for a beat. "You follow your heart."

"My heart wants Wyatt. That's easy. It's the whole I'm-moving-a-thousand-miles-away thing that's hard."

"It was hard before things started up with Wyatt though, wasn't it?"

Swallowing, I nod. "I love Hartsville. I love the family and friends I have here. I'd love nothing more than to stay."

"Then why don't you?" Mollie asks softly.

I scoff. "If only it were that easy."

"What if it was? Cash and I figured it out. You and Wyatt can too. We're in the middle of cattle country, for crying out loud. There're more horses per square mile than there are people. And isn't your job, well, taking care of horses?"

"It is, yeah. But I like a challenge. Something I haven't seen or done before."

I can picture Mollie nodding.

"I get that. You want a job that's going to challenge you, but that also feeds your soul. The position at Ithaca University definitely challenges you—"

"But it doesn't feed my soul one bit. In fact, it makes me feel kinda dead inside."

This is the first time I'm walking through this out loud. God bless Mollie. She's super smart, and if anyone understands the ambitions I have, it's her. She operates a gigantic cattle ranch *and* owns a cowboy boot company. She also understands that work has to have meaning in order for it to be enjoyable. Or at the very least, worth the sacrifice.

"Right. So let's take Ithaca University off the table. Are you comfortable with that?"

I glance at the door. "My parents are going to flip their shit."

"They'll get over it when they see how happy you are in your new job. How do *you* feel?"

Honestly? "I'd feel, God, so relieved if I didn't have to go back to New York."

"There's your answer."

She's right.

Mollie is absolutely *right*.

I'm terrified to turn down the job. I'm also already mentally drafting my resignation letter, which makes me feel —again—*relieved*. Facing Dad won't be easy. Disappointing my mentors and professors will suck. You know what will suck more, though? Living a life that's not mine.

Deep down, I know a life in Ithaca isn't right for me, even if Wyatt weren't in the picture. He's just making that decision easier, clearer.

"Maybe that's the right move." I hardly believe what I'm saying. "What do I do about a job, though?"

"We brainstorm. Talk to everyone and anyone in a hundred-mile radius. We'll come up with something. We always do, don't we?"

She's talking about the little found family we've made on the ranch—how, come hell or high water, the Lucks and the

Rivers and the Powells work together to find a solution and make things work.

I feel all mushy inside, knowing they have my back.

Dad and my professors will forgive me. But I'll never be able to forgive myself if I don't go after what I want.

I want to stay in Texas and be with Wyatt and rock some sort of veterinary surgeon position that doesn't require me to sacrifice my happiness.

"We do figure it out, yeah," I say.

I hear the smile in Mollie's voice when she replies, "Keep the faith."

———

I climb into bed at seven thirty. Not super early by ranch standards, but compared to last night's late bedtime, it makes me feel like I'm in third grade again, when Mom and Dad would put me to bed while it was still light outside.

I'm beat. I can barely keep my eyes open as I read a book on my Kindle. But when I shut off the light at quarter past eight, I can't fall asleep. Mostly because I'm thinking about what I'd be doing right now if I were in Wyatt's bed instead of my own.

I get why he wanted me to be at home tonight. I still kinda hate him for it, though. Because I'm pretty sure we'd be fucking right now, the fire crackling in the fireplace as Wyatt and I sampled every position under the sun.

An ache blossoms to life between my legs. The soreness is gone now, thank goodness. And Wyatt and I took a long, hot shower before he drove me home this morning. But I swear I can still feel him inside me.

Or maybe that's just wishful thinking.

I toss and turn. My knees and back throb, which is what happens when I'm this tired. I need to sleep. If I could just—

Tap, tap, tap.

I bolt upright, my stomach pitching, and I smile when I see a familiar shadow darkening the window across from my bed.

He didn't.

Oh, but Wyatt Rivers definitely did. He's definitely here, and I am definitely going to make him fuck me in my bed like he said he would.

A shiver of anticipation darts up my spine as I tiptoe across the room and open the window.

"Hi," he whispers, holding up a hand.

In reply, I grab the front of his shirt and pull him inside.

"Careful!" he hisses, and I can tell he's fighting laughter when he lands on his feet.

I go up on my toes and kiss his mouth. "Did you come to rescue me?"

"That's not what I came to do, no." His hands find my ass, and he presses me against his erection.

"You missed me."

"Obviously." He leans down to suck on my neck. "You miss me, Sunshine?"

I grab the hem of my T-shirt and pull it over my head. I'm not wearing a bra, and the moonlight streaming through the window catches on my bare breasts. "So much, Wy. I can't sleep."

Even in the dark, I can see Wyatt's jaw tic. "I can't stay away."

We attack each other. He fists his hand in my hair, and I push off his jacket. He pulls me in for a hard, hot kiss, and I shuck off my shorts. No underwear.

He backs me toward the bed, and I climb onto the mattress, careful not to make a sound. I watch Wyatt toe off his boots and take off his jeans and briefs. His dick stands upright, as huge and swollen as I remember it.

My clit pulses. Mouth salivates.

I bite back a cry when he slips a hand between my legs and parts me with his fingers.

He quietly curses at the slickness he finds there. "You been thinkin' about me, huh?"

"Obviously," I pant.

"Good."

The idea that we could be caught—that my parents are sleeping just down the hall—is terrifying and also arousing in the extreme.

I feel naughty. Dirty even. And I like it.

I like it even more when Wyatt climbs on top of me, using his knee to part my legs.

There is no preamble. No foreplay. He hikes my knee up to his side and lines up his bare tip to my entrance. I feel the hot drip of his pre-cum as his whole body tenses and he pushes all the way inside me on a hard, punishing thrust.

The fullness is almost too much to bear. But Wyatt doesn't give me time to catch my breath. Instead, he holds on to the headboard with one hand and holds the other over my mouth. He pumps into me with a slow, silent savageness that has me curling my toes.

"Make one fucking sound," he whispers. "I dare you, Sunshine. I dare you to get us caught. What do you think your daddy would do if he saw us like this? His sweet little girl being fucked hard by her real daddy and *liking* it."

I bite his palm. He lets out a small scoff, settling his body on top of mine. The enormous weight of him pins me to the mattress. I can hardly breathe.

I love it.

I love the feeling of being surrounded. I'm at Wyatt's mercy, yes. But he'd never hurt me.

He'll always keep me—us—safe. And, God, I love him for it.

I love you, I love you, I'll stay for you, I silently chant in time to his thrusts.

At the crest of a stroke, he swivels his hips, his pubic bone pressing against my clit, and my own hips punch forward, seeking. Hungry.

This hunger is killing me.

Wyatt leans down to suck my nipple into his mouth. A bolt of hot, almost-painful lust cracks through my center when he bites it, then soothes it with slow, lazy strokes of his tongue. I moan. He goes still.

"You gonna make me put my dick in your mouth to keep you quiet? Aw, yeah, Sunshine. Yes, you are. You can't do as I say and keep quiet, then I'mma make you stay quiet."

I don't have time to think. Next thing I know, Wyatt is pulling out of me and kneeling between my legs, his cock in his hand.

"Get up," he whispers.

I hesitate.

"Get up, Sally. Face me and get on all fours. I ain't playin'."

I *really* like it when he bosses me around. I do as he said, rolling over and pushing up so that I'm on my hands and knees, facing him. Leaning my weight on my left hand, I reach for him with my right.

"Yes, Daddy," I whisper.

My eyes have adjusted to the darkness, so I can see his nostrils flare as I wrap my hand around his dick and give it a slow, firm tug. Just how he taught me.

"Say it again. Call me that again." He pumps his hips into my grip.

"Yes, Daddy."

"Fuck," he pants. "That's a good girl. Now put me in your mouth. You know how to do it, Sunshine. Show me what you learned."

Sucking in a sharp breath, he runs his hand down the length of my spine. His fingers slip between my ass cheeks and find my pussy.

He shoves his dick inside my mouth at the same moment he shoves his fingers inside me. I gag, my body jerking, but he doesn't let up. Now he's circling those fingers over my clit. He's pumping into my mouth.

"You look so beautiful with my dick shoved down your throat," he whispers. "So fucking beautiful."

Oh God, I'm in agony.

I want to come so badly—I am so, *so* aroused—it literally hurts.

He grabs my hair and pulls it. Grabs my breast and plucks at my nipple.

I *come*. His cock is still in my mouth, muffling the sound of my cry as the shock wave hits.

"Never again," he grunts as he comes in my mouth a second later. "I'm never letting you sleep in any bed but mine again."

CHAPTER 27

Wyatt

THESE HAPPY GOLDEN YEARS

"WAIT, wait. Did you just say you're *roasting* a *chicken*?" Sally stares at me in disbelief from the threshold. She's still in her jacket and boots, and she's carrying a brown paper bag in her hand.

"I cook now, remember?" Smiling, I drop down to a squat and peer inside the oven. "Smells fuckin' good."

"Smells amazing. But you know Mom is—"

"Making dinner at the New House. I know. But I wanted you to myself tonight, so thought I'd do something here."

Sally blinks. Her face is flushed from the cold. "I love this idea."

"Thought you might. Go get comfortable." I nod in the direction of our bedroom. Yes, now that Sally's shit is in my drawers and she has a favorite side of the bed, it's *our* room. Not quite sure how to break it to her, but we'll get there. "I'll open the wine. I think there's a new episode of *Forensic Files* out."

She smiles. My heart leaps. My sweet girl has a bit of an obsession with gruesome true-crime shows, and I love getting to watch them with her every night.

"Great. I'll be right back."

"No rush, Sunshine."

"Thank you, handsome. This is"—she swallows—"such a nice surprise."

What I don't tell Sally? That I'm making Ina Garten's famous "engagement chicken," which apparently was the meal Emily Blunt and John Krasinski shared before he proposed to her.

Am I trying to manifest that shit? Maybe.

Do I want to ask Sally to marry me? Absolutely. I know she's leaving, but we'll figure that out later.

Who the fuck am I, I wonder as I open the wine, *and what good deed did I do in a past life to deserve a life like this?*

True to my word, I picked Sally up first thing in the morning after I visited her that night at her parents' house. She's been at my place ever since—a week and a half now. Every minute we're not working, we're together, often naked and sometimes sleeping.

We've settled into a nice, if exhausting, little routine. We wake up early—sleepy morning sex with Sally is my favorite —and then we're usually out the door by four thirty. We grab breakfast with our families at the New House. Then we kiss and go our separate ways. With calving season coming up, we've both been busy.

Sometimes, we'll cross paths during the day. A few days back, she was in the kitchen, helping Patsy prep dinner, so I snuck away from the herd and helped them prep too. Yesterday, Sally and John B were on Lucky River Ranch, helping Cash examine a pair of quarter horses he'd recently purchased, so I got to hang out with her in the barn and at lunch.

For the most part, though, we only see each other at the end of the day. I rush home. Sometimes, Sally is there; sometimes, she's still out. When she's home, we'll hop in the shower together. When she's not, I'll clean up on my own and try to keep my dick in check while I wait for her.

During the week, we'll have dinner at the New House with our families. I wouldn't say things are great between John B, Cash, and me, but they're getting better. I think now that everyone sees I mean business—I'm dating Sally out in the open, and I'm looking after her, treating her right—they're coming around.

They know I'm treating her right because the woman hasn't stopped smiling since the first night she slept at my place. Neither have I.

The timer on my phone chimes. I turn off the rice and give it a stir, then check on the green beans in the pot beside it.

I'm filling the wineglasses with some Oregon Pinot Noir—another Mollie Luck selection—when arms wrap around my middle.

"Hi." Sally leans her head against my back and pulls me to her. She takes a deep inhale.

"Hi." I smile, glancing over my shoulder. "Are you smelling me?"

"I am. You smell delicious. How was your day?"

"Better now. You?"

"It was awesome. I successfully fixed a broken femur this morning, and then I got to ride on horseback with the Hanovers' herd during lunch. It was a pretty great day."

I turn around and hand her a wineglass, then hold up my free hand. "Hell yeah, it was great. Proud of you, Sunshine."

She gives me the high five I'm looking for. But instead of letting her arm fall, she grabs my hand and twines our fingers, going up on her tiptoes to kiss me. "I have something for you."

"Oh, yeah?" I hook a finger in the waistband of her sweats, smiling like an idiot.

I love this woman's hunger. She's voracious for experience, for food and sex and sleep, and I'm more than a little thrilled to be the one indulging her.

She bites her lip. "Well, you're gonna get that too. But I got you a present." Turning around, she grabs the big paper bag she brought in earlier and holds it out to me, eyes glittering with excitement. "Hope you like it."

I blink. When was the last time I received an actual gift? For my birthday, Patsy will always make my favorite Texas sheet cake, and my brothers will take me out to The Rattler to get hammered. Every so often, Ella will give me the little arts-and-crafts projects she does at school. As a matter of fact, the tie-dye butterfly she made out of a coffee filter and a clothespin still hangs on my fridge.

I can't remember, though, when someone actually bought me something.

Setting my wine on the counter, I take the bag. I see there's a rectangular box inside wrapped in cowboy-boot-print paper.

"Cute," I say, removing the box from the bag. It's heavy.

Sally leans a hip into the counter. "I can't take credit for the wrapping. They did it at the store."

My heart dips. "Which store?"

"That adorable little bookstore in Lubbock. Drove out there today after lunch because only the best will do for Wyatt Rivers."

She's throwing my line back at me—the one I made about the fancy cowboy hat I bought for the potluck because I wanted to look good for her—and I love her cleverness, the way she cares, so damn much that I can hardly breathe around the happy swelling inside my chest.

"You didn't have to." My voice is husky.

"I wanted to." Sally nods at the package. "Open it."

I try to keep my hands from shaking too much as I carefully insert my finger underneath the seam of the wrapping paper and pull up the tape.

Sally chuckles. "You can tear the paper."

I don't want to tear the paper. I want to fold it up. Keep it forever, a memory of this moment.

The paper falls away, revealing a box set of all the *Little House on the Prairie* books.

I don't know whether to laugh, cry, or holler with delight.

My throat closes in.

They're just fucking books.

But when I glance up at Sally, it's clear we both know they're so much more than that.

"Since you and your mom enjoyed these stories so much, I thought you and I could revisit them," Sally says, and I notice her eyes get a little misty too. "Could be a cute way of keeping her memory alive?"

Her thoughtfulness.

Her insistence that I don't bottle shit up or sweep my grief under the rug.

Her bravery, confronting things that aren't easy to face.

I'm speechless.

Me, the guy who has a line for everything. The guy who can't help but crack a joke, deliver a verbal blow, tease the hell out of whoever I'm talking to.

I'm so fucking in love with this girl that I literally can't speak. For a split second, I worry I'm having a heart attack.

Please, God, don't let me die just when shit's getting good.

But you know what? My heart keeps beating. My lungs keep filling with air. My blood keeps pumping, making me feel more alive than I ever have.

More scared, yes. But I'm still standing, aren't I? Talking about Mom, revisiting my past—well, it hasn't killed me yet.

Holy shit, I'm actually okay.

"Thank you," I manage.

Sally sets down her wine and gently takes the box set from my hands. "You're welcome. Do we start chronologically?" She unwraps the plastic from the books. "Or do we dive right into your favorite? I do love *Little House in the Big Woods*, but *Farmer Boy* is, well, you. For us though, maybe *These Happy Golden Years* is the best way to go? I don't remember there being explicit sex in it, but we can make some up to add some literal and figurative spice? Jesus, listen to me. You've turned me into an absolute perv."

"Sally—"

"I know, I know. Not like you mind. I don't either, if I'm being honest." She surveys the books, running her fingertips over the spines. They're gingham, the color of Easter eggs—pastel blue, powder pink, violet. "They're so pretty, aren't they?"

"Sally—"

She looks up, drawing her brows together when she takes in my expression. "Shit, this is too cheesy, isn't it?" Her cheeks flush. "Or does it hit too close to home? I'm sorry. I was hoping it might make you feel better—"

"*Sally*—"

"Wyatt, really, it's okay—"

But she can't finish that thought because I'm grabbing her, one hand on her hip, the other sliding onto her face. Guiding her chin up, I lean down and angle my mouth so her top lip rests in the divot between my own. She closes her eyes.

I lick into her mouth, tasting my—her—toothpaste. We've used the same kind forever. But now we're using the same tube.

Weird I find that romantic?

I finally break the kiss, desperate for air, and rest my forehead on hers.

"So you don't hate the books then," she says thickly. Joyfully.

I scoff, my breath rustling the dark brown hair that falls into her face. "I fuckin' love 'em, Sally. Almost as much as I love you."

Her eyelashes flutter against my cheeks as her eyes fly open. I meet her gaze. This close, I can see the flecks of auburn in her irises that make them look like they're on fire.

My heart thunders, but somehow I'm able to keep my

voice even when I say, "Don't act so surprised, Sunshine. I'm in love with you. Been in love with you for a long, long time."

She opens her mouth. Closes it. Opens it again. "Really?"

The genuine surprise in her voice makes my chest cramp.

"Really. I realized it that day at the river right after my parents died, but I think I'd fallen for you way before then."

"My God." Her eyes well with tears. "Your tattoo…oh my *God*, Wyatt. Why didn't you tell me?"

I lift a shoulder, like I haven't been agonizing over that question for years. Decades. "You had so much to do. So many things to accomplish. You've always aimed so high, and I wasn't gonna stand in your way."

She fists her hand in my shirt. "Don't make me quote the corniest-slash-best love song ever written."

"What's that?"

Sally searches my eyes with an urgency that makes my pulse hiccup. "Ever consider you could never ever hold me back, even if you tried? You're not a roadblock, Wyatt. You're the wind beneath my fucking wings."

I erupt in a roar of loud, relieved laughter. "That's a great song."

"It's the best song. But I want you to know—I need you to understand"—she gives my shirt an angry pull—"I was in love with you too. Have been since…forever really."

My eyes burn. My body trembles, my gut a swirl of anger, sadness, relief. "We messed that one up, didn't we?"

She shakes her head, squeezing her eyes shut as her tears overflow. "You give me confidence. You make me laugh. You listen. You're always there for me, Wyatt." She opens her eyes. "All while you've been dealing with some heavy shit."

I swallow. "I thought you'd just leave again."

"What if I'm done leaving?"

My stomach plummets. We're finally talking about this. *Finally.*

"I can't ask you to stay."

"I don't need you to."

"Sally." Frustration grips me by the throat. "You have to go to New York. You made so many promises to yourself. I won't let you break them. And I promised your daddy—"

"That you wouldn't keep me here." Sally scoffs. "Of course my dad made that insanely inappropriate ask of you. I'm sorry."

"He's right."

"He's not though!"

My pulse seizes at her sudden outburst. I don't know what to do or say, so I just cup her face in my hands and thumb away her tears as she speaks.

"He's not right," she says, a little calmer. "I just—I can't leave you, Wyatt. I won't."

"What if I come with you?"

Her eyes bulge. Everything inside me heaves. Maybe she was ready to hear that I loved her, but she's not ready to hear I'd drop everything—my family, my job, my plans for the future—to be with her.

But then a small smile breaks out on her face. "You'd do that?"

"Stupid question."

"That's...wow. One hell of a gesture."

"I'm one hell of a boyfriend."

"Ha."

"All you need to do is ask, Sunshine. I'd say yes in a heartbeat."

I wait for her to ask as she studies my face, smile fading. I can see her wheels turning, the little divots between her brows a dead giveaway that she's deep in thought.

At last, she says, "But you have to stay, Wyatt. You belong here."

"Not if you're somewhere else."

Her eyes go soft. "I want to stay, Wyatt."

My heart riots. I want that too. So bad that it hurts. But she has to go back to Ithaca. I won't let her give up the job she's worked her whole life for.

I won't be the reason she lives a small life in a small town when she could make a big difference somewhere else.

I choose my words carefully. "I'll figure something out, okay?"

She twines our fingers. "*We'll* figure it out. Now that we're finally on the same team, let's not fuck it up."

But later, when we're making love in the dark, I find myself wondering how I can already miss her when she isn't even gone yet. Because Sally *is* leaving. She has to.

I just have to figure out a way to convince her to let me come with her.

CHAPTER 28

Sally

LOVE IS A COWBOY

I'M dead asleep when my phone rings.

Opening my eyes, I can't see a damn thing. The darkness is inky-black, complete.

I know before I even pick up my phone that it's Dad calling. The only numbers I don't silence overnight are Dad's, Mom's, and Wyatt's.

"You up, Sunshine?" Wyatt asks sleepily beside me.

"I'm up. Sorry."

"It's all right. What kinda emergency we got?"

I yank my phone off the charger. "I'm about to find out."

"Sorry to bug you, honey," Dad says when I answer. "But there was a fire over at the Wallace Ranch."

"Oh my God." My hand goes to my chest. "Is everyone okay?"

"Guess it was a small fire and they have it contained, but two of their horses were badly injured, trying to escape. Ava Bartlett is asking for you again."

"I'll be there ASAP."

Wyatt is already sitting up and turning on the lamp on his side of the bed. He rubs his hands over his face, the muscles in his arms and back bulging.

First, I take care of this emergency. *Then* I take care of the ever-present, always-raging desire I have for my boyfriend.

"Sounds good," Dad replies. "I'll meet you there. I have your supplies ready to go."

My heart twists. Despite his faults, Dad is a good man. A thoughtful one.

"Thanks."

"Drive careful."

"I will. Love you."

"Love you too." I hang up to see Wyatt getting out of bed. "What are you doing?"

"I'm coming with you."

He's naked—we're naked a lot these days—and I can't help but smile at how pale his butt is compared to the rest of him.

He has a really, really nice butt—bulbous, well-muscled, with a pair of freckles on the lower-left cheek.

"You don't have—"

"But I want to. If there was a fire, they're gonna need the extra hands. Besides, you ain't drivin' alone in the dark." Wyatt nods at the windows. "And, yeah, ever heard of competence porn?"

I'm grinning as he rounds the bed and holds out a hand, which I take. He pulls me out of bed.

"I have. I think about it often when I'm with you."

"You're the definition of it when you're workin'." He reaches around to grab my ass. "You'd best save some energy for me when you're done, 'cause I got a feeling I'm gonna be real hot and bothered by then."

"I think I can do that."

We're dressed and out the door in under five minutes. Wyatt holds out a glass bottle of Coke as we're trundling down the dirt road that connects Lucky River Ranch to Highway 21.

"I know it's not the same as a cup of coffee, but it'll get the job done," he says.

Grinning, I open the glove compartment and find the brass bottle opener we've used since—sheesh—even before we started mixing our Coke with Jack Daniel's.

"Thank you, handsome."

"Welcome, Sunshine."

I steal glances at Wyatt during the ride. He's wearing a backward baseball hat and his sherpa-lined jean jacket, and I watch his Adam's apple bob as he drinks his Coke.

I love this man. I love that he's with me right now. I fantasize about us doing this all the time. Not the middle-of-the-night-wake-up thing, because that sucks. But the going-to-work-together thing. We can do that here.

I just need to figure out what work I'd be doing exactly.

"What?" Wyatt asks when he catches me looking.

I shake my head. "I just like looking at you."

"Most people do."

Rolling my eyes, I smile as I reach across the console to swat his shoulder. "I regret the ego boost. You clearly don't need it."

"I might not need it, but I sure as hell don't mind it." He turns his head to look at me, dropping his empty bottle into the cupholder between us. "You all right?"

God, I hate how he picks right up on my moods. How he pays attention and how he cares.

I love it. I love everything about this man, and not having a solid plan for our future together is making me sick with anxiety.

"We're gonna be okay, right?"

Wyatt's chest barrels out on an inhale. He switches hands on the wheel and puts his right one on my leg. The motion is familiar now; he's done it plenty lately. Still makes my heart skip a beat the way it did the first time he touched me this way.

"We're gonna be okay, Sal."

We smell the smoke before we even turn onto the Wallace Ranch. Wyatt frowns as he guides the truck up to the horse barn. The lights are off; several windows are broken.

There are dozens of people, all of them milling around with flashlights and phones in their hands.

Wyatt and I hop out of the truck. He immediately finds Beck, who explains what happened. Apparently, the fire was started by some bad electrical wire in one of the stalls. The staff was able to put out the fire, but the barn sustained significant damage.

Side note: I love how Wyatt and Beck's little pissing contest has been put to bed. In true cowboy fashion, they've silently agreed that there's no time for grudges or awkwardness. This is ranch business—cowboy business—and that always comes first.

Dad is already here. He's standing with Ava and Vance in the gravel outside the barn's entrance.

"Structure is fine." Dad nods at the barn. "But the damage to the interior is extensive."

Ava nods. "Luckily, we got all the animals out. All but the two horses are okay. If y'all don't mind, I'd like to get a move on. We're keeping the injured animals in the arena up the hill."

Wyatt nods. "We're following you."

We climb back in the truck, and together with Dad and Ava, we form a little caravan that moves quickly through the silent dark.

The arena is massive—and massively impressive. I can smell the new lumber and fresh paint as I hop out of the truck. I've been to rodeos plenty, and I'm always impressed by the barrel racers I've seen. The Wallaces must really be serious about their program if they rolled this much money into a training facility.

Wyatt wordlessly moves to help Dad and me unload the equipment we need from the back of Dad's pickup.

Pays to date a cowboy, I think to myself as I put on my headlamp and walk into the dimly lit, soaring space of the arena. Especially a cowboy as knowledgeable and smart as Wyatt. I don't need to tell him to grab the portable X-ray. I definitely don't need to tell him to keep his footfalls quiet as we approach the animals in the makeshift stalls on one side of the arena.

Ava nods at the stall to the left. "This poor baby won't put weight on his front leg. And I think that one"—she motions to the next stall—"has issues with the back left leg."

I loop my stethoscope around my neck. "Did anyone see what happened?"

"No, but I can guess. The horses panicked, and these two ended up getting trampled."

"Any burns?"

"None that I saw, no."

My stomach clenches. I meet eyes with Wyatt.

He approaches the first horse before me. He's not being rude; he's just making sure I'm not also going to get trampled by a skittish, injured colt who weighs as much as a car.

"Hey, buddy." Wyatt keeps his voice low and soft.

The colt is a beautiful animal, its shiny black coat gleaming in the overhead lights. But the rapid rise and fall of his sides are a dead giveaway that he's in pain.

"We're just here to help. You're hurting, aren't you? You're gonna be okay."

Wyatt moves slowly, holding up his hands. When he reaches for the horse, the colt whinnies and pulls away, his eyes wild.

My cowboy, however, won't be deterred. "You got the best surgeon in the world here to take care of you. That's right. You're gonna feel so much better after she helps you."

Wyatt strokes the horse's back in steady, careful movements, and slowly but surely, the horse calms down.

Meanwhile, I'm bursting with...I don't even know what. Worry for the horse. Adoration for Wyatt.

Excitement that I get to do what I love, with the man that I love.

I belong here. Deep down, I think I've always known that, but Dad's dreams for me overshadowed my desire to return to Texas and make a life here.

After a few minutes, Wyatt has the colt literally eating out of his hand. Because again, Wyatt is a cowboy, and he thought to stuff apples into the pockets of his jacket on his way out the door.

Rubbing the colt's nose, Wyatt glances at me over his shoulder. "I think he's ready for you, Dr. Powell."

Blinking, I put the tips of my stethoscope in my ears. "Thank you, Mr. Rivers."

Out of the corner of my eye, I catch Ava leaning into Dad and asking, "Do they always refer to each other that way?"

"That appears to be...new."

I don't have time to decipher Dad's tone. I get to work, listening to the colt's heart and stomach, while Wyatt strokes him, keeping him calm.

He gets skittish when I bend down to examine his injured leg.

Wyatt puts a hand on the colt's neck to keep him steady. Then he looks down and says, "It looks like a compound fracture."

I frown. "How can you tell?"

"A few years back, Ryder's horse broke his leg in three places trying to jump a fence." Wyatt nods at the injury. "It looked a lot like that—the swelling, that dislocated bone there."

I confirm as much with a series of radiographs that show a gnarly break in the horse's front-right radius.

"Good call, Wy," I say, mentally calculating the amount of anesthesia we'll need for a horse this size.

Even Dad says, "You really know your shit, don't you?"

"Learned from the best." Wyatt looks at Dad. "And by that, I mean you. And Garrett."

I smile. "You got a world-class education in cowboying—that's for damn sure."

"Not as fancy as yours—"

"But just as important." I glance at Dad. "All right, y'all, it's gonna be all hands on deck. We're going to have to use plates, screws, and cables to fix this guy, but I'm almost positive we can do it."

Ava looks like she's about to cry. "I'm so relieved to hear that I can't even tell you. Thank you, Sally. Thank all y'all for coming out tonight."

Wyatt and I meet eyes.

We're always looking at each other this way, aren't we? Finding each other across the room. Checking in with each other.

It's the best, most ridiculous thing ever.

"Happy to," Wyatt says. "We're in our element."

———

When the colt is sedated, Wyatt crouches by my side. Together, we talk through what my plan is for the repair. He asks a lot of questions—*Why put the screw there? What can the cables do that a plate can't?*—and time flies as I answer them.

Dad and Vance join us in the stall as I begin to operate. We all chat amiably as the surgery progresses. When I start to sweat, Wyatt somehow rummages up a bottle of water *and* a straw, so I'm able to drink it without taking off my gloves.

He chuckles when I'm inserting the screws with a drill. "No wonder you like all those murdery shows. You'd make an excellent serial killer."

I laugh, the ache in my knees and eyes easing ever so slightly. "I do the opposite of dismemberment." I gesture to the horse's leg. "Look, I literally put bodies back together."

"Which means you know how to take 'em apart, too, don't you?"

I crank my drill. "Keep talking shit, and you're gonna find out."

He smiles, and I do too. By the time the surgery is done and I'm wrapping up the colt's leg, I've laughed so hard and talked so much that I'm exhausted beyond belief, but also buzzing with energy.

This is what happiness feels like, I think as Wyatt hands me an enormous cardboard cup of coffee and an egg-and-cheese biscuit from Mrs. Wallace's kitchen.

I think the same thing when Wyatt digs his thumbs into the sore muscles at the bottom of my neck while Dad and Vance prep the next horse for surgery, the mini massage making goose bumps break out on my arms.

Meanwhile, Ava fills me in on Pepper's recovery. She's doing so well that I give Ava permission to let her out of box rest.

The realization crystallizes with sudden, startling clarity. This sense of belonging, of being appreciated, of community —*that* is what I'm missing in Ithaca. The connection I feel to this place and these people is what makes my work here so satisfying.

Dad's never worked anywhere else, so maybe he doesn't understand how awful it is to practice surgery in a place that values prestige over people, success over saving lives.

In Hartsville, people focus on the right things.

They spend their time and energy doing right by their neighbors, their families, their animals.

They're proud people, and they should be. There's a real sense here that we're all in this together, which makes the work feel so much more meaningful, like it matters. Like I matter. At the big universities where I've worked, it feels very dog eat dog, like everyone is out for themselves.

That's just not who I am. That's not who Mom and Dad raised me to be. And maybe me choosing community and character over a fancy job title will make them proud.

Sure as hell makes *me* proud. And that's ultimately what has to matter, isn't it?

"You need me to give you a *Rocky* pep talk, or are you good?" Wyatt asks. "I know you're running on fumes."

"I'm good. You've gotta be wiped too, Wy. You don't have to stay. I know your brothers—"

"Are fine. I like watching you screw…things in."

"You're funny."

"You got this."

I grin. "I do."

———

Ava just stares at the filly, slowly shaking her head. "You're a miracle worker, Sally."

"Let's not speak too soon. I'm cautiously optimistic about this one—"

"Which means this sweet girl's gonna be just fine." Wyatt nods at the horse.

The filly's surgery was thankfully less complicated than the colt's. Turned out, she had broken ribs and a fractured tibia, which didn't require any plates to correct.

I'm thrilled with how it went. I'm also dead on my feet as I watch Dad and Vance clean up the stall.

"I truly can't thank y'all enough." Ava's gaze catches on mine. "You really are talented. When the Wallaces asked me to start their training program here—"

"Training program?" Wyatt asks.

"They're hoping to get involved in the barrel racing

circuit," I explain. "Breed horses, train riders. A little bit of everything."

Which, come to think of it, could be an opportunity worth investigating. I've operated plenty on racehorses.

"But, yeah," Ava continues, "I didn't realize the level of expertise y'all would have in Hartsville in terms of veterinary care. I've truly never seen anything like it, and I feel like I've seen it all."

"How long were you on the circuit?" I ask.

Ava gets a wistful look in her eyes. "Five years, but I feel like I'd trained my whole life for it."

"You miss it?"

"Yes and no. I was ready to be done. When I got pregnant with my daughter, I knew it was time."

"Oh!" Wyatt lights up. "How old is your daughter?"

"She's three."

I look at Wyatt. "We need to introduce her to Ella, don't we?"

"My brother also has a three-year-old little girl," Wyatt explains. "Fun age."

"Very fun. And very intense."

"We'll have to get y'all together."

Ava smiles. "I'd like that."

"Are you trying to set Ava up with Sawyer?" I ask when Wyatt and I are safely out of earshot in his truck.

Wyatt chuckles. "Hell yeah I'm trying to set Ava up with Sawyer. They both have three-year-old girls. They're both lonely."

"How do you know Ava's lonely? No, wait. How do you even know if she's single?"

He shrugs. "She's not wearing a ring, and I haven't heard of a husband or boyfriend hangin' around. I'd bet good money she's single."

But me? I'm taken. And I think I might be slowly coming up with a plan to make sure that never, ever changes.

———

Wyatt, Dad, and I head back to Lucky River Ranch later that morning. We have lunch with everyone at the New House. After inhaling Mom's chicken potpie, I wilt against Wyatt's shoulder. I feel like I need toothpicks to keep my eyes open.

Cash wipes his mouth, rising from his chair at the table across from us. "Why don't y'all head home? We got the herd handled."

I feel Wyatt go still. Cash offering to cover for his brother so Wyatt and I can rest—*together*—is a big deal.

"You sure?"

"Long as these clowns don't cut up too much." Cash knocks the baseball hat off Duke's head.

"Dude!" Duke says. "Don't mess with the hat. I'm havin' a bad hair day."

Mollie grins from her chair beside Cash's. Ella is in her lap, and Mollie is patiently braiding her long blonde hair into two plaits. "That some bedhead you have going on?"

"Wait, who the hell are you gettin' in bed with?" Ryder asks.

Duke just smirks. "Gentlemen don't kiss and tell."

"Good thing you're no gentleman," Wyatt replies.

"What's a gentleman?" Ella asks.

Cash leans down to press a kiss to her cheek. "Me. I'm a gentleman."

"Not always," Mollie replies with a smirk of her own.

Cash gives her nape a squeeze. "I won't elaborate in polite company, but you ain't wrong, honey."

Wyatt bends his neck and looks down at me. His eyes are bloodshot, but he still smiles at the inside joke we silently share between us—Wyatt's no gentleman either.

You turn me into an animal, he says, the skin at the edges of his eyes crinkling.

Wouldn't have it any other way, I reply, turning my head so I can kiss his arm through his shirt.

"But, yes, a break is what Sally deserves for performing yet more miracles," Cash continues.

"Wyatt performed some miracles of his own," I reply.

Cash arches an eyebrow. "Do I want to know more?"

"He got the horses in a good place. Calmed them down so I was able to do my thing with no issues," I reply. "He's the best surgical assistant I think I've ever had. Other than Dad, of course."

"Really?" Cash looks at his brother in disbelief.

"I've never had an assistant bring me a breakfast biscuit before or look so good doing it, so, yes, really."

Wyatt pops his cuffs. "Y'all are gonna make me blush."

"Go home." Cash waves us away. "Y'all did good today."

At Wyatt's house, we take a quick shower. I know I'm exhausted when I'm too tired to have hot shower sex with my very hot boyfriend, despite him helping me come to the realization earlier today that happiness is not success or big salaries, but community and caretaking and dating cute cowboys.

This particular cowboy has turned my world upside down in all the best ways.

We fall into bed and pass out hard. Next thing I know, late afternoon light is streaming through the windows. Wyatt is awake, his head turned on the pillow so that our eyes meet.

His look is so piercingly blue that my heart turns over.

"Hungry?" His voice is gravelly with sleep.

I reach for him. "Yes."

———

Later, after dinner, we plop on the couch with our laptops to catch up on work. As foreman, Wyatt is overhauling large chunks of the ranch along with his brothers, and his responsibilities include keeping up with a heinous amount of emails, spreadsheets, invoices, and projections.

I type up my notes from today's surgeries and email them to Dad, Vance, and Ava. I check the shipment status of some surgical supplies I ordered earlier this week.

Then I draft a letter of resignation and digitally sign it with today's date.

My stomach churns when I attach it to an email to my adviser and press Send. I close my laptop and let out a deep breath.

Then I smile.

I have no fucking clue what to do next when it comes to my career. Do I form an official partnership with Dad? Start my own practice? Ask Ava to hire me?

I don't know.

I just know my work—my life—is here now.

My heart has always been here in Texas. I just had to open my eyes and see that for myself.

Wyatt glances at me, the glow of his laptop screen catching on the straight slope of his nose, the fullness of his lips. "Somebody's happy."

Do I tell him what I just did? I could. I probably should. But part of me wants to surprise him with a grand gesture. Wyatt went to enormous lengths to ensure our first date was one to remember. It was cute, how big of a deal he made it. And he lost his mind when I gave him the *Little House on the Prairie* books. I also know my adviser is going to freak out when he gets this letter, and I might have to wade through some very unpleasant shit before my resignation is official.

And, yeah, I have to tell my parents. I feel like it would help lessen the blow if I came up with a plan, however preliminary, for my future employment.

I decide not to tell anyone my news for the moment.

Tonight, I'm going to celebrate having a great day, filled with great people, by doing what I love—my cowboy.

I could go for some true-crime TV, too, just because.

"Very happy," I say, and I mean it. "Wanna watch some *Forensic Files*?"

"As long as I'm not your next victim, sure."

CHAPTER 29

Wyatt

DESPERADO

I CLEAR MY THROAT. "SO..."

Sawyer glances at me over his shoulder and smiles. "So..."

Ordinarily, I'd want to slap that stupid, knowing smile off his face. It's early—the bright orange ball of the sun is just breaking over the horizon—and so cold that I can see my breath. I wouldn't say I'm cranky at this time of day, but I sure as hell don't feel like dealing with my brothers' bullshit.

But today?

Today, I just smile back, even though my stomach is a knot of nerves. "If y'all wouldn't mind me takin' a minute of your time, I have something I'd like to talk to you about. All of you."

The five of us are on horseback. We're bringing the herd out to graze in a pasture not far from the New House. I once heard someone give Sawyer parenting advice, saying that you should talk to your kids about tough topics in the car. No one can escape, and you're also driving, meaning you don't have to look anyone in the eye as you bring up horrifically uncomfortable shit.

Figure the same applies to being on horseback. I can

pretend to be busy keeping an eye on the cows, while telling my brothers the news.

Cash reins in his big black horse, Kix. "Everything all right?"

"Everything is great."

Duke drapes his forearms over the pommel of his saddle. "You knocked up Sally, didn't you?"

"Would you hush?" Ryder turns to me. "But I bet it's twins. We do run in the family."

I roll my eyes. "Y'all—"

"Sally and Wyatt, sitting in a tree," Sawyer singsongs. "First comes friendship, then comes boning, then comes baby in the baby carriage and maybe marriage?"

Even Cash is grinning, which I take to be a good sign.

"What happened to growling at me?" I ask him.

Cash splays his hand. "John B and Patsy ain't left yet. You're still showin' up to work. And, yeah, I see how happy you and Sally are when you're together."

I just stare at him.

"I'm allowed to change my mind," he says with a shrug. "Sometimes, people surprise you."

I shake my head. "Mollie teach you that?"

"She's taught me a lot of things, yeah."

"What's Sally teachin' you?" Sawyer asks, a twinkle in his eye.

Taking a deep inhale, I look out across the pasture. The rising sun turns everything it touches to gold—the nearby cliffs; an enormous, ancient oak to our left; the knobby cacti that spike up from the brush along a split-rail fence.

I can smell the earthy scent of the Colorado River above the even earthier odors of the herd. Cows low. My horse nickers, but he otherwise ignores the way Sawyer's mare flicks him with her tail.

I know this land better than anyone. I was born here, and I always assumed I'd die here too.

Maybe I will. Maybe I won't. Doesn't really matter anymore though. 'Cause as long as I do right by Sally, I'm gonna die a happy man.

I'll miss Texas like crazy. I'll always miss my family. But that's what planes are for, right?

I clear my throat, squinting against the growing light. "Think y'all could get by around here without me?"

Silence.

My heart drums in my throat as my brothers stare at me, wide-eyed looks on their faces.

"That mean what I think it does?" Cash asks at last.

I dip my head. "I'm moving to New York with Sally. That's only if she'll let me, of course—"

"She's gonna let you." Sawyer reaches over and claps a hand on my shoulder. "I'm so fucking happy for you, Wy."

"But really, is Sally pregnant?" Cash asks.

I laugh. "No, she's not pregnant. She wants to be, then, yeah, I'm more'n happy to make that happen. But that's not why we're moving in together. And moving together. *Hopefully* moving together. I wanna do things right." I glance at Cash. "Which is why I wanted to talk to y'all first. Our family, this ranch—you're my world. I don't want—" Christ, I'm gonna cry. "I wouldn't leave if I didn't have to. But I gotta follow my girl, you know? I gotta help her make her dreams come true because, well, Sally *is* my dream."

Sawyer squeezes my shoulder. "Then you gotta follow your girl."

"We have so much going on here." I gesture to our left, where a construction site is just visible. That's Mollie's new studio going up, along with part of the road that will eventually link the former Luck Ranch with the Rivers Ranch. "I understand that this is a terrible time for me to duck out—"

"But you do what you have to do." Cash's tone is kind, which makes the tears fall faster. "I understand."

Wiping my eyes, I sniffle. "You mean that?"

It suddenly seems silly to me that I ever expected this conversation to go any other way. Of course my brothers are going to support me. Even Cash. If anyone has learned about the power and the importance of love, it's him.

"Yeah, I mean that. I know making this decision couldn't have been easy for you."

"It wasn't." I straighten in the saddle. "At the same time, it was the easiest decision I've ever made. Do I wish Sally and I could be together here in Hartsville? Hell yeah, I do. But that's not the hand we've been dealt, so I gotta play the cards we do have the best I can."

Sawyer's lips twitch. "You would make that metaphor."

"You would fall right the fuck off that horse if I pushed you."

His eyes glimmer. "I dare you."

"Sally'll fix him right up," Ryder says.

I nod. "She does have a way with a drill."

"That's not funny," Sawyer replies.

Duke guffaws. "It kinda is though."

"You haven't told her any of this? Sally?" Cash asks, one eye shut against the sun.

"I haven't. Kinda want to make it a big thing. Wear an *I Love New York* shirt or something. Really show her I'm serious about being there for her, that I'm excited to support her. Had to get y'all's blessing first, though, because I know this is a decision that affects all of us. I know she's gonna want to see that y'all will get along just fine without me."

Cash sniffles.

My turn to stare.

"Yeah, I'm gonna miss your ass." He lifts his shoulder and uses it to wipe his nose. "I'm also happy for you. Really fucking happy, Wy. Mom…you know she's celebrating up in heaven, right? Just yelling at the top of her lungs, *Fucking finally!*"

I'm laughing and I'm crying, and so are all my brothers.

Conversations about my parents have always made me feel a gut punch of grief. And the grief is still there. But I also feel... a little more at peace now than I did in the past. Like deep down, I know that while I might miss Mom like crazy, talking about her isn't going to kill me.

The grief is not going to kill me.

"I've been thinking about her a lot lately." I reach for my rope when a steer starts to stray from the herd. Drop my hand when he gets back in line on his own. "She and Dad had to make a lot of sacrifices. Not just for us, but for each other too. Dad inherited this huge ranch, and I'm not sure Mom ever pictured herself becoming a rancher too. But she did it because she loved him. He made it work because he loved her. And they were happy. At least I *think* they were happy, from what I remember anyway."

Cash gets a faraway look in his eyes. "They were happy. Things weren't perfect, obviously. But I feel like they were okay with the sacrifices they'd made." He glances at me. "Just like you're gonna be okay with yours."

"You're also not moving to the moon," Sawyer adds.

Cash nods. "You can still be a part of things here. We're gonna need a new foreman, but maybe we can come up with a new role for you. Strategic planning or some shit? I don't know."

Duke smiles. "Mollie is rubbing off on you. I like it."

"She's got a brain for business, that's for damn sure." Cash looks at me, his hat casting half his face in shadow. "And she'll help us think of a way to keep you involved, Wyatt. Because I know you want to honor Mom and Dad's legacy."

I'm just shy of bawling. "I do want that, yeah."

"We all do," Duke says. "So it's important we make our dreams for the ranch come true together. You being in New York won't change that."

"Do you promise not to call me a Yankee asshole?"

Duke thinks on this. "That is a promise I don't feel comfortable making, no. You gotta give us *something* to work with."

"And you"—I glance at Sawyer—"will you fly up with Ella to visit us?"

He smiles. "Are you kidding? She'll get a kick out of getting on an airplane to visit her uncle Wy."

"I am her favorite."

"No, you're not." Cash makes a face. "I am."

Ryder points at us. "Wrong and very wrong. I'm the favorite."

"If by favorite, you mean *least* favorite, then, yes, you're correct," Duke replies.

"Have you thought about what you're gonna do up there?" Cash asks.

I slip my sunglasses on. "I have. I'll figure out something. Don't imagine they have operations like this one in upstate New York, but there's bound to be work available for a country boy somewhere."

Sawyer grins. "You could have some babies and raise 'em up. That's always an option."

"Y'all are really pushing this baby thing."

"Ella needs cousins." Sawyer looks at Cash. "You and Mollie makin' any progress on that front?"

One side of Cash's mouth kicks up. "We're givin' it a go."

My heart twists. I'm gonna hate not being here for all of this. I know Sally will too.

But that just means we'll be visiting Hartsville often. She loves my brothers as much as I do, and I know she'll make every effort to be here for the big moments and the not-so-big ones too.

There are multiple major airports in Texas with multiple flights a day to and from New York. We're going to make this work.

We have to.

And who knows? Maybe she and I will eventually end up back in Hartsville down the road. Her parents are here, too, and they're going to want to have a hand in raising any babies Sally and I do have.

Because *of course* I want to have babies with Sally. Can't believe I didn't realize it was a possibility until now.

More than a possibility. A certainty. Because I am gonna make this work.

I am gonna make Sally my wife.

"I love y'all," I say. "Thank you. For understanding. And for, well, putting up with me all these years."

Cash gives me a look. "You definitely owe us. You were fuckin' unhinged in your twenties."

"Good thing I'm in my thirties now." I pass the reins from my right hand to my left. "I got a favor I'd like to ask. Would y'all help me ask Sally?"

"To marry you?" Duke furrows his brow.

"I feel like I should ask her if she'd let me come to New York with her first and show her I have y'all's blessing to move," I say with a chuckle. "We've only been dating for, like, two and a half seconds."

Ryder shakes his head. "But you've been friends for two and a half lifetimes."

"Wyatt's right." Cash tips his hat in my direction. "Let's not scare sweet Sally off by rushin' things. When he bares his heart, it's supposed to be a big, romantic gesture, not an ambush."

"Agreed," Sawyer says.

Cash flashes me a smile. "Lucky for you, Wyatt, I got some ideas."

CHAPTER 30

Sally

SHOTGUN, SIDE OF SMOKED TURKEY

"IS THIS THE DRESS?" I ask, doing a small spin in front of Mollie and Wheeler.

Wheeler lets out a low whistle. "Honey, that is *the* dress."

"If there was ever a dress to wear while declaring your undying love for your best friend, that's the one." Mollie claps her hands before she pulls me in for a hug. "I am thrilled you're staying in Hartsville. I keep wanting to pinch myself. Obviously I was thrilled you'd landed that gig at Ithaca University, but I know I'm not alone when I say I was hoping you'd stick around here for the long haul. We love you, friend."

"I love you too." Stepping back, I smooth the exquisite crepe fabric of the dress over my thighs. It's fire-engine red, a shade that matches my favorite Bellamy Brooks boots. It feels like buttery silk as it swishes against my bare legs.

Smiling, I examine myself in the full-length mirror that's tucked into a corner of Mollie's former bedroom in the New House.

When I officially resigned from Ithaca University during a call with my adviser a few days back, I decided to put together a little last-minute Friendsgiving celebration so I could share the happy news—well, hopefully happy—with everyone. I want the chance to explain myself.

I also want Wyatt to see how committed I am to our relationship. By publicly declaring my intention to stick around, I hope he sees just how much I want to be with him.

Just how much I love him and how proud I am of the community we're building here in Hartsville.

To be honest, I've gone back and forth a million times as to whether or not this whole thing is a good idea. What if Dad flips out? What if I embarrass myself—or worse, embarrass Wyatt?

Mollie convinced me to go for it. She was the first person I confided in after I hung up on that call with my adviser. When I floated the idea of making the already-grand gesture of passing up a dream job even grander, Mollie was immediately on board.

"Cash is allergic to drama," she said. "But Wyatt? I mean, the guy agreed to fake date you even though he knew he was never gonna be able to keep it in his pants. Wyatt *lives* for the drama. You wanna go big, I say you go *big*. Love your man out loud, friend. Live your best damn life out loud."

Which is how I ended up in this dress, a Gucci number I borrowed from Mollie's closet. It's special, it's sparkly, and it's giving me just the boost of confidence I need to, well, go big.

"You look fabulous," Mollie says. "And you don't look *too* too nervous."

"Well, that's a surprise, because I'm so nervous that I feel like I'm going to vomit. I promise I'm gonna try real hard not to ruin this dress, Mollie."

She just smiles and tucks my hair behind my ear. "Don't worry about the dress. Worry instead about how Wyatt is gonna break you in two when he takes you home tonight."

"That man is feral in bed, isn't he?" Wheeler asks wistfully.

Mollie is still smiling. "That's what Miss Sally asked for—

to have fun with feral cowboys. And look what happened! You asked the universe for what you wanted, and lo and behold, you got it."

"You're forgetting the twenty years I wanted Wyatt, but didn't so much as lay a finger on him. I didn't think he'd ever be into a girl like me. More than that, I was afraid I'd end up losing him if we ever did become more than friends."

"But because you finally had the guts to ask for him anyway"—Mollie snaps her fingers—"it happened."

"It did." A burst of excitement—of joy and anticipation and heady disbelief—rockets through me. "I feel like I'm in the twilight zone. Like, I'm making such a mess of things. I don't know what I'm going to do about a job. Yeah, I'm practically living with Wyatt, but we haven't talked about moving in together—"

"He wants you to move in," Wheeler says. "You know he does."

Mollie solemnly nods. "It is known that Wyatt Rivers would have put a ring on Sally Powell's finger yesterday."

I want to protest, to wave off their comments.

Instead, I smile. They're right.

This all feels so, so right.

"Point being, I had a plan—a very good, very sensible plan—and now I have no plan, other than to make a life in Hartsville with Wyatt."

Wheeler shrugs. "Sounds like a solid plan to me. You'll figure out the rest."

"If y'all want to make it work, you'll make it work," Mollie adds. "I know it can happen from personal experience."

I am so happy, I might burst. "That's the hope."

"We'll let your dad know we're actively working on the job part." Mollie winks. "I get that you're anxious about how he's going to react."

Anxious enough to feel like I'm about to pass out, yeah.

"I just wish he'd trust me. I've never made a bad decision or disappointed him. I'm not making a bad decision now."

Mollie grabs my hand. "I'm proud of you for sticking to your guns."

Let's hope Dad feels that way too.

———

Mom and I have been prepping food for Friendsgiving for days now, but I still spent the morning in the kitchen at the New House, taking care of last-minute tasks—setting the big farm table with the prettiest china and glassware, squeezing lemons for the maple bourbon sours I'll serve, taking the turkey we smoked yesterday out of the fridge to come to room temperature.

I'm back in the kitchen at half past four in my red dress, the plan being that everyone arrives around five o'clock. Wyatt had a meeting with Cash and their contractor to discuss plans for the new horse barn they want to put up on the Rivers' side of the ranch, so he's been gone all afternoon.

I can't wait to see him.

Really, I can't wait to see his face when I tell everyone I'm staying in Hartsville. He's going to be so, so happy. I wonder if he'll ask me to move in with him.

I wonder how Mom is going to react to Dad's reaction. She's been nothing but supportive of my relationship with Wyatt, but I also know she's so proud of my education and the future I had lined up for myself. Then again, she did encourage me to follow my heart when I we talked that afternoon in the kitchen. Surely, she'll be happy for me—for us —right?

I put on an apron to protect Mollie's dress. My hands shake as I stuff them into a pair of potholders and take the gigantic eighteen-pound turkey out of the oven. Reheating it has made the kitchen smell insanely delicious, like hickory smoke and the caramelized onions I made. My stomach grumbles, despite the nerves that have taken up residence there.

"Wow, that smells good."

I nearly drop the turkey at the sound of the voice behind me. Setting the roasting pan on top of the range, I turn and see Dad step into the kitchen.

He's carrying two reusable grocery bags. I know without asking what's in them—Mom's pecan pie, some kind of Thanksgiving-themed gift for Ella, and the linen napkins Mom pressed for me that match the china.

My heart twists when I see how tired he looks, the rings around his eyes deep purple. For half a heartbeat, my resolve wavers. Last thing I want to do is stress Dad out more than he already is. He works so damn hard and worries so much.

But I can't take that on as my problem anymore. It's not my job to fix that, just like it's not his job to live my life for me.

"I'm glad Mom invested in the Big Green Egg," I say, referencing the egg-shaped smoker we used for the turkey. "I think this is gonna be delicious. How are you?"

He sets down the bags. "I'm all right. Long day, but that's nothing new. Your mom wanted me to drop these things off while she was in the shower back home. I've been looking forward to your Friendsgiving all week."

"I have too." Reaching behind me, I untie the apron and pull it over my head. "I think this could be a fun tradition, you know? A little more casual than Thanksgiving, but you still get the good food and the good wine. Plus, you get to choose your guests. Kind of the best of both worlds."

That's when I realize Dad is staring at me. Specifically, he's staring at my red dress, a hard expression coming over his face.

"Awfully dressed up for a casual dinner," he says.

My stomach drops a hundred stories. "It's still a special occasion."

"Only other time I've seen you get this dolled up was when you went to the potluck with Wyatt—you know, when you swore up and down that the two of you were *just friends*."

Oh Lord. Dad is onto me, because *of course* he is. He knows me better than almost anyone.

"What's going on, Sally?" He flattens his palms on the island countertop. "Please don't lie to me this time."

I meet his eyes. The saliva in my mouth thickens. "Tonight is the celebration of a new beginning. I'm"—*just keep breathing*—"not taking the job at Ithaca University."

Silence.

Terrible, awful silence that rings with dad's judgment. His disapproval.

My face burns. I can't go back now though. In for a penny, in for a pound.

"Hear me out?" I ask.

A muscle in Dad's jaw tics. "Okay."

"I've realized something since coming back to Hartsville. I always felt there was a piece missing from my life in Ithaca, but I could never really put my finger on it. I loved my work, but there was this…I guess this sense of loneliness I felt? Isolation? Our professors put so much pressure on us to do more surgeries, do more research, really push ourselves to be the best. But for what? It was always about the bottom line there. The grants we could get, the press, the accolades. I felt like it wasn't about the animals or even the people, you know? And while Ithaca University was a good fit for my residency, I don't think it's a good fit for the rest of my life. I want to take what I learned there and bring it here—"

"You have a higher calling than that."

A flare of anger ignites in my gut. "What higher calling could there be than to serve my community? Than to feed my soul by doing work that's meaningful, alongside people I love?"

"Trust me when I say you don't want this life—"

"Trust me when I say that just because we live in the same *place* doesn't mean we're going to have the same *life*."

Dad blinks, clearly taken off guard by my vociferous defense of the choice I'm making. I've never spoken to him this way.

Come to think of it, I'm not sure I've ever defied him, not even when I was little.

"You have to trust me," I say. "I wouldn't be staying in Hartsville if I didn't think there was opportunity for me to make a real difference. But I love the friends and family I have here—"

"You fell in love with Wyatt, and that's why you're staying." Dad grimaces. "Just say it."

"I did fall in love with him. But he's not the reason I'm staying. Not the *only* reason."

Dad's hand curls into a fist. "This is a mistake. I told him—"

"I know what you told him."

"What kind of man lets his partner pass up the opportunity of a lifetime?"

"Wyatt doesn't know—"

"I can't believe he betrayed me this way."

"No one betrayed you!" I scoff. "Don't you see? This is a good thing, Dad. Your daughter choosing happiness is a good thing."

He glances at me, and the furious glitter in his eyes makes my breath catch. "I disagree. You know how much I regret not doing more with my life. The opportunities I missed out on, the chance to save lives, the money…you can have all that, and you don't want it?" He scoffs. "Who the hell do you think you are?"

Then he abruptly turns and heads for the door.

"Dad—"

He holds up a hand. "Let me be, Sally."

"Where are you going?"

"I said, *let me be*." He grabs the door and yanks it open.

I jump when he slams it shut.

Well, that went way, way worse than I'd thought. I understand why Dad would be disappointed. But to get angry like that? To blame Wyatt, assume the worst about him?

That's taking it a step too far.

My legs feel like rubber as I ball up the apron I'm still holding, toss it onto the counter, and follow him. But I'm already too late. By the time I'm out in the yard, Dad is peeling out of there in his pickup truck, the tires kicking up gravel.

I try to think. Where would Dad be heading? I don't think he'd tuck tail and go back home. He's too pissed to do that.

I bet he's looking for Wyatt.

Oh God, what is Dad gonna do to Wyatt?

If I had to guess, my boyfriend is either still at the ranch office or in the barn, putting up the horses.

I decide to head for the barn. Running back inside to grab my phone, I throw on my jacket and head into the deepening twilight. Praying all the while that I'm not too late.

CHAPTER 31

Wyatt

CRACK SHOT

SURVEYING OUR MATCHING T-SHIRTS, Ryder shakes his head. "I feel like a member of some stupid, shitty-ass boy band."

"Then you can go *bye, bye, bye*," Sawyer singsongs as he zips up his jacket.

Ryder curls his lip. "Since when are you a Backstreet Boys fan?"

"That's an *NSYNC reference, thank you very much," Sawyer replies. "I put on boy-band playlists when Ella's in the car with me. I feel like they're harmless enough, right? There's a reason why girls love them."

"That reason ain't these shirts," Ryder says with a groan.

I'm laughing as I zip up my own jacket. "You have to wear it for ten minutes. Fifteen, tops. Y'all remember how it goes, right? We line up in the kitchen—keep your coats on, don't forget that—and then when we have Sally's attention—"

"We strip down and hump the floor." Duke nods. "Got it."

Sawyer, Ryder, Duke, and I are having a quick little meeting at my place before we head over to the New House for Sally's Friendsgiving. Cash spent the day with Mollie, but he's on his way back to the ranch, and I was sure to give him marching orders when we spoke earlier this morning.

When Sally proposed the get-together, I immediately knew it was the perfect time to lay it all on the line and let her know I was willing to go to the ends of the earth to keep us together.

Cash ordered the T-shirts, Sawyer picked up the champagne, and I wrote draft after draft of the things I wanted to say to her in front of our families and friends.

Feels a lot like a marriage proposal. But I don't mind that one bit. Figure the more practice I have, the better I'm gonna be when I do pop the big question.

If I had my way, I'd pop it sooner rather than later. I figure we'll see how tonight goes, and I'll come up with a plan from there.

Sawyer chuckles. "Ella is gonna lose her damn mind. Speaking of, I'm gonna run and grab her from the sitter. Meet y'all at the house in fifteen?"

"Sounds good. And Sawyer?" I ask.

"Yeah?"

"Thank you." I swallow. "Thank all y'all."

"I get the farmhouse when he leaves," Ryder says.

He and Duke are still living in the bunkhouse while renovations start on some potential housing for them on our family's side of the ranch.

Duke shakes his head. "You're gonna have to fight me for it."

"I'm still here," I say.

Ryder pulls me in for a hug. "You ready?"

"I've been ready for years. Let's do this thing."

Sawyer takes his truck to his place while the rest of us pile into one of Lucky River Ranch's new F-350s and head to the New House. I've been using this truck all day, which explains why my thermos is in the cupholder and my Beretta rifle is underneath the seat.

Duke puts on *NSYNC and cranks the volume. "You're welcome, Ryder."

"Dude, shut up."

"Twenty bucks says you'll be singing the chorus by the time we get to the house."

"That's twenty bucks you're gonna lose."

Duke, being Duke, sings at the top of his lungs when the "Bye Bye Bye" chorus comes on. I join in, laughing, and lo and behold, Ryder joins in, too, all three of us smiling like the idiots we are as we drive through the autumn twilight.

Sounds stupid, but I feel like my heart grows wings. I could fly I'm so happy.

I could fly because I'm free.

No more hiding. No more running in circles, trying to stay busy so I don't have to face my past or the fact that I let the girl I love go.

Funny how I found that freedom in commitment. That's truth for you, I guess. No matter what your truth looks like, if you're living it, you're gonna feel good.

Really fucking good.

We pass the corral and the horse barn. Frowning, I turn down the music when I see that the barn's floodlights are on. They operate on motion sensors, meaning they only come on when there's movement nearby.

"Y'all were at the barn last, right?" I ask my brothers.

Duke glances out his window. "Left not an hour ago. No one's supposed to be out there."

I point at the barn. "Let's check it out real quick."

My brother guides the truck down the hill and into the little valley where the corral and barn sit.

My stomach somersaults when I see the barn's side door is flung wide open. I put the truck in park and immediately reach for my rifle underneath my seat.

Meeting eyes with Duke in the passenger seat, I give him a curt nod.

We open our doors at the same time. The three of us pile out into the cold and I take the lead, raising my rifle so that it's tucked firmly into the ball of my shoulder.

My heart is hammering. Something's up. I feel it.

"Hello?" I shout, carefully releasing the safety so that it doesn't make a noise. "Who's in there?"

No answer.

"We're comin' in," Ryder adds. "And we're armed."

We round the corner of the barn. Pressing my cheek against the butt of the rifle, I keep my stride steady as I slip through the open door.

A figure moves in the shadows, put off by the overhead lights. My finger sits on the trigger.

"Come out," I say. "Right now."

I nearly pass out from relief when John B emerges from the dark. I immediately put the safety back on and drop the rifle, letting out a breath. "Jesus Christ, John. Why didn't you—"

But then he grabs the rifle out of my hands with a quickness I didn't know he was capable of at his age. He raises it, aiming the barrel at my chest. "Just who I was lookin' for."

I'm so taken aback—this is so out of character for him—that it takes a full beat for my brain to unscramble the events as they happen.

First, John B puts his hand on the trigger.

Second, he closes his left eye, aiming for my heart. Did he release the safety? My heart is pounding so hard that I could've missed the telltale click. And the light in here is too dim to see.

Third, John says, "Tell me you didn't break your promise."

My heart thumps in my ears. "What?"

Duke, Sawyer, and I exchange glances. None of us has any idea what the fuck is going on. We stay put, my brothers hovering just behind my left shoulder.

Could the three of us take John out before he pulls the

trigger? He's getting on in years, but he's still a born and bred country boy. He got his first rifle at five and has been a crack shot since six. Or so the story goes.

We've hunted together plenty, so I know the man only raises a gun when he means business. He ain't gonna miss if he fires.

I squint, straining to see whether the safety is engaged or not. Still can't tell.

"You promised me you weren't going to keep her in Texas. You lied to my face, boy."

What the hell?

"I didn't lie to you," I reply slowly. "Sally is still going to New York."

John B just chuckles, a low, sinister sound. "Quit your lying already. She just told me."

"Told you what?"

"Quit *lying*, Wyatt, or so help me God—"

"John, please." Duke steps forward, his hands held up. "Let's all keep a cool head here, all right? I think there's a misunderstanding—"

"There's definitely a misunderstanding," I say, anger mingling with the fear coursing through my veins. "I have no clue what you're talking about."

A flicker of doubt moves across John's eyes. "Sally didn't tell you she's not taking the job at Ithaca University?"

A bomb detonates inside my skull. At the same time my heart hammers against my breastbone, leaving me short of breath.

Sally isn't taking the job? Since when? Why? And how can I feel so relieved and so terrified, all at once?

Then I remember the cryptic way she kept saying she wanted to stay in Hartsville the other day. But she made no mention of going so far as to quit her job.

I feel Duke's and Ryder's eyes on me.

"She didn't tell me, no," I manage.

John hesitates, his finger falling from the trigger. I can see the mental gymnastics he's doing to have it all make sense.

"I can prove it to you actually." I put my hand on my zipper.

John immediately puts his finger back on the trigger. "Keep your hands where I can see 'em."

"John—"

"You'd best listen." He moves toward me, rifle still raised.

I back up, my hands held high.

"I would never let Sally quit her job on my account," I manage. "You know this about me. I love her more than words can say, but I'd never—you know I'd never ask that of her. I'm a man of my word, John. Please, let me prove it."

"We all can prove it," Ryder chimes in. "Just give us a minute. A second."

But John keeps stalking toward us. We keep backing up until we're moving out of the barn and into the night, the four of us standing in the dirt path between the corral and the barn.

A flash of light catches my eye. I turn my head to see approaching headlights.

Cash's Ford.

At the same time, I hear a scream.

Sally.

My Sally.

She appears at the edge of the circle of illumination that's put off by the floodlights over our heads. She's breathing hard, her eyes wet with tears as she takes in her dad, the rifle, and then me.

"Stop!" she screams again. "Dad, put down the rifle right now."

Cash's truck jerks to a stop beside the barn.

"Not until he swears he's gonna keep his promise," John replies. "Let her go, Wyatt."

Sally shakes her head as she comes to stand beside me.

"You're insane, Dad. Seriously, if you don't put the gun down, I'm calling the cops." She digs her phone out of her pocket and holds it up.

I hear a truck door open. Close.

Sally grabs my hand. I twine our fingers.

John keeps the gun pointed at my chest.

"I swear to God, John, it's not what you think," I say.

"You're lying, Wyatt," he replies.

"Dad, please, stop," Sally begs. "This is ridiculous. *Put* the gun *down*. He's right—"

"What's going on here?" Cash's voice, sharp and loud, cuts through the night air.

John's eyes remain locked on mine. "This son of a bitch did my daughter dirty—that's what."

I feel Cash's stare. "Wyatt—"

"I can explain." My voice sounds desperate, even to my own ears.

Sally steps forward. "*I* can explain. I didn't tell Wyatt about the job, Dad. I didn't tell anyone except Mollie, because I was hoping I'd get to surprise y'all with the news tonight at dinner." She looks at me. "I wanted it to be this big, special moment because it is a big moment. It is special. Or it was supposed to be."

I look back, heart thumping. "What news?"

"I refused the job offer," she says simply, like she isn't wildly altering her life course. All our life courses. "I'm staying in Texas. No, I don't know what I'm going to do about a job, and, yes, I'm working on figuring something out. But I'm staying because I've discovered I need a sense of community—a feeling of being connected to people—that I haven't found anywhere else. Turns out, my dream doesn't have anything to do with one specific job like I thought it did. My dream is serving my hometown. Working alongside people I know and love." Sally sucks in a deep inhale and meets my eyes. "I'm sorry you had to find out this way, Wyatt."

"Wait, wait." John B blinks, finally lowering the rifle. "Wyatt really didn't know?"

Once again, I find myself speechless. Sally isn't taking the job. She's not moving to New York.

Which means—

My God, she's actually staying.

We're staying in the town I was born and raised in. The town where I want my children to be born, where I want to raise them.

Joy swoops through me.

"He didn't know," Sally confirms. "That's proof this was my choice."

Without thinking, I grab my zipper and yank it down. "I have proof of my choice too."

Sally's eyes go wide as they take in my white T-shirt. It's one of those simple *I Love New York* shirts, a red heart in the place of the word *love.*

"Wyatt"—her voice cracks as her eyes flick to meet mine—"what's this?"

I hear more zippers being pulled behind me, and then Ryder appears at my elbow. "Surprise! We're forming a boy band."

Sally looks at his shirt, Duke's too. And then she laughs.

She covers her mouth with her hand and howls, tears leaking out of her eyes.

John still has my gun in his hands, but I don't care. I curl an arm around Sally's neck and pull her against me, pressing a kiss into her hair.

"You and I are apparently on the same wavelength, Sunshine. Same night you were gonna tell me you were staying in Texas was when I was gonna ask you if I could join you in New York. Show you I had my family's blessing. Show you that I was excited to follow you wherever your dreams took us. I was never gonna make you choose between your job and me."

Cash chuckles. "That's pretty dang sweet."

I hear another car door opening, and I look up to see Mollie climbing out of Cash's truck. "Everything okay?"

"Not okay that you didn't tell me Sally's news," Cash replies. "But, yes, it's safe for you to come out. Right, John?"

Sally's father has a flabbergasted look on his face. He doesn't say a word.

Instead, he watches Sally sob into my new T-shirt, my brothers discreetly wiping their eyes around us.

"I can't believe you'd move for me," Sally manages.

"Aw, Sunshine, can't you though? I can't let you out of my sight as it is. You really think I could handle living halfway across the country from you?"

"I'm glad you can't."

"You sure?" I ask, even though I already know the answer. "About the job?"

Sally nods. "I'm sure. I've never been surer of anything in my life."

"Okay." *Okay.*

My God, I feel so much better than just okay.

"You look beautiful, by the way. Love the dress. But love you more."

John B clears his throat. Every head swings in his direction.

That's when I see that he's crying, tears streaking down his cheeks. My chest contracts.

"I believe I owe y'all an apology." He sniffles. "I didn't—I assumed the worst about all of you, and I'm sorry."

Sally gives him a look. "Dad, you pulled a fucking *gun* on my boyfriend."

John B's voice wavers when he says, "I wasn't gonna actually shoot anyone. Safety's still on, see?"

He holds up the rifle, the floodlights glinting off its polished barrel. I let out a breath when I see that the safety is —*my God*—indeed engaged.

Cash steps forward and holds out his hand. "I'd still like to take it, please."

"I'm sorry." John passes my brother the rifle, then covers his face with his hands. "I'm so, so sorry, honey. You're right. I should've trusted you. I didn't understand—I only wanted the best for you. I was trying to save you from having the regrets I do. I thought I was doing the right thing. I'm sorry."

Sally glances up at me. "Are you okay, Wy?"

"Not gonna lie. I'm a little shaken. For a second there, I thought...well..."

"I promise I wasn't gonna shoot," John says. "Did you not see the safety was on?"

I shake my head. "Too dark."

"I'm sorry," he repeats.

"But I do feel better now that I know it was on," I say. "Still not right what you did, John."

He scoffs. "Of course it wasn't right. I just—y'all gotta understand how my regrets have eaten away at me over the years. I never want my daughter to have to wonder about what-ifs."

Sally's expression softens ever so slightly. "I'd wonder *what if* for the rest of my life if I took the job in New York, Dad."

"I see that now."

"Do you really?" Sally presses. "Because if you ever pull a gun on my boyfriend again, even if you don't mean to shoot—"

"I promise, Sally." John's voice breaks. "I understand. I'm sorry, and I'll keep saying I'm sorry until you believe me."

Sally looks at him for a long beat before she turns to my brothers. "And y'all? Are you guys okay?"

They nod.

Dropping my hand, Sally moves toward her dad. I hold my breath, half expecting her to slap him, give him another verbal dressing-down at the very least.

Instead, she pulls him in for a hug. "You have a lot of work to do on yourself, Dad," I hear her murmur.

"I know," he replies. "I'll do it. I promise you, honey, I'll do better."

Mollie claps her hands. "All right, y'all. No one is dead, and Sally and Wyatt are gonna ride off into the Texas sunset together. I think this calls for a celebratory drink."

"Or five," Sally says. "I've got a pitcher of bourbon sours back at the house if anyone's interested."

"Don't gotta ask me twice," Duke says, elbowing past me.

I hold out my hand to Sally. "Our sunset awaits."

Smiling, she walks toward me and takes my hand. "No one I'd rather ride with than you."

"I think you just mean ride," Sawyer says. "As in there's no one you'd rather ride, period."

I roll my eyes. "Seriously?"

But Sally just laughs.

CHAPTER 32

Sally

HIGHLY RECOMMEND

TUCKING my hair behind my ears, I take a deep, steadying breath and recite the lines I've practiced a thousand times over the past few weeks.

I've researched the barrel racing circuit, and I feel that I can help you build a world-class competitive training program that would truly put the Wallace Ranch on the map.

In addition to veterinary services, I can help create training regimens that would ensure the safety of racers and their horses while also promoting top-notch performance in the arena and beyond.

Yes, I'm willing to travel. And, yes, I have a cowboy friend who's particularly skilled in all things related to riding and who would be more than happy to lend a hand whenever we need it.

Yes, that cowboy has a brother who also happens to be a single parent if you're interested in making a new friend yourself.

I'm seated in the Wallace Ranch's swanky new office, a shingled building not far from the enormous arena where I performed that pair of surgeries back in November.

It was only a little over a month ago, but it seems like it was yesterday. Also seems like it was from another lifetime, in the era before Wyatt officially asked me to move in with him.

Before we spent the most joyous fucking holiday season ever together. Seriously, December was one nonstop party. Between us celebrating our decision to stay in Texas, to us celebrating moving in together, to us toasting our very first Christmas tree as a couple, I felt like I was practically swimming in good tidings and cheer.

I also feel like I'll be celebrating the fact that Wyatt was willing to move to New York with me for the rest of my life. I know how much Texas means to him, and I know he would've missed his family terribly. But he was willing to move anyway.

That kind of love will always make me weak in the knees.

Throughout December, my friends—namely Wyatt and Mollie—helped me brainstorm some ideas for the future of my career. I kept coming back to the Wallaces and their budding training program. Their facilities are top-notch, and more importantly, so are the people who work there. Beck and I were able to smooth things over a few weeks back when we ran into each other at The Rattler. I blushed so hard that I was sure my face would catch fire as I explained myself to him, but luckily, he was cool about it. He's genuinely a good guy, and I have no doubt he's going to make someone very happy someday.

Now I find myself waiting outside Ava Bartlett's door at eight a.m. the Monday after New Year's. A leather folio rests in my lap. Inside, I've got several copies of my updated résumé, along with printed references from the professors and surgeons I've worked with.

There's also a letter from Dad. After tempers cooled and I felt like we were on semi-decent footing again, I asked him to write me a recommendation. He had his first therapy appointment just after Thanksgiving, and I know he's working hard to win back my trust, Wyatt's too.

Not gonna lie. When I read his recommendation, I cried like a baby. He didn't hound on my credentials the way he would in the past, name-dropping the schools I attended or the famous professors I worked with.

Instead, he talked about my "heart-first" approach to veterinary care. How my practice is made richer by the bonds I have with the people around me. He said my technical proficiency is second to none, and so is my bedside manner. I care for animals, and I care for the community they're a part of too.

As cheesy as that last part was, I had to print out another copy because I cried so hard while reading it that my tears soaked the page.

A door to my left opens, and Ava emerges with a warm smile. "Hey, Sally! So happy to see you. Come on in. Pardon the mess. We just moved into these offices, and I'm still getting settled."

We sit across from each other at a wide white desk, the two of us exchanging pleasantries for a few minutes before I open my folio.

"Thank you again for meeting with me. I have a proposal I'd like to make."

Ava nods eagerly. "I'm all ears."

"I'm just going to dive right in and say that I'd love to be a part of the program you're building here. I've worked plenty with the horses y'all breed, and I'm seriously impressed by what I've seen. I believe, with the right people in place, Wallace Ranch has the potential to be a world-class training facility. I'd like to be one of those people."

Ava's smile grows. "Go on."

I give her enough specifics to let her know I've given my proposal a lot of thought. I float the idea of Vance and me forming a veterinary care team unit that provides both clinical care and expertise in diet, training programs, and preventative medicine.

"Obviously, my main role will be performing surgeries as needed," I say, wrapping up. "But I'd like to make that role a bit more dynamic by incorporating all these other elements. I'd like to flex my muscles a bit, be part of the action."

Ava's smile hasn't wavered. "I love this idea, Sally. Really, truly love it. You make a very compelling case, especially considering I've witnessed you perform several miracles on our horses. It would be a dream to have you on our team."

I flush, chest filling with excitement. "Thank you."

"Let me chat with the Wallaces and get their thoughts. But you bet your bottom dollar that I'm gonna push hard for you. I know an opportunity when I see one, and talent like yours is a major opportunity for us. Thanks for bringing this to me, sincerely."

We shake hands, and I leave the ranch feeling like a million bucks. Even if I don't get the job, I'm still proud of myself for taking such a big swing. I'm learning that it's the people who have the balls to ask for what they want who ultimately get it.

So I'm going to keep asking for what I want and hope for the best.

On the way home I get a call from Dad, asking for help at a small ranch that's about twenty or so miles down the road. I head in that direction, and next thing I know it's late afternoon, and I'm itching to get back home to Wyatt.

Will I ever not rush home to see him? If I leave now, I can probably grab a shower with him. Then we'll hang out, maybe watch whichever serial killer documentary just came out on Netflix. Then we'll make some dinner if we don't feel like going to the New House.

And then, of course, we'll get naked after that.

Yeah, life in Texas is good. Really, really good.

It's almost four by the time our farmhouse comes into view. I smile when I see Wyatt's truck parked out front. Only when I pull up beside it do I see that he's in the front seat.

He's wearing a cowboy hat, a denim jacket, and a knowing smirk I want to kiss right off his handsome face.

How is this my life?

He rolls down his window after I hop out of my car. "Get in."

"What?" I say, laughing. "Why?"

"We're gonna celebrate you gettin' a job."

Rolling my eyes, I cross my arms over my chest. "I didn't get a job. Yet."

"But you will. What'd Ava say? That she couldn't verbally give you an offer, but she sure as hell isn't letting you slip through her fingers?"

"Something like that." I blink. "You're good."

"Yep. Now get in."

It's all I can do not to giggle as I climb into his truck and immediately reach across the front bench to grab Wyatt's shirt.

Yanking him to me, I hover my mouth an inch off of his and say, "Hi."

"Hi."

"How was your day?"

"Better now."

We have this exact conversation every day. And every day, it makes me feel like I'm floating.

I kiss him, and he slides a hand onto my face and kisses me back. I love how we can still do this, shamelessly make out with each other, despite the fact that we've been dating since November and it'd be so much easier—simpler—to just skip straight to sex.

Wyatt, though, takes his time with me. Always has.

I'm the one to finally break the kiss. Falling back in my seat, I put on my seat belt. Wyatt presses a button on the dash, and the opening notes of "Yellow" by Coldplay fill the car.

I reach over to turn it up. "I love this song."

"I know."

"Where are we going?"

He puts the truck in drive. "You'll see."

I get a weird sense of déjà vu as Wyatt drives across the ranch. We're heading to the river, I know that much.

He parks in our usual spot at the top of the bluff that over-looks the water. Above it, the sky is a kaleidoscope of colors—orange, neon coral, lavender, powder blue.

"I forgot what a perfect place this is to watch the sunset," I say.

Wyatt reaches into the back seat and pulls out a six-pack of Cokes—glass bottles, naturally—and a fifth of Jack Daniel's.

"Too cold to skinny-dip." He pops the tops off a pair of bottles and takes a sip from one, then the other. "But figured we could get naked in the truck instead. Don't worry, we'll cuddle first." He pats his lap.

The memory hits me—the afternoon I picked up Wyatt right after his parents died. I was listening to Coldplay that day. "Yellow," if memory serves.

I blink, my eyes smarting. With the Cokes and the Cold-play and the Colorado River, is Wyatt re-creating that day?

He's revisiting a moment that was both terrible and wonderful in equal measure.

He's not afraid to go back there anymore.

My eyes flick to his neck. My heart thunders when I see that he's not wearing his gold chain.

I don't want to read too much into that. But Wyatt *always* wears that thing, and the fact that he's not today—

Oh my God.

He pours a good amount of Jack Daniel's into each of the Cokes and hands one to me.

"Cheers, Sunshine." He holds out his Coke.

I absently touch my bottle to his. "Cheers, handsome."

I sip. The sweetness of the Coke mingles with the fire of the Jack Daniel's on my tongue.

Then a big old smile splits my face. Yeah, Wyatt is definitely re-creating that day.

"You get it then," Wyatt says. "The song and the drinks..."

"I get it." I look down at my Coke, then look up at him. "Cute."

"Cute? That's all I get?" he teases.

Careful not to spill my drink, I all but launch myself across the bench and climb into his lap, Sally Field in *Smokey and the Bandit*–style. Looping an arm around his neck, I pull him in for another kiss. "You know you're gonna get more than that, cowboy."

His eyes flash with heat. "I got a question to ask you first."

"Oh, yeah?" I ask, like my heart isn't in my throat and my thoughts aren't a riot of hope. "Talk to me."

"That day you picked me up, you said you'd be my sunshine anytime." He searches my eyes. "What do you think about being my sunshine forever?"

I stare at him as the realization takes shape.

"Really?" I manage, vision blurring with tears.

"I know it seems fast—"

"Yes. So fast. And also not fast at all."

"We've only been dating for a couple of months. But I'm not gonna waste another twenty years playing it safe. We can get married next month, next year, or ten years from now—I don't care." With a grunt, he reaches for the glove compartment. Opening it, he pulls out a small velvet box. "I just refuse to go another day without putting a ring on your finger."

He flicks open the box with his thumb. The breath leaves my lungs when I see the *gorgeous* yellow diamond solitaire that sparkles on a thin gold band. It's classic, beautifully proportioned, and so very me.

"You know Cash got Mom's engagement ring," Wyatt explains, "and I got her wedding band. But I still wanted the band to be a part of *your* ring, so Mollie gave me the name of her jeweler, and I had him redo the band and added the yellow diamond. Because, yeah, you're my sunshine. I hope you like it."

I try and fail to formulate any sort of coherent response.

Instead, I sob and pull my fiancé in for a teary, salty kiss, both of us crying and laughing and *happy*.

So damn happy.

"That a yes?" he asks.

I manage a nod. "That's a yes, Wy. I love it. I love you. My God, do I love you."

My heart skips several beats when he takes the ring out of its box. It looks impossibly delicate in his huge, blunt-tipped fingers, and I shiver when he slides it onto the fourth finger of my left hand. The diamond winks at me, its fire clear and bright.

"You're the only one I wanna cook for," he says. "The only one I wanna take wholesome literature and turn it into spicy prairie porn with. The only one I want to watch terrifying serial killer shows with. You're the only one, Sally."

"And you're the only one my dad's ever held at gunpoint," I say, and he laughs, a big, booming sound. "I never thought I'd have that kind of epic love story, but I'm glad we do."

"*We.*" He threads our fingers together.

"We're a package deal now, yeah." I lean in and bite his neck. "So how do you feel about making some spicy prairie porn of our own right now?"

More laughter. My heart soars.

Squeezing my thigh, he replies, "I could be convinced."

I grab his hat and drop it onto my head. "Saddle up, cowboy."

Tied Up

SALLY SQUEEZES MY HAND, hard, making my heart dip.

"You all right?" I ask. "If you need a break, just say so."

Her eyes are closed, a slight grimace on her face as the artist adds some dimension to the Coca-Cola bottle he's tattooing on the inside of my fiancée's forearm.

"I'll be okay," she replies. "Just—please tell me we're almost done."

The tattoo artist wipes Sally's arm with a cloth. "Almost done," he says with a smile. "Looks great."

I smile too. "It's not as slutty as mine—"

"I wouldn't dream of even trying to compete." Sally cracks open an eye and grins. "You win the slutty thigh tattoo contest, no question."

The artist laughs. "I like y'all."

"But it is really, really cute." I give her hand a gentle squeeze. "I think you're gonna like it."

Her grin broadens into a smile. "I think I'm gonna love it. Mostly because I love you."

"I love you more." I point at the sun tattoo on my own forearm. "I win that contest too."

Sally bites her lip, a soft look coming over her face. "Can't believe it took me so long to put two and two together."

"But you did. And now look at you. You got my ring on your finger and my tattoo on your arm."

"*Our* tattoo. I brought the Coke—"

"And I brought the Jack." I chuckle. "Fair point."

Looking at my fiancée in the artist's chair, I'm struck by how fucking gorgeous she is. Her long, dark hair is fanned out around her head, and her full lips are pulled into that pretty smile of hers. Getting tattooed definitely doesn't feel great, but she's being incredibly brave—she hasn't complained once.

I still can't believe Sally Powell is getting a *tattoo*. One inspired by our relationship. One that I have inked on my skin too.

Yet another pinch-me moment. I keep having those lately now that Sally and I are together. We're *getting married*.

When we sat down last week with Patsy and John B to start planning the wedding, I legit started to cry I was so happy. That made everybody else cry, and then we were all hugging and laughing, joking that we'd have to have the reception in the Wallaces' new arena because everyone and their mother was gonna want to attend the wedding.

Ava officially extended a job offer to Sally not long after they first spoke about it. Sally of course immediately accepted it. The title is head of veterinary programs, but Ava is letting Sally decide what that entails. So far, Sally's enjoyed exploring her interests while caring for the Wallaces' stable of racehorses. She's happy, so I'm happy too.

As for me, I'm enjoying my role as foreman at Lucky River Ranch more than ever. I think opening up—being honest— has led me to shed my class-clown persona. I don't have to wear a mask or pretend to be someone I'm not, and because

I'm finally able to take myself seriously, I think other people do too. My brothers included.

Go figure—it feels really fucking good to let your guard down every once in a while.

Feels really fucking good to turn to your fiancée and say, "After this, dinner and *Forensic Files* at home?"

Sally moved in with me the day after I proposed. I love having her at the house. Love the little routine we've settled into as a couple.

Most of all, I love waking up next to her every day. Didn't think happiness this big, this overwhelming, existed. But here we are.

"I love that idea, yeah," Sally replies.

The artist finishes the piece, then gives Sally instructions for how to care for her new ink. She stands in front of the full-length mirror beside the chair and smiles as she turns her arm this way and that, admiring the tattoo that matches mine.

Sidling up behind her, I drape my arms across her torso and murmur into her neck, "You love it?"

"I love it."

"Home?"

"Yeah." She turns her head to nudge my jaw with her nose. "Home."

———

Back at the house, I help Sally out of her jacket, then shoulder out of mine. Sally watches me, a hot gleam in her eyes that I've come to know well. Awareness gathers between my legs as I hang my jacket on the rack beside the door, then take off my hat.

"Keep that on." My fiancée licks her lips. "Okay, change of plans. We're skipping *Forensic Files* and playing poker instead."

I smirk. "Poker? Really?"

"A special kind of poker." Sally grabs my hand. "The kind I'd only play with you."

I let her pull me into the kitchen. "I'm interested."

"Thought you might be."

Grabbing a deck of cards from the junk drawer by the door, I toss them onto the kitchen table. "What are the rules?"

"Simple." Sally sits at the table and begins to shuffle the cards. "You win a hand, you keep your clothes on. You lose, you take 'em off, one item at a time. You in?"

I pull out a chair and sit, my dick going full salute as I watch my girl confidently deal a hand of Texas Hold'Em. "Yes, ma'am, I am."

She bites her lip, glancing at me across the table. "Should we up the ante? Whoever is naked first orgasms last?"

I let out a bark of laughter. "Sure." Although I think we both know I'd never come without making Sally come first.

Sally and I have played Hold'Em several times since that fateful night at the potluck, but I'm still pleasantly surprised when Sally wins the first hand, then the second. First, I take off my shirt—putting my hat back on, of course, because my girl gets what she wants. Sally's nipples harden to tight, visible points as she takes in my naked chest and stomach. She literally moans when I rip off my belt next, followed by my jeans after she wins yet another hand.

Finally, I win a hand, and I nearly bite off my own tongue when Sally pulls off her sweater, revealing a barely-there pink bra that *does* something to me.

Adjusting myself through my briefs, I bite out, "Your jeans. Those come off next."

Luckily, I win the hand, and then Sally is sitting across from me in just her bra and panties. Well, her socks, too, but I figure those don't really count at the moment.

I win the next hand too. But when Sally moves to take off her bra, I shake my head. "Naw, Sunshine. The panties—

those gotta go. Take 'em off, then scoot your chair back. Yes, just like that. Now open those pretty legs of yours."

Her lips twitching, Sally does as I told her, scooting back just far enough that I can see her bare pussy. She glistens in the light overhead, making my mouth water.

My dick throbs. "If I win this next hand, I want you to touch yourself."

"That's not in the rules," Sally says with a smirk.

"It is now."

I win.

Holding her cards in one hand, Sally reaches between her legs with the other. "Touch myself like this?"

Her fingers circle her clit. They move easily, her pussy slick, swollen.

"Bend your knee. Put your foot on the edge of the chair so I can see you better." I pull my cock through the slit in my briefs and watch, my breath caught in my throat, as Sally spreads herself wider, then slips a finger inside herself. "Good girl. You like it when Daddy tells you what to do, don't you?"

"Uh-huh," she pants, hips beginning to roll against her hand.

I give myself a slow, easy tug. "How 'bout this? I win the next hand, I fuck your mouth. You win, I fuck whatever you want me to."

She's biting her lip again. "Yeah. Okay."

I thumb my head, working the pre-cum over my skin. "I'll deal."

As luck would have it, Sally bluffs her way to a win. Throwing up one arm, she continues to finger herself with her other hand. "You can fuck me here, please."

"Yes, ma'am."

Then I stand. I pull off my briefs and I move around the table. Then I grab her. I set her on the edge of the table and step between her legs.

Kissing her mouth, I murmur, "Put me inside you, Sunshine."

She reaches between us and curls her hand around my dick, giving me a tight pull before lining me up at her entrance. "Guess you come first? Since you won?"

I shake my head and push into her, gasping at the feel of her soft, wet heat. She's already tightening around me, her orgasm close.

"That ain't gonna happen and you know it."

Laughing, she curls an arm around my neck and rocks her hips, riding my dick as I begin to thrust. "Let's come together then."

Thumbing her clit, I nod. "Stay with me."

"I'm almost there."

"I know."

"I won't be able to—"

"I *know*." I kiss her, hard, my thumb moving faster. "Ever consider I'm doing this on purpose? You go first, always."

She smiles against my lips. "Okay."

She comes a beat later with a shout I capture in a kiss. She pulses around me, milking me to my own orgasm. I can barely breathe as I come down and rest my forehead against hers.

I feel my cum leaking out of her.

"I like that game." My voice is husky.

Sally laughs. "I do too."

———

A few days later, we head for the Wallace Ranch for a good old-fashioned barn raising. Really, the town is coming together to repair the barn that was partially destroyed by that fire. There will be music, kegs, tons of food, and of course some dancing.

Sally and I are excited, mostly because Ava and Sawyer

JESSICA PETERSON

will finally get to meet. Sawyer said he'd be bringing Ella with him, and Sally told me Ava planned on bringing her daughter too.

"Really, it's kind of perfect when you think about it," Sally says as she climbs out of my truck. "Think they'll hit it off?"

"I do, yeah. Sawyer gave me some pretty great speeches about falling in love and shit, so I think he's at the very least open to dating."

Sally smiles, grabbing my hand. "I think Ava is too. She's such a lovely person, and I'd love for her to end up with a good guy like Sawyer."

The barn raising is in full swing. A band plays beside a nearby corral while a long table, covered in a checkered tablecloth, is set with more food than I think I've ever seen—and that's saying something, considering the epic spreads Patsy puts out for breakfast, lunch, and dinner every day on Lucky River Ranch.

Sawyer is already here, tool belt hanging from his hips as he works inside the barn. I can just glimpse him and Ella through the open doors. His daughter is at his side, holding a pink plastic hammer in her hand. So freaking cute.

"Oh! There's Ava." Sally waves at her. "Great, she's coming this way. Let's introduce them."

"Hey, y'all!" Ava says brightly. "Thank you so much for coming. We're blown away by this turnout!"

"Welcome to Hartsville, where everyone's nosy as hell but always willing to lend a hand." I nod at the kegs. "The fact that there's free beer doesn't hurt."

Ava smiles. "Least we could do."

"So, Ava"—Sally cuts me a look—"Wyatt and I would like you to meet someone."

"Oh?" Ava's brows pop up. "This sounds fun."

"It's Wyatt's younger brother. He has a three-year-old too," Sally says.

Ava's smile deepens. "Let's do it."

She follows us inside the barn.

"Sawyer!" I bark.

"Uncle Wy! It's Uncle Wy and Auntie Sally!" Ella cries, running over to wrap each of us in a bear hug.

Turning away from the framing he's working on, my brother smiles when he sees me. "Hey, Wyatt. Sally, it's always a pleasure seeing yo…" His voice trails off as he looks up and locks eyes with Ava. His eyes go wide, and a flush erupts on his neck and works its way up to his face.

"Hey!" Ava says, and that's when I notice she's blushing too.

She looks like she's seen a ghost.

"It's…good to see you." Sawyer tugs a hand through his hair. It's his tell, the one that says *I'm nervous as fuck*. He laughs. "Been a minute."

"Yeah." Ava laughs, too, but it sounds funny, like she's out of breath. "Wow. What are the chances?"

Stomach twisting, I pull my brows together. "Wait, do y'all know each other?"

Sawyer's running his hand up the back of his head now. "Funny enough, we do."

———

Thank you so damn much for reading WYATT! I sincerely hope you enjoyed it. **Need more Sally+Wyatt in your life? I've got you covered. Check out the bonus epilogue I wrote for them, which is available on my website at jessicapeter son.com.** The epilogue may or may not include a pair of blue cowboy boots and a white dress! Enjoy.

Be sure to grab SAWYER, the next book in my Lucky River Ranch series. If you're in the mood for more small town goodness, check out I WISH I KNEW THEN, the first book in my Harbour Village series. Happy reading!

I'd love to keep in touch! Follow my not-so-glamorous life as a romance author on Instagram @JessicaPAuthor

Acknowledgments

The Lucky River Ranch crew has changed my career and my life in so many awesome ways. 2024 was by far my best year yet, and that's largely because I'm surrounded by some of the best people on the planet who accept me as I am and cheer me on. I love each and every one of y'all, and I can't thank you enough for showing me and my books so much love. THANK YOU!

First up, I have to thank the ladies I work with day in and day out. Jodi and Meagan, I adore y'all. Thank you for being the best damn assistants and friends a gal could ask for.

To the ladies (and Charlie) at Valentine PR: I love, love, LOVE working with you! So many exciting things have happened in my life because of you. Can't wait to see where 2025 takes us! Shout out to Tracy, as always, for helping me with my PR packages. So appreciate you making each one beautiful!

To Najla Qamber and her team: y'all rock. Your work is second to none, and you make my job SO much easier. You always, always get the vibes right!

To my editors, Rachel, Joni, and Jovana: I am grammar's worst nightmare, but for some reason, you put up with me and fix all my mistakes. Y'all are the smartypants-es I need in my life.

Huge shout out to my alpha readers, Nina, Chasity and Meagan, and to my beautiful beta team: Catherine, Logan, and Logan (or Logan squared, whichever you prefer). Your feedback on early drafts of this book truly brought the story to the next level. THANK YOU!

To my Facebook Reader Group admins, Kenysha and Tara: thank you so very much for holding down the fort while I disappeared into my writing cave. Y'all rock.

To Mandy Stewart and the team at Fred & June's books: thank you for spreading the word about my stories locally here in Charlotte. I adore working with y'all!

To booksellers everywhere: thank you for doing the Lord's work. Books are more important than ever, and I see the difference you're making in the world. Thank you!

To all the Instagram, Facebook, and TikTok girlies who have shown this book an overwhelming amount of love: thank you for helping spread the word about my books! I've loved getting to know each of y'all, and hope to squeeze you soon at a signing!

And most of all, to my readers: I get to live my dream every day because of you. I appreciate your support more than you'll ever know. Thank you from the bottom of my heart!

I also have to give a shout out to my little family. I've never worked harder in my life trying to balance my roles as mom and author, but I'm so grateful I have a whole world outside my work to get lost in. I love you!

Also by Jessica Peterson

THE LUCKY RIVER RANCH SERIES

Texas cowboys do it best.

Cash (Lucky River Ranch #1)

Wyatt (Lucky River Ranch #2)

Sawyer (Lucky River Ranch #3)

Duke (Lucky River Ranch #4)

Ryder (Lucky River Ranch #5)

THE HARBOUR VILLAGE SERIES

Small town romance with a smoking hot southern twist.

I Wish I Knew Then (Harbour Village #1)

I Wish You Were Mine (Harbour Village #2)

I Wish We Had Forever (Harbour Village #3)

THE SEX & BONDS SERIES

An outrageously sexy series of romcoms set in the high stakes world of Wall Street.

The Dealmaker (Sex & Bonds #1)

The Troublemaker (Sex & Bonds #2)

THE NORTH CAROLINA HIGHLANDS SERIES

Beards. Bonfires. Boning.

Southern Seducer (NC Highlands #1)

Southern Hotshot (NC Highlands #2)

Southern Sinner (NC Highlands #3)

Southern Playboy (NC Highlands #4)

Southern Bombshell (NC Highlands #5)

THE CHARLESTON HEAT SERIES

The Weather's Not the Only Thing Steamy Down South.

Southern Charmer (Charleston Heat #1)

Southern Player (Charleston Heat #2)

Southern Gentleman (Charleston Heat #3)

Southern Heartbreaker (Charleston Heat #4)

THE THORNE MONARCHS SERIES

Royal. Ridiculously Hot. Totally Off Limits…

Royal Ruin (Thorne Monarchs #1)

Royal Rebel (Thorne Monarchs #2)

Royal Rogue (Thorne Monarchs #3)

THE STUDY ABROAD SERIES

Studying Abroad Just Got a Whole Lot Sexier.

A Series of Sexy Interconnected Standalone Romances

Lessons in Love (Study Abroad #1)

Lessons in Gravity (Study Abroad #2)

Lessons in Letting Go (Study Abroad #3)

Lessons in Losing It (Study Abroad #4)

About the Author

Jessica Peterson writes romance with heat, humor, and heart. Heroes with hot accents are her specialty. When she's not writing, she can be found bellying up to a bar in the south's best restaurants with her husband Ben, reading books with her adorable daughters Gracie and Madeline, or snuggling up with her 70-pound lap dog, Martha.

A Carolina girl at heart, she fantasizes about splitting her time between Charleston and Asheville, but currently lives in Charlotte, NC. You can check out her books at www.jessicapeterson.com.

Made in the USA
Monee, IL
27 December 2024

75507689R00215